Praise for the novels of Lee Tobin McClain

"Lee Tobin McClain dazzles with unforgettable characters, fabulous small-town settings and a big dose of heart. Her complex and satisfying stories never disappoint."
—Susan Mallery, *New York Times* bestselling author

"Fans of Debbie Macomber will appreciate this start to a new series by McClain that blends sweet, small-town romance with such serious issues as domestic abuse.... Readers craving a feel-good romance with a bit of suspense will be satisfied."
—*Booklist* on *Low Country Hero*

"[An] enthralling tale of learning to trust.... This enjoyable contemporary romance will appeal to readers looking for twinges of suspense before happily ever after."
—*Publishers Weekly* on *Low Country Hero*

"*Low Country Hero* has everything I look for in a book—it's emotional, tender, and an all-around wonderful story."
—RaeAnne Thayne, *New York Times* bestselling author

Also by Lee Tobin McClain

The Off Season

Cottage at the Beach
Reunion at the Shore
Christmas on the Coast
Home to the Harbor

Safe Haven

Low Country Hero
Low Country Dreams
Low Country Christmas

Look for Lee Tobin McClain's next novel
Forever on the Bay
available soon from HQN.

For additional books by Lee Tobin McClain,
visit her website, www.leetobinmcclain.com.

LEE TOBIN McCLAIN

first kiss
at
christmas

HQN

HQN®

Recycling programs
for this product may
not exist in your area.

ISBN-13: 978-1-335-47703-3

First Kiss at Christmas
Copyright © 2021 by Lee Tobin McClain

Secrets of Summer
Copyright © 2021 by Lee Tobin McClain

This edition published by arrangement with Harlequin Books S.A.

For questions and comments about the quality of this book,
please contact us at CustomerService@Harlequin.com.

HQN
22 Adelaide St. West, 40th Floor
Toronto, Ontario M5H 4E3, Canada
www.Harlequin.com

Printed in U.S.A.

CONTENTS

FIRST KISS AT CHRISTMAS

To My Readers

CHAPTER ONE

KAYLA HARRIS CARRIED a bag of snowflake decorations to the window of her preschool classroom. She started putting them up in a random pattern, humming along to the Christmas music she'd accessed on her phone.

Yes, it was Sunday afternoon, and yes, she was a loser for spending it at work, but she loved her job and wanted the classroom to be ready when the kids returned from Thanksgiving break tomorrow. Nobody could get as excited as a four-year-old about Christmas decorations.

Outside, the November wind tossed the pine branches and jangled the swings on the Coastal Kids Early Learning Center's playground. A lonely seagull swooped across the sky, no doubt headed for the bay. The Chesapeake was home to all kinds of wildlife, year-round. That was one of the things she loved about living here.

Then another kind of movement from the playground caught her eye.

A man in a long, army-type coat, bareheaded, ran after a little boy. When Kayla pushed open the window to see better, she heard the child screaming.

Heart pounding, she rushed downstairs and out the door of the empty school.

The little boy now huddled at the top of the sliding board, mouth wide open as he cried, tears rolling down round, rosy cheeks. The man stood between the slide and a climbing structure, forking his fingers through disheveled hair, not speaking to the child or making any effort to comfort him. This couldn't be the little boy's father. Something was wrong.

She ran toward the sliding board. "Hi, honey," she said to the child, keeping her voice low and calm. "What's the matter?"

"Leave him alone," the man barked out. His ragged jeans and wildly flapping coat made him look disreputable, maybe homeless.

She ignored him, climbed halfway up the ladder, and touched the child's shaking shoulder. "Hi, sweetheart."

The little boy jerked away and, maybe on purpose, maybe not, slid down the slide. The man rushed to catch him at the bottom, and the boy struggled, crying, his little fists pounding, legs kicking.

Kayla pulled out her phone to report a possible child abduction, eyes on the pair, poised to interfere if the man tried to run with the child.

One of the boy's kicks landed in a particularly vulnerable spot, and the man winced and adjusted the child to cradle him as if he were a baby. "Okay, okay," he murmured in a deep, but gentle voice, nothing like the sharp tone in which he'd addressed Kayla. He sat down on the end of the slide and pulled the child close, rocking a little. "You're okay."

The little boy struggled for another few seconds and then stopped, laying his head against the man's broad chest. Apparently, this guy had gained the child's trust, at least to some degree.

For the first time, Kayla wondered if she'd misread the situation. Was this just a scruffy dad? Was she maybe just being her usual awkward self with men?

He looked up at her then, curiosity in his eyes.

Her face heated, but she straightened her shoulders and lifted her chin. She was an education professional trying to help a child. "This is a private school, sir," she said. "What are you doing here?"

The little boy had startled at her voice and his crying intensified. The man ignored her question.

"Is he your son?"

Again, no answer as he stroked the child's hair and whispered something into his ear.

"All right, I guess it's time for the police to straighten this out." She searched for the number, her fingers numb with the cold. Maybe this situation didn't merit a 911 call, but there was definitely something unusual going on. Her small town's police force could straighten it out.

"Wait. Don't call the police." Tony DeNunzio struggled to his feet, the weight of his tense nephew making him awkward. "Everything's okay. I'm his guardian." He didn't owe this woman an explanation, and it irritated him to have to give one, but he didn't want Jax to get even more upset. The child hated cops, and with good reason.

"You're his guardian?" The blonde, petite as she was, made him feel small as her eyes skimmed him up and down.

He glanced down at his clothes and winced. Lifted a hand to his bristly chin and winced again.

He hadn't shaved since they'd arrived in town two days ago, and he'd grabbed these clothes from the heap of clean but wrinkled laundry beside his bed. Not only because he was busy trying to get Jax settled, but because he couldn't bring himself to care about folding laundry and shaving and most of the other tasks under the general heading of personal hygiene. A shower a day, and a bath for Jax, was about all he could manage. His brother and sister—his *surviving* sister—had scolded him about it, back home.

He couldn't explain all of that, didn't need to. It wasn't this shivering stranger's business. "Jax is going to enroll here," he said.

"Really?" Another wave of shivers hit her, making her teeth chatter. Tony didn't know where she'd come from, but apparently her mission of mercy had compelled her to run outside without her coat.

He'd offer her his, but he had a feeling she'd turn up her nose.

"The school is closed on Sundays," she said.

Thank you, Miss Obvious. But given that he and Jax had slipped through a gap in the playground's loosely chained gate, he guessed their presence merited a little more explanation. "I'm trying to get him used to the place before he starts school tomorrow. He has trouble with..." Tony glanced down at Jax, who'd stopped crying and stuck his thumb in his mouth, and a surge of love and frustration rose in him. "He has trouble with basically everything."

The woman shook her head and put a finger to her lips, then pointed at the child.

What was that all about? And who was she, the parenting police? "Do *you* have a reason to be here?" he asked, hearing the truculence in his own voice and not caring.

She narrowed her eyes at him. "I work nearby," she said. "Saw you here and got concerned, because the little guy seemed to be upset. For that matter, he still seems to be."

No denying that. Jax had tensed up as soon as they'd approached the preschool playground, probably because it was similar to places where he'd had other bad experiences. Even though Jax had settled some, Tony could feel the tightness in his muscles, and he rubbed circles on his nephew's back. "He's been kicked out of preschool and day care before," he explained. "This is kind of my last resort."

She frowned. "You know he can hear you, right?"

"Of course he can hear, he's not..." Tony trailed off as he realized what she meant. He shouldn't say negative things about Jax in front of him.

She was right, but she'd also just met him and Jax. Was she really going to start telling him how to raise his nephew?

Of course, probably almost anyone in the world would be better at it than he was.

"Did you let the school know the particulars of his situation?" She leaned against the slide's ladder, her face concerned.

Tony sighed. She must be one of those women who had nothing else to do but criticize how others handled their lives. She *was* cute, though. And it wasn't as if *he* had much else to do, either. He'd completed all the Victory Cottage paperwork, and he couldn't start dealing with the program's other requirements until the business week started tomorrow.

Jax moved restlessly and looked up at him.

Tony set Jax on his feet and gestured toward the play structure. "Go ahead and climb. We'll go back to the cottage before long." He didn't know much about being a parent, but one thing he'd learned in the past three months was that tiring a kid out with active play was a good idea.

Jax nodded and ran over to the playset. His tongue sticking out of one corner of his mouth, forehead wrinkled, he started to climb.

Tony watched him, marveling at how quickly his moods changed. Jax's counselor said all kids were like that, but Jax seemed a little more extreme than most.

No surprise, given what he'd been through.

Tony looked back at the woman, who was watching him expectantly.

"What did you ask me?" Sometimes he worried about himself. It was hard to keep track of conversations, not that he had all that many of them lately. None, except with Jax, since they'd arrived in Pleasant Shores two days ago.

"I asked if you let the school know about his issues," she said. "It might help them help him, if they know what they're working with."

"I didn't tell them about the other schools," he said. "I didn't want to jinx this place, make them think he's a bad kid, right from the get-go. He's not."

"I'm sure he isn't," she said. "He's a real cutie. But still, you should be up front with his teachers and the principal."

Normally he would have told her to mind her own business, but he was just too tired for a fight. "You're probably right." It was another area where he was failing Jax, he guessed. But he was doing the best he could. It wasn't as if he'd had experience with any kids other than Jax. Even overseas, when the other soldiers had given out candy and made friends, he'd tended to terrify the little ones. Too big, too gruff, too used to giving orders.

"Telling the school the whole story will only help him," she said, still studying Jax, her forehead creased.

He frowned at her. "Why would you care?"

"The truth is," she said, "I'm going to be his teacher."

Great. He felt his shoulders slump. Had he just ruined his nephew's chances at this last-resort school?

MONDAY MORNING, KAYLA welcomed the last of her usual students and stood on tiptoes to look down the stairs of the Coastal Kids preschool. Where were Tony and Jax?

She'd informed two of her friendliest and most responsible students that a new boy was coming today and that they should help him to feel at home. If he didn't get here in time for the opening circle, she'd tell all twelve of the kids about Jax.

But maybe his uncle had changed his mind about enrolling him.

Maybe Kayla's mother, who was the principal of the little early learning center, had decided Jax wasn't going to be a good fit and suggested another option for him. That would be rare, but it occasionally happened.

Mom said Kayla fretted too much. Probably true, but it was in the job description. Kayla felt a true calling to nurture and educate the kids in her care. Sometimes, that meant worrying about them.

The Coastal Kids Early Learning Center was housed in an old house that adjoined a local private school. Kayla's classroom was one of three located upstairs, and from hers, she could see down the central staircase to the glassed-in offices. Her mother was welcoming a few stragglers, but there was still no sign of her new student.

She turned back to face her students. "Good job sharing," she said to redheaded Nicole, who was holding out a plastic truck to her friend. "Jacob, we don't run in the classroom. Why don't you look at the new books on our reading shelf?"

After making sure all the kids were occupied with their morning playtime, she stepped out into the hall. If she could flag down her mother, she'd try to find out what was going on with Jax.

And then Tony came into the school, holding Jax's hand. Kayla sucked in a breath. Wow. He cleaned up *really* well. Not that he was entirely cleaned up; he still had the stubbly half beard that made him look a little dangerous, and his thick, dark hair was overlong. But he wore nice jeans and a green sweater with sleeves pushed up to reveal muscular forearms. He knelt so Jax could jump onto his back for a piggyback ride, then stood easily, and Kayla sucked in another breath. There was something about a guy who was physically strong.

He stopped and spoke to Kayla's mother—she'd been occupied with another parent right inside the office, apparently—and then, at her gesture, headed up the stairs toward Kayla's classroom.

Maybe it was the fact that the school was dominated by kids and women, but Tony seemed very, well, *large*. He took the stairs two at a time, still carrying Jax on his back. "Sorry we're late," he said as he came to the door. "Here you go, buddy. You met Miss Kayla before."

He bent to set Jax down, but the boy clung to him like a monkey.

That wasn't surprising, but Kayla had seen every reluctant-new-kid trick in the book. She was ready. "We have a special day for you, Jax. If you like trucks and cars, we have a whole tub of them, and friends who like to play with them, too."

Jax turned his face away and clung tightly to his uncle. *Should I come in?* Tony mouthed to her.

"Better if he comes in on his own," she said quietly, then stepped to Tony's side to be closer to Jax, who still clung to Tony's back. "Jax, honey, after playtime, and circle time, would you like to have the job of feeding our hamster?"

The little boy peeked in her direction for a nanosecond, then buried his face against his uncle's shoulder.

"Come on, buddy," Tony said. "Get down, and we'll go see the hamster." He peeled the boy's hands apart, releasing their death grip on his neck, and swung him to the ground.

Immediately, Jax crouched and grabbed Tony's leg and clung to it. "You come, too."

"Is that okay?" Tony asked her. He knelt and, by holding Jax's hand, managed to get the child to stand on his own two feet.

Having a parent or guardian come in with a new student wasn't ideal, but Jax seemed to have a *lot* of separation anxiety. Which made sense, if he'd had bad experiences at other schools. Kayla made one more try. "How about if we show Uncle Tony the hamster when he comes back to get you?" she suggested. "He'll come back. Moms and dads— and uncles—always come back."

At her words, Tony winced. Jax stared at her for a half second, then his face contorted and he flung himself to the floor, his legs kicking, grabbing desperately at Tony's ankle.

"His mom didn't come back," Tony explained to Kayla over the child's ear-splitting screams.

Kayla pressed a hand to her mouth. "I'm so sorry. That was just the wrong thing to say, then." Behind her, she heard the kids in her class murmuring and gathering around the door. Another kid's tantrum always drew an audience.

Tony knelt and patted his nephew's back. "It's okay, buddy," he said, his voice a low rumble. "You're okay."

"Not okay!" Jax wailed.

Kayla blew out a sigh and looked from Jax to the cluster of children in her care. A couple of them looked upset. Kids this age were starting to develop empathy, which was great, but it also meant that meltdowns could be contagious.

She glanced down the stairs. No help there. "I'm going to get the other kids busy," she said to Tony. "If he can settle down, maybe bring him in for a bit and stay with him?"

He nodded, and she went into the classroom, half closing the door in an attempt to give Tony and Jax some privacy.

She never failed with kids, but she'd failed with Jax this morning. She shouldn't have made an assumption about his family life. With a college degree in early childhood education and three years of full-time experience here at Coastal Kids, she knew better.

She would make it up to him. That was central to her identity as a teacher. It had nothing whatsoever to do with his uncle's concerned brown eyes.

CHAPTER TWO

TO TONY'S RELIEF, he and Jax made it through the three-hour preschool class, but only because Tony held Jax in his lap the entire time. Any hint of backing off, and the tears started up again.

Despite her thoughtless comment about parents always coming back, Kayla seemed to be a good teacher. The kids hung on her, or tried to, but she had a gentle way of detaching and redirecting them that Tony watched closely, hoping he could use a similar strategy with Jax. She actually taught the kids, which Tony hadn't realized even happened in preschool; today, they were learning the letter X, and she had the children form the letter with their fingers and lie down with arms and legs outstretched to make an X shape with their whole bodies.

"Who has the letter X in their name?" she asked.

A precocious-seeming little girl named Pixie shouted out "Me, me!" Kayla had her hold up the name card from her cubby to walk around so each child could point to the x in the middle of her name.

"Anyone else?" she asked, smiling at Tony and Jax.

Jax's mouth curved up just a little, which was a relief; he remembered. Tony had written Jax's name for him many times and had him spell it out with magnetic letters on the fridge in their old place. He was never sure how much Jax retained.

Kayla pulled a name card off a cubby, and sure enough, it said "Jax."

"Do you want to walk it around like Pixie did?" she asked Jax gently.

He shook his head.

"Not even if Uncle Tony walks with you?"

He hesitated, then shook his head again.

"Then, let's see…can we have a volunteer?"

The other children clamored to be the one chosen, and as the class continued, with Jax refusing to participate, Tony's heart hurt for his nephew.

It was Tony's fault the child was in this state. If he hadn't fought with Jax's mother, she might not have returned to her druggie boyfriend and lifestyle. Jax would still have the mom he missed so much.

As the rest of the parents came in and greeted their children, talked with each other and marveled over the construction-paper stars the kids had loaded with glitter, Tony held Jax against his chest and sighed.

He had no idea of how to handle Jax's fears. He was at the end of his rope, which was why he'd agreed to join the Victory Cottage program.

He just hoped Kayla would have some ideas up the sleeve of her oversize red Christmas sweater.

As the other kids and parents trickled out, Tony stood, too, but Kayla put up a hand like a stop sign. "We need to talk."

Great. Was Jax getting kicked out of another school on day one?

And would the boy be glued to Tony's side for the rest of his life? He had a vision of Jax as a teenager, then a grown man, wrapping himself around Tony, unable to let his uncle out of his sight. The image would have been comical, except it wasn't.

"Come on downstairs," Kayla said. "We'll sit and talk, and Jax can play with one of the other kids. Mom set it all up."

Mom, Tony realized as he carried Jax downstairs, was Miss Meg, the principal of the school. Once she and Kayla stood side by side, the resemblance was unmistakable.

"Hi, Jax," Miss Meg said cheerfully. "I've got a friend to play with you while Uncle Tony talks to your new teacher."

Jax turned his face into Tony's chest.

"He has a dog," Miss Meg said. "A really big, really lazy dog."

Jax lifted his head at that and looked past the woman.

"Come on in here." Meg bustled ahead, gesturing, and Tony followed her into a room where a boy about Jax's age— and, indeed, a large dog that looked like a bloodhound— sat waiting.

"I'm Davey," the boy said to Jax. "You can play with my dog, but you have to listen to me, cuz I'm older than you. I'm in kindergarten."

Jax, who hadn't responded in the least to Kayla's nor Tony's pleas, nodded and wiggled to get down.

"His name is Sarge," Davey informed Jax, beckoning him closer. "His ears are soft." He lifted one of the dog's floppy ears.

Tony started to follow his nephew. Jax wasn't accustomed to dogs, and this one, for all its apparent gentleness, was pretty large.

A hand on his arm stopped him. Kayla.

"Maybe let them handle it?" she suggested in a low voice. "Kids are good with each other, sometimes better than we can be."

Tony hesitated. The last thing Jax needed was another scare, another setback. But Jax looked more engaged than

he had all day, listening to the other boy's running mono-
logue. "Right, okay," Tony said, and followed Kayla to a
small table.

"Sorry about the little chairs," she said as she pulled
one out.

Tony raised an eyebrow. No way was he sitting in one of
those. He'd break it. He looked around and spotted a stack
of folding chairs. "Okay if I grab us a couple of those?"

She nodded, and he brought them over, keeping an eye
on his nephew. Jax knelt in front of the bloodhound now,
touching its ear with a hesitant finger.

Meg brought in a laptop and sat near the two boys. "You
two talk," she said to Tony and Kayla. "I'll look out for
the boys."

Which was nice, but it seemed like the whole school was
getting involved in Jax's problems. That didn't bode well,
in Tony's limited experience.

"Hey," Kayla said as soon as they were both seated, "I
apologize again for what I said about mothers. I'm sorry
for your loss. Was Jax's mom young?"

"She was." And he didn't want to talk about it. "Do you
think this is going to work, with Jax? I'm sorry he dis-
rupted your class."

"Of course it'll work." Her voice was matter-of-fact and
confident, and her face was kind, and it felt as if she was
lifting part of the burden off his shoulders. "We just have
to think of some strategies."

"Really? Like what?"

"He can bring a lovey, if he has one."

What was a lovey? He must have looked blank.

"A favorite stuffed animal or blanket?" She straightened
and frowned. "Does Jax have one?"

"Oh. Yeah. It's actually...his mom's sweater." When

Tony had opened his door that awful day, to find Jax crying on his doorstep, the child had been clinging to Stella's sweater. He slept with it every night.

Kayla swallowed. "Wow. Well, he can certainly bring it if it's a comfort. Also, we can start with short visits, if he doesn't want to stay the whole time. He could bring a picture of you, or…" She hesitated. "I don't know if a picture of his mom would help or hurt. How recently did you lose her?"

"Three months ago. I'm not sure a picture of her would help." He looked away. The two boys were still occupied with the dog. Meg, the principal, was typing something on her laptop, and a woman who looked like a janitor was sweeping dirt into a dustpan near where the boys sat.

"Kids pick up on our feelings," Kayla said hesitantly.

He turned back toward her. "What are you saying?"

"Just that…you've had a loss, too, and you seem a little…"

He forced his expression to stay bland as his blood pressure rose. "A little what?"

"Tense," she said. "You seem tense. Are you getting some help?"

Talk about nosy. He wasn't going to share his innermost thoughts with a preschool teacher. "I'm fine." He stood. "Jax, time to go."

Kayla stood, too. She didn't apologize for her intrusive question, just studied him with a raised eyebrow. "I hope you'll bring Jax back tomorrow."

He wanted to say no, but what choice did he have? Jax needed something, and Tony sure wasn't providing it. He forced himself to make nice. "Look, I appreciate your ideas and that you're open to working with Jax. We'll be back. I just… Jax is tired and hungry, and he doesn't do well then."

He rounded up his nephew. "Thanks for everything." He threw the words back in the general direction of the two women and the little boy, and then hurried Jax toward the school's exit, not sure exactly why he felt like he had to escape, fast.

SYLVIE SHAFFER HAD always loved to clean—loved housework, really. So getting the job as the janitor at the Coastal Kids school was an amazing stroke of luck.

It would put her in contact with Jax every day. She could keep an eye on him like her boyfriend, Big Bobby, wanted her to. She could make sure Jax didn't know anything incriminating about the day his mother had died.

She finished sweeping the hallway just as Jax and his uncle emerged from the lunchroom-slash-conference room. They seemed to be in a hurry, and that was just as well. After giving them a quick smile, she looked away. She didn't *think* the boy would recognize her—she'd dyed her hair and cut it—but best not to take the risk.

She wished she could pick Jax up and hug him. They said when you saved a life, you were ever after responsible for that person. She didn't know if she'd exactly saved his life, but she'd gotten him out of harm's way at a dangerous moment. Maybe that was why she felt emotional toward the boy. Or maybe it was because she'd never had kids of her own. Now, at thirty-two and with a much older boyfriend, it didn't look like she would ever have that chance.

She stole another glance in their direction. The uncle was kneeling, zipping up the child's coat.

Jax stared at Sylvie, eyes round.

Uh-oh. Did he recognize her?

Kids were like animals; they sensed things. She bent

down to pick up her dustpan and hurried away from the pair, tense until she heard the door close behind them.

A voice from the office area startled her. "How's it going so far?" That was Miss Meg, her new boss. The woman was in her early fifties but looked younger. She'd probably made better life choices than Sylvie had, fewer mistakes. "You settling in okay?" Miss Meg asked her.

Sylvie nodded. "I just need to mop. Then I'll be done with the downstairs."

"That's great," Meg said, smiling, "but I meant settling into town. Did you find a place to stay?"

Sylvie leaned on her broom. "I did. I'm at the Chesapeake Motor Lodge. Ria, that's the manager, she gave me a deal for the month of December and let me start a few days early."

"Good." There were questions in Miss Meg's eyes, but to her credit, she didn't ask them. Things like "Why are you available to take a temporary job in a town that's new to you?" were legally off the list for bosses to ask.

Still, Sylvie needed to be friendly so she could keep this job. "Pleasant Shores seems like a real nice place," she said. "The downtown's so cute. And I like that it's on the water."

The people seemed friendly, too, even to an outsider. It was too bad Sylvie couldn't open up to anyone.

"It's a wonderful place to live." Miss Meg shifted her laptop and file folders to her other arm. "The job is only three hours per day, and you've been here that already. You're welcome to work a few hours overtime, but you don't have to. You can wait and work on the upstairs tomorrow."

"I'll probably do that. Thanks." She headed for the supply cupboard. The school was pretty clean, but it was obvious that the person she was filling in for had cut some corners. Apparently she'd worked right up to her due date.

"Oh, and Sylvie," Miss Meg said, "I can introduce you to some people, if you'd like to make some friends. Once you're settled."

"That's nice of you, but there's no need." Sylvie focused on pulling the mop and bucket out of the closet so she wouldn't have to look at Miss Meg.

She hoped her reticence wasn't suspicious. Wished she could be honest and take Meg up on the offer, actually. Wished she'd grown up in a nice town like this.

When Big Bobby had told her he wanted her to spend time in a shore town to keep an eye on young Jax, she'd agreed immediately. Mostly because she always did what Bobby said to do, but partly because things hadn't been going so well between them. A break might do them both good.

Part of her wondered whether that was what Bobby had in mind. Had he drummed up the excuse of needing someone to stay close to the child, just to start the process of breaking up?

Would that be a bad thing?

She squirted disinfecting floor cleaner into the mop bucket and started to fill it with water. She'd work a little longer, make a few extra bucks.

Working hard would prevent her from thinking too much.

TUESDAY AFTERNOON, trying to make up for another disastrous morning at preschool, Tony took Jax to the local toy store. It was an old-fashioned-looking small shop in a row of them, on the main street of Pleasant Shores.

"I'll buy you one thing," he said to Jax as they walked in, "but something that doesn't cost much. We have to watch our money."

He figured it would be way too hard for a four-year-old

to understand budgets and money, but to Tony's surprise, Jax nodded as if he were familiar with the concept. Which he might be; Stella had usually been short on funds.

"Can I help you?" The clerk, or maybe the owner, approached without a smile. She had short-cropped hair, a knee-length dress, and sensible shoes. Tony would have pegged her for a nun from a conservative order if she hadn't been working in a toy store.

"We're just looking," he said, hoping to avoid the high-pressure sales pitch used by some smaller stores.

"Let me know if I can help you." She looked Tony up and down, turned, and walked away.

What was *her* problem? But despite the unfriendly sales clerk, the store was a kid's wonderland. Of course, it was decorated for Christmas, with fake cotton snow and colored lights. There was a life-size Santa figure in one corner and a big Christmas tree in another. Even on a weekday afternoon, there were five or six other customers in the shop.

Jax visibly perked up as he looked around at the bounty of toys: stuffed bears and big Tonka trucks, blocks and boats and board games. He hurried from aisle to aisle, and Tony followed, enjoying his nephew's excitement. But the abundance also made him realize that Jax didn't have all that many toys, and he regretted the child's deprived background. Maybe if Tony had been able to help Stella more, financially, she wouldn't have gotten so angry and desperate.

Jax knelt beside a shelf of wooden boats, touching them reverently. Tony stood beside him, partly to make sure he was being gentle with them, and partly to check the price tags. What he saw made him step back. "Almost fifty dollars for a toy boat?" he said. "Sorry, buddy, that's too much for us."

Jax bit his lip and Tony thought he might cry, but then he swallowed hard and nodded.

"They're handcrafted replicas of real historical crabbing boats," the tight-mouthed shopkeeper informed him. "Make sure your son is careful."

Tony opened his mouth to say something not so nice, and then shut it again and simply nodded. He wished he could buy Jax everything, buy him happiness, but he knew from experience as well as his online social work studies that money and toys didn't heal kids.

They wandered on, and fortunately, Jax got interested in some more moderately priced playthings. A father and son waved from the counter, and Tony recognized the boy as belonging to the preschool class. "Hey, Jax, there's a new friend," he said, trying to encourage his nephew's social skills. Maybe if Jax got more familiar with the other kids, he'd actually enjoy preschool.

But when Jax saw the other boy, he hid his face against Tony's leg. Oh, well. One thing at a time.

There were some small military figures of a sort Tony used to play with as a kid, made of green plastic. Tony knelt and looked through the basket, remembering the various poses and weapons. Back then, all the soldiers had been male, a fact Stella had complained about as a toddler. He remembered her bringing in a couple of her baby dolls and insisting that they be allowed to participate. The memory of her dolls, dwarfing the toy soldiers and ordering them around in Stella's childish lisp, made him smile.

"Hey, we could afford a few of these," he said over his shoulder to Jax.

No answer. Jax wasn't there.

Tony leaped to his feet, his knee bumping the basket of soldiers and knocking it over as he looked around wildly, his heart hammering. "Jax! Jax, where are you?"

"He's over here," the father of Jax's classmate called,

pointing to the aisle where Jax had been before, looking at the boats.

Tony rushed over and found Jax walking toward him, his chin trembling. Tony's shouts must have scared him.

"You can't do that, buddy!" He knelt in front of Jax. "You need to stay close by me." All of a sudden the place felt too hot, too crowded. "Look, we need to leave. We'll come back and get you something another time."

He expected a protest from Jax but didn't get it.

Remembering that he'd knocked over some toys, he took Jax's hand and walked to the soldier aisle, but a young clerk was putting the basket back, all refilled.

"Sorry about that," Tony said.

"No problem. Happens all the time."

Tony still felt overly hot in his heavy coat, and he noticed that Jax was sweating, too. "We'll come back another day, buddy," he said, and they walked out into the refreshingly cool air.

"Hey! Sir!" It was the cranky shopkeeper, yelling behind him. From the other direction, a uniformed police officer approached.

Jax knelt and wrapped his arms around his knees.

"This is the man," the shopkeeper said to the officer, her voice shrill. "He stole an expensive toy!"

Jax started to cry as the police officer stopped in front of them. While the officer was at a respectful distance, the shopkeeper stood inches away from him and Jax.

"You're scaring him," Tony said. "Back off."

"You're using him to steal," she accused.

He knelt and picked Jax up. "What?"

And then he felt the large lump beneath Jax's coat. "What's this, buddy?"

Jax ducked his head and tried to twist away.

Uh-oh. Tony set him down, knelt in front of him and unzipped his coat enough to extract the fifty-dollar boat.

"There, you see? They stole one of our special replicas." The shopkeeper sounded triumphant.

Tony took Jax's chin in his hand, forcing the teary child to look into his eyes. "You can't do that, Jax. That's stealing, and it's wrong." He held up the replica toward the shopkeeper without breaking his gaze from his nephew's. "You need to say you're sorry."

"I'm sorry," Jax choked out and then threw himself into his uncle's arms. Tony stood, then picked Jax up and held him on his hip like a much smaller child.

"I apologize, too, ma'am," he said. "I should have been watching him more closely. If the toy's damaged, I'll pay for it."

"You certainly will." She examined the boat from every angle.

Tony felt like a complete failure. Had Stella allowed Jax to shoplift, or at least, had she not taught him that it was wrong? Was Tony depriving Jax too much, causing him to steal?

"You have to nip that kind of criminal behavior in the bud," the shopkeeper said. Which was basically what Tony had been thinking.

But he didn't like hearing it from this negative woman's mouth. "Ma'am, he's four years old."

"That's where it starts," she said tartly.

Blood pounded in Tony's ears. "You might be in the wrong line of work, if you don't like kids."

Two high pink spots appeared on her cheeks. "Well, I never heard such a thing." She turned to the police officer. "Are you going to let this thief stand here and insult me?"

Tony opened his mouth, ready to give her a piece of his

mind, but a glance at his nephew's tearful face stopped him.
He pressed his lips together and shifted Jax to his other hip.

"I'll take it from here, Therese," the officer said.

The father and son from the preschool came out of the
toy store and joined a small crowd that Tony only now noticed had gathered to watch the little drama. He sucked
in a breath and let it out slowly. *Calm, calm,* he repeated
mentally, something he'd learned to do in tense situations
overseas. "I'll pay for the boat," he said to the woman,
reaching for his wallet.

"Never mind. That won't teach the right lesson. At least
I know that much."

Tony ground his teeth.

"You can get back to your shop," the officer said to the
woman, "unless you want to file a report against a four-
year-old."

She made a disgusted sound and marched back into the
store.

"Nothing to see here, folks," the cop said, giving the little crowd a firm stare, and they began to disperse.

Tony now needed to deal with his crying nephew. Did
he punish Jax or comfort him?

An image of Kayla, the pretty preschool teacher, flashed
through his mind. She'd probably know just how to handle
such a situation.

She wasn't here, though, and Tony was. And maybe it
was wrong, but Jax's heartbroken, weakening sobs made
him choose compassion. He stroked his nephew's hair.
"Come on, buddy. It's all over. You said you were sorry."
Then he looked at the cop. "I apologize for all this. Thanks
for defusing the situation."

The officer nodded and held out a hand. "Evan Stone."

"Tony DeNunzio. And this is Jax."

Jax peeked out at Evan and then buried his face again, letting out a couple more sobs.

"He's afraid of police officers," Tony explained. "He's... he's had some bad experiences with them."

Understanding crossed the man's face. "Are you the new Victory Cottage family?" he asked.

Was it that obvious? Tony nodded.

"Good program," Evan said. He reached into his pocket and pulled out a small badge, a plastic imitation of his own larger police one. "Okay if I give this to him?"

"Sure thing." He set Jax down and knelt beside him. "Officer Stone has something for you," he told his nephew. Wind whipped through the street, and Tony zipped Jax's coat up tight again.

When Jax saw the little badge, his eyes lit up.

"You can wear it," the officer said, handing the toy badge to Tony to pin on. "But remember, no taking things from stores unless you pay for them."

Jax nodded seriously and then watched as Tony pinned the badge onto the outside of his coat.

It was more than any of the beleaguered officers back home had been able to do for Jax. Benefit of a small, crime-light town, maybe. "Thanks," he said to Evan, "and again, I'm sorry about what happened. I'll keep a closer eye on him."

"No problem."

As he stood, noticing a few lingering pedestrians who'd watched the interaction, Tony realized he was wearing his long green army coat and that he hadn't shaved. Again.

The unpleasant shopkeeper glared at them from behind the door of her shop, hands on hips.

He made a vow to himself. He was going to clean up and make nice and try to fit in throughout his Victory Cottage stint. He had to, so he could help out his troubled nephew, not mess his life up more.

CHAPTER THREE

ON TUESDAY EVENING, Kayla walked into the Gusty Gull and squinted through the loud, beer-scented darkness until she found her friend Amber sitting at the bar, surrounded by men. Of course.

"Am I late, or were you early?" she asked as she slid onto the barstool beside Amber. "Scoot, guys, she's married."

Amber laughed and waved the guys away. "They know it. They're just fooling around. Look, they bought you a beer." She slid an untouched glass in front of Kayla and pulled her own soda closer.

"Thanks, I could use that." Kayla settled on her stool and looked around the bar. A favorite of the locals, the Gusty Gull was one of the few bars in town that was open year-round, rather than just during the tourist season. A cluster of fishermen—actually, not just men, there was Bisky Castleman with them—occupied a big table along one side of the room. Eighty-something Henry Higbottom held court, as usual, at the other end of the bar, telling what looked like a long, involved story to a couple of women.

In a corner, a group of twenty-something women seemed to be having a wedding shower or bachelorette party, judging from the balloons and the volume of their laughter.

Amber studied her phone and then put it away, chuckling. "Paul's over at the gym teaching a bunch of kids to play basketball, and he says he's losing his mind. So glad you asked me to come out tonight."

"Anytime. Is Davey over there, too?"

"Yep," Amber said through a smile. "And speaking of Davey, I heard from him that you have a new kid at school."

"That's right." And it was one of the reasons Kayla needed this beer she was sipping. Again today, she'd had no success at reaching Jax. He'd clung to his uncle throughout the entire class, despite the raggedy sweater and small photo book Tony had brought along in an attempt to ease his fears.

Amber studied the menu written on the chalkboard above the bar. "Davey said the new boy's dad is scary."

Was Tony scary? "He's big."

"Oooh, I like." Amber looked at her and raised an eyebrow. "Details, please."

Kayla rolled her eyes. "Stop. You've got your own big man."

"I do, and he's perfect." Amber smiled. "Soooo perfect. But even if you love your own dog to pieces, that doesn't mean you don't think the puppies in the pet store are cute."

"Comparing Paul to a dog now?"

Amber laughed, a loud, happy sound that made various people around the bar look their way and smile. Amber was popular, and most people in town knew about her health history and were glad that she was strong and well.

"Anyway," Kayla said, "Tony's not my new student's dad, he's his uncle. Some kind of sad story there, but I'm not sure what it is. They're staying in Victory Cottage."

"Oh." Amber nodded. She, of all people, was familiar with the place and its role in the community; she'd helped Mary Rhoades, the program's benefactor, with the original purchase of the property. "I hope Victory Cottage can help him like it's helped the other residents."

"Me, too." The first resident, William Gross, was happily settled in the community after falling in love with Bisky Castleman. In fact, they were expecting a child together. There had been one other resident so far, a woman, who'd benefited from the program and gone back to her hometown.

The bartender came over, looking frazzled, and they both ordered appetizers and another drink.

"So the new guy," Amber persisted afterward. "Is he single?"

"I don't know. He seems to be Jax's main guardian."

"Could he be the one?" Again, Amber waggled her eyebrows up and down.

Kayla looked up at the ceiling. "I wish I'd never told you that ridiculous New Year's resolution."

"It's a great one. I want you to do it."

"Forget about it."

"No, I feel responsible, since I contributed to one of your bad dates." Amber had at one point told her now-husband, Paul, to see other people, and he'd gone out with Kayla.

And spent the whole evening talking about and pining after Amber. Which was par for Kayla's course.

The bartender brought their appetizers, and after Amber took a delicate bite of a fried clam, she continued pushing Kayla. "I can't even believe it's true. How can you be twenty-five and never been kissed? I mean, you've got the long blond hair and the bodacious bod."

"You mean I'm fat." Kayla crunched on an onion ring.

"Nope, you're just not skinny. Most guys don't like skinny."

Kayla shrugged. She didn't worry about her weight one

way or the other; that was one good thing her mom had done for her. She'd never be the tall, thin model type, nor delicate like Amber, but she was healthy and active and had worn the same size since high school.

"Hey, ladies!" A couple of men from the fishermen's table came over, one standing by Amber, the other by Kayla. "You want some company?"

"Not me." Amber held up her left hand. "Married."

The man beside Kayla smirked at his friend, then boldly reached for Kayla's left hand and held it up. "No ring here."

She jerked her hand away. "I still don't want company," she said firmly, and turned away from the guy.

"Sorry! Jeez. Didn't mean to bother you." The two men headed for the other end of the bar.

"That was cold!" Amber studied Kayla. "And I've seen you do that before."

"Do what?"

"Shut men down."

Kayla shrugged. "I'm not interested in him."

"You don't even know him! He's cute. Give him a chance. Or if you don't like how grabby he was, smile at his friend."

"Oh, well…not tonight." Kayla shoved aside her beer and took a sip of water.

"You need to practice," Amber insisted. "You're so sweet with little kids. Try being sweet with men."

Kayla snorted. "Not sure grown men would appreciate being treated like preschoolers."

There was a shout from the other side of the bar, where a table of college-age guys roared as one of their number stood and shook himself. On their table, a pitcher was on its side. Beer dripped onto the floor.

"Not much more mature than preschoolers," Amber said dryly, nodding at the laughing, jostling group of guys.

Kayla laughed and clinked glasses with Amber.

But she wasn't laughing quite so much inside. Was Amber right, that she was cold? It wouldn't be the first time someone had said so.

The trouble was, she didn't know if she could overcome the past enough to joke around with a guy in a bar the way Amber did so easily.

Let alone find someone who'd give her her first kiss.

If she didn't start somewhere, though, she'd never fulfill her resolution to kiss a man before the year ended…which was a step toward what seemed like the impossible dream of a husband and family of her own.

FRIDAY AT DINNERTIME, Tony held Jax's hand as they trudged through a chilly wind, headed for Pleasant Shores' small downtown area. It would have been smarter to throw together something to eat at home, since Jax was already hungry, but Tony couldn't face the prospect of another evening alone at the cottage.

He'd experienced plenty of loneliness when he'd been stationed overseas. The roller coaster from high stress to boredom and back again had brought out the worst in some of his fellow soldiers, and Tony hadn't liked partying to let off steam the way a lot of the others did. He'd spent a fair number of weekend nights alone in his barracks, reading a spy novel and missing his family and friends stateside. That was why he'd decided to earn his college degree online— so he'd have something to do during the long stretches of downtime.

Even so, being alone with a preschooler 24/7 made him

crave adult interaction in a way he never had during his soldiering days.

Maybe he'd be able to strike up a conversation with a waiter or counter worker. Pathetic.

He'd been on the path to getting settled in his hometown, had just scored a new job as a counselor at the VA, when his sister had been killed and he'd become Jax's full-time guardian. Jax was so troubled that it was hard to find sitters, let alone a steady day care, where he could be comfortably left. Tony had deferred the job and stayed home with his nephew.

At least back home, he'd had some family and a few old friends. Filmore, Pennsylvania, was a struggling rust-belt town with a serious drug problem, but there were good people trying to solve it. His sister was one of them—she ran the fire department, which these days mostly meant getting naloxone to people who'd overdosed. His brother was a force for good in the community, too; he'd started up a street ministry to help the homeless. Having finished his degree in social work online while serving overseas, Tony had planned to join their fight by working at the VA.

All of them had seen the town's problems firsthand, among friends and especially their sister Stella's struggle with drugs. When she'd been killed, both his brother and his sister had tried to help with Jax. But Tony was who Jax wanted. Tony had been named Jax's guardian in a handwritten will they'd found in Stella's things. That made sense, because he'd spent a couple of his military leaves with Stella and Jax and had moved in with them when he'd gotten out. He and Jax were close.

But he'd never approved of Stella's lifestyle, and he hadn't found the best way to communicate his concern to her. Instead, he'd started multiple yelling fights with her for neglecting her son, which had led to her moving out, getting back together with one of her several drug-dealer boyfriends, and getting shot.

Tony's fault.

So caring for Jax was the least he could do, and the Victory Cottage program offered his best hope of that. The fact that Tony knew no one in town and had no one to talk to was insignificant.

They strolled through the downtown area, all decorated with twinkle lights. Jax tugged at Tony's arm and pointed at a shop sign, lit up in the gathering darkness. Goody's Ice Cream.

"Not now, buddy. We need to get a real dinner first."

"Here." Jax planted his feet.

"Later, if you eat your dinner." Tony knew all too well what would happen if Jax consumed nothing but sugar. He'd made that mistake a few times.

"Here!" Jax bellowed and threw himself down onto the icy sidewalk, where he kicked his legs and banged his head on the ground and wailed.

"No ice cream for dinner." He knelt beside Jax. At least this meltdown wasn't about grief; it was just a normal cranky and hungry four-year-old thing. "Stop that, buddy, you'll hurt your head."

"I. Want. Ice. Cream!"

Tony looked around, wondering whether to pick Jax up and carry him back to the cottage or to let this spectacle play out on the street. It was a ten-minute walk home under normal circumstances, but with a struggling, screaming kid, it would take longer.

In the window of the ice cream shop, an older woman in an apron crossed her arms and frowned. Pedestrians stared and then looked away.

And then, like a vision, there was Kayla, dressed in workout clothes and a woolly red hat. Even though she probably couldn't help, since Jax hadn't warmed up to her or her class all week, it was good to see a friendly face.

Kayla veered off from the friend she was jogging with. "Jax! Tony!" She approached them like she was going to swoop Jax up and then stopped abruptly, looking at Tony. "Um, can I help?"

Tony sat back on his heels. "I wish you would," he said wearily. "He wants ice cream for dinner, and he didn't like hearing 'no.'"

"Ooooh." Kayla looked at the ice cream shop and then at Jax, whose cries had ever so slightly decreased in volume. She knelt and lightly rubbed Jax's arm. "Hey," she said, her voice quiet. "I can't talk to you and your uncle if you're so loud."

Jax paused, hiccupped, and then resumed the tantrum.

"I can just take him home." Tony stood. Jax had stopped banging his head, and he was warmly dressed; he wasn't really hurting himself, just wearing himself out. Which meant he'd sleep well tonight.

Tony could have peace and a break. Although, a break to do…what? Watch bad TV? He'd read all the books he'd brought already.

"Goody's does have real food." Kayla stood, too. Apparently she'd come to the same conclusion as Tony, that Jax wasn't doing himself any harm. "The crab cake sandwiches are to die for, and the fries are greasy, but really good."

Tony's stomach rumbled. "Should I give in, though? Won't that reinforce the bad behavior?" He didn't really know; he was just echoing what some of his advice-giving friends and siblings had told him.

Jax rubbed his eyes and sat up, still crying dramatically, but not so loudly.

"Maybe make a deal? If he goes in and behaves and eats real food, he could have some ice cream?" She smiled. "I have to recommend the chocolate milkshakes. They're heavenly." She kissed her fingertips and gestured toward the shop.

Her pink cheeks and sparkly eyes took Tony's attention away from his nephew and his guilt and his aloneness. He smiled for the first time in a long time. "That good, huh?"

"Better. You should try one."

"If the teacher says so, how could I disagree?" He raised an eyebrow at her.

Their gazes held for just a moment too long.

She broke first, laughing a little, looking down at Jax. "He's listening," she said.

Tony knelt beside his nephew. "Okay, kiddo. Miss Kayla says they have healthy food here." If crab cake sandwiches and greasy fries could be considered healthy. "Come in and sit and eat your supper nice, no crying. If you do that, you can have ice cream for dessert."

Jax hiccupped, considering.

Tony pulled out a pocket pack of tissues and wiped at his nephew's messy face.

"Miss Kayla, too?" Jax looked up at his teacher.

Tony caught his breath. It was the first sign of liking that Jax had made toward Kayla. Toward anyone outside his family, actually.

Kayla looked surprised and then gave Jax a big smile. "That's very nice of you."

Tony stood. "I'd be honored if you'd let me buy you dinner."

Her cheeks got pinker, and Tony wondered if it had

sounded like he was asking her out. "You've put up with a lot from us this week. Just consider it a thank-you."

Her forehead creased, and she glanced off in the direction her friend had headed. The woman stood waiting, pointing at her watch. "I'd like to join you," Kayla said, "but I should really get back to my workout."

"Jax and I would love the company." He didn't want her to go back to her workout; he wanted her to join him and Jax for dinner. His eyes skimmed her figure and he briefly noted how well she filled out a pair of running tights. "You don't need to work out."

She flushed again.

He could have kicked himself. That remark had probably sounded as sexist as anything a sleazy politician would say. "Your call, of course. I appreciate your help." He busied himself with helping Jax to his feet and adjusting his hat, and then turned toward the ice cream shop. "Come on, buddy. Let's go in before we freeze."

"Can she come?" Jax asked.

His hand on the door of the shop, he looked at Kayla and raised an eyebrow. He really did hope she'd join them. It would be good for Jax. Yeah. That was what his eagerness was all about.

"Oh, well, I can work out anytime, but how often do I get to have dinner with Jax?" She gave the boy a light touch on the head, not hugging him or doing anything to scare him off.

Jax stared up at her, eyes wide, and then his face creased into a smile. He reached up and took her hand. It looked like the kid was getting a sudden crush.

Given that Kayla had rescued Tony from carrying a screaming four-year-old across town, he felt the same way. "After you," he said, and held the door for her.

KAYLA WALKED INTO Goody's ahead of Tony and Jax, inhaled the familiar scent of fries and crab cakes, and looked around the crowded dining room.

Oh, great.

It was just Kayla's luck that Primrose Miller, the biggest gossip in town, was there. Having dinner with Mary Rhoades and…was that her mom? Really?

Word was sure to spread. But, Kayla reflected, why should she care? It wasn't like it would hurt her reputation, having dinner with the new, handsome man in town. Maybe it would enhance it. She waved to the trio and then turned back to Tony and Jax, pointing to the chalkboard menu and offering advice on Goody's best specialties.

They stood in line, ordered, and then snagged a table to await their dinners. Jax, placated with a packet of crackers, was quiet, with no trace of his former upset.

She studied the little boy as he chewed the food and looked out the window, his face tired but relaxed. He was such a cute child. She was thrilled that he'd reached out to her. Maybe that meant she'd be able to connect and help him.

"Hello!" Primrose Miller called as she buzzed over to their table in her electric wheelchair. "I thought I'd come and greet two new members of our community. Make you feel welcome and invite you to church. But maybe that's already happened." She paused for a split second and then looked from Tony to Kayla and back again. "Are you two seeing each other?"

"No!" Kayla said.

"No!" Tony added at the same time.

He didn't have to sound so adamant about it, but then again, that was typical for Kayla. Friend zone, permanently.

She sighed. "How's it going, Ms. Miller? You said you haven't met Tony and Jax yet?"

Primrose hadn't, so Kayla made introductions. They chatted for a few minutes, and then Primrose got a text that her ride was outside and headed for the exit, waving.

Their food arrived, further calming Jax, so that by the time Mary and Mom stopped by their table on the way out, the child was half-asleep in Tony's lap, ice cream apparently forgotten. At the approach of the two older women, though, Jax tensed and clung more tightly to Tony, turning his face away. What had happened to him to make him so scared of people?

Mary greeted Tony, whom she must have met because she ran the Victory Cottage program. "Word of your romance is spreading around town even as we speak," she told him, eyes sparkling.

Tony looked startled. "What?"

Kayla's cheeks heated and she hurried to explain. "Because Primrose saw us. She's sort of the town crier."

"I hope I didn't cause you any problem, inviting you to have dinner," he said. "Honestly, I was just glad to see a friendly face. I don't know many people in town yet."

The implication being, once he'd made some friends, he wouldn't be inviting Kayla to join him and Jax. That figured.

There was a knock on the window. Kayla's former student Davey was there, and right behind him, his parents: Amber and her husband, Paul.

Jax lifted his head and gave Davey a half smile. Mom noticed it and gestured for Amber to bring him in, so Amber, Paul, and Davey soon crowded around their table, as well. Jax took in the looming adults and buried his face in Tony's chest, but when Davey climbed on the chair beside him and started a knowledgeable discussion of ice cream flavors, Jax seemed to forget his fears.

After it was explained that Paul and Amber had helped Mary purchase the Victory Cottage property, Tony expressed his thanks to all three of them. "It had to be a lot to organize. It's been a godsend for me and Jax." He glanced down at his nephew. "I was at the end of my rope, so I appreciate your setting it up."

"It helped me," Paul said. "I needed a volunteer gig as a part of the program I was in—Healing Heroes—and Mary let me work on Victory Cottage. It was nice, because I could do it while taking care of my son."

"I almost forgot." Tony looked at Mary. "I need to talk to you about the volunteer side of Victory Cottage. I'm not sure how I'm going to manage just now, because Jax isn't comfortable being at the preschool without me. Being anywhere without me, really."

"Hmm." Mary frowned. "We'll have to give that some thought. Unless…" She looked at Kayla's mother.

Mom smiled. "Are you thinking what I'm thinking?"

"Male influences are important for young children, and hard to find," Mary said. "Weren't you just lamenting that even your new janitor is a woman?"

"I was. This would be perfect."

Tony looked confused.

Kayla, though, saw where this was going. "I don't think—"

"It's a perfect solution," Mom interrupted. "Tony, how would you like to volunteer in Kayla's classroom during your time at Victory Cottage?"

CHAPTER FOUR

MIDMORNING ON SATURDAY, Sylvie sat in the chair outside her room at the Chesapeake Motor Lodge, having a smoke and trying to decide what to do with her day.

What would she have been doing back in Filmore?

Saturdays, Big Bobby usually spent with his friends or his ex-wife and youngest son, though he usually came home in the evenings. He insisted he wasn't involved with his ex-wife. It was just that, having a teenager still at home, he wanted to be there for his sports events and such, in a way he hadn't been able to for his older son, Little Bobby. Sylvie agreed with that. Kids came first.

He'd brought her to his little frame house the very night they'd met, eight years ago, and she'd ended up staying. Once she'd pulled herself together, she'd enjoyed giving the place more of a woman's touch. She often occupied herself with cleaning or fixing something, decorating or planting flowers. She liked to bake, too. None of which she could do in a motel room, obviously, even one that had a little kitchenette.

The other thing she liked to do was walk. Maybe she'd take a walk this morning, get the lay of the land. Bobby wanted her to find out where Jax lived so she could keep an eye on him over the weekend, but that seemed a little excessive to Sylvie. Give the boy and his uncle their privacy.

"How's it going, Sylvie?" Ria Martin, the owner of the

motel, walked down the sidewalk that ran along the front of the block of rooms, clipboard in hand. "Everything to your liking?"

"It's great, thanks," she said. "Hope you don't mind my smoking. I'm trying to quit, but I'm not quite there yet."

"As long as it's outside, it's fine. And good for you, trying to quit. Got plans for the day?"

Sylvie stubbed out her cigarette. "Mustering up the energy to go for a walk."

"Oh, hey, do you want company? I *really* need to walk." Ria patted her thigh. "These aren't getting any smaller."

"Uh, sure. Company would be great." Sylvie wasn't used to this kind of casual friendliness. Being the girlfriend of a man involved in the drug trade, however small-time, had made folks in Filmore cautious around her.

Sylvie didn't feel great about it, herself. In fact, she hated it. But Big Bobby had saved her from the streets eight years ago, and back then, she hadn't been in a position to be picky. Hadn't even understood what he did for the first year or so she'd been with him.

"I'll go get on my walking shoes," Ria said. "Meet up by the front office in ten, does that work?"

"Sounds good."

When Sylvie came into the front office, Ria was hugging a handsome man who held a white cane. She turned and beckoned. "Sylvie, this is my husband, Drew Martin. Drew, Sylvie Shaffer. She's staying in suite 6 for the month of December."

The man reached out a hand and Sylvie grasped it. "Pleased to meet you," he said. "You have people in the area?"

"No, not really." Sylvie waved a vague hand. "Just needed a break."

"Pretty place to take one." He turned toward Ria. "I'm

working the afternoon shift at the museum. See you tonight."

"Can't wait," she said, her voice a little husky.

He pulled her in for another quick kiss, and then Sylvie
and Ria set out walking toward a bike path that Ria said
ran along the bay.

"It's nice to see a married couple that likes each other,"
Sylvie said, just to make conversation.

Ria laughed. "We do. We've had our rough patches,
though. Are you married?"

Sylvie shook her head. "Serious boyfriend."

"He okay with your coming here for the month?"

"He's fine. He wanted me to come." Then she bit her
lip. She wasn't supposed to talk about her task of keeping
an eye on Jax.

Ria looked curious. She didn't ask any questions, but
Sylvie found herself talking on. "He loves me, but I think
he might be seeing someone else," she explained as they
crossed Bay Street. "Me being away, it gives him more
freedom."

"Are you okay with that?" Ria asked quietly.

Sylvie opened her mouth and then closed it again. Nobody had ever asked her that question. Most of the good
people in Filmore kept their distance from the likes of her
and Bobby, while Bobby's own cronies, who knew her
background, just thought she was with him for his money.
Thought she was lucky to have him. "I don't know," she
said slowly. "Guess that's something I'll think on, while
I'm here."

"It's a good place to think." Ria gestured out toward
the bay. Low winter sun reflected on it, silvery. Along the
shore, ice had built up around the pilings, making what

looked like fanciful, lacy statues. "Can't look at the bay without realizing there's a bigger picture."

"True enough." Sylvie decided she'd like to walk out here every day. Do some thinking.

"I'm trying to remember where you're from," Ria said. "I know it's on the motel paperwork, but I honestly didn't pay much attention."

"Filmore, Pennsylvania. Small city, halfway between Johnstown and Pittsburgh."

"Filmore…" Ria snapped her fingers. "Isn't that where the new Victory Cottage family is from? Do you know them?"

Why had she let down her guard? "I don't," she said, thinking fast. "They probably live in a different part of town."

"But you've met?" Ria looked curious.

"The little boy goes to the school where I got the job. So tell me about the best places to eat around here. How's the Gusty Gull?"

Ria, agreeably enough, let the conversation be turned. But Sylvie considered it a warning. If her reason for being here came out, Big Bobby wouldn't be happy. He might even be really, really angry.

She'd only seen him that way a few times, but that had been plenty. She needed to keep her mouth shut and keep her distance from these friendly small-town people, for sure.

THE SESSION WITH Jax's new counselor didn't start well.

Tony had wanted a woman, figuring that was what Jax was missing in his life. Plus their male counselor in Filmore hadn't seemed to connect with Jax. And okay, he got a woman. But she was old, way past retirement age in Tony's estimation. Could she be up to date on what counseling was supposed to be these days?

Jax clung to Tony and refused to talk, and no wonder. He wasn't used to older women. He'd never known his grandparents, who had died before he was born.

Unfortunately, choices were limited in a small town like Pleasant Shores. And counseling was part of the program. Elizabeth Cramer, Dr. Liz as she preferred to be called, was basically it.

"Like I told you on the phone, it can take Jax a while to get comfortable with new people," Tony said as his nephew clung to him in full monkey position, arms and legs wrapped around Tony's torso.

Dr. Liz waved a hand. "Nothing I haven't seen before. He can stay right there as long as he feels like it, and then we'll open up the play area when he's ready."

Jax lifted his head at her words and took a quick look around. Tony did, too. The office was set up like a living room, with bookshelves and a couch and comfortable chairs. There was a desk, but Dr. Liz didn't sit behind it. Instead, she perched on the edge of one of the chairs.

She smiled at them. "Let me just open a session record, and we'll get started," she said, and her fingers flew over the keyboard of a small, flat laptop. "Anything changed since your intake?" They'd done that by phone, before he'd arrived.

"We're settled in," he said, "and Jax has been in preschool for the past week. Which… Well. Mixed success." He was learning that you didn't want to say anything a child shouldn't overhear, and he didn't want to discourage Jax about his lack of progress in preschool. He also wanted to ask her opinion of him volunteering in Jax's classroom, but again, he wasn't sure bringing it up in front of Jax was the best idea.

"Good, I'm glad you've gotten him started in that direction. It'll be good for him to socialize." She set the laptop aside, picked up a photo from her desk, and held it toward them. "Jax," she said, "do you like dogs? I have a picture of mine."

Jax didn't budge, so, to be polite, Tony leaned forward. At the sight of the dog, Tony couldn't restrain a laugh. "That's…interesting looking. What breed?"

Jax turned a little, and Dr. Liz shifted so he could see the picture, too. "He's a mix," she explained. "Mom was a bulldog, and dad was a feisty Pomeranian."

Tony studied the photo. "So that explains…"

"The stocky body and the tufted ears, yes. Apparently, the mix is in demand, except the pups can turn out a variety of ways. This particular way wasn't quite what customers wanted, and he ended up at a shelter." She smiled fondly at the photo. "It's okay to laugh. I know he's funny looking."

At that, Jax loosened his grip on Tony and turned to look at the photo. He studied the strange looking dog, his face serious. "Is he nice?" he asked finally.

Dr. Liz didn't make a big deal of Jax's talking. "He's very nice. Would you like to meet him?"

Jax's eyes widened and he nodded.

"Wait here," she said. "No allergies or historical problems with dogs, Uncle Tony, correct?"

Tony remembered then that she'd asked something about animals during their phone intake discussion. "That's right."

She disappeared through the side door of the conference room. A minute later, she came back with the dog they'd seen in the picture. She sat down on the carpet, pulled a tug toy out of her pocket, and waved it in front of the little dog until he grabbed one end and tugged.

Jax sat upright in Tony's lap now, watching.

"We tug gently for a little dog like this, so we don't hurt his teeth," Dr. Liz explained in a conversational tone. "When he gets tired, he likes to climb into a lap." She used the toy to guide the dog into her lap, where he rolled onto his back for a belly rub.

Jax scrambled down and stood beside Tony, watching.

"Even with a little dog, it's important to be careful," the therapist went on. "You don't want to jump around and yell right at first. Dogs don't like to be surprised, any more than you do."

Jax nodded solemnly. That, he could definitely understand. "Can I pet him?"

"Sure thing. Come over and use two fingers right at first. Touch his chest or side, not the top of his head."

Jax dropped to his knees and did exactly as instructed. The dog turned and carelessly slurped Jax's hand, making the boy laugh.

It was a good sound. Tony smiled and Dr. Liz did, too.

"What's his name?" Jax asked.

"Mixter," she said. Gently, she lifted the dog out of her lap and set him on the floor in front of Jax. She pulled a basket of dog toys from beside her chair, putting that in front of Jax, as well. "You can sit on the floor and see which of these he wants to play with today, if you'd like."

Jax sat down instantly, and Dr. Liz came back to sit in her chair across from Tony.

"Thank you," he said to her. "I doubt he'll talk about anything deep today, but at least he's getting comfortable." Tony was definitely getting a more positive impression of Dr. Liz. She seemed to know what she was doing.

"That's our goal. And we don't talk deeply with kids much, anyway. Their concerns come out through play, as I'm sure you know from working with his other therapist."

"Yeah." That guy hadn't been anywhere near as quick to get Jax to relax. Of course, he hadn't had a dog in the office.

"I'll talk to *you* instead," she said, smiling at Tony. "Are you settling into town okay?"

He nodded. "It's a nice place."

When he didn't elaborate, she tilted her head to one side, her eyes shrewd behind horn-rimmed glasses. "I'm a therapist," she said. "You can be honest."

"I know." He laughed a little, feeling surprisingly nervous. "I mean, I'm trained as a counselor, as well. But I guess I'm as slow to warm up as Jax is."

"Fair enough. Are you meeting people? Do you think you and Jax will be able to make some friends through the preschool?"

"I think so." He told her about Davey, how he and Jax seemed friendly already, how Davey's parents had been involved with Mary's Healing Heroes program, the forerunner of Victory Cottage. "Actually," he said after making sure Jax was occupied with rolling a soft ball for Mixter to trot after, "it was brought up that I could volunteer in Jax's classroom. Since he's having trouble letting me out of his sight just now. Do you think that would be a good idea or a mistake?" He'd hesitated to agree, saying he wanted to talk to the counselor first. It had been to give himself the chance to think about it, but now that he'd met Dr. Liz, he actually wanted to know her opinion.

She tapped a pen against the arm of her chair, looking thoughtful. "It might work," she said. "Especially if there's the option to increase the distance gradually. Maybe you could extend out to other classrooms as time goes on, so

Jax knows you're in the building, but he can start to gain some independence."

"Good idea. Although..." He paused, feeling embarrassed.

"What is it?"

"I'm not great with kids," he confessed. "I don't know if it's how I look or how I act or what, but I don't have that kind of..." He waved a hand, unable to describe it. "That way with them, like what you just did with Jax."

"You'll get there," she said. "We can discuss it when you come in for your appointments."

Tony frowned. "I'd like to focus on Jax in these sessions," he said. "My issues aren't the important thing."

She gave him that piercing look again. "I beg to differ. You need to take care of yourself, deal with your own concerns, so you can help Jax."

Mixter trotted over, and Tony ran a hand over the dog's soft back. "I know, you're right. I just meant that Jax takes priority. I'm here to help him heal."

"Of course," she said, and for a minute, they both watched as Jax enticed the dog back to his side with a toy and the two of them rolled on the floor together, tugging. Then she spoke again. "People do better when they're not sacrificing everything for their kids. When they have some goals of their own."

It reminded him of what Kayla had said that first day at the preschool. "Someone, Jax's teacher actually, said kids can sense our anxiety."

"That's true. So give some thought to that for our next session, what goals you might have for yourself for your time here in Pleasant Shores."

"I will." Tony wasn't arrogant enough to think he had no issues. And he used to have goals: he'd wanted to make a difference, to help the people in his hometown, like his siblings did. He'd even begun to think he might like to set-tle down with a good woman, start a family.

But now that he was Jax's guardian, everything had changed. What were his goals now?

And did he have any hope of achieving them?

ON TUESDAY AFTER CLASS, Kayla, Tony, and Jax walked to-gether down toward the bay. It was an unseasonably warm day, windy, with a blue sky and a few scudding clouds.

Kayla had been worried on Monday when Jax and Tony hadn't shown up at class, but he'd called Monday night. They'd missed class because of an appointment with their new family therapist. And the therapist, apparently, thought it would be fine for Tony to volunteer in the class. Even a good thing.

So they'd come to class today, and Jax had stayed glued to his uncle, just like he always did, although he *had* given Kayla a couple of shy smiles. Progress. The plan was for them to discuss Tony's volunteer role after class, and since it was so nice out, they'd decided to walk and talk. It was a way to kill two birds with one stone, since she'd been want-ing to scope out an area where she could bring the kids on a field trip. Tony and Jax could help her.

She kept up some friendly chatter as they walked, point-ing out shops and seabirds and a big yellow cat. Tony obvi-ously could tell that she was trying to engage Jax, and he told her about a cat that lived in their neighborhood back home and a pet shop they'd visited with Jax's aunt. Jax smiled a little and seemed to relax away from the pressure of the classroom situation.

"I know I was foisted on you," Tony said as soon as they reached the bike path that led along the bay. "I'm sorry about that, and if you don't want me, you're always free to turn me down. Although," he added quietly, as Jax ran ahead, chasing a seagull, "I hope you'll allow Jax to continue doing the class, even if it means I'm tagging along."

"No, it's fine." She'd talked to her mother about the volunteer thing, expressed her hesitation about having Tony join the class as an assistant, but she hadn't been able to budge Mom from the notion that the kids needed a male influence.

It was true; having a man in the classroom would, or could, bring a different and valuable perspective. It was just strange and uncomfortable to have this giant, burly male suddenly a part of her class every day. Especially when Amber kept reminding her that he'd be a perfect candidate to fulfill her resolution about finally getting her first kiss. She blew out a breath and tried to clear her head. "Let's talk about what you could do."

"Not much," he said, kicking a stone. "I'm not the best with kids. Stay close, buddy," he added to Jax, who returned immediately to Tony's side.

"Hey now." Her teacher instincts kicked in at Tony's self-deprecating words. "Don't put yourself down. Look how much Jax loves you."

"He doesn't have much choice."

"Right, but you're good with him. I've watched you." Then her cheeks heated. She didn't want to admit, to herself but especially to him, exactly how much she'd watched him since Jax had joined the class.

"You're the one who's good. I admire the way you talk to the kids, and keep discipline without being mean, and teach them. I definitely can't live up to that."

He smiled over at her, and there was what seemed like real admiration in his eyes. It made Kayla's heart speed up. Ridiculous, but… She glanced again. No, she hadn't imagined it. He was looking at her with at least some kind of warmth.

"Well!" She rubbed her hands together. "It's fine if you just want to observe the first few days. If you see a kid struggling, help them out. Encourage sharing."

"Break up fights," he joked. "I get it. I can strong-arm them."

She glanced at his muscular arms. Yes, he could. He surely could.

She cleared her throat. "You could read them a story, maybe. To get them used to you, and you used to being in front of a class. I'm guessing you read to Jax some."

"I can't do voices like you do," he warned.

"You could learn." Kayla felt like she was encouraging an insecure preschooler. "Or how about music? Do you play an instrument?"

"He sings and plays his lay-lee," Jax piped up.

"You play the ukulele?" Kayla asked, delighted.

"Hey now, buddy," he said, mock-scolding Jax, "that's just between us." His cheeks were red.

He was cute when he was embarrassed. And she could only imagine how cute he'd be playing a tiny ukulele, as big and gruff as he was. "Maybe when you get to know the kids better, you'll be brave enough to play a song for them," she teased.

"Uncle Tony's brave!" Jax looked up at her. "He has medals from fighting bad guys."

"Wow, that's cool," she said, meaning it. So Tony was a veteran. Interesting.

"Which doesn't mean I can sing in front of preschoolers." As Jax knelt to study a tiny crab, scuttling at the edge of a puddle, Tony winked at Kayla. "What you do, that takes real guts."

It was her turn to blush. She was terrible about reading men, but...*could* he be just the slightest bit interested in her? Oh, she had no illusions that someone who looked like Tony would be drawn to her for the long-term, but maybe he at least wasn't *not* interested.

Remembering a phone call from Amber made her face feel hotter. Amber had literally crowed Friday night after seeing them together at Goody's. "He's the one, he's the one," she'd chanted. "First kiss, coming up!"

There was no way a guy like Tony would kiss someone like Kayla. But she couldn't deny the notion had its appeal.

A group of women walked toward them, two pushing baby carriages, one holding the hand of a young child, and Kayla felt a pang of longing.

That was what her desire to kiss a man was all about, really. She wanted to marry, have a family, as all her friends were doing.

"Kayla? Kayla Harris? Oh, my gosh, it *is* you!" The woman with the young child stopped. Then the other two did, as well, and Kayla's heart sank to her toes.

These three girls had made her life miserable throughout middle school, until Mom had let her transfer to the private school in Pleasant Shores. She hadn't seen them, except from a distance, since.

The woman who'd spoken, Norleen Michaelson, flicked a glance at Tony and raised an eyebrow. "I didn't know you were married, let alone that you had a child," she said, then knelt in front of Jax. "Look how cute you are, little man!"

Jax reeled back and clung to Tony's leg.

"Aw, how sweet," she said, rising gracefully to her feet and smiling at Kayla, then Tony.

Kayla wasn't sure whether the woman was sincere, but she tried to take the high road. "Jax is one of my students," she explained, "and this is his uncle, Tony. Tony, this is Norleen and Lisa and Pam."

He greeted them all. "You went to school together?" he asked.

"We've been friends since we were in preschool," Norleen said.

Friends, sort of, until their paths had diverged and then Norleen had become a middle-school bully. "We were in school together until I changed to a school in Pleasant Shores," Kayla clarified. "Do you three still live up the coast?"

"We do," Lisa said, indicating herself and Pam, "but Norleen and her daughter just moved here, to Pleasant Shores. We came down to see her new place."

Kayla's stomach lurched. Norleen was living here, in town? She covered her reaction by smiling in the direction of Norleen's daughter, who'd knelt beside a puddle and was poking at a crab with a reed. "Your daughter's cute. What's her name?"

"Rhianna. Say hi." She nudged at her daughter with her foot, and the little girl looked up and waved, then gestured to Jax.

To Kayla's surprise, and judging from his expression, to Tony's as well, Jax went over and knelt beside the little girl.

"I just got divorced," Norleen said. "I'm getting back on the dating scene, which is a challenge for a single parent." She looked from under her lashes at Tony as if waiting for him to agree with her. Was she seriously testing the waters two minutes after meeting Tony?

Norleen had perfect dark hair and was dressed in skinny jeans and a leather jacket that clung to her slender figure.

Just like in middle school, she was still way prettier than Kayla, still more poised around boys.

"We need to get going. Nice to see you ladies." She didn't owe them an explanation, not when they'd been so awful to her in school.

"Nice to meet you," Tony said. "Come on, Jax."

"Hope to see you around," Norleen called after them as they walked on.

Kayla felt awkward. Was Tony waiting for her to provide an explanation for brushing off her old schoolmates?

But no way. She didn't want to admit to handsome Tony what a bullied loser she'd been in school.

Her insides churned. Norleen, the ringleader of the mean girls, was now living in Pleasant Shores. Hopefully she'd changed and grown up; hopefully she wouldn't make Kayla's life miserable the way she had in middle school.

CHAPTER FIVE

DURING HIS YEARS in the military, Tony had been in plenty of scary situations. But he couldn't remember the last time he'd been this nervous. Jax tugged him toward the entrance of the Coastal Kids Early Learning Center, while Tony dragged his heels.

You're assisting in a preschool class. You've met all the kids. Don't be ridiculous.

During circle time, Jax actually sat beside Tony rather than in his lap. That was progress, and Tony would be glad if he weren't so nervous.

Kayla addressed the students. "We have a new helper in our class, students!" she said cheerfully. "Mr. DeNunzio will be helping us over the next few weeks."

"Hi, everyone," he forced himself to say, waving. "You can call me Tony. DeNunzio's hard."

"*Mr.* Tony," Kayla corrected immediately. "Let's all say 'Hi, Mr. Tony'!"

"Hi, Mr. Tony," they chorused dutifully, and to Tony's ears, doubtfully.

"Mr. Tony's going to read to us sometimes," Kayla said. "Maybe he'll even contribute to our music days."

Why had Jax confided that he played the ukulele? He was barely a beginner, on the ukulele that Stella had in the house. Because that had comforted Jax, right at first, Tony had watched a few videos and taught himself a couple of simple songs. Tony waved a hand. "Maybe, but not today."

She seemed to be restraining a laugh. "But not today."

When playtime started, Tony tried to do as Kayla did, walk around and comment on what the kids were doing, ask questions. But there was none of the eager conversation he overheard when Kayla greeted a group. Instead, the kids had wary, one-word answers to everything he said.

Kayla smiled at him encouragingly. "You're doing fine. Just keep an eye on everyone. They'll get used to you. I'm going to work with the group that's struggling with their letters."

She'd gathered those kids in a way that didn't single them out, but made them feel special, which Tony admired. And he knew that having him here to help with the other kids would enable her to focus on that group, so he redoubled his efforts, squatting to appear smaller, softening his voice, and forcing himself to smile more.

He was making progress when Pixie Smith threw up right into the plastic airplane another boy had been playing with.

That boy took one look and started retching, too.

Tony had no idea how to help a kid who was vomiting. During the past three months, Jax hadn't vomited.

Although, from the green look on his face, that might be about to change.

"Hey, Kayla," he called, and knelt beside Pixie. "It's okay, honey. We'll get you cleaned up."

She vomited a little more, crying, and Tony grabbed for a toy towel from the little kitchen and used it to wipe her face.

She cried harder and twisted away from him.

"Okay, Pixie. Come on." Kayla, who'd apparently taken

in the situation with just a glance, arrived with damp cloths and wiped Pixie's face. "Everyone else, go to the book area and get a book, then on your squares."

The kid who'd been gagging, Joey, abruptly threw up.

The rest of the class was too fascinated by the drama to do as Kayla had said.

"Come on, everyone else, get a book. Go to your squares. Now." Tony didn't think to use his nice voice, and the kids responded, hurrying to get books. They looked at him fearfully, though, and Jax clung.

"Here, wipe Joey off." Kayla handed him one of the cloths. But when Tony turned toward Joey, the child screamed and cringed.

So he wouldn't be helping with actual kid cleanup—fine with him, truthfully—but maybe he could be helpful another way. He turned toward the door. Jax was hanging on his leg, so he picked up his nephew and strode to the classroom door. "Sylvie?" he called. Not seeing the janitor, he trotted down the stairs. "Sylvie?"

"Yes?" She came hurrying out of the lunchroom.

"Can you come help me clean up some vomit?" he asked. "Kayla's room."

"Oh sure. Let me bring up supplies."

"Thanks. I need to go back up."

"Go," she said.

Jax was staring at her, his eyes wide. As Tony carried him upstairs, he continued watching the janitor.

Back in the classroom, Tony tried to do damage control. "Janitor's on her way," he said to Kayla, who was kneeling beside the two sick children.

"Did you notify my mom?" Kayla asked.

"No. I should have thought of that."

"It's fine, the janitor's most important. But could you let Mom know, please?"

Good. At least he could help a little, even if the kids were terrified of him. "Sure. Jax, want to sit on a square with the other kids?"

Jax shook his head and clung more tightly onto Tony.

On the way downstairs, he passed Sylvie headed up. He hurried to the office and informed Miss Meg of the situation, and she stood, looking concerned. "We need to get those children's parents here," she said. "Most likely, Pixie just ate something that didn't agree with her, but just in case. We don't want an infection going through the whole class, if we can help it."

"Do you want me to call them while you go help out?" He could handle phone calls way better than he could handle upset kids.

She shook her head. "Numbers are confidential. You go help Kayla out, and tell her I'll be right up."

So he headed back into the classroom, got Jax to sit on a carpet square with the other kids, and helped Sylvie clean up the mess. Kayla calmed the children, and Miss Meg came in and got the sick ones down to the office.

Tony felt totally inadequate.

When he'd been in the military, he'd been considered a good person to have around when things got rough. He was decisive and read situations well.

But he'd been basically useless in a preschool emergency.

It was a little bit ridiculous, and he'd probably see the funny side of it later. All the same, it was a good reminder, especially when you added it on to his failure on the family front with Stella.

He was a bad bet, and Kayla, or anyone, would be better off without him.

ON WEDNESDAY AFTERNOON, Sylvie put on her walking shoes and headed downtown at a brisk pace.

She needed to cheer up after her conversation with Big Bobby.

She'd only been trying to be funny, telling him about the incident at the school. Bobby liked kids and she thought he'd be amused to hear about the chain-reaction throwing up, and how Jax's uncle had turned nearly as green as the kids.

But she'd made the mistake of mentioning that Jax had looked at her funny, that there was a chance he'd recognized her. Bobby had flipped. "Keep your head down!" he'd ordered. "Stay out of that classroom!"

"But I'm working there," she'd argued. "I have to do my job."

"You can make excuses. Just watch the kid from a distance." And then he'd delivered the kicker. "And don't get involved with anyone in the town. Keep to yourself."

She'd agreed, because that was what you did with Big Bobby. He was old, out of shape, but he could still be a scary guy, and he knew people who were even scarier.

After hanging up, she'd sat in her motel room, getting more and more blue. If she wasn't to make any friends in this friendly town, it was going to be a long month.

She'd finally decided to go out for a walk. Nothing Bobby could object to there.

The sun shone over the downtown's cobblestone streets, weakly, a winter sun. Some of the shops were closed for the season, but unlike the shut-down storefronts in Filmore with their broken-out windows, the shops here all had cheerful seasonal displays. The pedestrians mostly smiled at one another.

Not for the first time, Sylvie wondered what her life would have been like if she'd grown up in a place like this.

It wasn't a luxury town, at least not during the off-season. From what she could see, people worked hard. But it was clean, relatively crime free, and just so pretty, with scenic views of the bay from multiple spots in town.

She strolled by a quaint bookstore shaped like a lighthouse, and on impulse she walked inside. Since Bobby didn't want her to make any friends, maybe she'd buy some books to read.

The place was neat and appealing, with a little sitting area and shelves with labels like "Bestsellers" and "Pets" and "Local Interest." Sylvie's spirits lifted. She'd spend a little time here, browse around. She liked to read and didn't do enough of it. While she was here in Pleasant Shores, she vowed, she'd read a book a week, maybe more.

"Hi there, Sylvie!" Her landlord, Ria, waved from the check-out area, where she'd been talking to the cashier, an older woman. Beside them, a teenager leaned on the counter, paging through a magazine. It took only a quick glance to realize they were all related. "Three generations?" Sylvie hazarded a guess, walking over.

"Uh-huh," Ria said. "This is Julie, my mom. She works here at the bookstore. And this is my daughter Kaitlyn. I don't know if you've met. Sylvie is staying at the motel, in suite 6," she explained to the other two.

The teenager gave a semifriendly wave.

"Welcome to Pleasant Shores," Julie said.

Sylvie wished she could stay and chat. But, conscious of Bobby's orders, she smiled but didn't linger. "It's nice to meet you. I'm just looking for a book or two." She headed toward the book displays.

Then, under cover of studying the latest releases, she

couldn't help but watch as the three women talked and joked. What would it be like to be Ria, to be close to both your mother and your daughter, to live near them? Sylvie had no kids, and her own mother hadn't wanted her around—had as much as told her to leave if she didn't like the current boyfriend. She'd done just that at eighteen and had managed okay for a few years, until she'd lost a job and a roommate at the same time. With too much time, too little good company, and no money, she'd drowned her worries in drinking and a few drugs and gotten evicted. She'd been lucky to land with Big Bobby. Things could have gone a lot worse for her.

Now that she was away from Filmore, though, Sylvie was beginning to realize how much her mistakes had cost her.

Another older woman came out from the back of the store, striking, model-thin, with long white hair. "Shoo, you three," she said. "I'll take over. Aren't you getting your nails done or something?"

"Yes, although what good that's going to do me, working at the motel and filling in for the cleaning people, I don't know," Ria said.

"Oh, Mom, c'mon, don't back out now. Your nails look terrible. I'm embarrassed." The teenager grabbed her mother's hand and pulled her toward the door, beckoning to the woman Ria had introduced as Julie. "Come on, Grandma, we have to go!"

The trio left, and Sylvie realized she'd been staring at them like a hungry kid looking into the window of a bakery. What was it about Pleasant Shores that made her long for things she'd never had, never even thought to want?

She studied the books in front of her and realized she'd ended up in the religious and inspirational section. *Not* where she belonged, but one of the books caught her eye.

Resolutions for Superwomen. The cover portrayed a super-hero with her fist clenched and raised high. Sylvie flipped the book over and scanned the back cover, then, carrying it with her, wandered over to the science fiction section.

The white-haired woman stayed at the counter for a few minutes and then headed out onto the sales floor. There were only a couple other customers, and she checked with each one before lighting on Sylvie. "I'm Mary, the owner of Lighthouse Lit. Are you finding what you need?"

"Yes, thanks. Just going to pick up a novel and then head out."

"Very good." She looked at the book in Sylvie's hand. "Oh, the superwomen book! We're reading that one for our book group this month. Are you local?"

"For the moment," Sylvie said. "I'm staying at the Chesapeake Motor Lodge, filling in for a janitor at the Coastal Kids Academy." She pressed her lips together. Why was she revealing so much about herself? Bobby wouldn't like it.

"Oh, wonderful. There's a women's book group that meets here at the shop, and we're discussing that next week, if you'd like to join us."

Sylvie had heard of book groups, but she'd never known anyone who belonged to one. They weren't common in Filmore. "Look…like I said, I'm a janitor. I wouldn't fit."

"We have all kinds of women in the group," the woman said. "We have business owners and teachers and women who fish for a living. It's good to hear from various per-spectives. Anyone who likes to read is welcome."

"Thanks for the invitation, then." Sylvie felt doubtful, but Mary seemed sincere. "I'll think about it."

Maybe she *would* come to the book discussion. That was educational, not social, right? So she wasn't exactly break-ing Bobby's rules. She grabbed a novel off the shelf, one that featured a female character in battle gear on the cover. "I'll take these two books," she told Mary.

They headed for the counter where Mary rung up the books and slid them into a bag, along with a flyer for the book discussion group. "Have you found a church home for while you're here, dear?"

Sylvie almost snorted. No one would have asked such a question back home. "No, I haven't."

"You were looking at the spiritual books, weren't you? I thought it might be an interest." Mary walked with Sylvie to the door of the shop. "If so, there's a lovely church just down by the bay, Catholic. That's where I attend. And right beside the Chesapeake Motor Lodge, there's a small Protestant church that's very friendly. I think services are at nine and eleven o'clock on Sunday mornings." She patted Sylvie on the back. "Welcome to Pleasant Shores."

As Sylvie walked toward the bay, swinging her bag of books, she felt herself smiling. Maybe she *would* go to church, and to the book group, too. What was to stop her? Nobody knew her here. And Big Bobby never needed to find out.

JAX WAS SCREAMING. Tony jolted awake, struggled free from the covers, and leaped out of bed.

He glanced at the clock—2:00 a.m., Wednesday night or rather Thursday morning—and rushed across the hall. Jax sat up in his bed, eyes and mouth wide open, his wails echoing in the tiny room.

"Buddy, buddy, it's okay." But was it? Tony searched the room as Jax continued to scream. The window was securely shut and locked, no one visible outside, no intruders hiding behind the rocking chair or underneath the bed.

He did a quick sweep through the rest of the upstairs—

nothing—and then hurried back into Jax's room and turned on a small lamp. The screaming was slightly less in volume, but still earsplitting. He sat down on the bed and pulled Jax into his arms, noting that the boy was stiff and sweating, his breathing and heartbeat rapid.

Was he hurt? Having a seizure? Tony checked Jax's head and hands and feet, but there were no visible injuries. He felt Jax's forehead. No fever.

"Wake up, it's okay." He stroked Jax's damp hair and rubbed circles on his back, but the boy continued a rhythmic, fussy cry, eyes wide but unseeing. "You had a bad dream," he said, turning Jax to face him. "Jax! Wake up."

There was no change in Jax's rigid posture, no recognition in his eyes. It was as if he were in a trance. Thoughts of rushing him to the ER came to Tony, and he started to stand, but suddenly, he flashed back to a childhood memory. Stella had had similar episodes as a toddler, and since Tony had been a light sleeper, he'd usually been the one to comfort her.

How old had he been, he wondered as he carried Jax back to his own bed. Maybe eleven or twelve, and Stella had probably been just around Jax's age.

The weight of Jax in his arms reminded him of how it had felt to carry Stella as a toddler. Of course, Tony himself had been smaller, so it had been more of a struggle, but a welcome one. Remembering how proud he'd felt when he'd managed to comfort her, get her to stop crying in the middle of the night, made his eyes prickle.

She'd trusted him to help her feel better. She'd always let him tuck her back into her bed and had gone immediately back to sleep.

If only he could go back in time and redo everything from those days forward. If only he'd helped Stella when she'd gone through her difficult teen years, rather than going off to the military, leaving his struggling parents to cope with her adolescent rebellion. If only he'd been as patient with her as a young mother as he'd been with her as a child. Maybe he could have done more to help her get into a better lifestyle, been less critical of her weaknesses.

He settled Jax beside him in own big bed, both of them leaning back against the headboard. Jax was quieter now, just making a low fussy sound. He was warm against Tony's side, the mingled smell of sweat and bubble bath a comfort.

"Hey, Jax, buddy, wake up. You had a bad dream."

Jax shook his head like he was clearing cobwebs from it, looked at Tony with actual awareness...and burst into wide-awake tears. "Mommy, Mommy, want Mommy," he cried as if his heart were broken.

Pain wrapped around Tony's chest, and he pulled Jax into his lap. "Uncle Tony's here," he said.

Jax pounded Tony's chest with a small fist. "I. Want. Mommy!"

Tony hugged Jax closer, effectively restraining the flailing arms, and rocked him back and forth. "I know, buddy. I miss her, too."

It was true, he realized as he cuddled the child close and used the sheet to wipe his tears. Through all the guilt and anger, he just plain missed Stella. He missed her laugh, her funny way of imitating people's voices and mannerisms, her obvious pride in her son.

Jax could have had her with him, still, if it wasn't for Tony and his wretched temper.

He closed his eyes as if that could shut out the pain of his failures, and eventually, he felt Jax relax against him. The child's breathing grew more regular; hopefully, he'd fall back to sleep and stay asleep. His forehead felt a little warm, and he was sweaty. Had he caught the bug that his classmate, Pixie, had had?

Should Tony call a doctor or the hospital?

If there was anything lonelier than being a single, inexperienced caregiver with a sick kid in the middle of the night, Tony didn't know what it was.

For some reason, an image of Kayla flashed into his mind. He wondered what she would say about Jax's nightmare and overheatedness. Given how competently she'd handled the vomiting episode in the classroom, he had the feeling she'd know exactly what to do.

Which was a ridiculous thought. Why had Jax's teacher come to mind in the middle of the night?

Because she's calm and competent and smart, probably. *And pretty.*

And that brought a different kind of image: Kayla, waking up beside him in the night, blond hair messy with sleep, reaching for him...

His stomach tightened and his pulse thrummed. *If only...*

Not happening, he told himself sternly. Not ever. He shook off his thoughts of Kayla and studied his nephew. Jax was breathing steadily now, eyes closed, lashes dark against his damp, flushed cheeks. The moon sent silvery rays through the half-open blinds, making the room feel too bright for sleep, but Tony didn't want to get up and close them for fear of waking the boy.

Instead, he reached for his phone and typed in "toddler wakes up screaming" and learned that in all probability Jax had had something called a night terror. That he wouldn't remember it in the morning, and that Tony shouldn't have woken him up, because that could lead to disorientation and make the child more upset.

Exactly what had happened. Was there any end to the number of kid-related things he didn't know?

He put down the phone and settled back against the pillows.

He had to do better. Had to prioritize Jax even more, rather than thinking about the job or the program or, God forbid, a woman like Kayla.

He'd call her tomorrow and tell her he and Jax wouldn't be in. It wasn't as if he was a terrific help in the classroom, such that the late notice would cause a problem. He'd call Jax's therapist and tell her about the night terror, get her advice, see if he needed to bring Jax in for an extra appointment.

He'd failed Stella, but he wasn't going to fail Jax.

KAYLA SHOULD HAVE known it was going to be a bad day when the new student who showed up was none other than Norleen Michaelson's daughter.

"Surprise!" Norleen cried as she and little Rhianna—who was adorable—showed up at the door of the classroom.

Kayla, busy getting the children ready for their field trip of walking down to the bay, managed to stifle her negative emotions and welcome Rhianna properly. It wasn't easy, though.

Mom had let her know that a new student and parent were coming along on the field trip; she just hadn't mentioned it was Norleen. If she had, Kayla might have thrown a tantrum worthy of one of her students. Being around Norleen brought back way too much hurt and shame.

If there were any small blessings, it was that Tony wasn't here today. He'd called yesterday morning to say that Jax had a slight fever and might have picked up the bug that had taken Pixie down. He thought he should keep Jax home.

Apparently, one day had stretched into two, because he and Jax were nowhere to be seen this morning.

They headed down the street that led to the bay, the children walking as instructed, two by two, holding hands. Two mothers who'd come along for the trip walked in front, chattering like the old friends they were.

That left Kayla to walk in back with Norleen, who'd decided to come along to make sure her daughter adjusted okay to the new class.

You're a grown-up, Kayla reminded herself. *Norleen is, too. She has no power over you.*

"So tell me," Norleen said, "that guy you were with the other day. Is he your boyfriend?"

"No." Kayla didn't say more, even though Norleen looked at her with an expectant expression. She didn't owe Norleen an analysis of her own love life or anything else, and moreover, she didn't want to give the woman any ammunition.

"Is he single, then?" To Kayla's jaded eyes, Norleen seemed to be almost salivating.

"I don't know." Kayla looked up the line of kids. The ones in the front were speeding up, making the line stretch out too long. The mothers, still chatting, had simply stepped aside and let the children go in front. "Russell and Tate, slow down," she called.

The two little boys in question looked back and slightly slowed their pace. One of the mothers turned and walked backward. "Sorry, we'll keep a closer eye on them," she called back to Kayla.

The sun shone brightly, and the kids who'd been sent to school dressed for winter weather were pulling off their hats and gloves and unzipping their coats. A breeze whipped off the bay, still a block away. It tossed Kayla's ponytail and cooled her warm face, bringing with it the fragrance of saltwater and, more faintly, fish.

It soothed her, the natural beauty of her adopted hometown. She was taking the children to experience the wonder of the bay, Norleen's daughter included. She didn't have to flash back to schoolgirl bullying, and she didn't have to respond to any of Norleen's questions or jabs. She just had to do her job and let the rest go.

Norleen wouldn't be around much after today, Kayla assured herself. She'd fade into the group of parents who dropped their children off at nine and picked them up at twelve.

Behind them, she heard a shout. "Hey! Hey, Kayla!"

"Miss Kayla!"

The out-of-breath male voices belonged to Tony and Jax, and as Kayla turned, her stomach knotting with some emotion she couldn't identify, they caught up. "I'm sorry we're late," Tony said. "Jax said he didn't feel well today, and I was going to keep him home again, but when he realized it was field trip day he made a miraculous recovery."

"That's a familiar trick." Norleen stepped in front of Kayla. "I'm Norleen. We met the other day, remember?" She stuck out a hand.

Tony shook it politely and then turned back to Kayla. "Sorry we missed yesterday. Jax had a night terror and was up most of the previous night. I was afraid he might be getting sick."

"That sounds rough." Kayla reached down to pat Jax's shoulder, then looked back at Tony. "Do you know what caused it?"

"You might not know this, not being a mother," Norleen said, "but kids do have nightmares. It's not a big deal." She smiled at Tony.

Kayla gritted her teeth. No, she didn't have kids, but did Norleen have to rub that in?

"What can I do to help with the class?" Tony asked.

Kayla thought. "Why don't you take Jax up to find a partner? There's a group of three."

"My daughter's in that group, he can partner with her," Norleen said quickly. "She's new."

"Sure. *If* he'll let go of me." Tony offered a wry grin. "What else?"

"Russell and Tate are showing a little too much interest in the irrigation ditch," she said. "Make sure the kids stay on the sidewalk."

"Will do." And he moved up the line, stopping at the threesome and miraculously, getting Jax to take Norleen's daughter's hand.

Kayla should have been happy about that, but she wasn't.

She'd managed to separate her painful school years from her adult life. Most of the difficulty had taken place up the coast; few people in Pleasant Shores knew what had happened.

She just wanted to keep it that way, and for some foolish reason, she especially wanted to keep her youthful embarrassment and misery from Tony. Didn't want to see the pity in his eyes.

Having Norleen here threatened to breach the wall she'd put up between those years and her current happy life.

Soon they were at bayside, and Kayla did a solemn safety talk and explained the plan for each child to find five treasures: a stone, a shell, a leaf, a pretty stick, and some kind of surprise. That got them excited. "But no getting in the water, or catching live creatures, or pulling up plants," she cautioned. She taught them the word "ecosystem" and explained the need to be gentle with their natural resources before sending them off to explore the grasses and shells. The mom helpers showed their mettle, keeping close watch on the children, which allowed Kayla to circulate and talk with the kids about what they were finding.

It also allowed Tony and Norleen to stand talking, getting to know each other.

As Kayla walked back and forth with the kids, she caught snatches of their conversation. "New in town," and "single parent," and "tough divorce" were some of the words she overheard.

Annoyed, Kayla perched on a dock far away from them, and kids trickled over in groups of two or three. She helped them decide if they'd achieved their part of the treasure hunt, marveled over their finds and told Russell and Tate that no, seagull droppings didn't qualify as a good surprise item. She pulled a big bottle of hand sanitizer from her bag and made the boys use it.

The sun made jewels on the bay, and a few fishing boats bobbed nearby. Seagulls perched atop the wooden pilings, cawing their concern about the small humans invading their territory.

It didn't matter if Tony and Norleen became close friends, did it? Tony was out of Kayla's league and always would be. Norleen, meanwhile, was even prettier than she'd been in middle school, and although she still seemed a little hostile, she'd at least learned some restraint. That full mouth of hers wasn't twisted in a sneer the way Kayla remembered it, and she hadn't said one openly mean thing. Maybe she'd changed.

Kayla had changed, too, thank heavens. She'd gotten a life, a good life. And if that life didn't include the husband and kids she'd hoped for, well, you couldn't have everything. Look at Norleen, going through a divorce already, at a young age. Look at Tony, suddenly a guardian to his nephew because his sister had died.

She needed to stop feeling sorry for herself, and stop being unfriendly, too. She hopped off the dock and wove her way through the children, checking on them. She chatted for a few minutes with the moms, thanked them for volunteering their time to come on the trip. And then she went and stood beside Tony and Norleen.

"So maybe we can arrange a playdate," Norleen was saying.

Kayla's decision to be friendly faltered.

"Sure, if the kids get along," Tony said easily. He turned to Kayla. "I'm sorry I'm not much help today. You know you can give me orders, right?"

She smiled her appreciation. "I will. For now, everyone's busy and happy."

Norleen smiled over at Kayla. "You just look great," she said. "I'm so glad you got past that awful situation and that everything straightened out." She clapped her hand to her mouth. "Sorry! Bad choice of words. I didn't mean… I shouldn't have…" Her cheeks were flushed. "Kayla wore a back brace all through school. She had that curve in her spine, what was it called?"

"Scoliosis," Kayla gritted out. Even saying the word made sweat drip down her back.

Was Norleen really so socially awkward that she'd blurt out the thing that had made a misery of Kayla's school years? Or had she done it on purpose?

"That must have been hard on you," Tony said.

Kayla opened her mouth to respond, but Norleen jumped in. "Oh, it was. There were some boys who were taking bets on what it would be like to…" She trailed off. "Well. They were awful."

Now there was no doubt in Kayla's mind: Norleen was doing it on purpose. Deliberately bringing up Kayla's worst moments, moments she tried to keep stuffed way back in the depths of her memory. Moments she never told anyone about, because they were too embarrassing.

"A lot of kids teased me about the brace," she said, lifting her chin as she looked hard at Norleen. "Seems to me the girls were worse than the boys."

"Oh, there were some mean girls, all right." Was Norleen smirking? Because she knew Kayla wouldn't throw her under the bus in front of Tony?

And she was right: Kayla wouldn't. Nor would she stay in the company of these two another minute. Let them make friends and have playdates. She was going to move on and find someone else to kiss.

And she was going to do it soon. Like, this weekend.

Maybe it wouldn't be someone with Tony's appeal, but girls who looked like Kayla, girls with her background, girls with scoliosis, didn't get boys like Tony.

She'd go out with the mail carrier who'd been begging for a date for months. She'd join the other single teachers at the Gusty Gull and dance with anyone who asked her.

She'd avoid Tony, because she didn't want to see the surprise and pity in his eyes.

SATURDAY MORNING, Jax banged into Tony's bedroom and jumped on top of him. "Dec-rate! Dec-rate!" he yelled, over and over.

Tony blinked and propped himself up on his elbows and squinted at the time. 6:35 a.m.

He felt a brief longing for his earlier life, for Saturday mornings sleeping in after an evening at a social club with old friends.

But he couldn't be upset, because Jax was here and now and sounding excited and happy, like a normal kid. "Dec-rate! Dec-rate!"

Tony wrestled him into lying down and rubbed his cowlick. "It's too early. Go back to sleep."

The minute he let go, Jax bounced upright and started jumping on the bed. "Dec-rate! Dec-rate!"

No more sleep, then. "Go wash your face and I'll meet you downstairs," he said. "We'll have some cereal and talk about what to do today."

"Dec-rate! Dec-rate!" Jax chanted as he headed for the bathroom they shared.

Tony threw on jeans and a T-shirt, then headed downstairs to start a cup of coffee.

Jax's obsession with holiday decorating had started because the other kids in his preschool class had bragged about their Christmas trees and outdoor decorations. Tony and Jax had walked through town last night and sure enough, there were a couple of streets where the residents seemed to be vying for some highest-volume-of-decorations-per-square-foot prize.

When Jax had begged for an inflatable giant Santa, Tony had explained that they were only living here for a few months. They couldn't buy a bunch of decorations for Victory Cottage when they'd soon settle down back in Filmore.

Jax's face had fallen at that reference, and Tony had felt a little blue as well, thinking of returning to a place where they'd experienced such sadness. He'd quickly changed the subject and agreed to go to a Decoration Swap taking place at the community center today. Tony figured he'd get a small artificial tree and a few ornaments.

Jax ran and jumped and bounced downstairs, and over cereal, they discussed the day. "We'll get a few decorations and come back and put them up," Tony said. "But it's too early. The swap doesn't start until ten. Cartoons first." He didn't feel great about using the TV as a babysitter, but he needed a few quiet minutes with coffee and the news. One of his many imperfections as a guardian.

"Okay," Jax agreed. "Can Miss Kayla come with us? To the swap?"

Tony liked the idea a little too much, and that made him hesitate instead of giving the immediate "no" he should have.

Hope brightened Jax's face. "Can she?"

"No, it's her day off," Tony said. "We'll go by ourselves."

"But I want her to come." Jax looked at Tony with big puppy dog eyes. "Can you ask her?"

"I don't want her to feel pressured," Tony explained.

"What's pressured?"

Tony definitely needed more coffee. He clicked on the TV. "Look, the Muffinheads!"

Thank heavens four-year-olds were distractible.

He poured Jax more cereal and thought about the boy's request. Inviting Kayla to the swap didn't make any sense, but still, Tony was intrigued by the idea.

She'd acted strange yesterday during the field trip, cool. Seemed as if she didn't much like the new mom in the class, and she definitely hadn't wanted to talk about wearing a brace and having scoliosis. Understandable. That would be hard on anyone, but especially a girl.

Tony could relate to wanting to put the past behind you. Everyone had things they weren't comfortable with in their past, and Tony was no exception. Kayla probably didn't want to think about an embarrassing and awkward time.

Tony's own history was darker.

He didn't want to think about how he'd failed to fulfill

his father's deathbed request that he take care of the family. About his relationship with his sister and how it had pushed her out of the family home and into that dealer's arms.

He'd never know exactly what had happened that last day. Had she seen something she wasn't supposed to see? Had she just been caught in the cross fire? Fought with her boyfriend and made him angry—angry enough to kill?

Most of all, he wondered how much Jax had seen and how the boy had ended up on Tony's doorstep. Who would have known to bring him there? Had his sister gasped it out with her last breath?

The police were making limited progress on the case. Tony called every few days, and so far, no arrests.

The problem was, drug-related violence ranked second only to overdoses as causes of death in Filmore. The police were overburdened. Tony and the rest of the family might never get the answers they wanted.

Next door, he could hear dogs barking, and he glanced out the window to see a couple of pit bulls racing around the yard while a woman watched, laughing. The little blue house was some kind of training facility, he'd heard.

Jax brought his bowl into the kitchen and leaned against Tony's leg. "Is it time yet?"

Tony smiled at a four-year-old's notion of time. "No, buddy. The swap doesn't even start for a couple of hours."

"Miss Kayla?" he asked, his voice hopeful.

Tony rubbed a hand over his nephew's head. He'd caused so many problems for this little boy. Shouldn't he make Jax as happy as he could? "Tell you what," he said, "I'll text her. That way, if she happens to want to come, she can come. But no fussing if she doesn't," he warned.

"Thanks, Uncle Tony." Jax leaned in, and Tony put an arm around the boy, love filling his heart.

Whatever he could do to make a Christmas and a life for Jax, he'd do. Including bothering Jax's pretty teacher.

The fact that texting Kayla made his own heart pound a little faster…well. Tony didn't want to examine that reaction too closely.

KAYLA WALKED INTO the Decoration Swap feeling strangely exposed.

No reason, really. She'd been to the community center many times before, had been thinking about coming to the swap anyway. Half the town usually showed up; even those who didn't know about it beforehand or hadn't planned to attend couldn't miss the large blowup decorations on the lawn, mostly a little bedraggled, and all available for a small donation.

Inside, tables were labeled: some held Christmas ornaments, others wreaths, and still others tabletop decorations and ceramics. It was a mishmash of items people wanted to get rid of, whether due to lack of space, outgrowing the item, or simply realizing the purchase had been a mistake. That meant a big proportion of the decorations were of the tacky variety, but that was part of the fun.

Primrose Miller sat at the doorway beside a big Santa head cookie jar that was rapidly filling up with donations. "Just give what you can," she said to everyone who came in. She also gently forced everyone to sign in with at least an email address, guaranteeing further communication from the town council.

Kayla greeted Primrose and bent to sign the sheet.

"Miss Kayla! You came!" Jax ran to her, nearly knocking her over in his enthusiasm, then wrapped his arms around her.

"Gentle, buddy, gentle!" Tony approached and knelt beside his nephew. "You can't just run into people like that."

"It's fine. Hi, honey," she said to Jax, rubbing the top of his head. She was just glad that Jax was so warm toward her, after his rough start in town and in her class. Judging from Tony's pleased expression, he felt the same.

Her faced heated, though, when she saw how closely Primrose was watching the exchange.

"I'll finish signing you in," the older woman said with a meaningful smile. "You three go have fun."

"Um, thanks." She looked quickly at Tony, wondering if he'd noticed Primrose's wink, but he was focused on Jax.

She'd been surprised to get Tony's carefully worded text: Sorry to bother you, but Jax asked if you could join us at the Decoration Swap. Don't feel obligated.

If there had ever been a less enthusiastic invitation, Kayla didn't know what it would be. But since she'd been thinking about coming anyway, and she wanted to support Jax as he came out of his shell, she'd decided it couldn't hurt. Jax was an adorable little boy, and the fact that he'd lost his mother and was still grieving—at the holidays, no less—wrung her heart.

"Thanks for coming," Tony said now. "You can see somebody's thrilled."

Indeed, Jax had taken her hand and was staring up at her with the kind of adoration that would make anyone's day.

And she wasn't going to say the words that wanted to burst out: "And I can see that somebody's *not* thrilled, too."

Oh, well. She'd always been the most popular with the under five set. "What are you men looking for today?"

Jax giggled. "I'm not a man. And we want a great big Santa!"

Kayla glanced up at Tony, laughing. "Sounds like you'll need some help hauling that back to the cottage."

"We're shopping for a small artificial tree and some ornaments," he said, looking at his nephew with an expression he probably thought was stern. "We talked about this, Jax."

Moderate decorations made more sense, given that their stay in town was temporary. But she was suddenly aware of how lonely it could be for Victory Cottage residents during the Christmas season. "Will you be having any company over the holidays, or going home to visit?" she asked Tony and Jax.

"Aunt Pam might come," Jax said doubtfully. "She came to our old house." A shadow crossed his face and then was gone.

"That's right," Tony said. "And if she doesn't come to see us, we'll go to see her after Christmas. Uncle Vince, too." He looked at Kayla. "My brother and sister," he said. "They're both single, and they work a lot at this time of year, but we're hoping they can both get away."

"Mommy got mad at Uncle Vince," Jax said solemnly. "He yelled at her."

Kayla looked quickly at Tony and saw him wince.

"Look at all the Christmas trees!" she said, hoping to change the subject away from what seemed painful. "How big of a tree are you looking for?"

He smiled his gratitude at her. "That's where we disagree," he said. "Jax wants one that touches the ceiling, and I want one I can carry home. We walked down, so I think I'm going to win that argument."

"Smart strategy." They strolled into the part of the center that held multiple artificial trees, bigger ones set up on the floor, and smaller ones on a couple of tables along the wall. People wandered among the trees, measuring, discussing, and greeting friends.

"How about this one, buddy?" Tony pointed to a three-foot tree on the table, already decorated with candy canes and red balls.

"This one!" Jax ran toward the biggest tree in the place, which was where several other children had clustered.

Tony and Kayla followed, and Kayla bent close to examine it. "Oh, man," she said, "that's one of those where you have to stick every branch into the right hole. They take forever to put up."

"Color coded?" he asked.

"Looks like it."

"Bad memories," he said with a rueful grin. "No way. Jax, this one's just too big."

As Jax and Tony continued to discuss the question, Kayla felt a tap on her shoulder and turned to see Amber.

"Having fun?" Amber took her by the arm and pulled her out of earshot. "Did you come with them?"

"No!" Kayla said. Then she smiled. "But I *did* meet them here, at Jax's request."

"Uncle Tony doesn't seem too sad to see you here," Amber said. "He's the one, I can feel it!" She leaned closer and chanted "Kiss! Kiss! Kiss!" into Kayla's ear.

"Shh!" Kayla glanced back over her shoulder to make sure Tony couldn't hear. "Actually, he doesn't seem too enthusiastic about spending time with me. I think he's just trying to encourage Jax to warm up to people."

"Men are funny," Amber said. "Not always in touch with their feelings. You know I had to help Paul along the way."

Kayla laughed outright. "Seems to me you needed a little help yourself, admitting you were madly in love with the guy."

"Mom, look what Daddy said we can get!" Little Davey tugged at Amber's hand. "It's a Santa that sings real loud whenever anyone walks by!"

Amber made mock-horrified eyes at Kayla and let herself be dragged away.

Tony and Jax were dickering over a couple of trees—smaller than Jax's first choice, and bigger than Tony's. The issue now seemed to be that one was evergreen, frosted with tasteful artificial snow—that was Tony's choice—and one made of shiny silver foil needles, which Jax preferred.

"Which do *you* like better, Miss Kayla?" Jax asked.

Kayla winked at Tony. "I like the shiny silver one, of course!"

"See, Uncle Tony?"

"Thanks a lot," he groused, but in a good-natured way. "Now when anyone sees that tree and calls us out for having bad taste, I'll blame you two."

"Nobody's going to see the tree but us, and maybe Aunt Pam," Jax said, his face thoughtful. "Right? 'Cause we don't have any friends here."

Kayla's heart caught. "I hope I can come see it once it's decorated," she said. And then her face heated. *Way to invite yourself over.* It wasn't Tony who'd wanted her to come today, it was Jax.

Now, the child was smiling up at her. "You can come see," he said. "Maybe tomorrow?"

"Um, well, we'll see." Maybe Tony was planning to have cozy playdates around the Christmas tree with Norleen and her daughter.

Although it *was* Kayla they'd called to accompany them, not Norleen.

"We'd love to have you come," Tony said.

"Maybe she could help us decorate!" Jax suggested.

Great. "That's for you and your uncle to do," she said quickly.

"We don't want to take too much of Miss Kayla's time," Tony added. "And we *do* have friends. Remember, Davey's coming over for a playdate real soon."

"Davey's here," Kayla said to Jax before Tony could expand on the idea of playdates, including the potential one with Norleen's daughter. "I think he's talking his mom into getting a Santa decoration." She pointed in the direction Amber and Davey had gone.

"Can I go see?" Jax asked Tony.

"Sure, buddy. Just don't leave this room. I'll be over in a minute."

They both watched as Jax ran over toward Davey, as carefree as any little boy. "He's getting so much better," Kayla said. There. She'd keep the conversation strictly on Jax.

"I can't believe he left my side like that," Tony agreed. "This place is good for him. And thank you again for coming. He really likes you."

"Of course. I have to get some decorations, too. Plus I brought in a few things that were…mistakes. I decorate the classroom every year, and sometimes I go overboard."

Tony nodded and then frowned. "It's hard to figure out how to make a Christmas for him. We don't have a big family, and I know he'll really be missing his mom this year."

"That must be hard." Her heart went out to the man as they drifted over to the refreshment area, where hot cider and hot chocolate and multiple fattening cookies and pastries beckoned. "Does he remember much about his past Christmases with her?"

"I don't know." He frowned, held up three fingers to the hot chocolate guy, and stuffed a ten into the donation bin. Then he carried the three drinks over to the end of a table.

"Stella—that's my sister, Jax's mom—she had a lot of issues, but she tried to give him a good childhood."

"What was the problem, if you don't mind my asking?"

"Drugs," he said briefly. "She was an addict. She was hurt on the job and got hooked on painkillers, then graduated to heroin and fentanyl."

"And that's what…"

"No." He looked away, his jaw tightening. "She was shot."

"Oh, Tony, I'm sorry." She touched his arm, bare where the sleeve of his flannel shirt was rolled up, then pulled her hand quickly away. "How awful."

"I regret things I did wrong every day," he said and then pressed his lips together.

Kayla wondered what those regrets were, but she wouldn't probe. His family's issues were his business.

Kayla understood not wanting to talk about the past, all too well.

The silence got a little awkward, and at the cry of "Uncle Tony!" they both turned. Jax and Davey were dragging a mailbox decoration, taller than they were, in their direction.

Bless kids for providing a distraction.

"Uncle Tony, look! It's a Snoopy mailbox like from the TV show. See, it goes up and down, and there's that bird inside."

As Tony leaned down to discuss the find with Jax and Davey, Kayla spotted Norleen across the room, and her heart sank.

It wasn't just the flicker of annoyance that Norleen seemed to be everywhere Kayla and Tony were. It was the memories she evoked, of that horrible time in Kayla's life and especially of that one bad incident.

Kayla could still remember the horrible feeling of Rufus Jones pushing her back against the wall and trying to plaster his lips to hers while a couple of his friends watched and laughed. Meanwhile, his hands had been pulling up her shirt—probably not with sexual intent, but rather wanting to see and show his friends her brace.

She had twisted away and taken off running, and Rufus hadn't come after her. He was scrawny and harmless, and anyway, he'd been laughing too hard.

It had been a small thing, over in a couple of minutes. But every time she'd gotten close to kissing a man since, Rufus's shiny freckled face, the smell of his teenage-boy sweat, the laughter of his friends...all of it had welled up in her mind and she'd lost the mood and found a way to escape the situation.

It was ridiculous, she knew. It wasn't as if she'd been abused. So many people had suffered so much worse.

Kayla had never seen a counselor about it, never even told anyone, because what would be the use? It was a dumb problem.

It was just that the experience had shaken what little confidence she'd had. The teasing had gotten worse, and she'd retreated farther into her shell.

Jax came to lean against her. "Do you like my mailbox, Miss Kayla?"

"I do like it," she said, smiling at the adorable boy. "But what does Uncle Tony say?"

Tony gave her a wry grin that made visible a dimple on his left cheek. "Uncle Tony's a sucker," he said. "I'm going to need a truck to haul everything home."

Kayla opened her mouth to offer to drive them or help but then closed it again. She'd already inserted herself enough into their lives, and she couldn't continue doing that.

Not when the risk of getting attached—and hurt—was far too great.

CHAPTER SIX

SYLVIE COULD COUNT on one hand the number of church services she'd attended, outside of a few weddings and funerals. But on Sunday morning, with no plans for the day, she remembered Mary's suggestion and walked across the motel's icy lawn to the little white church next door.

It was a small, simple building—just a sanctuary and a wing of classrooms, and according to the signs, something called "Fellowship Hall" downstairs.

She walked into the sanctuary and was pleasantly surprised. Unlike the dark and gloomy churches she'd seen, this one was light and bright. There was a round stained-glass window up front, but the other windows were clear, offering views of the Chesapeake, the scudding clouds and blowing trees. Evergreens hung all around the sanctuary, the Christmassy fragrance mingling with the scent of candle wax. People greeted her and slid down the pew to make room.

The service was informal and easy to follow, the Christmas carols familiar, the sermon interesting and not too long. After the final blessing, as she started to collect her things, she realized that she'd never once felt out of place. And that, for a drug dealer's girlfriend with a rough background, was unusual.

The organist played a quiet medley of Christmas hymns as people lingered in the aisles in little groups, chatting.

Reluctant to go back to her lonely motel room, Sylvie paused halfway to the exit to watch a group of kids running through the pews, most dressed in cute Christmas clothes. She was glad to see that Jax was among them; he just wore a blue sweater and jeans, not a Christmas outfit, but he was playing, interacting with the other kids. He did glance over toward his uncle often, probably reassuring himself that the man was still there. Understandable, given what he'd been through.

Jax saw her, stopped running, and stared. Was he remembering? Sylvie shrugged into her jacket and put up the hood, heart rate accelerating. When she glanced back at Jax, another kid had come up behind him, waving a chain of Christmas bells, and Jax laughed and ran off with him.

There was a buzzing sound behind her, and she turned to see a gray-haired woman riding a bright-red motorized scooter. "I'm glad you came to church, dear," the woman said, reaching out a hand to clasp Sylvie's. "You're the new janitor at the Coastal Kids Academy, isn't that right?"

"I am." Sylvie inclined her head and pushed back her hood to better see the woman. "But…have we met?"

"No, and that's why I hurried up here to catch you. I like to welcome visitors to our church. I'm Primrose Miller." She held out a hand.

"Thank you, Ms. Miller." She bent forward to shake the proffered hand. "I'm Sylvie. Sylvie Shaffer."

"Well, we're pleased to have you here, Sylvie. Did you hear the pastor mention the luncheon after services? Would you like to come?"

Around them, people were drifting off toward the back of the sanctuary. The organ music stopped, and a few people clapped.

"Oh, well…" Sylvie lifted a shoulder. "I heard the pastor mention it, but it's potluck, right? And I didn't bring anything."

"That's not a problem." Primrose turned her scooter toward the back of the building. "The church provides the basics. People do bring sides and desserts, but it's not a requirement. We always end up with way too much food."

"Well…" Sylvie caught a whiff of ham cooking and her stomach growled. "It does smell good."

"Come on," Primrose urged, smiling at her. "You can sit with me and my friends."

"All right. Thank you. You're very kind." Sylvie followed Primrose into the church's hall and listened, amused, to the woman's ongoing commentary on people they met. "That's Erica and Trey Harrison. They adopted the baby your landlady's daughter had—"

"Wait, Ria's daughter Kaitlyn? But she's so young!"

"No, Kaitlyn's sister, Sophia. She's off to college now, but she's been very involved with the child. His name is Hunter." Primrose nodded with satisfaction. "When I was young, girls who got pregnant were sent off, or kept hidden. Nowadays, it's better. Why, everyone in town has a stake in that baby and his well-being. He's got more people to love him than most other babies being raised by their natural families."

"That *is* nice." Sylvie knew plenty of young mothers who hadn't had the benefit of marriage.

"And that's Bisky Castleman," Primrose said, nodding at a very tall, very pregnant woman. "She's pretty old to be having a baby, if you ask me. But then again, no one *does* ask me." She chuckled. "Anyway, I was the first to know, outside of her husband and daughter."

The woman in question put an arm around a man even

taller than she was. As she looked up at him, laughing at something he said, Sylvie's heart twisted.

What would it be like to have a man everyone approved of, to be gossiped about just in a normal way, like Primrose was doing? To be pregnant at an older age, and to be happy about it?

"Bisky's daughter, Sunny, is off in college."

A woman about Primrose's age glared at them. Why? What had they done?

But Primrose took it in stride. "Hello, Goody. No, I'm not gossiping, or not too much anyway. This is Sylvie, and the poor thing is staying at the motel, filling in for that janitor who left on a maternity leave. I'm just telling her who's who."

The woman named Goody gave Sylvie a sour smile, turned, and walked away.

"Don't worry," Primrose said, "Goody's not friendly to anyone. But she runs the local ice cream parlor, and the milkshakes there are the best." They reached the buffet table, laden with ham, scalloped potatoes, and multiple vegetable dishes. Plates of cake and pie were visible at the end of the line.

A pretty, artistic-looking brunette approached them. "Can I help you fill your plate, Primrose?" she asked, giving Sylvie a shy smile.

"Thank you kindly, Gemma. Beef or ham and whatever vegetables are left. I'm going low carb." She wrinkled her nose. "Well…except for cake. I'll have a tiny piece of cake. How's Isaac?"

"We're all doing well, Primrose. How are you? Who's your friend?"

And Sylvie, busy filling her own plate, was introduced

again. There was no way she'd remember everyone's name.
But it was kind of Primrose to take her under her wing.

As Sylvie followed Primrose toward a table, carrying
both of their plates, Ria called to her. "Come sit with us,
Sylvie!"

Sylvie couldn't get over how friendly this community
was. Or maybe it was just the fact that no one knew her and
her disreputable history. "Thank you, but Primrose asked
me to sit with her."

"Go, go," Primrose urged as she pulled her scooter up
beside a table filled with women about her age. "Sit with
the younger people. You'll have more fun."

"Well…" Sylvie felt at a loss. It was lovely to have people
be so friendly, and she didn't care, honestly, where she sat.

"I'll send the pastor over to say hello." Primrose winked
and took her plate from Sylvie.

What was that all about?

"Over here." Ria beckoned her to a table where the two
women Sylvie had met in the bookstore—Julie, Ria's mom,
and Kaitlyn, her teenage daughter—were already sitting,
along with Ria's handsome husband, Drew. Sylvie was soon
swept up in stories about the motel and the town and up-
coming Christmas activities.

As they were digging into dessert—Sylvie had chosen
pecan pie with real whipped cream, and it was fantastic—
the pastor slid into the chair next to her and introduced
himself as Steve. He was good-looking in an all-American
way, with sandy hair and muscular shoulders and a nice
smile. "I hear you're new in town," he said. "I'm glad you
came to church."

"I enjoyed the service." Something made her want to
joke with him. "Almost as much as this pie."

He laughed. "If I can even come close to Julie White's pecan pie, I'm doing the Lord's work."

"Did I hear my name?" The older woman at the table turned toward them.

"Your pie is fantastic," Sylvie said, scraping the last bite from her plate.

"She says it's better than my sermon," the preacher said.

Julie patted Steve's hand. "You just keep practicing, and one day, your sermons will be as good as my pie." She turned back to her conversation with Ria and Kaitlyn.

The pastor's eyes were warm and open and friendly as he asked Sylvie more questions, enough that she got a little spooked. Pleasant Shores' friendliness was nice, but she needed to remember her real life and her purpose for being here. Not to mention Bobby's orders about staying uninvolved. She kept her answers to his questions short and vague.

Finally, he stood. "I need to go mingle, but let me know if you'd like a visit, or you're welcome to stop into the church office anytime."

"Thank you." She watched him leave and then turned to Ria. "Was that...why'd he ask if I'd like a visit? Is that what pastors here do, or was he hitting on me?"

Ria laughed. "I'm pretty sure he'd do that for anyone. He's a real nice guy. Although..." She looked in the direction the pastor had gone. "Actually, I'm not sure."

"He's interested," Kaitlyn said without looking up from her phone.

"Do you think so?" Sylvie asked, a little flattered. Nobody in Filmore would dare to flirt with Big Bobby's girlfriend. "He *is* good-looking."

"You should stop in and see him," Ria urged. "He's a

nice man, and he's really wise. If nothing else, he'd be a good friend or a spiritual mentor."

Kaitlyn snorted.

"He would!" Ria said.

"That's not what he's after," Kaitlyn said.

Julie swatted her granddaughter. "Everything's not about love and romance, the way your generation thinks it is."

"But love and romance are pretty important." Drew put an arm around Ria and tugged her closer. "Right, sweetheart?"

"Drew! We're in church!" But Ria was smiling. "What kind of impression will Sylvie get?"

"A good one," Sylvie said. It was a cozy and fun feeling, being a part of this church and family group.

Then misgivings pushed in on her. It was *too* cozy. What would Big Bobby think?

She had to admit that her relationship with him hadn't been right in a while. He'd sent her here to Pleasant Shores without a qualm, and she'd heard little from him. She knew he was spending time with his son but wondered who else was keeping him company.

The kicker was, even if he was seeing someone else, she didn't feel too upset about that. Nor did she miss the man all that much. She was fond of him, and grateful, but the romance had definitely faded.

People were walking around now, going up to get seconds on dessert, talking with friends, or starting to clean up. She noticed Jax and Tony were seated at the end of a long table with another family. They seemed to be having a good time and settling in here, just as Sylvie was.

If anyone asked, if Big Bobby asked, she could just say she was keeping an eye on the two of them. Couldn't she?

On the way out, she stopped to visit with Primrose.

"Did you talk with the pastor?" the older woman asked, eyes sharp and interested.

"I did," Sylvie said slowly. "He was very…friendly."

"Of course he was," Primrose said. "The man is lonely, and you're a pretty woman."

Was she pretty? It had been a long time since anyone had told her so. "You're sweet."

"I'm observant," Primrose corrected. "There's a difference. Are you headed home?"

"I guess I am. How about you?"

"I am as well," Primrose said. "I promised myself that I'd get to cleaning my kitchen. It's disgraceful, but I have trouble finding the energy to work on it."

"Would you like some company?" Sylvie asked impulsively. "I like to clean."

Primrose looked startled. "You want to come over?"

Sylvie winced. "Sorry. I guess I invited myself."

"No, I'm glad," Primrose said as they moved toward the elevator. "I was just surprised. Especially since it's cleaning we're talking about."

"I'd love to come," Sylvie said. "I have nothing planned for this afternoon, and it's gloomy to sit inside a motel room."

"If you're certain, then that would be lovely." Primrose smiled. "Thank you, dear. I ride the church van, and you're welcome to ride along."

"Or I can take you in my car. It's just over in the motel parking lot."

"Even better, dear."

They took the long way around to the parking lot because it was more accessible to Primrose's scooter. "People think I'm too nosy and full of gossip, you see," Primrose said, her voice bubbly. "For the most part, people don't want to come visit me."

Sylvie could see how folks would think that—Primrose *did* seem to know everyone's business—but she shrugged. "You've just been nice to me, even though I'm a stranger. I appreciated the invitation to lunch."

"You're a sweet girl," Primrose said.

As she helped Primrose into the car and then followed her instructions to fold up her mobility scooter, Sylvie reflected that, once again, she was doing exactly what Big Bobby had told her not to do: she was getting involved with the people of Pleasant Shores.

Not only that, but she was enjoying it. What would Bobby think?

On Sunday afternoon, Kayla looked around the outlet mall's food court, crowded with Christmas shoppers. She finally saw Amber and Erica waving from a tiny table beside the windows.

Artificial evergreen garland, decorated with tinsel and red ribbons, hung from the ceiling, and signs on the walls proclaimed sales. The smell of fries and cinnamon buns and the sound of "Grandma Got Run Over by a Reindeer" filled the air. Kayla wove through the family groups and finally plunked her tray on the table. "I see we're all going healthy," she said, laughing at Amber's huge paper basket of onion rings and Erica's pizza slices. Her own fast-food tacos smelled fantastic, and she dug in.

Beside them, a toddler whacked her baby brother with a plastic sword and then, scolded by her mother, burst into tears.

Some surrounding shoppers frowned at the shrill noise,

but Amber and Erica grinned at each other. "You as glad as I am to get away from kids?" Amber asked her sister.

"Yep. I mean, Hunter's only a year and a half, but it's like he senses Christmas in the air. He doesn't want to nap or go to bed. I think he's afraid of missing something."

"Davey's wild," Amber said.

"He's on a constant sugar high," Erica said, "because you won't stop baking cookies."

"Me and Hannah both." Hannah was Amber's college-age daughter, now home for Christmas vacation.

"How about the kids in your class, Kayla?" Erica asked. "Are they driving you up the wall yet?"

"Getting more excited every day." Kayla dipped a tortilla chip in salsa. "And yesterday—" she lowered her voice, conscious of the little ones around her "—Pixie announced there's no Santa Claus."

"What?" Erica's mouth dropped open.

"Oh, no!" Amber was laughing.

Kayla nodded. "I had to do major damage control, and I still got phone calls from parents."

"Kids at that age are adorable," Amber said, "but you couldn't pay me to do your job."

"I love it." Kayla wiped salsa off her fingers. "The truth is, I wish I had kids at home to get away from. You're both lucky."

"You're right," Erica said quickly. "I'm glad for a break, but I'm grateful for Trey and Hunter every day."

"Same, with Paul and Davey," Amber said. "Speaking of families and romance and babies…how's your goal coming along?" She raised her eyebrows.

"Don't—" Kayla began, and then sighed and didn't bother finishing the thought. She didn't know Erica as well as she knew Amber, but she doubted there was much point in trying to keep a secret between the sisters.

"Can't we just tell Erica?" Amber asked. "Please?"

"Stop being that way," Erica scolded. "Some people actually have a sense of privacy. You don't have to tell me your secrets, Kayla."

"It's fine," Kayla said. "She's talking about my New Year's resolution to kiss a man this year." She took a big bite of taco.

"Aw, that's…" Erica frowned. "Wait, why did that need to be a resolution?"

"Because she never did it before! Isn't that ridiculous?"

Erica poked her sister's arm with a pizza crust. "No, it's not ridiculous! Just because *you* were kissing boys at twelve—"

"Eight," Amber said. "Howard Goldbloom. Behind the bushes outside of the school."

"See? *That's* what's ridiculous." Erica turned to Kayla, who was laughing. "Did you have a particular reason to wait? Like a religious belief?"

"No, nothing like that." The family at the next table had gotten their two kids calmed down, the mom holding the toddler while the father lifted the baby high, then swooped him down low, then lifted him again. "Actually," she said, "it was Rufus Jones."

"You *did* kiss a guy? I thought—"

"He *tried* to kiss me. But it really wasn't about kissing. He just wanted to see my brace and show it to the other kids." She explained about the scoliosis, surprising herself, because she rarely talked about it.

"Is that why you wear those baggy sweaters?" Amber asked. "Because of the brace?"

"No!" Kayla stared at her. "I haven't worn it since I

was sixteen." Couldn't people tell she didn't wear a brace anymore?

Erica play-punched her sister on the arm. "Her sweaters are cute."

"They *are* cute," Amber said, rolling her eyes. "*Davey* loves them."

Kayla looked down at herself. She was wearing a loose green sweater with a Christmas elf on it. "Are they bad?" she asked, stricken. "Tell the truth."

"No!" Erica said firmly. "They're adorable."

Kayla thought back, frowning. "I did get in the habit of loose clothes when I wore my brace. Kinda my formative fashion years, you know? And then the kids love seasonal stuff." She had a whole collection of autumn, Easter, and other holiday tops.

"There's nothing wrong with them," Amber said. "Not at all. It's just that…they're too big. You've got this amazing figure, and you never show it off."

"Not flat like us." Erica gestured down at herself. She was almost as thin as Amber was.

"It takes all kinds." Kayla shrugged. "I'm a curvy girl. Always have been." And she just didn't think a whole lot about her figure.

But the sisters' comments did make her think. Was she dressing wrong for her age and body? Was she stuck back in her teenage years, fashion-wise?

"You know," Amber said to Erica, "we're going lingerie shopping next, right?"

"Right." Erica looked at Kayla. "We agreed to buy pretty lingerie for each other for Christmas. Since we both have scars to cover."

"And husbands to impress," Amber added. "That's the main thing. Not the scars."

The sisters' eyes met and held for the briefest moment. Amber's scars were from cancer surgeries, and she was open about that. Occasionally, she talked about her higher-than-usual risk of recurrence.

It sounded like Erica might have had surgeries, too, but Kayla didn't want to be intrusive and ask.

She didn't need to. "I had preventive surgery," Erica explained. "I have one of those genes that makes reproductive cancers super likely."

"We all do, or did," Amber chimed in. "Me, Erica, and Mom."

"And since both Mom and Amber got cancer," Erica went on, "my doctors wanted me to go ahead and have a hysterectomy." Her voice tightened a little at the end.

Amber put a hand over her sister's. "Which was a wise decision," she said. "I helped talk her into it, because I sure didn't want her to go through what I went through." She swallowed. "And I didn't want to lose her like we lost Mom."

"Oh, wow, I'm so sorry," Kayla said, her heart aching for the sisters. "That all sounds really hard to cope with."

"We're lucky to have each other," Erica said.

"Even if we drive each other crazy sometimes." Amber stuck her tongue out at Erica, lightening the mood.

Their conversation got more general then, as they finished up their food and walked out into the mall. But Kayla couldn't stop thinking about what they'd said.

Amber and Erica had gone through a terrible challenge and come out strong. They'd both found families.

So what was Kayla's problem that she let one bad experience in middle school—not even that bad, either, not like a lot of women endured—keep her from finding happiness?

They stopped in front of a trendy store with improbably

built mannequins dressed in bright red bras and tiny underwear and Santa hats.

"Come on, let's get you some push-up bras!" Amber pulled Kayla inside. "That, and some V-necked sweaters, and the men will be lining up to kiss you!"

"Shh! I can't!" Kayla protested weakly. She didn't want to admit that she'd never even been inside a store like that.

"The sweaters don't have to be tight," Erica said. "Just... not baggy."

"They can even have elves and reindeer on them, as long as they fit." Amber flagged down a saleslady. "She needs a bra fitting. She's buying like six new bras."

The woman's eyes lit up. She grabbed a tape measure and draped it around her neck. "Right this way," she said.

Beckoned from ahead by the saleslady, and nudged from behind by Amber, Kayla went into the fitting room and learned she'd been wearing the wrong size bra for years, "like most women," the lady assured her.

Amber had followed them into the fitting room area and was waiting outside the door. "What size?" she asked, and the saleslady told her before Kayla could protest.

Someone in the next cubicle called out a question, and the saleslady stepped out. "I won't go far," she promised Kayla before she walked away.

"Stay there," Amber called as Kayla started to pull on her sweater. "Don't get dressed." She was soon back with an armload of bras the likes of which Kayla had never seen before.

Kayla tried on the plainest-looking one, white with a little lace, and studied herself in the mirror. Her face heated.

She used to play in front of the mirror as a little girl, like most kids. But once she'd gotten the brace, she'd avoided looking at herself.

Now…wow. The bra lifted everything up instead of flattening her down and it was…sort of impressive. Sort of too much, too.

She studied herself full-length. It was a body that wasn't at all like those on TV or in magazines, and it was worlds away from the mannequins in the shop windows. But she definitely had cleavage, and hips, and a decently nipped-in waist.

She turned around and looked over her shoulder. *That* was the best part: her strong, straight back.

"Now, put this on and look at the difference," Amber said. She tossed a novelty top over the transom. Kayla held it up and had to laugh; it said "Get Lit" and sported a flashing Christmas tree.

It was also two sizes smaller than Kayla's usual.

"I can't wear this," she called out to Amber. "It's too small, and it's inappropriate."

"Just try it on and show us. You don't have to buy it."

"Did anyone ever tell you you should be in sales?" But Kayla put on the sweater and studied herself in the mirror.

She frowned and turned sideways. She didn't look half bad.

"How's she doing?" Erica asked from her own fitting room.

"Let us see," Amber said, and Kayla opened the door.

"Oh, that's so cute!" Erica said, peeking out of her cubicle.

"See! You're a knockout." Amber smiled with satisfaction, and beckoned the sales clerk over. "She'll take five of those bras, plus that sweater."

"Whoa, slow down!" Kayla was laughing. "I'll take two bras but not the sweater. Can't wear a top that suggests drinking in front of the kids," she added.

"They won't get it," Amber argued.

"But their parents will." Kayla went back into the fitting room and changed into her regular clothes, which now felt frumpy. Maybe, if they hit a less risqué store, she *would* buy a couple of new, better-fitting sweaters for work.

The thought of Tony seeing her in more body-skimming clothes made her heart pound. Would he notice? Would he like how she looked?

She walked out of the cubicle to see Amber and Erica next to each other on a big round bolster in the waiting area, studying each other's phones.

"See, Davey had such a good time making Christmas cookies with me and Hannah." Amber smiled as she scrolled through photos, holding the phone so Erica could see it.

"That face!" Erica looked up and saw her. "Come look at Davey. He's covered with frosting."

Kayla looked and laughed, and then looked at photos of baby Hunter in several of his latest Christmas outfits, of which he apparently had many.

"Let's go!" Amber said eventually. "We still have to shop for Crabby Christmas. You can get something sexy to wear to the cocktail hour," she said to Kayla. "But this time, get your own date," she added jokingly.

It had been at Crabby Christmas, last year, that Kayla had had her awful date with Paul, now Amber's husband.

"Or you can come with me and Trey," Erica said. "I'm definitely getting a new dress."

"Thanks." But all of a sudden, Kayla didn't want to be a third wheel. And she didn't want to be there with someone else's boyfriend.

She wanted a real date to Crabby Christmas. And not just any real date, she realized as she paid for her new bras. She wanted her date to be Tony.

Which probably meant she'd have to ask him. But could she possibly muster up the courage?

CHAPTER SEVEN

LATE SUNDAY AFTERNOON, Tony sat on the couch at Paul and Amber's place, watching football and drinking a second beer.

Paul lazed in the recliner, and the boys ran around in circles, living room to kitchen to dining room, shouting and waving plastic light sabers.

It had been a nice afternoon. They'd run into Paul, Amber, and Davey at the church lunch, and Paul had invited them to come over to keep them company while Amber went shopping. "It'd be a help," Paul had said. "Jax and Davey get along well, and with kids, it's one plus one equals zero." Which Tony hadn't understood, but now he did: when two kids played happily with each other, the adult responsibility for entertaining them reduced to zero.

Tony was just thinking he and Jax should leave, go home and get some dinner, when the front door opened. Amber came in with a flurry of shopping bags…and Kayla. The two women were laughing and talking, faces pink with the cold, and in the moment before she noticed him, Tony just sat and admired Kayla. She seemed to embody all the fun and goodness he wanted. He couldn't have it, no, but it sure was nice to look at.

"Miss Kayla!" Jax rushed to her and hugged her legs.

Kayla's forehead wrinkled and she glanced up and spotted Tony. "I didn't know—" She broke off and focused on Jax, ruffling his hair and kneeling to speak to him.

But Tony could finish her sentence: she didn't know Jax and Tony would be here, at Paul and Amber's. He and Jax had walked over, so there was no car to give a warning. And it seemed possible, based on the guilty smile on Amber's face, that *she'd* known but hadn't told Kayla.

What was up with that?

Paul hugged his wife and then started tapping his phone. "Everyone, stay for dinner," he said. "I'm cooking. Which means I just now—" he flourished his phone "—ordered pizza."

"Told you," Amber said to Kayla.

"We can't stay," Tony said quickly, standing. He didn't want to put Kayla in an uncomfortable spot. "We've been here all afternoon."

"But I want Jax to stay," Davey said.

"Yeah, Uncle Tony. Can we stay?" Jax asked.

The two sets of pleading eyes were hard to resist.

"Don't go!" Amber was piling packages in a chair. "I'd love to get to know Jax better."

"One plus one equals zero," Paul reminded him.

Kayla didn't make a plea either way, but she didn't look too upset at the prospect, so Tony agreed. Only to get more concerned as Jax continued to hang on Kayla, holding her hand, leaning against her when she sat down, even clinging to her leg when she tried to get up.

Tony called Jax over and talked with him, tried to distract him by encouraging him to play with Sarge the bloodhound, and decided he'd definitely talk to the therapist about this at their appointment tomorrow. He needed to find out if Jax's growing attachment to his new teacher was a bad thing.

As for his own growing attachment...he didn't have to ask a therapist. He knew it wasn't wise.

He'd always figured he'd meet a great woman, settle down, start a family. But he didn't deserve that, not now, not when he'd failed to protect his sister. Not when he was the reason Jax had lost his mother.

His responsibility was to take care of his nephew and help him heal, not to think about his own needs and desires.

"So, um, a hurricane hit the house, is that it?" Amber joked. She'd leaned back against Paul and his arms were wrapped around her from behind. They both looked so happy that it made Tony's heart hurt with jealousy.

He looked at Kayla to discover she was watching them, too, but he couldn't read her expression.

"Hey, we were babysitting," Paul said. "You know men can't multitask."

Tony looked around the house and realized that, indeed, there were toys strewn across the floor. Sarge was eating chips from a bowl on the coffee table. Jax and Davey had gone back to chasing each other.

"We'll clean it up, promise," Tony said to Amber as Paul shooed the dog away from the food.

"I was kidding. We had such a good time shopping, I couldn't be mad no matter what I found at home." She winked at Kayla. "We got some great stuff, right?"

Kayla's cheeks went pink. "Uh-huh," she said, and knelt to pet the bloodhound.

"What did you get *me*?" Davey asked Amber.

"Now, why would you think I got you something?" she teased.

As Davey tugged at her and begged her to tell him what she'd gotten him, Jax frowned like he was thinking hard. Then he looked up at Kayla. "What did *you* get *me*?"

Uh-oh. "Hey, Jax. Miss Kayla is your teacher. She's not like Miss Amber. She's not part of our family. She doesn't buy us presents."

"She's not your mommy," Davey further explained.

Amber put a hand on Davey's shoulder and, when he looked up at her, shook her head.

Kayla bit her lip but didn't speak.

Jax frowned. "My mommy died," he said slowly. "That means her body stopped working and we can't see her 'live anymore."

Tony's throat tightened. It was the explanation he'd given Jax, and repeated several times, coached by the therapist they'd visited back in Filmore.

"My mommy died, too," Davey said. "She got real sick."

Jax looked puzzled. "Miss Amber is your mom."

"Miss Amber is my *new* mom."

"Oh." Jax looked speculatively at Amber, then at Kayla.

Tony had to step in, or Jax would start to have dreams that could never be realized. "Your mommy loved you very much," Tony said. That was something the therapists wanted him to emphasize to Jax. "It's not your fault she died."

He caught Kayla looking at him. She gave him the tiniest nod, which made sense. She was trained in early childhood education, which probably meant she was trained in how kids tended to think about death—namely, how they tended to think it was their fault.

"We talk to my mommy every night when we pray," Jax told Davey.

"Us, too," Davey said. Then he glanced up at Paul. "Not every night. Sometimes I forget." He squatted, and Sarge came over to nudge his hand with his big muzzle. "Sometimes," Davey added, "I forget what she looked like, but Daddy shows me pictures and then I remember."

Paul sat down on the floor and pulled Davey into his lap, and Amber perched on the couch, watching them with a mix of love and pain in her eyes.

Jax went over and leaned against Sarge. "I heard a big bang," he told Davey. "My mom fell down and didn't get up."

Tony sucked in a breath. Jax had never said that before. Was he starting to remember the day of the shooting?

Kayla pressed her hand to her mouth, just for a minute, and sank down onto a chair. She didn't speak, and Tony appreciated that. Lots of people couldn't handle this sort of discussion from kids. He could barely handle it himself.

"Why didn't she get up?" Davey asked.

Jax looked up at Tony.

Immediately, he knelt, then sat on the floor beside his nephew. Jax scooted right into his lap.

"Do you want to tell about it?" Tony asked. He dreaded it, and moreover, he wasn't sure it would be a great thing for Davey to hear about. His biggest priority, though, was Jax. These difficult conversations didn't ever come up at predictable times, but from all his reading, he knew it was important for Jax to discuss his mom's death if he felt the need, for him to know the subject wasn't taboo.

"It's okay if you don't want to talk about it," Amber said quietly.

Jax looked up at Tony. "You tell."

"Sure, buddy." He closed his eyes for the briefest second and then opened them again. He looked at Amber, then at Paul. "It's a sad story," he said, giving them the chance to withdraw their son.

"Sometimes things are sad," Paul said. "It's better to face it." It was tacit permission to go on.

Tony nodded, took another breath, and reached for a child-level explanation. "Jax's mom was walking to the car and a bad person shot her with a gun. She was hurt so much that she died."

"Mommy told me to run and I ran," Jax said.

"You were there? Oh, honey." Kayla reached over and squeezed Jax's shoulder, her eyes filling with tears.

Tony and Amber looked both shocked and sympathetic. Davey leaned back into Paul's arms.

Tony was floored, not because it was such a shock, but because Jax had never talked about that day before.

"Maybe if I didn't run she wouldn't be shot," Jax said, his voice thoughtful.

"Buddy, listen. You couldn't have stopped the bad man. You did what Mom said to do, and that was just right." Tony was reeling inside. He'd have to notify the police that Jax was regaining his memories. Or maybe he'd always remembered, but he was starting to talk about it.

He'd call the therapist before their appointment tomorrow, give her a warning and get her perspective on how to handle this new development. And she'd know the best way to help Jax process what he was remembering.

The doorbell rang. It was the pizza delivery, and everyone mobilized to pay the guy and set the table and put out drinks. The boys asked if they could eat in front of the TV, and the adults instantly agreed.

"Another beer?" Paul held out a can to Tony, eyes compassionate.

"Better not, thanks." Tony definitely needed all his wits about him, in case Jax talked more about the day his mother had died.

The boys settled, the four adults sat around the table, nibbling at their pizza. Nobody seemed to have much appetite.

"So Jax witnessed his mother being shot?" Amber asked quietly.

Tony nodded. "This, tonight, was the most he's said about it. I suspected he must have seen, but we didn't know for sure."

"Did the police just find him on the scene?" Kayla asked. "That's so awful."

"I've dealt with a few of those," Paul said. "Former cop," he added, looking at Tony. "Tragic stuff. Hard on a kid."

"That it is." Tony sighed and pushed his plate away. He probably wasn't going to find another group of people as knowledgeable as these. "What's weird is that someone brought him to my porch and left him. We don't know who."

"Like a Good Samaritan?" Amber asked.

"We think so," Tony said. "The shooting happened in a rough part of town, and there was drug involvement and probably more than one shooter. Jax is lucky to be alive, and he probably owes his life to that person, whoever it is."

"Breaks my heart." Kayla shook her head. She hadn't eaten a bite. "The things kids live with."

Jax and Davey laughed uproariously at something on TV. They were both leaning against the couch, stuffing pizza into their mouths, Sarge between them.

"Kids are resilient." Amber gestured toward the boys. "Remember that, Tony. He'll be okay."

"I hope so." But the thing that worried him, in addition to Jax's memories, was his growing attachment to Kayla.

She was a good woman, a kind woman. The type of woman who would have made a good new mom for Jax if the situation were different.

But Tony couldn't drag her into it, couldn't ask her to

be involved with a household that included a man who'd forced his own sister, basically, to her death.

LATE TUESDAY AFTERNOON, Sylvie walked into the back room of DiGiorno's restaurant, feeling anxious. She liked wrapping Christmas gifts, and loved the cause of helping underprivileged kids, but here she was, doing it again: getting involved in the community against Bobby's wishes.

Going against Big Bobby Morrano's wishes would, or should, make anyone nervous. But Sylvie's heart cried out for connection and a new start.

She'd do the volunteer gig today, but she'd keep her distance, she decided. She wouldn't aim to make a bunch of new friends or connect more closely with those she'd just recently met.

"I didn't know you were coming," Primrose Miller called from one of the three tables. "Come sit with me. We need two at a table, and my partner backed out."

Sylvie smiled and greeted the woman. She'd enjoyed helping Primrose do some cleaning Sunday afternoon. Even Big Bobby couldn't object to her befriending an older church lady, could he?

Kayla and her mother sat at one of the tables, and two gray-haired women who looked like twins sat at the third. Each table had a big plastic box of red, green, and silver wrapping paper, scissors, tape, and ribbons.

She walked over to say hi to Kayla and her mom and thanked them for inviting her. They in turn introduced her to the other women, who were indeed twins, and who thanked her for volunteering. "I lured her here with food," Kayla joked, then turned to Sylvie. "Once we work an hour or two, they'll bring in calzones or pasta or something else good. I promise."

"Sounds wonderful. I love Italian food." And she was getting a little tired of the limited meals she could prepare for herself in her kitchenette, with its two-burner stovetop and microwave.

The room, really a big banquet hall, had a window facing the bay, and Sylvie strolled over. Today was gray, with only a couple of boats out and gulls swooping overhead. Although the bay wasn't displaying its classic beauty, Sylvie found she liked its variability.

She watched the boats and daydreamed. Maybe, one day, she'd go out on a boat, experience the Chesapeake the way the fishermen did.

"We'd better get started," Primrose said, and Sylvie looked around and saw that the other women had begun wrapping the boxes and toys that were propped beside each table.

She hurried back to the table she was sharing with Primrose. "Sorry, I got caught up in the scenery," she said.

"That's understandable. We love our beautiful bay." Primrose leaned over in her scooter and plucked tape and a roll of glittery Christmas wrapping paper from the bin. "If you don't mind cutting, dear, I'll tape. It's not easy for me to reach all the way across the table."

"Of course." Sylvie took the roll of wrapping paper from her, eyeballed the size of the boxed doll on the top of their toy stack, and then cut a big sheet of paper for Primrose to use. "Is this something you guys do every year?"

Primrose nodded. "The restaurant sponsors it, and people from the community and the churches buy the gifts. It's pretty informal. Anyone can participate."

"There aren't many poor kids here in Pleasant Shores, are there?" Sylvie hadn't seen any poverty, at least not like back home. Most of the homes here on this side of Pleasant Shores were modest, but well-kept, and most people seemed to be employed. You didn't see shady characters hanging around in parking lots and on street corners, setting up drug deals.

"Oh, yes, we have people in need," Primrose said. "Head over to the docks sometime, on one of your walks. Some of the families over there really struggle. It's hard to get by with a small fishing business, these days."

"Is it safe to walk there?"

Primrose looked at her strangely. "Of course it is."

They continued working, and as the stack of wrapped toys grew beside their table, it brought back a memory.

Her mother had taken her and her brother to a similar event at a church one year. She and her brother must have been under ten, but they were old enough to sense that the people who ran the event weren't real friendly, at least to their family. A couple of the hosts had exchanged harsh words with Mom, who'd grabbed Sylvie and her brother by the hand and dragged them away before the toys could be distributed. "Guess we aren't the right kind of poor people," she'd said bitterly.

There hadn't been any Christmas presents that year. Most years, for that matter. And since Sylvie had spent most of her adult life with Big Bobby, whose relatives didn't accept her, she hadn't gone to many family Christmases, either. A couple of times, she'd made the drive to visit her brother in Baton Rouge, but the truth was, she'd felt out of place. She wished she and her brother were close, but they weren't.

"Sorry I'm late!" The deep voice cut through the female chatter and sent a funny feeling down Sylvie's spine.

It was the pastor, striding in, greeting everyone. And

was it her imagination, or did his eyes light up a little when he looked at her?

"Let's see, who's wrapped the most presents?" He went from table to table, checking their stacks, talking and laughing.

"At least we've been working, unlike you." Kayla smiled at the pastor, making it clear she was joking with him.

"Right! I've been remiss. What's my job?"

"You carry these wrapped gifts over to the tree and bring us our next batch of toys."

"Yes, ma'am." He gave her a little salute and picked up a stack of boxes beside their table.

"Arrange them artistically, Pastor Steve," Kayla said.

Sylvie watched their interaction and wondered. Kayla was pretty, and not that much younger than the pastor. Maybe he liked her. Maybe they had a thing. She'd *thought* Kayla liked Jax's uncle, but it would be hard to resist someone like Steve.

As the other women joked comfortably with the man, Sylvie blew out a sigh and tried to focus on cutting paper and helping Primrose wrap. But her eyes kept straying back to the pastor, whose rugby shirt showed his broad shoulders and chest and trim midsection to good advantage.

It was wrong of Sylvie to compare Steve with Big Bobby, who was aptly named. She'd always found his burly physique attractive in its own right, his sizable belly notwithstanding. And love wasn't all about looks, anyway. It was about what was inside.

What's inside the pastor is probably pretty impressive, too.

After a while the staff of the restaurant started carrying in dinner, and they all stopped working and moved over to the long table to eat.

Sylvie inhaled the fragrance of marinara and garlic, the

yeasty smell of the calzones, and her stomach rumbled. "Somebody stop me or I'll eat eight of these."

"No need for you to stop, you're thin," Kayla said. Kayla was *built*, as they said, with the kind of curves and hips men loved. "Now, me, on the other hand… I'd better limit myself to one."

"You're gorgeous," her mother scolded. "Eat as much as you want."

That was nice. A mother-daughter relationship that was supportive.

Her own mother hadn't ever criticized the way Sylvie looked, but that was because she'd barely paid attention to Sylvie at all. Too caught up in her own problems, too busy trying to manage money, support the family, and avoid her boyfriends' fists.

Mom hadn't chosen men well, and her frequent bruises and sprained wrists were the result.

Sylvie had chosen better, she'd always thought. Big Bobby wouldn't marry her, and hadn't always been faithful. She'd contemplated leaving him, multiple times, but she'd never felt secure to manage on her own. Besides, it was hard to imagine starting over.

But Big Bobby had never raised a hand to Sylvie. And he supported her financially, which was huge considering she didn't have a lot of skills. She'd worked over the past eight years, but never at anything resembling a career. Mostly, she'd done custodial work, which didn't pay enough for her to live in the kind of nice little house Bobby had.

"The kids are going to love this," Kayla was saying when Sylvie tuned back into the conversation. She gestured to the tree and wrapped gifts. "They were so cute at last year's party. I thought they'd grab for the biggest packages, but they were mostly so polite, looking out for each other."

"Do you have any kids?" Sylvie thought to ask. This was the first time she'd had a real conversation with Kayla; mostly, they'd stuck to practicalities of working together at the school.

"No." Kayla looked around the group. "Or rather, I have twelve of them this year. Some years, even more."

Her perky tone seemed a little forced, and Sylvie wondered at it. Kayla obviously loved kids, and she was a pretty girl, and sweet. Why didn't she have a family, then, if she wanted one?

"How about you, dear?" Primrose asked. "Any children?"

The pastor looked up as if curious about her answer.

"No kids," Sylvie said. "I love them, though."

"Are you married?" Primrose persisted.

The twins glanced at each other, and Kayla's mom rolled her eyes. They obviously weren't on board with Primrose's nosiness, but what could you do? She meant no harm.

"No," Sylvie said, "I'm not married." She could have said that she had a long-term boyfriend and lived with him, but she didn't want to go into it and possibly earn these people's disapproval. She felt a twinge of disloyalty to Bobby, but after all, he was the one who'd wanted to avoid tying the knot. She was just telling the truth: she wasn't married.

"I was never blessed with a husband or children, either," Primrose said. "It can make you bitter, or better." She glanced around the group. "I know, that sounds trite. But I have it needlepointed on a pillow at home, and it's a good reminder."

"Being single gives you time to help the community, Primrose," the pastor said, "and for that, we're all grateful."

"This community is my family," Primrose said.

"You're lucky, then." Sylvie half wished she could stay in this community herself. She loved it here.

She didn't miss Bobby, not really. She could admit that to herself, now that she was away from him. Things had been cooling between them for a while now. He was less loving toward her, and it didn't bother her in the least. She was generally glad when he was gone from the house, even when it stretched into an overnight absence that he didn't explain when he came home.

Could she end it? But the thought of that filled her with fear. Bobby didn't like to be rejected; he liked having Sylvie around.

Besides, she'd never saved up any money, which was just plain stupid of her.

Maybe she could change that.

Sylvie poked at the rest of her food. Primrose followed the twins back to their table and sat talking with them, and Kayla and her mom got back to work. All of a sudden it was just Sylvie and the pastor lingering at the dinner table.

For whatever reason, that made her nervous. She stacked dishes and started to stand.

"You don't have to bother with that," the pastor told her. "They'll wait until we're done with our activity and then clean everything up at once."

"Oh, well, I like to be busy. And my partner's otherwise engaged." She gestured toward Primrose, deep in conversation with the twins.

"I can take over for her for a bit," he said, "if you're eager to get started." He stood and headed for the table where she and Primrose had been sitting.

Now she was stuck. Reluctantly, she took her seat at the gift-wrapping table again, now with the pastor beside her.

He smelled of something fresh and woodsy, and when their arms brushed, he felt warm. She stood, feeling nervous again, and started cutting big squares of wrapping paper to fit each toy.

They worked for a few minutes in silence. "You didn't stop in to see me at the church," he said finally.

She laughed a little. "I'm not much of a church person." She pulled out a chair across the table from him and sat down at what felt like a safer distance.

"A church person." He studied her. "I'm not sure what that means."

"I had a rough background. You wouldn't approve."

He lifted an eyebrow. "Are you saying you're a sinner?"

The blunt question startled her. From a lot of men, that would have qualified as a come-on, but Steve didn't seem to mean it that way. "Definitely," she said. Just living with Bobby for all these years, without benefit of marriage, would qualify her for the label.

"The church specializes in sinners." He wrapped a box and deftly folded and taped the ends.

"Does it, now?" That was pretty different from what the self-righteous church people Mom had gotten mad about were like. Different, too, from the curious stares she'd gotten at the few funerals to which she'd accompanied Bobby.

"We're *all* sinners, Sylvie," he said. "It's just part of being human in this fallen world."

Their hands brushed on the package exchange, and it didn't feel accidental.

"Are you preaching at me, Pastor?" she asked, going on the offensive because she felt uncomfortable.

"I'm off duty tonight," he said. "I'm here as a civilian, not a pastor." He paused, then added, "I'm just a man. Like any other man."

Clear blue eyes met hers and held.

Sylvie's breath got a little quicker. It took some effort to look away.

Oh, if only, she found herself thinking. She barely remembered how to flirt, but she liked Pastor Steve, and he seemed to like her.

But this was different from developing a nice friendship with Primrose. Getting involved with the local pastor—even getting a little friendly with him—was definitely something Bobby wouldn't approve of.

And anyway, she was here to keep tabs on a little boy, make sure he didn't know anything incriminating about the day his mama had died.

That was what was important. Not any little dissatisfaction she might feel with her own life, nor any tug toward starting something new.

"If you're trying to start something," she forced herself to say, "you should know I'm already..." She started to say *living with someone*, but at the last minute, switched it to "seeing someone else."

The pastor nodded. "I'm not surprised," he said. "And I'm going to be honest. I think you're a very attractive woman. But I would never cross a line you don't want crossed. What's important is that you feel some of the comfort the church has to offer. I'd like to talk to you about your faith and put you in touch with some of our people and groups."

"Why?" The question seemed to burst out of her.

He smiled. "I'm good at spotting a seeker," he explained. "Goes with the job description. Sometimes I meet someone who seems like they could really benefit from everything the church has to offer."

She lifted an eyebrow. "Aren't you supposed to say that everyone could benefit from the church?"

"Sure. Most people could, in my opinion. But some just seem especially hungry for it. That's what I sense from you."

"Hungry for church? Me?" She pretended his words were funny rather than piercing. "You must have gotten that wrong. I'm just hungry for another calzone."

He chuckled at her joke, and then his face got serious. "I do want you to know that I'm there. The church is there, should you need it."

She wanted to believe that. Wanted to take advantage of it. But how would that fit in with her real life?

It wouldn't. She stood, conscious that the movement was abrupt. "Listen," she said to the room in general, "I'm going to have to take off." And giving a few quick waves and goodbyes, she hurried out of the restaurant and into the cool evening darkness.

She needed air, and distance, so she didn't make a big mistake.

CHAPTER EIGHT

TODAY WAS THE DAY. Christmas wasn't for almost two weeks, but this was the last day of preschool. That meant it was time for the preschool Christmas party…and for the debut of Kayla in her new, properly sized sweater over a properly fitting bra.

Even alone in the classroom, she barely wanted to take off her coat. But she forced herself to do it. Then she stood on tiptoes before the small mirror on the wall, trying to see how it looked.

Of course, she'd studied herself in the full-length mirror at home, and had decided she looked just fine. The sweater wasn't formfitting, not exactly. It was no different from what most women her age wore, even women older than she was. Even her mother.

"What are you doing, honey?" It *was* her mother, at the doorway of the classroom.

Kayla's cheeks heated as she spun to face her. "Nothing! Just checking to see if…if I got toothpaste on my sweater."

Mom came into the room. "You didn't. That's pretty." She looked around. "Everything ready for the party in here?"

Kayla breathed a sigh of relief. Maybe her change of style wasn't going to be as noticeable as she'd feared. "Ready as I can be. There are two moms coming, and Tony should be here any minute, so we'll be fine."

"Good. I have to admit, I'm glad we have an extra-long break instead of going right up until Christmas like the public schools do. I've got the movie and the popcorn machine ready to go downstairs, at eleven."

"Perfect. We'll all be ready." Two hours of party was a lot for little kids, so they'd decided to gather them all in the common room for the last hour of the school day. "I'm going to try to keep the actual party short. We're doing circle time and story time first."

"Good luck with that." Mom turned her head, called "coming," and hurried down the hall. All the teachers were rushing to finish preparations for their classroom parties, and from the noise downstairs, it sounded like excited kids were starting to come in.

Kayla was buzzing almost as high as they would be, because today was the day she planned to ask Tony to Crabby Christmas.

She'd gone back and forth about it. Should she make a move?

She liked him a lot. He was a rare man who was masculine, but could take feedback and try to improve, rather than getting defensive or thinking he already knew it all. He was good with Jax, and increasingly, with all the kids. He was handsome, *really* handsome. And a little haunted, which, okay, had its appeal.

So she'd gotten coaching from Amber and had figured out what she was going to say. If she didn't do it today, no telling when she'd see him again.

Yes, today was definitely the day, and the only question was, when? If he got here early, maybe she'd do it right away, get it over with. If he said no, they'd have a lot of distractions that would get them comfortable with each other again, and then he'd go off with Jax for Christmas break.

The thought of that pierced a tiny, painful hole in her heart.

She was checking her basket of small gifts for the kids when there was a sound behind her. "We're here!" Jax called. He ran toward her and then stopped, staring at her. "You look pretty, Miss Kayla."

So maybe her change of style *was* visible. She couldn't help glancing at Tony, who was unfastening his jacket.

He'd definitely seen her, but he didn't say a word.

Which was fine. Good, really.

She hugged Jax and helped him take off his jacket. "Could you put one of these gifts from the basket on every kid's seat?" she asked him, and his face lit up, just as she'd known it would. He loved being given little jobs. And keeping Jax occupied would give her time to pop the question to Tony.

When she reached him, her courage failed. "You ready for today?" she asked, her voice hearty, not warm and romantic as she'd planned.

"I don't know." He hung his coat and Jax's backpack and smiled at her. "I've never been to a party at a preschool before."

"There's nothing like it," she said honestly. "Be ready for excitement and lots of running around. Maybe some tears, too."

"Vomiting?" he asked with a mock cringe.

She laughed. "Let's hope not, but no guarantees."

"I'll do my best. Just tell me what you need me to do, and if I'm making any mistakes, give me a nudge. Or kick me."

"Okay, I will," she joked.

"You do look nice," he said. "Jax was right. Pretty sweater."

Her face flooded with heat. "Thanks."

She should ask him now. *Ask him.*

"Would you want to—" she started.

"Hi, everybody!" It was Norleen and her daughter, and if Kayla had wondered about the tightness of her sweater, seeing Norleen's left her in no doubt that her own was fine. "We're excited!" Norleen gushed. "So glad I could come in and help!"

"Me, too," Kayla said with zero enthusiasm. She hadn't seen much of Norleen since the trip to the bay and the brief encounter at the Christmas decoration swap. And she hadn't missed her one little bit.

"What were you saying, Kayla?" Tony asked.

"Nothing. Tell you later."

Norleen raised an eyebrow. "Secrets?" She studied Kayla. "You look different," she said. "Did you lose weight?"

Kayla hoped her cheeks weren't as red as her sweater. "Are you kidding? It's the holidays. If anything, I've gained."

Tony went to negotiate a truce between Jax and Rhianna.

Norleen stayed, studying Kayla. "I'm serious. You look different. You didn't get enhancement, did you?"

Kayla frowned at the woman. "Enhancement?"

"A boob job." Norleen gestured at her chest. "I never noticed you were quite so…busty."

Kayla hunched her shoulders, her face flaming. "No way!"

"Oh, sorry!" Norleen laughed merrily. "My mistake. And lucky you! I've always been so skinny. I was jealous of you in school."

Indeed, Norleen's snug sweater clung to a narrow chest and flat abs. Her figure was as different from Kayla's as could be imagined.

"Merry Christmas!" Pixie and her mom called from the doorway as they came in, and more kids followed.

Glad to end the one-on-one with Norleen, Kayla greeted them and helped them hang coats, keeping her shoulders caved in so as not to show off her so-called *enhanced* chest. If she'd brought another bra and sweater, she would have rushed off and changed. What had she been thinking, wearing something that looked so different to school? Were all the kids noticing? Was Tony?

"Here, Miss Kayla, my mommy made you a present," little Noah said, handing her a glittery gift bag.

"We made bark," another girl said, rattling a clear quart jar of pink and white candy. Then the rest of the kids swarmed around Kayla, either giving her gifts or looking to see what the others gave.

She was touched by all the kids who'd brought her small gifts: homemade Christmas ornaments, cookies, a gift card. She thanked them quietly, not wanting to make a big deal of it to the kids who hadn't brought anything.

The presence of the kids, their simple joy, calmed and uplifted her, as always. She straightened her shoulders and forgot about what she was wearing and how she looked.

The kids were what was important. No matter what else happened, no matter what kind of games adults wanted to play, little kids were always sincere and open.

She gathered the children into a circle and got them to listen to a story and practice some of the letters in *Christmas* and *holiday* and *Kwanzaa*. They sang two of the carols they'd learned. Tony had finally brought in his ukulele, and he strummed along to "O Christmas Tree."

It wasn't easy keeping their attention, though, especially when parent helpers started setting up for games and refreshments. Pixie's mom dumped out individual bags of chips, while Norleen unveiled a tray of cupcakes, personalized with a letter for each kid's name. "All peanut free, soy free, gluten free," Kayla heard her telling Tony.

Rather than finding out whether or not he was impressed, Kayla released the children to the parent-helpers' charge.

"First party game," Pixie's mom said. "Look around, and you'll see bows through the classroom. Your job is to run around, and don't touch the bows!"

Kayla blinked. Oh, well. She'd given the moms free rein with the party and welcomed the break. It would be interesting to see what they did with it.

"Yay!" The kids started running, randomly and speedily, around the room, where Pixie's mom had placed all kinds of bows, from package size to the huge type people used when they were gifting someone a car.

The kids were all full of energy, and this was definitely a way for them to use some of it. They ran, bumping into each other and laughing.

Pretty soon, though, the kids started crashing harder into each other. Some fell, and others accused one another of touching the bows.

Dealing with her second teary child, who'd thwacked his head on a bookshelf while dodging a bow, Kayla looked up to find Tony kneeling next to them. "Any way I can help?"

She cuddled little Caden next to her, wiping his face with a tissue. "I think I've got it covered. Until the next casualty."

"This is some party." He surveyed the wild, running kids. Norleen was fussing with the cupcakes, and Pixie's mom was red-faced and sweating, trying to get the kids to run more carefully and slow down, to no avail.

Go to Crabby Christmas with me.

Kayla looked over at Tony. This was her moment. She

could ask him. They were in a little pocket of isolation, possibly the only one they'd have today.

But she couldn't make herself blurt it out, and a minute later, the noise level rose to deafening anyway, and not in a happy way. At least three kids were screaming at each other. "Could you...try to help me fix this?" she asked Tony instead, waving a hand toward the children.

"It's a bad game," he said frankly. "There's no way to win."

"Well, games that you win aren't the best for preschoolers, games with one winner, anyway." Another child came toward them, crying, and Kayla shifted Caden out of her lap to make room. She looked up at Tony. "Do you have any suggestions before they kill each other?"

Tony looked blank. "Umm, not really."

Pixie's mom rushed over. "I'm sorry," she said, sounding out of breath. "I'm terrible with games. I should never have volunteered for them."

"Could you get them started on the next one?" Kayla asked. Maybe it would be something calming.

"This is the only one I have planned," Pixie's mom said, looking ready to cry herself.

The shouting accelerated.

Tony put his fingers to his lips and made a piercing whistle that brought all the kids to an immediate halt. "Okay, kids, that game's over. Now let's play stick the bow on Miss Kayla! Everyone grab a bow!"

That was a huge hit, although it left Kayla feeling bruised. At least they were all running into her now, rather than each other. "How about a game of Santa, Santa, Reindeer?" she suggested. "It's like Duck, Duck, Goose."

"Yeah!" several kids yelled. The familiar game was more successful, and then Norleen broke out the cupcakes. Tony got everyone small cups of water, and Kayla took charge of hand washing while Pixie's mom talked on her cell phone.

Mom came through the door to check on them. "Fifteen more minutes until we gather for the movie," she said. "How's it going in here?" She looked across the classroom. "My goodness, is that Norleen Jenkins?"

"Uh-huh."

Mom shook her head. "She's certainly grown up since the two of you played dolls together as preschoolers."

"You registered her, didn't you?"

"Over the phone," Mom explained. "I always wondered how things would turn out for her. She never had a lot of opportunities."

"You're kidding, right?" Kayla stared at her mother. "She seemed on top of the world in middle school."

"She got pretty good with fashion and makeup," Mom admitted. "But she didn't have the smarts—either that or she didn't apply herself. No help from her family, and no thought of college. I always thought she was jealous of you."

"Norleen, jealous, of me?" That was rich. But of course Kayla had never told her mother about the bullying; even when Mom had guessed, Kayla had refused to name names.

"From what she said on the phone, she's still struggling. I'll try to talk with her sometime."

Mom's compassionate attitude was far from anything Kayla could manage. "You do that," she said. "I'll bring the kids down in a few."

After Mom left, Kayla turned back toward the classroom. It was almost time for the class to end. Asking Tony to Crabby Christmas would be now or never.

They got all the kids seated, eating cupcakes and drinking water. Some soothing Christmas music helped.

Tony stood, surveying the kids, and Kayla walked over

to his side. "So," she began, her heart racing, "have you heard about Crabby Christmas?"

He frowned. "I think there was a sign up at Goody's," he said. "What is it?"

"It's a fun event," she said, and launched into an explanation. "See, there's a cocktail hour for adults, childcare provided, and then everyone goes over to Goody's for a visit from Santa."

"Sounds fun."

Kayla opened her mouth, hoping her question wouldn't come out all breathless.

"It sounds *really* fun," Norleen said as she approached from Tony's other side. She must have been eavesdropping.

Kayla felt like strangling the woman.

"Hey, I have an idea," Norleen said. "We should go together, with our kids!"

"Jax and I are game," Tony said. "We basically never have any plans." He looked over at Kayla. "What about you? Can you come? It would make Jax really happy."

Kayla pushed up the corners of her mouth into a fake smile while she debated what to do. On the one hand, she really, really didn't want to spend an evening in Miss Did-You-Have-A-Boob-Job's company. On the other hand, the thought of Norleen and Tony and their kids going together... no. Just no. Even if that was exactly what Norleen was angling for.

"Sure," she said. "I'd love to go."

THE AFTERNOON AFTER the preschool Christmas party day, Tony opened the door of Victory Cottage at 1:30 p.m. to greet Evan Stone, the local police officer who'd come to his defense at the toy store when he'd first arrived in town.

Jax and Norleen's daughter, Rhianna, were running

around. Tony had been trying to hustle Norleen out the door to no avail; she'd insisted on staying to help him clean up.

He'd only meant to invite her daughter over. He hadn't asked Norleen to stay for a late lunch. But she'd lingered, finally ending up at the table, cooing over the peanut butter and banana sandwiches. She'd kept a continual conversational patter going. It was so great they could get together with their kids. It was so hard to be new in town, and single. She couldn't wait until Crabby Christmas.

All of it had added to the headache that had begun during the hours helping to supervise excited kids.

"Come on in," he said to Evan.

Rhianna and Jax stopped in their tracks, staring at the big, uniformed police officer.

Norleen came out of the kitchen, wiping her hands on a dishcloth. "Well, hello!" she said to Evan, her voice husky. "I don't think we've met."

"Norleen," Tony said, "this is Officer Evan Stone. Evan, Norleen Michaelson and her daughter, Rhianna. And I'm sure you remember my nephew, Jax."

"He gave me a badge!" Jax said. Apparently, he'd forgotten the events leading up to the gift. Probably just as well.

"Pleased to meet you all." Evan knelt to their level and gave the kids a friendly smile. "Hi, there," he said to Rhianna. "I'm Officer Stone."

"I'm Rhianna." The little girl stared at him. "Did you come over to arrest Jax and his dad?"

"Rhianna!" Norleen scolded.

"Police officers chase bad guys," Rhianna said.

"Nobody did anything bad. I'm just here for a visit." Evan turned toward Jax. "Glad to see you, too."

Jax nodded, but his lower lip trembled as he took a step back. Police officers brought bad things to mind for him, and now that Rhianna had reminded him about the bad guy connection, the impact of an officer in uniform seemed to hit him.

Tony stepped closer to his nephew, and Jax reached out for his leg and clung on. He'd been a little out of sorts, a little more clingy, since Sunday, when he'd remembered more about the day his mother was shot. His therapist had told Tony that might happen, but it still wrung at his heart. No child should have to experience what Jax had experienced, see what he'd seen. And Tony was bound and determined to make it up to him.

"Officer Stone's here to have coffee with me," he reminded Jax. "That's why you have a friend over now, too."

Jax nodded, still clinging on.

"You said you wanted to show Rhianna your room, right?" Tony stroked Jax's hair.

Jax's grip on Tony's leg loosened slightly. "Uh-huh."

"What toys do you have?" Rhianna asked. "I brought some, in my backpack." She picked it up.

Jax frowned. "I have trucks."

"I like trucks," Rhianna said. "At home my dolls ride in trucks."

Jax looked doubtful. "My trucks crash. A lot."

"That sounds fun!" Rhianna tugged at Jax's hand. "Let's go!"

And the two children thundered up the stairs.

Meanwhile, Norleen wasn't making any move toward leaving. Tony turned toward her, wondering if he was going to have to push her out the door. "I can bring Rhianna home in a couple of hours, or you can pick her up." He hoped his hint wasn't too broad or downright rude, but subtlety didn't seem to work with Norleen.

"Oh, sure. I guess I should be going."

Do you think? "Thanks for letting Rhianna come play with Jax."

"Sure thing." She seemed to take forever finding her coat and purse. "It was nice to meet you," she said to Evan. Then she looked at Tony. "Thanks so much for having us over."

"Sure." Tony felt like he was herding her to the door. She kept staring at him, and alternately at Evan.

Finally, though, she left, and he closed the door behind her with the sense of having escaped a piranha.

"Pretty lady," Evan commented.

"Uh-huh. Come on into the kitchen. Sorry about the mess." Tony wondered briefly what Norleen had been doing in here; she'd said she'd clean up while Tony supervised the kids, but the remains of their lunch still littered the table. He led Evan over and shoved the dishes to one side. "Coffee?"

"Sure. Thanks." Evan sat down. "Looks like some bad weather coming in."

"Get much snow here?" Tony stuck the cup beneath the brewer and pushed the button, watched the coffee stream out.

"Can. We had a beast of a storm last winter, which was my first here. Apparently that's the pattern, one or two big snows. Where are you from?"

"Filmore, Pennsylvania. We got a fair amount of snow."

"Ah, Filmore. I know it by reputation."

Tony set another cup brewing and brought Evan's to the table. "Reputation isn't great," he said.

"Right. Lots of drug issues?"

He nodded. "That's part of what I need to talk to you about."

"Okay." Evan's eyes narrowed slightly.

Tony brought his own cup to the table, sat down. "I don't know how much time we'll have before the kids come back in, so let me jump right into it," he said. He quickly explained the situation: the shooting, Jax's nonmemory of the day's events, and his mysterious appearance on Tony's doorstep. "So our therapist thought it would be good to talk to you," he explained. "She suggested, and I agree, that it's smart for someone local to know the situation, due to the dangers involved."

"So you think he was there on the scene?" Evan asked.

"I wasn't sure, but then on Sunday, he said…" To his horror, Tony's throat tightened. He took a gulp of hot coffee and nearly choked on it, and by the time he'd stopped coughing, he'd gotten himself together. "Sorry. He said he heard a big bang and saw his mom fall down."

"Ahhhh." Evan shook his head. "It's bad what kids go through." He frowned. "Is there any way word could get back to Filmore that his memories are returning? Did other people hear what he said on Sunday?"

"Paul and Amber heard, and Kayla, and Davey, but… no. No one there has connections to Filmore." Tony thought about it. "My sister, and maybe my brother, might visit during the holidays. But they're on the good side, trying to make things better in Filmore. And they love Jax."

"What's the status of the case?"

Tony blew out a disgusted noise. "No progress. I talk to the Filmore police pretty often, and my sister who lives there puts a lot of pressure on them. But they're overwhelmed."

"Yeah. Everybody's understaffed." Evan sipped coffee. "Have you told the Filmore cops that Jax is remembering?"

"No, I didn't." Tony wasn't sure how to explain. "I just have a feeling there are a few bad seeds on the force there. I could be wrong, but… Jax's safety is my priority, even if he doesn't share information that could help with the case."

"Smart." Evan frowned. "I've heard a few things about Filmore. The police aren't in control. At best. At worst…"

"They're being paid off by some gang or cartel." Tony sighed. "It's possible."

The children raced into the room. Jax hurled himself into Tony, and Tony hugged him. "Hey, buddy," he said, "are you having fun? Sharing your toys?"

"He shared," Rhianna said.

"Uncle Tony! She says she has video games at her house. Can we go over?"

"Not right now, buddy. Maybe another day, if Rhianna's mom says it's okay."

"I already asked her, before we came," Rhianna said. "She wants you to come. She says if you come over, she'll make a cake!"

Tony wondered why Norleen was so nice. Overly so, to the point of it being uncomfortable. "We'll see," he said. "Jax, run back and play a little longer while I finish talking to Officer Stone."

"Okay," Jax said glumly. "But she only wants to play dolls."

"Then you be kind to your guest and play what she wants to play," Tony said.

"Okay." Jax sighed and trudged toward the stairs.

"Come on, we can do more truck crashes with the dolls," Rhianna suggested, showing that she had some of her mother's persuasive abilities.

Jax brightened. "Okay," he said, and they climbed the stairs.

Evan and Tony watched them go. "Cute kids," Evan said. "Does the therapist think he'll remember more?"

"She says it's fifty-fifty. I'm to keep lines of discussion

open if he does, because we don't want him keeping it inside or thinking he's not allowed to talk about it."

"Right. Poor little guy." Evan shook his head. "I'm glad you contacted us, just in case anything comes up. I'll let the department know." He held up a hand, forestalling Tony's question. "I can vouch for the honesty and morals of every person on the force."

"Every person?" Tony asked, skeptical.

Evan's face broke into a little smile. "All four of us."

Oh, right. The good thing about a small town. "That's fine, then."

Evan stood. "Stay in touch, and let us know if anything worrisome happens."

As they walked out, Evan spoke, clearly trying to lighten the mood. "We have a big celebration coming up in town this Saturday. Crabby Christmas. You planning to come?"

"I am," Tony said slowly. "How about you?"

"Wouldn't miss it. It's the place to be in Pleasant Shores, our biggest event of the season."

And Tony was slated to go with Kayla, which sounded pretty good...and Norleen, which didn't. Tony stopped at the door. "Is it a date kind of thing?"

"It can be," Evan said.

Tony thought about it. "Then...it might be, you could help me out with a problem." He was seeing Amber and Paul tomorrow, and he'd try to get them to help him evade Norleen and spend time with Kayla. But the way Norleen was, it would be better to have all hands on deck.

CHAPTER NINE

FRIDAY EVENING, TONY knocked on the door of Paul and Amber's place.

Beside him, Jax hopped on one foot and then the other, a big smile on his face.

Clearly, Jax was starting to feel at home here. Tony was, too.

It would be hard to leave at the end of their three-month stretch.

There was an obligatory "woof" from Sarge, and then the door flew open. "Come on!" Davey yelled at top volume. "Hannah's here and we're decorating gingerbread boys!"

Jax looked up at Tony.

"It's okay," Tony said, encouraging Jax. "You're allowed."

Davey turned, then looked back over his shoulder. "Come on!" He ran toward the back of the house.

Given how Jax had been acting lately, Tony expected him to demur and cling, but he sprinted off after Davey without a second glance. Sarge paused to sniff Tony's hand before trotting after them.

"Hey, Tony. Paul's upstairs showering. He just got home from work, but he'll be down in a minute." Amber gave him a half-hug. "Come in the kitchen and meet my daughter. She's going to supervise the boys' cookie decorating so we can have a civilized glass of wine."

Tony held out the bottle he'd brought.

"You didn't have to," she protested. "We invited you."

"Just contributing to the festivities." He followed Amber into the kitchen, where a college-aged woman, obviously Amber's daughter, was stirring food dye into bowls of frosting.

"Hannah, this is Tony, Jax's uncle and guardian," Amber said. She pulled a corkscrew out of a drawer and deftly opened the wine he'd brought.

Hannah gave him a friendly smile. "Good to meet you."

"She said we can put on as much frosting as we want!" Jax's eyes were round with the thrill of that.

"You do what she says, okay?" He squeezed Jax's shoulder. "Thanks for this," he said to Hannah. "Jax will love it."

"Davey, too, and me," Hannah said. "I love kids."

Amber hugged her daughter and then turned to Tony. "Come on, we'll hang out by the fire." She snagged three wineglasses plus the open bottle and headed out of the kitchen.

Tony looked at Jax. "I'll be in the living room, where we came in, if you need me."

"Okay. I'm not scared." Jax climbed onto the chair beside Davey's, seeming to forget about Tony, which was a beautiful thing. The child was bouncing back from his memory-induced clinginess, continuing to gain independence.

"Sarge will 'tect us," Davey said, reaching down to rub the dog's drooly muzzle. "He was a police dog." He wiped his wet hand on his pants, grabbed a plastic knife, and spread a big dollop of blue frosting onto a cookie.

"Davey! Wash your hands," Hannah scolded, then smiled up at Tony. "Beware the blue gingerbread boy," she whispered.

"Will do." He followed Amber into the living room and,

at her gesture, sank into a comfortable chair near the fire. She poured him a glass of wine.

Tony looked around at the ceiling-height tree, heavily decorated with ornaments and lights and tinsel. Not showy like a magazine, but colorful and messy, with plenty of obviously homemade ornaments and a crooked star. Red and green stockings hung along the mantel, each labeled with a name: Paul, Amber, Davey, Hannah and Sarge.

Around the base of the Christmas tree, an electric train made its leisurely way around a track dotted with buildings and snowy landscapes and tiny figures.

It was so cozy and family-centered that his heart hurt. He blinked and refocused on the mantel. "The dog gets a stocking?" he asked.

"Of course!" Amber laughed. "Didn't you ever have a dog?"

"Just a hunting dog that stayed outside," he said. "We never, um, got it gifts."

"It's a whole new world of dog ownership," she said. "Sarge definitely gets more gifts than either Paul or I do."

Paul came down then, and they drank wine and listened to the kids and talked. Soon enough, the subject of tomorrow's big event, Crabby Christmas, came up. Tony admitted he was going with Kayla and Norleen.

"Some guys have it that way," Paul said, chuckling. "Hard to believe you just got into town."

"Why both?" Amber asked.

"Norleen is…forceful." Tony spread his hands. "I don't know how it happened. I'd rather just go with Kayla, but I didn't know about the event. Didn't know to ask her."

"Seize control, man," Paul said. "I didn't, and it almost cost me way too much." He glanced over at Amber, his eyes warm.

"As well as giving both me and Kayla a really bad time at last year's event," Amber said. "Make sure she has a better time this year, will you?"

Tony sensed there was a story there. "I'll try. But if the two of you see any way to distract Norleen or find her someone else to dance with, I'd welcome the help."

"On it!" Amber pumped her arm. "I would love to see you and Kayla get together."

"That's not what I..." Tony stopped, confused. If he didn't want to start anything serious with Kayla, why was he conspiring for it to happen?

"That wasn't the worst thing that happened that weekend," Paul said, obviously still thinking about last year. He looked at Amber. "Remember?"

"I'll never forget." Amber turned to Tony. "We had the most terrifying experience. Davey actually went missing."

Tony put his wineglass down without taking another drink. He'd always known missing children were a tragedy, but now that he'd taken on guardianship of Jax, the horror was no longer abstract. "What happened?"

"His maternal grandparents decided to take custody of him without letting me know," Paul said. "We worked it out, but it was dicey before we found him."

Amber leaned forward so she could see into the kitchen, holding a finger to her lips. "To this day he doesn't realize he was basically abducted," she said, keeping her voice low. "He just thinks he had a surprise car ride with Grandma and Grandpa."

"So...was it kind of a misunderstanding, or an actual crime?" Tony had dealt with some child abduction and custody cases in his counseling practicum, and he knew how difficult they could be. "Did you press charges?"

"No charges, and yes, we get along pretty well now,"

Paul said. "They just needed some clear boundaries. And some therapy."

"Wow." Tony should have realized that even a perfect-seeming family like this one had its shadows in the past.

"Anyway." Paul brushed his palms together like he was brushing away those experiences. "Crabby Christmas. They have a childcare area during the first part of the evening, the cocktail hour. People get dressed up. It's fun." He grinned and winked at Amber. "That's when to make your move, if you're going to make one."

"Stop," Amber said, laughing. She turned to Tony. "It *is* nice. They do a good job with the kids so the adults can have fun."

Tony frowned. "I would have said that Jax wouldn't go to strange childcare providers, but I could be wrong. He went to your daughter right away."

"He did. How's he doing, anyway, overall?" Amber finished her wine and held out her glass to Paul. "Just a tiny bit more, and then I'll switch to water."

"He's doing pretty well." Tony thought of the last couple of days and realized that Jax had slept soundly, and hadn't had any meltdowns. No repeat of the night terrors, either. "The counseling helps, and so does the preschool class. He's getting attached to Kayla, for sure."

"That's good. Kids are more resilient than we are." Paul poured more wine all around and then turned on a speaker. Low, jazzy Christmas music surrounded them, and the smells from the kitchen were getting ever more enticing.

Tony breathed it all in, appreciatively. "This is nice," he said. "Thanks for inviting us over."

"Do you have plans for Christmas itself?" Amber asked.

Tony shook his head. "My sister and brother plan to come on the twenty-seventh, so we'll do our celebrating then."

"Oh, no, you can't skip the holiday itself with a kid!" Amber's eyes rounded with concern.

"She's right," Paul said. "Even last year, when he was four, Davey knew exactly when Christmas was and what to expect in the way of gifts and activities."

"We're having a big dinner here and you're welcome to come." Amber tapped her fingers on her chin. "Maybe I'll invite Kayla and her mom, too."

That idea gave Tony's heart a lift. To be able to see Kayla on Christmas...

And yeah. It wasn't only Jax who was getting attached to her. Tony was, too.

"Have you met Bisky yet?" Paul asked. "She does a Feast of the Seven Fishes on Christmas Eve, and I know she'd welcome you."

"I don't want to impose." Tony shook his head. "We'll go to church and have a quiet Christmas Eve."

"If you want, but lots of people come after church. Or they leave the party and go to midnight Mass." Amber smiled at him. "Pleasant Shores isn't the kind of place where you can spend a holiday alone."

"That's nice, but I haven't even met this Bisky."

"She's super friendly. She'd love to meet you."

"It's a huge gathering," Paul said. "All ages, all types. Jax would have a good time, too." He reached over and patted Amber's knee. "Pretty special to us."

Amber smiled, then looked at Tony. "He proposed to me there, last year."

"Wow, sounds...public," Tony commented.

"Tell me about it. It wasn't my style, but it was hers, so I did it. Hannah helped me make it work." Paul nodded toward the kitchen. "And it was totally worth it."

"I can see that." It was good to meet such a happy couple.

Amber reached over and took Paul's hand. "So you'll come?" she asked Tony. "Here for Christmas Day, and Bisky's for Christmas Eve?"

Tony frowned. It was a lot. Too much, too kind, and he felt guilty. But he had to at least make life good for Jax. "To Christmas Day, here, for sure, and we thank you," he said. "About the other event, we'll have to see."

Fortunately, Jax and Davey ran in with trays of cookies and there was no chance for Amber to apply pressure. Sarge loped behind them, stopping to snag a cookie that fell from Davey's tray.

Paul scolded the dog, shaking his head. "He was a good drug detection dog at one time," he explained to Tony. "Now…he's a lazy bum."

"Daddy! He's not lazy!" Davey sounded indignant as he knelt in front of Sarge. "He does all kinds of tricks for food."

"You're right," Amber said, rubbing Davey's shoulders. "He's a good dog, even if he *is* a cookie monster."

Jax handed his tray of cookies to Tony, and Tony praised the messy, overladen cookies. He couldn't imagine eating many of them, but the fact that Jax had gotten to decorate them was everything. He didn't know whether Stella had ever done that with Jax, what kind of Christmas activities she'd managed in the midst of her complicated, difficult lifestyle.

Jax leaned against Tony's leg. "I wish we had a dog and a mommy and a family," he said.

The words brought a lump to Tony's throat. He didn't have an answer; he just stroked Jax's hair. Sarge came to sit beside Jax, who rubbed the big dog's ears.

Tony wanted all this for Jax. Wanted to have Christmas

traditions and a warm, cozy home. Wanted Jax to feel secure and loved, not just by him, but by a whole family.

The real comfort would be if Jax did have a mom, but because of Tony, he didn't.

Tony's determination to help Jax grew stronger than ever. He had to make it up to his nephew the best he could.

KAYLA ARRIVED AT Crabby Christmas a few minutes late on Saturday night. She'd spent too much time changing her clothes, and she still wasn't exactly satisfied with her last-minute conservative choice. But she *was* looking forward to her friends, and Tony.

Maybe especially Tony.

The fact that Norleen would be with them dimmed her excitement a little. But Kayla was determined to be friendly and civil to the other woman. Middle school was in the past.

DiGiorno's restaurant had morphed from a big Italian eatery to a fairyland. Candles adorned the tables that surrounded the big dance floor, and tiny white lights lined the ceiling. The big windows faced west, and though the sky was mostly dark, a glow of purple, pink, and orange remained along the horizon, a testimony to the beauty of the Chesapeake Bay sunset.

People stood in clusters, talking, drinking soda, and wine, and cocktails, and eating finger foods and cookies from pretty tables around the edges of the room. Laughter rang out frequently above the Christmas music played by a small band in one corner. Bisky Castleman, resplendent in a sparkly red maternity dress, was making her way to the front of the room.

She grabbed the microphone from a stand in front of the musicians. "We're going to speed things up and start the dancing, folks," she called. "Who's ready?"

Good-natured commentary went back and forth. Kayla remembered that much from last year: Bisky was a lot of fun as an emcee.

Kayla spotted Amber and Erica and waved to them. There was Primrose Miller, her hair piled high atop her head, a shimmering silver sweater making her look festive.

"Kayla!" It was Norleen's voice, audible from across the room. The woman wore a spectacular, formfitting royal blue dress.

Kayla thought of the red sheath she'd bought for this occasion…and left at home. She'd tried it on, and it had looked fine, but it had emphasized her curves and after how she'd felt at the preschool party, she'd realized she just wasn't comfortable with that. So here she was in black, serviceable pants and a sweater…not even one of her new ones, but a loose old favorite. She hoped no one would notice that she was underdressed.

"Over here," Norleen called again.

Kayla started toward the other woman and then stopped, because there was Tony, standing close to Norleen. Uh-oh. She'd known she was going to be a third wheel on their date, but she hadn't thought through how awful that would feel.

Maybe she should just stop coming to Crabby Christmas. This might be an even worst disaster than her date last year with Paul, who'd gone on to marry Amber.

"Miss Kayla!" Both Rhianna and Jax ran to greet her, and she knelt and let them run into her arms, smelling their sweaty-kid scents, feeling their overheated excitement. What a relief. Kids made sense, and she loved their uncomplicated joy.

She scooted back and studied them, enjoying Rhianna's

fancy velvet dress and Jax's red sweater. "You two look like Christmas elves."

"We're not elves!" Jax laughed.

"I'm kind of an elf. This is a new dress." Rhianna twirled.

They didn't notice or care about what she was wearing. They just wanted to have fun at Christmastime, and that was as it should be.

She looked up at Tony, who'd come over to greet her. He looked fantastic in dark slacks and a soft green sweater that looked like cashmere. Although he wasn't wearing a suit like some of the men, he looked dressed up and even a little festive.

And handsome. Really, really handsome.

Norleen greeted her effusively. "There you are! I was wondering if something came up. I thought you might not be able to join us."

You wish was what went through Kayla's mind. She stopped herself from saying it, though. She was going to take the high road.

Honesty made her admit to herself that there was a little cowardice mixed in with her principles. She didn't intend to give Norleen any ammunition. That was what was behind her choice of clothing; she didn't want Norleen to have the opportunity to make any more snotty remarks about the size of her chest.

She focused on the children. "Are you having fun?" she asked.

Jax nodded, but Rhianna glanced over toward the room's exit. "I wish we could go play games," she said.

"The kids are getting along so well, ever since our play-date," Norleen said, leaning against Tony's arm.

A weight seemed to press down on Kayla. "The kids"

sounded like what you'd say when you were a couple. And she hadn't known they'd gone through with it and had a playdate.

Now they were here together, a great looking pair with same-age kids. Wouldn't it be sweet, perfect really, if they got together?

"But they can't go to the childcare room, which is sad." Norleen bit her lip and looked up at Tony. Kayla could swear she was batting her eyelashes. She could also swear that the lashes were fake, because who had real eyelashes that long?

"Why can't they go to the kids' playroom?" Kayla asked, trying to stifle her jealousy.

Tony stepped away to talk to someone, and Norleen came closer, leaning down to speak into Kayla's ear. "They're short a childcare person. Someone got sick or something. That's why the kids are still out here. Only when they have one more person will they have the right ratio, where Jax and Rhianna can join in." She looked expectantly at Kayla. "Gosh, and I was really hoping to get a break tonight. A single parent doesn't get that many."

Kayla knew manipulation when she saw it, but she also liked to help out. If the kids needed her…

"Could you do a shift in the childcare room?" Norleen asked. "I mean, with you being a teacher and all…"

Kayla was tempted to refuse Norleen's bold request. She wanted to at least mingle with the adults and see her friends. And she didn't want to support Norleen's pushy, annoying behavior.

She also didn't want to leave room for Norleen to move in harder on Tony. Even if their pairing off was inevitable, Kayla just wasn't a good enough person to want to help that happen.

She looked away from Norleen and saw that both Jax

and Rhianna were watching her, eyes pleading. "Will you come help, Miss Kayla?" Jax asked.

"Please?" Rhianna begged.

That settled it. "Sure, I'll help," she said, standing up.

Why not, after all? It would give her something to do, something she loved doing. It would help the children. And if it allowed Norleen and Tony to get to know each other better, if that was what they wanted, then so be it.

"You're the best!" Norleen gave her a hug and air-kiss, the smell of her perfume almost making Kayla choke.

Kayla backed away, beckoning to the children. She'd go before Tony got back and politely argued against her going. "I'll take them back there and scope it out. You and Tony have fun."

"Yay! Thanks, Miss Kayla!" Jax crowed. The kids each grabbed one of her hands and tugged her toward the child-care room.

People smiled indulgently to see the dressed-up little children dragging her along. No one looked surprised. She was Kayla-the-preschool-teacher. Always ready to help out. Always good with the little ones.

This was her life, taking care of other people's kids, and it was a good life.

In the smaller banquet room that was serving as a child-care area, two teenagers were in charge—Bisky's daughter, Sunny, and Ria's daughter Kaitlyn, also home for the holiday break. They looked harassed. The children were running around, high on the Christmas spirit and probably sugar; on one of the tables, there was a big platter with crumbs and a couple of broken cookies remaining.

"Thank heavens you're here," Kaitlyn said.

"Let me guess," Kayla said. "You started off with refreshments."

"Bad idea?" Sunny asked.

"No big deal. It's nice of you girls to help." Kayla surveyed the scene. There were crafts on one table, a couple of bins of toys on another, and a Christmas movie playing on a big screen. "Want me to take charge, help you get organized?" she asked the teenagers.

"Yes, please!" Kaitlyn said.

"I wish you would," Sunny added.

The kids continued running around, now with Jax and Rhianna added to the mix. That made fourteen kids of mixed ages, which was a lot for a small room.

"Okay. Let's each grab a little one before the bigger kids run over them." There were three toddlers, and Kayla swung a pretty two-year-old girl she didn't know onto her hip while the teens grabbed the other two. "Kids, grab a toy or a coloring sheet," Kayla said to the remaining children. "Sunny will help you with the toys, and Kait with the coloring sheets and crayons. Then we'll sit on the floor and watch the movie." This part of Crabby Christmas didn't go on long, and after this was Santa. So Kayla felt it was best to keep things calm and quiet.

Once the kids had settled down, Kayla had time to think, and that wasn't a good thing, necessarily. She regretted that she hadn't gone for it and worn the red sheath. Maybe then, she wouldn't have accepted being relegated to the childcare room. Maybe then, Tony would've noticed her a little.

More than that, she regretted that she wasn't going to have the chance to dance with Tony. By the time she'd finished her "shift," as Norleen had called it, the adult cocktail-and-dancing time would be over.

There was a little flurry at the door. "What on earth?" Amber came into the room, Erica beside her, holding little

Hunter. "Kayla, why are you here and not out there with the grown-ups?"

Kayla shrugged. "They were short a person."

"We needed help," Sunny added. "We didn't know what we were doing, and Kayla got things under control."

"Fine, it's under control." Erica set Hunter down beside the other kids. "She can leave now."

"She can't," Kaitlyn said, "because there's some rule about ratio of kids to adults. We were on the wrong side of that."

"No. Just no." Amber shook her head. "I want Kayla out there having fun. She does enough childcare in her day job."

"I'll take over. I don't mind," Erica said.

"That's not necessary," Kayla protested. "You should get the chance to have a good time."

Just then Hunter, Erica's son, ran over to her. "Mama stay!" he cried, and clung to her.

"See?" Erica said, hugging him. "No way am I getting to leave now." She paused and looked at Kayla. "You know, Tony's dancing with Norleen and she's got him in a death grip."

"Like an octopus," Amber added. "She's practically strangling him. Are you going to leave him to that fate?"

Was she? Kayla didn't want to compete. Didn't want to be anywhere near Norleen, who kicked up all of her fears about mean girls.

But then again, she'd just been complaining to herself about staying back here with the kids the whole time.

And now, the image of Tony and Norleen dancing was stuck in her head.

"He's desperate, from what I can see," Erica said. "He needs to be rescued."

"You two are pushy, you know?" Kayla said, but she

had to admit, she was glad they'd come in. Tony wasn't the only one who needed rescuing. Kayla needed to be rescued from herself, her tendency to concede the game, especially to someone like Norleen, without even trying to play.

Amber walked Kayla out, holding her arm, but instead of turning toward the main hall, Amber steered her toward the ladies' room.

"What's wrong?" Kayla asked. "I mean, I can wait for you, it's fine."

"This is about you." Amber tugged her inside and did a quick stall check. "Good, we have the place to ourselves. Why didn't you wear the dress we picked out when we went shopping?"

Kayla shrugged. "It didn't look right."

"It looked spectacular!"

"I look too chesty in those kinds of clothes. I have it on good authority."

"Who told you that?" Amber tilted her head to one side.

"Doesn't matter."

"Who?" Amber demanded.

"Norleen," Kayla said finally. "She asked if I had breast enhancement surgery."

Amber hooted. "Get outta here! I can't believe that witch! You don't look like you had surgery."

Kayla shrugged. "She noticed right away."

"Why would she think that was okay to say? Where's she coming from?"

"Directly from middle school," Kayla said grimly. "She was cruel to me then, when I had scoliosis and wore a brace, and she seems to think it's okay to dish out some of the same stuff as an adult." She looked at herself in the mirror, drab in black. It wasn't that no one else was dressed as casually as she was; she'd noticed people wearing everything from evening gowns to jeans. But most people at least looked like they were going to a holiday party, not a funeral. "I wish I could go home and change," she said.

"No time. Just give me five minutes to work on you. You did wear one of the good bras, right?"

Kayla laughed. "I did. Truthfully, wearing a bra that fits feels so much better than wearing a smasher."

"Of course it does." Amber pulled the scrunchie out of Kayla's hair, put it on her wrist, and wetted her hands. "Bend over," she said, "and let your hair fall down." Kayla did as she asked, and Amber ran her wet hands through it. "Now stand up," she ordered. Kayla did, and Amber tossed her hair back so it looked kind of wild, and then pulled hairspray out of her purse. "Close your eyes," she said, and sprayed through.

"Wow," Kayla said when she looked in the mirror. "Not in preschool mode now."

"We've only just begun." Amber took the scrunchie and played with the bottom of Kayla's sweater, making it asymmetrical and caught up to one side. That had the effect of giving her a waistline, at least.

"Now," Amber said, "we're trading jewelry. Take yours off."

"You can't wear this little stuff," Kayla protested. Her necklace was tiny pearls, and her earrings were plain pearl posts.

"You shouldn't either, and it's more important for you. I'm so mad at that Norleen I could spit." Amber was removing her large hoop earrings and glitzy necklace as she spoke. "Come on. Off with your pearls."

"Okay," Kaya said doubtfully, and took them off.

"Now, put mine on. Do you have lipstick?"

Kayla draped on the necklace, put the hoops through her

ears, and rummaged in her giant purse, finally coming up with some lipstick.

"Good. You'll look good in that bright pink. Put it on."

"There's a reason it was in the bottom of my purse," Kayla said.

"Yeah. And there's a reason you always look like a pre-school teacher."

"Okay, okay." Kayla traced her lips with the brighter color.

"Now, your eyebrows. I know you shouldn't share makeup, but I'm gonna guess you don't even own an eye-brow pencil?"

"That's right."

"Well, you should wear it, because it defines your eyes." Amber pulled some out of her purse and traced it lightly over Kayla's blond eyebrows.

Kayla looked in the mirror and lifted an eyebrow. "I look decent," she said.

"You look great. Most women here are overdressed. Oh, wait." Amber slipped off her strappy sandals. "What do you wear, an eight?"

"Seven and a half."

"Close enough. Give me your sensible shoes."

"You're kidding, right?"

"No, I'm not kidding. These things will kill your feet, but they look great."

"No." Kayla shook her head. "I draw the line there. For one thing, you'll look like a doofus, wearing my wedges with your dress. For another, I can't walk in high heels."

Amber considered, then nodded. "Okay. Fine. Come on."

They walked out, and on the edge of the dance floor, Kayla paused. There was Tony, dancing close with Norleen, and their attractiveness as a couple made Kayla's heart sink. No way would she look that good.

Then she caught the expression on Norleen's face as she looked directly in Kayla's direction. It was a triumphant smile. Kayla's fingers tingled with the desire to wring the woman's neck.

"Are you going to let her win?" Amber asked quietly.

"No, but… I'm just not that confident."

"Listen, I know what it is to be insecure, but you *are* good enough. You deserve happiness. And you're not going to have a repeat of your awful middle school experience, because Erica and I will *take her down* if she says or does anything mean. You just whistle, and we'll be right there at your side."

Kayla hugged Amber. "Thank you. You're a good friend."

"Hey, I figure after last year's Crabby Christmas, I owe you."

"That's for sure." Kayla squared her shoulders and headed toward Tony and Norleen.

CHAPTER TEN

As the song ended, Tony extricated himself from Norleen's arms and looked around the crowded dance floor. Where was Kayla?

"That was fun!" Norleen shouted over the noise of the crowd. She stepped close and kind of nuzzled against him. "Let's do it again!"

Norleen was a pretty woman for sure, but pretty wasn't everything. "I'm going to take a break."

"No way!" She clung on tighter. "Don't leave me alone!"

Since they were surrounded by friendly, noisy people, Norleen was hardly alone. But she was new in town, and he didn't want to be unkind. "Look, there's Pixie's mom," he said, pointing. "Why don't you go talk to her?"

"I'm staying right here with you." She pushed herself close to his side, took his hand, and actually wrapped his arm around her.

He untangled himself and stepped away. He tried to be nice to everyone, but he wasn't a total pushover. "I need to go find Kayla." He didn't know where she'd gone, but he definitely wanted to find her. She'd agreed to come to the event, and he didn't want to miss out entirely on the chance to spend time with her.

Norleen looked like she might turn on the tears. Great. Where was Evan Stone when you needed him? He scanned the crowd and spotted him. "Come with me," he ordered Norleen.

When they reached Evan, the man's face broke out in a big smile. "Just the lady I was hoping to find," he said with apparent sincerity. "Don't let Tony dominate your time. I deserve at least one dance."

Take two or three.

Norleen looked indecisive.

Evan reached out both hands. "Come on, I bet you're a great dancer. You can show me a thing or two," he added with a smile and a wink.

Norleen let go of Tony's arm and took Evan's hands.

Tony backed away. *Thank you*, he mouthed. He definitely owed the man a beer.

Now to find Kayla. He made his way through the crowd, smiling and greeting those he knew while staying focused on his goal. Unlike Evan, Kayla was short, not easy to spot above the crowd.

Finally he caught a glimpse of blond hair and headed toward it. Yes, there was Kayla, talking to a couple of guys. No wonder. She wasn't all decked out like some of the ladies, but she didn't need to be. Her simple, natural look was part of her appeal.

He was relieved when he broke through the crowd and reached her. He waited until she'd ended her conversation and turned to him.

"Hi, Tony," she said, her voice noncommittal.

"Would you do me the honor of dancing with me?" His face heated. Where did *that* awful line come from?

But she smiled and gave a little curtsy. "Yes, fine sir," she said, and that made it okay.

Kayla always made things okay, made you feel comfortable. Maybe that was why he'd so urgently wanted to spend time with her tonight.

A familiar fast song was starting up. Most people seemed to know it and came onto the floor, making it even more crowded. Groups of women put their hands in the air and laughed and danced their hearts out.

Kayla's eyes sparkled and her cheeks were pink. She moved with easy rhythm, and he was hard-pressed to keep his gaze above the neck, but he tried. Her hair whipped around, and he realized he'd never seen it loose before. What would it feel like, he wondered, to run his hands through it?

They touched hands, backed off, touched again. Tony liked to dance, and it was clear that Kayla did, too. He even managed to twirl her a couple of times despite the press of the crowd. When the song ended, people clapped and started to leave the dance floor.

"Uh-uh, don't stop yet, folks," Bisky called from the stage. "We've got a couple of slow songs before we head over to see Santa at Goody's. One last chance to hold your girl close, fellas."

Tony looked at Kayla. She bit her lip and backed away.

"Will you dance a slow song with me?" he asked.

Their eyes met and held, and it felt like he was asking her for something more than a dance.

"What about Norleen?" she asked.

"I'd rather dance with you." He held out his open hands.

She stepped closer, and he wrapped his arms around her as the little band started a popular slow song.

She fit against him perfectly. She wasn't tall; the top of her head was at chin level. She felt warm and womanly in his arms. They swayed together, and there was that sense of rhythm he'd noticed on the fast songs, now close up.

Around them, other couples were locked together. He caught a glimpse of Paul and Amber. Mary, the head of the Victory Cottage program, was in the arms of a tall, bald man who looked extremely happy. Norleen was wrapped around Evan, who didn't seem to mind.

It made his body happy to hold Kayla; he couldn't deny it. She was all female, and they were dancing pretty close. But that was an experience he'd had before, many times.

What he'd never experienced was the caring he felt—both for her and radiating from her. Long before this moment, he'd learned she was a wonderful person. Jax adored her; all kids did. She was unfailingly kind, but also fun and lively.

He rested his cheek on the top of her head and closed his eyes, just for a moment, savoring her. Yeah. This felt different. This *was* different.

Becoming Jax's guardian had made him more serious, and more choosy about women, too. Kayla lived up to his new higher standards and then some.

The song ended, but the band immediately segued into another slow song, and he kept his arms around Kayla. He hadn't imagined he could feel this good. "One more?" he asked her.

"Sure." She sounded a little breathless.

A minute in, he recognized the song and guilt slammed into him, guilt and sadness. He stepped away from Kayla, holding her upper arms for a few seconds, then letting go.

"I...I need to leave," he said. The people around him seemed to blur, all except Kayla, who was studying him, her expression curious.

"Sorry," he said. "I have to go."

"What is it?"

He couldn't tell her that the song everyone around them was dancing to was his sister's favorite song. Couldn't share with her the memories of Stella swaying to it every time it came on the radio, blasting it from her phone when she needed a lift. If he started talking about that, he'd break down.

He just needed to get Jax and refocus on his meaningful job of caring for his nephew. Not on holding an innocent, kind, good woman in his arms. She deserved better.

He turned away from Kayla's curious eyes and headed toward the children's area, only to find Paul and Amber emerging with Davey and Jax. Amber looked past him, at which point he realized that Kayla had followed him.

"We're taking the boys over to Goody's," Amber announced. "They want to go together. We'll meet you at the boat parade after."

He looked down at Jax, who was trying to get his arms into his coat sleeves. Tony held the coat for his nephew and then helped him zip it.

"Me and Davey are gonna see Santa!" Jax said.

"Do you *want* to go with Davey?"

Jax nodded vigorously. "Can I, Uncle Tony?"

Tony swallowed hard. Jax was getting better here, not needing to cling, and it was a good development. It meant he was healing. "Sure you can," he said, even though he kind of wanted to cling to Jax himself. To comfort his own sorrow about Stella by clinging to her son.

"Yes!" Jax pumped his arm and scooted over to where Davey was standing.

Tony felt a hand on his shoulder. "Come on," Kayla said, her voice firm. "Let's take a walk."

Kayla. All his feelings about dancing with her went to war with his anger at himself, leaving him confused. "I should really go with Jax," he said.

She nodded at Jax, who was following Paul and Amber through the now-emptying ballroom, talking a mile a minute to Davey. "Jax is fine," she said. "Come with me and tell me what happened in there."

He let his eyes close for just a minute. The temptation

to tell her was strong, but so was his shame about his role in his sister's death.

"Look, Tony, I'm not trying to make a move on you. I'm just being a friend. Something happened when we were dancing together, and I want to help, if I can." She crinkled her eyes at him. "So, a walk?"

"Okay," he said.

"Good." She guided him toward the coat racks with a gentle hand on his arm. She found her own red coat and stocking cap, which made her look like a kid. He grabbed his jacket and they walked out together into the chill. People were disappearing down the street toward Goody's, and the sudden quiet was disorienting.

They walked for a few minutes on the bike path beside the bay. Even through the cold air, he caught the faint fishy smell of a waterfront town. Water lapped against the pilings, rhythmic and soothing.

He tried to let his thoughts calm down, but they kept racing. Kept bringing back Stella's face, twisted in anger, that last time they'd been together.

"Look," Kayla said, "I know I'm being pushy, but I'd like to help. Won't you tell me what's wrong?"

"You *are* kind of pushy," he said, but in a joking way. Kayla's pushiness was of a completely different variety than Norleen's, because it came from a place of caring.

Should he tell her about Stella, about his role in her death? The therapist had encouraged him to talk about it. "It's not a pretty story," he said.

"That's okay. Come on, let's sit where there's a break from the wind. I can always talk better looking out at the water."

What else could he do? He followed her to a sheltered bench and sat beside her. Not close this time.

She just waited without speaking.

"That song they played last. It was my sister's favorite. The sister who died. Jax's mom." He looked out over the water. It was rippled but glossy, like an old-fashioned mirror, and the full moon made a path across it. He had the fanciful thought that if he could follow that path, he'd get to where Stella was. What would he say to her?

He'd apologize, beg her forgiveness, for sure. Tell her how Jax was doing.

His throat tightened. She'd loved Jax so much.

"Tell me about it?" Kayla asked.

He sucked in a breath and watched the water.

"You don't have to," she said. Her voice was gentle.

Why not? It was a way to make her back off, so he wouldn't have to push her away. "After I got out of the service, I moved back into our family home in Filmore, where Jax and my sister were living," he began.

"Your parents are gone?"

He nodded. "It's the house where I grew up. Old and run-down, and I thought I'd fix things up a little while I was getting my feet under me. Spend some time with Jax."

"That makes sense."

"I was the oldest, and Stella the youngest. She looked up to me in a way, but also kind of wanted to defy me. I was more like a father than a brother."

Kayla nodded. "Big difference between oldest and youngest sibling," she said.

"Yeah. She'd sneak out like a teenager after Jax went to sleep. He'd wake up in the morning and she wouldn't be there, and he'd come wandering into my bedroom to find me. That always made me mad. What if I'd had an early appointment and was gone some morning? I was interviewing for jobs, sometimes at the last minute."

"You're right. She should have let you know before leaving him."

"We fought a lot," he said. "And finally…" He paused, looked up at the sky, at the stars peeking out around clouds. "Finally, after a big blowup, she took Jax and left. Wouldn't answer her phone, didn't say where she was going."

"That must have been so scary!"

"It was, but she got in touch with our sister, let her know she was safe. Only…she actually wasn't." He sighed. "Two days later—actually, two *nights* later, it was after midnight—Jax showed up on my doorstep. No idea who brought him, but he was crying and upset and couldn't say what had happened. A little while later, the police came to let me know…" He swallowed. "To let me know Stella had passed. Shot down. Our address was on her ID."

Her hand came over to find his and hold it. "That must have been just terrible," she said.

"Yeah." He looked down at the ground, kicked at a rock. "I pushed her back into the drug lifestyle, and as a result, Jax doesn't have a mom."

She squeezed his hand, studying his face. He couldn't read what she was thinking, but she had to be disgusted by what he'd told her.

For the first time, he realized that Kayla was almost exactly the same age Stella had been. And although their lives had been completely different, Stella had also been so young. Too young to make good decisions, and she'd needed his guidance and support, not his judgment and yelling.

Was Kayla thinking about what that would be like, looking up to an older brother who ultimately betrayed her? He couldn't stand the innocence in her eyes, and he had to look away.

Farther down the boardwalk, people were clustering, ready to watch the boat parade. The first lit-up boat motored in front of them, a sailboat with colorful lights strung from the top of the mast down to the bow and stern. Next

was a little fishing boat, this one with white lights sparkling along the railings.

"Did Jax's therapists ever talk to you about reassuring
him it wasn't his fault?" Kayla was still looking steadily
at him, still holding his hand.

"Yeah." Another decorated boat came into view. "They
did, especially the new one, and I've talked to him about
it a few times."

"Good. I guess they told you that small children think
the world is centered on them. That's why they think everything is their fault."

"Uh-huh." He wasn't sure why she'd changed the subject. Maybe it was easier to talk about Jax than to react to
the story he'd told her, about his own culpability.

"But it really *isn't* their fault."

"Right."

"So Tony," she said, her voice gentle, "you're kind of
doing the same thing."

"The same… What do you mean?" He'd expected an
attack, but she just looked and sounded compassionate.

"I'm saying your sister's death isn't your fault, even
though you think it is."

Was she patronizing him? Faking kindness, covering the
truth of his transgression with sappy-sweet words?

Sweet words that, as he thought about them, insulted
him. "You're saying I'm like a little kid?"

"You may have made some mistakes in your relationship
with her, but she could have moved out and gone any number of other places. To a hotel, to your other siblings, to a
reliable friend's house. Or she could've stayed and tried to
work things out with you. You didn't kick her out, right?"

"No, I didn't. Though according to her, I made it intol-
erable for her to stay."

"Because you wanted her to be responsible for her son?"

She shrugged and stood. "To me, that seems like the kind of thing that needed to be said. Think about it."

Could she be right?

"Let's go over by the railing and watch the boats," she said. She took his hand and tugged, and he got to his feet and followed her.

The boats were passing by more regularly now, and closer together. All were strung with lights, some multi-colored, some white or blue. Between the moonlight above and the reflected light below, the effect was like a fairy tale. Jax had to be loving it.

And Tony loved it, too. Loved the beauty and the bay; loved having his burden of guilt lift just a little.

"You're mad at me," she said, looking up at him, her hair wild and silvery in the moonlight. "I shouldn't have psychoanalyzed you."

"I'm not mad. The opposite, in fact." He tugged her hand to make her face him and stepped closer. Reaching up, he let his fingers catch a strand of her hair. It was as soft as it looked.

Her eyes widened and darkened. Moonlight played across her features.

He touched her cheek.

He wasn't enough for her, wasn't a good bet. He'd done something awful to his sister and to Jax.

But tonight, in this fairy tale world, he could set all that aside. He could do what his heart wanted to do.

He leaned closer and pressed his lips to hers.

CHAPTER ELEVEN

TONY'S KISS WAS so gentle, so much a natural outcome of the night's events, that Kayla relaxed into it.

His lips were warm on hers. That was what she noticed the most, the warmth. In his lips, and in the circle of his arms. A gentle brush and then a light pressure. She could smell his after-shave, could feel his hand touching her hair, lingering there. She reached up to touch his dark, springy curls, so much coarser than her own flyaway strands.

And then she realized: *My goal! My first kiss!* It was happening before the year ended. She smiled against his lips and leaned her cheek against his chest, just for a moment. Her ridiculous goal, achieved.

"Let's walk." He tugged her to his side, and they strolled slowly toward the crowd.

Kayla's heart raced. Kissing Tony wasn't what she'd expected. She'd imagined something pushy and intrusive, probably because of the boy who'd attempted to kiss her in school.

But it had been nothing like that. More of an invitation than a demand.

And she wanted to follow up on that invitation. "Let's stop here for a minute," she said before they got close to the edge of the crowd. She turned away from the water, leaned back against the railing, and lifted a wondering hand to his face.

He caught her hand in his and pressed his lips to it, his eyes on her. "Sorry my beard is rough. I wasn't expecting any kissing."

"Me, either. And in fact, I shouldn't be doing that."

His forehead wrinkled and distress rose to his eyes, and she realized immediately what he was thinking: that she reviled him for his story, that he was a bad person, and that was why she shouldn't be kissing him. She'd gotten to know him so much better, she realized. She was starting to read his mind.

And she didn't want him to get the wrong impression. "Aren't you going to ask *why* I shouldn't be kissing you?" she asked.

"I can guess." He still looked troubled.

"I doubt that." She was still holding his hand, and she pulled it to her lips and kissed it, smiling at him. "Because technically, I'm your boss," she said. "Inappropriate to be fraternizing with a coworker."

"Ooohhh. I see." He smiled and then tugged her against his chest and kissed the top of her head. "I like fraternizing with you," he said, his breath warm against her ear.

She lifted her face to him. "Me, too," she said.

He nudged and crowded her until she felt the railing against her back, and put an arm on either side of her, trapping her.

For just a minute she felt that rush of panic that stemmed back to her time in middle school. But it was as if Tony sensed her distress, because he lifted one hand to touch her chin, then tangle in her hair.

He wasn't trapping her, he was just being close. And that closeness felt *wonderful.* She lifted up and pressed her lips to his.

His response was immediate, and his mouth moved on

hers, and it was suddenly not just warm, but hot. His lips were firm and it was very, very clear that he knew what he was doing. And Kayla realized that the first kiss had just been a practice round. This, this kiss on the bay with the wind picking up around them and the moon above, now *this* was what everyone raved about.

She lost track of time and didn't want to find it again. She wanted to stay here, in his embrace, forever. Her pulse quickened and her face heated and it got a little bit hard to breathe.

Finally, he lifted his lips and looked down at her with a crooked smile. "You're something else."

She felt like her mouth was swollen. Her heart raced. "Wow," she said, looking into his dark eyes. "Just wow. I didn't know it would be so...intense."

He laughed a little. "Intense for me, too."

"It was my first," she confided, feeling starstruck.

His forehead wrinkled. "Your first?"

"My first kiss," she said. "I'm glad it was with you." She felt so close to him, so emotional. That was what was really intense. Oh, she'd felt the kiss from head to toe, and she understood that part of it was physical attraction, but that wasn't all. She'd felt cradled in his arms, cherished.

His eyes widened. "Wow. Your first kiss?" He took a step back, and the breeze chilled the front of her, where he'd been keeping her warm.

His obvious surprise made her self-conscious. "Could you tell?" she asked shyly. Maybe she'd done a bad job of kissing. How would she even know?

"No, I couldn't tell, although..." He looked at her again, shaking his head. "It does make sense of some things. How come this was your first kiss?"

Now she felt like a freak. "There were some...reasons," she said.

"Did I push you into it?" His eyebrows drew together.

"No! In fact, I wanted—" She stopped herself. It wouldn't exactly be flattering to him to learn that he was part of a goal she'd set before she'd even met him. "I wanted to kiss you," she said.

The crowd down the boardwalk was getting noisier, and a couple of the boats were setting off fireworks, making small, bright flashes in the sky. The bay lapped against the pilings, and the rhythmic sound settled her.

Kayla took deep breaths of the cool night air. She needed to calm down. Needed to think about what had happened.

Needed to treasure and relive how wonderful it had been. She smiled up at him.

He put an arm loosely around her shoulders and turned them both toward the crowd. "Come on, we should join the others and check on Jax." He urged her forward. "I'm honored to be your first kiss."

There was something about the way he was reacting. "Honored" wasn't what she'd been looking for. And besides, he didn't sound honored. He sounded bemused, maybe upset.

Her starry-eyed feeling started to evaporate, replaced by familiar insecurity.

Someone like Norleen would have known how to kiss. And not just how to kiss, but how to act afterward.

Maybe you weren't supposed to act all happy and excited. Maybe you were supposed to play it cool afterward.

Maybe kissing Tony had been a mistake.

SYLVIE COULDN'T EAT much at the church lunch. She'd figured as much—her stomach had been acting up lately—so she'd only taken tiny portions of a few side dishes.

The best solution for a down mood was work. So, as

soon as she'd finished as much as she could, she took her plate to the kitchen. She found a coffeepot and carried it around, offering refills. Then she headed into the kitchen and started scrubbing pots and pans and baking sheets.

Big Bobby was pressuring her to come home and visit. He wanted to know what Jax had seen, what he remembered, what he knew.

Bobby wasn't mad. He just wanted her to come home for a couple of days so they could see each other and she could tell him what she'd learned.

His voice when they'd spoken was quiet, but there was an edge to it. He wasn't happy with her. If she wanted to please him, she should probably corner little Jax alone and interrogate him.

It said something about their relationship that she didn't care as much as usual about making Big Bobby happy. And she really, really didn't want to go back to Filmore, even for a short visit.

Nonetheless, she owed Big Bobby for taking her in all those years ago. For giving her a home.

Maybe making the five-hour drive would help her figure out what she wanted.

The kitchen got crowded as people finished their meals and helped to clean up. Sylvie didn't talk much—she just kept scrubbing pots—but it was comforting to hear the laughter and friendly jokes behind her.

Pleasant Shores was home to a lot of good people. You could trust them. And now that she was among them, she realized she wanted to spend more time around people like this.

Pastor Steve came to stand beside her, leaning back against the counter. "You seem preoccupied."

She gave him a quick smile and kept scrubbing. "I am."

Should she tell him any more? Or keep her troubles to herself, as she'd done all her life?

"Want to talk about it?" His smile was easy, his eyes kind.

"Just… I have to make a trip back home tomorrow. And I'm dreading it."

He nodded. "I'm sorry about that. Are you staying back home for Christmas, or celebrating here?"

She thought of what Christmas would be like in Filmore. Normally, she decorated the house. Bobby usually spent time with his ex-wife and kids on the day, so it was lonely for her. When he did come home, he often brought friends. Lots of drinking involved.

"What's it like here at Christmas?" she asked.

He picked up a clean dish towel and started drying the big stack of pans she'd washed. "It's real pretty. Friendly, too. Of course I love the Christmas Eve service the best—" he gave her a wry grin "—since I'm in charge of it. But there's also a parade in the park on Christmas afternoon that's fun to watch. All the kids bring their favorite new toy, and there's hot chocolate and cookies."

"That's sweet." She couldn't imagine such a thing happening in Filmore.

"It's nice for folks who don't have kids in the family, or people who are alone." He hesitated. "It's not easy being single on Christmas, but if you're in town, I guarantee you'll get invitations to dinner."

She'd figured she would. Or maybe she'd see if Primrose wanted to get together and cook a big Christmas meal. Maybe there were others they could feed. "It's a friendly town."

"Hey, Sylvie, Pastor Steve, if you don't need anything, we're out of here." The couple who'd been loading the big industrial dishwasher and wiping counters were shrugging into their coats. Only a few people remained in the dining area, and they seemed to be gathering their things to leave.

"We've got it covered," Sylvie said. "Just a few more trays to wash." She looked over at the pastor. "I'm sure you're busy. You don't have to stay."

"I'm actually not too busy. I'll help you finish up." He paused. "Unless you want to be alone?" His voice sounded strangely nervous.

It made her want to be nice to him. "Lord, no. I'm glad of the company. I go crazy in that motel room sometimes."

"We're a pair, then. I go crazy in the parsonage sometimes." He carried a stack of pots to a cupboard. Then he came back and stood a few feet away, leaning against the counter again. "I'm curious about you," he said. "I sense there are some hidden depths."

Back home, that remark would have made a lot of people laugh. Back home, she was just Big Bobby's girlfriend. "I'm just an ordinary girl." She hesitated, then added, "Who had a tough childhood and ended up in a relationship I don't want to be in." As soon as the words came out, she realized they were true. That was why she so dreaded going home tomorrow. She didn't know how to tell Big Bobby; didn't know if she could.

"Is it abusive?" Steve asked quietly.

"No, but…" She trailed off, took the drain plug out of the sink, and watched the soapy water swirl and disappear.

"Hard to leave?"

She nodded, relieved that he understood. "There are years of history. And some other stuff." She wanted to watch over Jax for a little longer, make sure he still seemed happy rather than troubled by memories. "I just have to go back and straighten a couple of things out. I hope to be back here for Christmas." She dried her hands.

"I hope so, too. But just in case you're not…come with me." He gave her hand a little tug, then headed out of the kitchen.

She followed him through the darkened halls of the church, wondering what he was leading up to. Was it a ploy to get her alone? Did pastors do that?

Would she mind?

They walked through an office containing an empty receptionist desk, a copy machine, and stacks of file folders and printer paper. Everything was a little messy. You could tell it was an active church.

At the back of it, a door was marked Pastor's Office.

"Wait here," he said, and disappeared into his office. A moment later, he came back out with a book. "Early Christmas gift," he said.

"What is it?" She took the book, flipped through it. Was it a Bible?

"It's a collection of Bible verses under headings, depending on what you're going through." He smiled at her encouragingly. "And tuck this in there. It's a card with my cell phone number. Call me if you need anything."

"Thank you." It was a sweet gesture, but there was a part of her that wished he wasn't acting like a pastor.

"You can build a new life, you know," he said.

A burst of anger surprised her. "People like you, in places like this, think it's easy to start over. But it's not."

"I never said it was easy, Sylvie," he said quietly. "Just that you *could* do it."

"Honestly? I don't know if I can." She spun on her heel so she wouldn't see his expression, wouldn't know if it was hurt or anger or just professional detachment.

Like it or not, she was a Filmore girl. And she had to go there tomorrow.

Tony sat in the waiting room of the therapist's office, Jax on his lap, feeling like a terrible person.

He'd kissed Kayla, a woman so innocent she'd never been kissed before. Tony, on the other hand, was older and maybe too experienced. He shouldn't have touched her.

And maybe he wasn't as experienced as he thought. Kissing Kayla had felt different—not physically, but in his heart. The way she'd looked at him had made him feel like a hero. That, he'd never experienced with any woman before.

Sadly, it wasn't something he could do again. Tony knew he wasn't a good bet for a relationship; look what he'd done to his sister.

Although… Kayla's words came back to him. She thought his sister's death wasn't his fault, thought he was being like a child for blaming himself.

Was he? But Tony couldn't get around the fact that if he'd stifled his criticism, Stella might be here today. Jax might have a mother.

To add to his guilt, Jax had regressed in the past twenty-four hours. He hadn't slept well, hadn't eaten well, had lapsed into some kicking-and-crying tantrums the way he'd so often done back in Filmore, after realizing his mother wasn't going to come home.

The regression made Tony realize that Jax had been doing much better, with a change of scene and new friends and these weekly therapy sessions.

Only now, he'd had a setback. Tony didn't know why.

Dr. Liz opened the door to her inner office. "Come on back, DeNunzio men. We're going to do some art today!"

Jax didn't look at her, and he didn't make a move to stand up. He just huddled close to Tony.

"Time to go play with Dr. Liz," Tony said. When Jax didn't move, Tony stood with Jax clinging monkey-like to his chest. "You're getting heavy, pal. Anytime you want to walk, you let me know."

Jax didn't respond, but once inside the office, he allowed Tony to put him down in a chair at the wooden table, one with a thick cushion that raised a kid to table height. "You want me to sit here, too?" he asked the therapist.

"Oh, yes. We're *all* going to draw." She pulled up a chair for herself and passed crayons and paper to Jax and Tony.

He sat down beside Jax. "I'm not too good at art."

"Just start with something simple. Maybe your house. Or your family."

Jax immediately started drawing. Tony did, too.

"So how's your week gone?" she asked.

"Jax hasn't been feeling too well," he said. "He's waking up in the night, and he has an upset stomach. I don't know what's set him back."

"It's nothing you did, Tony," she said. "It's normal given what he's been through. Grief is like a spiral for everyone, but especially for children. They touch on something important, then go off and think about other things, then come back to it. That can happen dozens, even hundreds of times."

"Wow." Tony focused on coloring in the house he'd drawn, a weak attempt at portraying Victory Cottage. "Is there anything we can do to make it better?"

"This. And talking. And time."

They all drew for a few minutes. Tony felt ridiculous playing with crayons, but he had to admit it was weirdly soothing.

He drew in a couple of figures, himself and Jax in the front yard. That looked lonely, so he added his brother and sister to the picture.

Jax looked over at his drawing. "You forgot Mommy," he said.

The words stabbed Tony. "Where should I put her?" He was wondering what Jax pictured: Stella in the sky, or in the ground, or just the same as living people.

"Maybe Jax would like to draw her in," Dr. Liz suggested.

Tony pushed the paper over to Jax. He grabbed a crayon and drew a person, or at least a four-year-old's version of one: head, stick legs, and eyes.

Only…she was laying on the ground.

Jax grabbed a red crayon and scribbled patches around her. "Blood," he said. Then he drew another stick figure, bigger than any of the rest. "That's the bad man," he said. Then he frowned and scribbled all of it out. His eyes filled with tears, and then he went into a full-on crying jag.

Tony pulled Jax onto his lap and let him lean against him. Jax's thumb was in his mouth, something Tony usually discouraged, but not now.

He held his nephew as his heart turned inside out. Jax, sweet, innocent Jax, must have witnessed Stella's death up close, if he'd seen her lifeblood flowing out of her. What could be worse for a kid?

If only Tony had taken a kinder and gentler approach with Stella. She'd been so young. His words had goaded her into leaving, and she'd been unequipped to be out there on the streets on her own. Sure, she'd *thought* she was grown up and fine; sure, she'd been the mother of a four-year-old child. But in so many ways, she'd been like a defiant teenager. You didn't take them at their word; you didn't let them run away and be on their own. You protected them, kept them safe until they grew up enough to get better sense.

With immense effort, he stopped himself from spiraling down into his grief and shame. Now wasn't the time. He had to focus on his nephew, not his own feelings.

Jax's tears still flowed, but he was quieting a little. His monotonous little bleats just sounded miserable, full of loss and grief.

Tony looked helplessly at Dr. Liz. "No progress," he said, keeping his voice low.

"This *is* progress. It's him processing what happened, and what better place than here, with you and me to help him?" She went over to her laptop and took a few notes.

Tony stroked Jax's hair and the crying wound down. He grabbed a couple of tissues and wiped his nephew's face.

"How are you doing, buddy?" he asked, and then added, feeling his way, "It's okay to be sad and cry."

Jax swallowed, wiggled his way down from Tony's lap, and climbed back into the chair with the cushion.

"Why don't you draw your family the way you wish it could be?" Dr. Liz suggested.

Jax drew, his tongue sticking out of the corner of his mouth, gripping the crayon tight. He drew two more of his head-with-legs people. "That's me and you," he informed Tony. He drew two more people, twice as big. "That's Mommy and Miss Kayla."

Uh-oh. Tony glanced at Dr. Liz, who was smiling and nodding.

Jax drew another shape, so big it covered most of the page. This one had four legs. "And that's a big dog."

"I like your big dog," the therapist said, her voice encouraging. "Can you tell me about him, or the people?"

"He 'tects us," Jax said seriously. "Like Sarge 'tects Davey."

"I see," she said thoughtfully.

Jax threw down his crayon like he'd completed a herculean task. Which, psychologically, maybe he had.

"Now, do you want to play with Mixter for a few minutes while your uncle and I talk?"

"Yeah!"

Dr. Liz disappeared into her back hallway and returned with the odd-looking creature. The dog trotted immediately to Jax, tufted ears high, tail wagging.

Jax ran to the basket of dog toys, selected a thick, knotted rope, and started playing tug with the dog.

The adults watched for a minute, and then Liz turned to him. "Any concerns about what happened here today?"

"Considering that he drew a picture of his mother bleeding on the ground, yeah."

The therapist nodded. "That means he saw her body, at least. No wonder he's having some post-traumatic stress."

"I hate it." Tony sucked in a breath, realized he was clenching his fists, and tried to relax. "I'm also concerned because he put Kayla, his preschool teacher, into the family picture."

"Speaks to him getting attached to her. Not a bad thing, unless she's going to abruptly disappear from his life."

Tony lifted his hands, palms up. "I don't know what's going to happen. This is supposed to be a temporary gig here."

She studied him shrewdly. "What's your relationship with the preschool teacher?"

He felt his mouth quirk up a little. "You see too much. I like her a lot. But it's not serious. It can't be."

"Because..." she prompted.

He wasn't ready to go there with her. "Just because."

Jax rolled on the floor with Mixter.

Tony reached over and picked up the picture Jax had drawn. "We're not going to be able to bring his mother back, or get Kayla a permanent spot in his life," he said slowly, "but maybe I could think about getting a dog."

Dr. Liz smiled. "I couldn't agree more. There's a therapy dog program here in town, and a shelter just up the coast." She searched for information on her phone, wrote it down, and handed it to him. "Addresses and phone numbers. But think hard before you take Jax there."

"Why's that?"

"Because, first of all, there won't be any window-shopping. If Jax goes with you, you'll take a dog home that day. I guarantee it."

"You're probably right."

"And it's hard to manage a scared new dog, and an excited little boy." Her mouth quirked up on one side. "Maybe his preschool teacher could come and help you out."

"Yeah!" Jax cried.

Tony looked down to see that Jax was playing much closer than he'd been before. "You were listening, buddy?"

"I wanna take Miss Kayla and go get a dog right now!"

It was the happiest and most animated that Jax had been all day. Tony would give a lot to keep him happy.

Even if it meant spending time with a sweet, compassionate woman he should never have kissed.

CHAPTER TWELVE

"I'M SO GLAD I ran into you," Kayla said to Sylvie as they headed toward a window table at Goody's. It was Monday, barely lunchtime, and the restaurant was hopping with Christmas week shoppers. "This isn't the best place for my waistline, but it *is* the place to be in Pleasant Shores. I can't believe this is your first time."

"Not the last, I hope," Sylvie said as they settled into their seats.

They'd encountered each other at Lighthouse Lit, Mary's bookstore. Kayla was taking advantage of the time off school by shopping for a gift for her mother, who went through a couple of books a week. Sylvie had been in the same section—cozy mysteries—and had given Kayla some suggestions about what her mother might like. They'd chatted for a few minutes about the book club selection, which they'd both read, and then Kayla had asked Sylvie if she wanted to join her for lunch.

She might not have done it, except that Sylvie looked blue. It had reminded Kayla that Sylvie was alone in town. Since the preschool had gone on break, she probably didn't see many people. Kayla knew the holiday season wasn't happy for everyone.

And indeed, Sylvie had taken her up on the offer instantly.

Now, she took a sip of chocolate milkshake and her care-worn expression changed into a happy one. "Wow. This is fantastic."

"Goody's milkshakes are famous." Kayla tasted hers. "Yum. Goody takes 'drink away your worries' to a whole different level."

The place was already crowded. Bags and packages surrounded most of the tables, indicating that Sylvie and Kayla weren't the only ones who'd been shopping. The residents of Pleasant Shores were big on supporting local businesses. And, apparently, on waiting for the last minute to get their Christmas shopping done.

In the slightest of nods to the season, Goody had draped ribbon around the cash register, and an artificial poinsettia sat beside it. That was all. The music playing was country, not Christmas. "Goody's a little Scrooge-like," Kayla told Sylvie. "So if you get tired of all the Christmas music and decorations, this is the place to come."

"I do get tired of it." Sylvie picked up a french fry and tasted it. "Wow, terrific fries, too. She doesn't need to decorate as long as the food's this good."

Kayla bit into a steaming crab cake and then fanned the air in front of her face. "Whew, that's hot." She swallowed and asked, "How do you like Pleasant Shores so far?"

"Love it," Sylvie said immediately. "That's why I'm putting off a trip home."

"Filmore, Pennsylvania, right? Are you staying there through Christmas?"

Sylvie shook her head. "No way. I'd honestly rather spend the day in my motel room than be back there."

"Trouble?" Kayla was ashamed that this was the first time she'd wondered what Sylvie's life was like outside her work at the school. "Family you don't want to see?"

"Not exactly," Sylvie said. "I mean, it's typical trouble. I think I need to break up with my boyfriend there, but that's easier said than done." She nibbled a fry. "How about you? You're dating Jax's uncle, right?"

"No!" Kayla's cheeks heated as she thought of the last time she'd seen Tony. The cool breeze, the moonlight, the Christmas lights on the boats…and most of all, the kiss.

That had made her feel like she *was* seeing someone. But Tony hadn't called or texted yesterday, and so far, nothing today. So maybe the kiss hadn't been as magical for him as it had been for her. Maybe she'd been bad at kissing. Maybe it hadn't meant anything to him, had just been the combination of the event and the opportunity and the season.

"Funny," Sylvie said, "I got the feeling there was something between you."

I got that feeling, too. But apparently Tony didn't. "All that's between us is Jax," she said firmly. "I'll do what I can to help the child. I feel so sorry for him, losing his mother to violence."

"That would be traumatic. Poor kid." Sylvie hesitated, then asked, "Do you…do you think he remembers anything about it?"

Kayla frowned. "It wasn't that long ago, so I'm sure he remembers her when she was alive."

"I mean, was he there? Did he see what happened?"

"Oh. Yeah, I think he was." Kayla remembered what he'd said that day at Paul and Amber's. "He was talking to another little boy about it, and he said his mother fell down and didn't get up. So he must have seen it happen." Her heart broke for the poor kid. "I can't imagine anything more awful than that."

"It *is* awful," Sylvie murmured. "I wonder if he'll have to testify in court. Wonder if he saw the killer. Do you think he did?"

Sylvie sounded strangely curious. "Did you know him back in Filmore?" Kayla asked.

"No. No, I didn't. I just wondered, you know?"

Kayla pushed her basket of fries away. "I have no idea what he may have seen. I hope, for his sake, it wasn't much."

Goody's door was opening and closing, people coming and going. Kayla hadn't been paying attention, but at the sound of a deep voice, something electric shot up and down her spine.

Tony was here. She glanced over and saw him and Jax joining the line to order food.

"Miss Kayla!" Jax ran over and hurled himself against Kayla's side. "We saw you in the window. Guess what, we're getting a dog and you can come help!"

"You're getting a dog? That's awesome!" Kayla smiled, pushed away from the table, and focused on Jax. Such a sweet, enthusiastic little boy, and resilient, too. She already missed her preschool kids, this one especially.

"Yeah!" Jax climbed into her lap, and Kayla melted at his easy affection. "Dr. Liz said we need another grown-up. Can you come?"

"There you are!" Tony strode across the restaurant. "Jax, you're supposed to stay beside me. I didn't know where you'd gone."

"I 'vited her to come with us." Jax bounced up and down, smiling broadly. "To get our new dog."

"Buddy, you're supposed to let grown-ups do the asking," Tony said, his face flushing. "Sorry, Kayla."

Why wasn't he meeting her eyes?

Immediately her mind raced to interpret his expression and actions. Whereas Jax, who loved simply and unconditionally, wanted to invite her on this most important of shopping trips, Tony didn't agree.

She'd give him a graceful way out, pretend she hadn't taken the invitation seriously. "You two need to have lunch," she told Jax, "so you have energy for dog shopping. Miss Sylvie and I were just finishing. You can have our table."

"Do we have time?" Jax looked up at his uncle.

"Sure do," Tony said. "Hi, Sylvie. Didn't mean to ignore you. Are you enjoying your time off from school?"

Sylvie smiled at Tony and Jax. "It's nice to sleep in a little, but I miss the kids."

Jax leaned against Kayla's leg and studied the woman, his sweet face going serious. "You were in my bad dream," he said.

"I'm sorry, honey." Looking distressed, Sylvie stood quickly and started gathering her paperware. "This has been fun, but I need to get on the road. If I don't see you folks again, Merry Christmas."

Kayla watched her toss her trash into the garbage and hurry away. There was something different about Sylvie. She seemed to have a lot going on beneath the surface.

"DeNunzio!" called Goody from behind the counter.

"That's our food. Mind if we sit down for a minute?"

"Go for it," she said, and a moment later, he returned with a tray holding two baskets of fish and chips and two milkshakes. Tony and Jax ate heartily for a few minutes. When they'd slowed down, Kayla asked Tony, "Is it true that you're getting a dog?"

"We're *looking* at dogs, at a place in town and then maybe at a shelter up the shore," he said. "Just looking for now."

"Right. The week before Christmas is exciting enough for kids without adding a new dog into the mix." She looked at Jax, who was bouncing in his chair. "Is Jax going too? Because…"

"I know, I know." Tony laughed a little. "I'm probably fighting a losing battle." He hesitated, then added, "Dr. Liz, our therapist, suggested I bring another adult to help with the dog and Jax. Any chance you've got time to do that?"

"Please, Miss Kayla?" Jax looked up at her, his brown eyes wide.

She did have time, but it probably wasn't wise to spend that time with Tony and Jax, considering Tony's nonreaction to their kiss.

She looked at Jax's eager face again. "Sure, I'll go," she said.

TWO HOURS AFTER encountering Kayla at Goody's, Tony listened to Jax crying in the back seat as he turned the car north. "Sorry to put you through this," he said to Kayla, who was in the passenger seat beside him.

"I wanted a dog!" Jax wailed.

"I know you did, sweetie." Kayla reached back to pat Jax. "You made the right call," she said to Tony. "None of the therapy dogs they had were ready or right."

"Which makes sense to adults, but not to a little boy." Tony sighed. "If the rescue Dr. Liz told us about doesn't have the right dog, we're in for a long night." He felt, rather than heard, Kayla stiffen, retraced what he'd said, and frowned. "I mean Jax and I. You don't have to be involved. This is already a lot to ask."

"It's fine." She opened her mouth like she wanted to say something else, and then closed it again and looked out the window.

Why did everything have to be so awkward with Kayla now?

But he knew why: because of that kiss on Saturday night. He hadn't been able to get it out of his mind.

It had been a mistake to do it, but he didn't regret it. The kiss was something to hold on to, that momentary feeling: swept away and excited, but also content. Holding Kayla had just felt right.

As a matter of fact, as soon as he and Kayla had started dancing, he'd caught a glimpse of what real love and a family life might be like. Looking around on the dance floor, he'd seen other couples sharing the same close embrace, the same look in their eyes. Married couples. Happy married couples.

He wanted it. Badly. With Kayla.

But he couldn't have it, not when he was so flawed, not when he'd failed his sister so badly, and Jax, too. So the goal today was to get Kayla's help with dog shopping and then gently, kindly, back away from her.

The thought of letting her go made him feel as desolate as the marshy area they were driving through, where dozens of tree trunks stuck up like bleak, bare posts. They'd lost their branches and died, killed by the salt water that was increasingly taking over the land.

Duck blinds and deer stands of various sizes stood in the distance. The Eastern Shore was mostly thought of as a vacation destination—he'd always thought of it that way himself—but parts of it were wild, cut off from mainstream civilization. Hunting was a popular pastime; in fact, Evan Stone had invited him to some local hunting event.

The place was complex, full of unexpected facets. Kind of like the woman riding beside him.

"Slow down!" Kayla said.

He braked. "What's wrong?"

"Sika deer. Look." She pointed at a couple of tiny deer standing by the side of the road.

He let the car glide closer and studied the small, spotted creatures. One lifted its head and looked at them, then went back to eating a patch of greenery that had survived the cold temperatures.

At the same time, both Kayla and Tony turned toward Jax. But he was sleeping, his head slumped to one side in his booster seat.

They looked at each other, and their gazes tangled. They'd both had the same thought. Tony wished he could have that permanently in his life: someone on the same wavelength, someone who thought of Jax in the same way he did. Wanting him to be able to see an interesting animal, but also wanting him to get the rest he needed.

Tony tore his gaze away from Kayla's and forced a practical, parenting tone into his voice. "Better not wake him up."

"There will be other deer. They're actually sort of common here."

Easy. She was so easy to get along with. He drove past the deer couple slowly and then picked up the pace.

"Look," he said, "I appreciate your coming today, when—"

"About that kiss," she said at the same time.

He had to smile even though it was awkward. They really *were* on the same page. "You first."

"I was just going to say, just because it was my first kiss, that doesn't mean you have to feel awkward or obligated in any way. I'm not expecting you to give me a ring or anything."

Talk about cutting right to the chase. He glanced over at her and saw that her cheeks were red. It hadn't been easy for her to say that.

"I wish I could be, you know, more to you." He was feeling his way. But it was easier to talk while driving than while sitting somewhere face-to-face. "I… It was great, Kayla, really. I just can't…" He trailed off.

Because what could he say? He'd already told her he felt guilty about everything.

And she'd accused him of thinking like a toddler.

"It's fine. No need to explain. Hey, slow down!" She pointed. "Aren't we supposed to turn on Boar's Neck Road?"

"Right. Hold on." He slowed and turned.

"Uncle Tony?" came a sleepy voice from the back seat. "Are we there?"

"Just about." And more than that, they were done with this awkward and difficult conversation, at least for now.

"Want me to go in and scope it out, sort of pave the way?" Kayla asked.

"That would be great." If there was paperwork to be done or a long line, getting started would cut down on the amount of time Jax had to be patient.

He watched her walk into the shelter, her blond ponytail swishing back and forth, her pace energetic. He remembered what her hair had looked like at the Crabby Christmas event, curling down around her shoulders.

He remembered what it had felt like. And every day, it seemed, he saw more ways she'd be a great partner to the right man.

Which wasn't him.

"C'mon, let's go in!" Jax's words pulled him out of his thoughts, and the child was matching words to actions, unhooking himself from his booster seat and climbing down.

"Stay in the car until I get you," he reminded Jax.

"Hurry! The dogs might be all gone!"

Tony doubted that, but he climbed out of the car quickly and opened the rear passenger door. "Hold my hand," he ordered. He was still learning to state and enforce all the many crucial rules involved with kids—and just how important they were. Jax was bouncing up and down, tugging at him; clearly, he'd been ready to run across the parking lot into the building with no thought of traffic.

Inside the shelter, Kayla was filling out an adoption form. "They don't hold dogs," she explained. "If we want one of theirs, we have to take it home today. I figured I'd fill it out for you just in case."

Tony knelt in front of Jax. "Remember, we're looking. We might not find the right pet for us today."

"I know." Jax rose to his tiptoes, trying to see past Tony into a room full of dogs in pens.

"Okay." Kayla stood. "That's mostly done. You can finish the rest of it if today goes well."

"Come on back," the worker said. She had frizzy gray hair and looked tired, but friendly.

In the kennel room, Jax couldn't contain himself. He raced from pen to pen, shouting, "I want this one! And this one! No, this one!" His movements whipped the dogs into a frenzy of barking.

"Jax!" Tony scolded. "Settle down. You have to be quiet and walk slowly, so the dogs don't get scared."

"I don't *feel* quiet." But he came obediently back to Tony's side.

The worker pointed out a kennel that held a grizzled-looking beagle. "Clyde would be nice for first-time dog owners," she said. "He does like to run away, that's the breed, but he doesn't run very fast anymore. He sleeps a lot."

Tony nodded, liking the dog's floppy ears and wrinkled forehead. Then he watched as Jax unsuccessfully tried to prod Clyde into action with fingers poking through the wire. "I'm not sure we're the best family for an older dog," he said.

"Now this is LuLu." The worker pointed to a dirty-looking poodle. "She's a real beauty when she's freshly groomed. Kind of a prima donna, too."

"She's for a girl," Jax announced, and walked right past her pen.

Tony had to smile. He'd been thinking the same thing.

Kayla and Jax both knelt by a small pen holding a brown mop of a dog. "This one's cute," Kayla said.

"Yeah, I like this one," Jax agreed.

The kennel worker shook her head. "Too small for a household with a young child," she said. "And he's actually pretty aggressive. Don't let him—"

But Jax was already extending his hand toward the kennel's wire fencing, and suddenly, the little mop lunged, baring his teeth. Jax yanked his arm away and tumbled backward. He stared at the dog, his lower lip trembling.

Kayla put an arm around him. "Some dogs aren't right for you, but that doesn't mean you did anything wrong," she reassured him.

"That's right," said the worker. "Tell you what, you take your time and look around. Let me know if you like any of the dogs, and I'll tell you more about them."

They walked around to see the rest of the dogs. There was a beautiful husky, but he cowered in the back of the pen. Another, a bulldog mix, seemed too old and rickety for a child with Jax's energy level. A Chihuahua barked fiercely at them, making Jax step back and cling onto Tony.

"This might not be our day, buddy," Tony said. He felt disappointed himself.

"Are there any other possibilities?" Kayla asked the kennel worker, who was at a big sink washing dog dishes.

"Well...there's Paddington, but I don't think—"

"We read stories about Paddington," Jax interrupted. "He's a bear."

The worker chuckled. "Our Paddington is kind of like a bear, too." She looked at Tony. "He's a large Saint Bernard, young, not even two years old. He's just coming out of quarantine today—we quarantine all our dogs for two weeks when they come in—so nobody's looked at him yet. But I don't think…"

"I wanna see Paddington," Jax said. "Please, Uncle Tony?"

"We may as well take a look, if he's available for adoption," Tony said.

"Oh, he's available. But I don't think he's quite what you want."

As she spoke, she led them to a little room, bare except for a bench and some dog toys. "You can meet him here," she said, still sounding doubtful.

A moment later, a big furry creature bounded into the room…and bumped straight into the wall. It yelped and then jumped back, cowering a little.

"It's okay, big guy." The kennel worker grabbed hold of the dog's leash. "I shouldn't have let you go right away. You need to get your bearings first."

Tony held Jax close and studied the dog as it moved clumsily around, sniffing everything. "What's going on with him?"

"He developed cataracts young," she said. "He's almost completely blind. His owner tried to return him to his breeder, but they didn't want him back. So they brought him here."

Kayla's eyes widened. "For being blind? You're kidding!" She reached for the dog and rubbed his large block of a head, and he graced her with a sloppy kiss.

"Can I pet him?" Jax asked.

"I mean, sure, he's gentle as a lamb, in the sense that he's not aggressive. But he's pretty high energy."

Kayla lifted an eyebrow. "Maybe on a par with a four-year-old boy?" she asked.

"I guess. He can knock you over if he bowls into you, and he does that pretty often. He requires a lot of grooming, too."

Jax grabbed the dog around the neck and clung on, and Tony and Kayla both jumped to intervene. "Gentle, buddy," Tony scolded, his heart pounding at the sight of Jax so close to the big dog's teeth.

"Oh, don't worry, Paddington loves affection," the worker said, and the dog proved it by licking Jax's face until he giggled.

Tony knelt in front of the dog and studied him, noting the cloudy white color of his pupils, running his hands over soft, wild fur. "He's good with kids, do you think? Have there been any problems with them?"

"We haven't seen him interact with any kids visiting the shelter yet, but I do know that the family that had him before had kids. He's used to them. In fact…" The worker stopped talking.

"What?" Tony looked up.

"Nothing. We're not supposed to say anything about the people who drop off their dogs here."

"It's hard to believe they were able to get rid of this guy," Kayla said. She'd progressed to rubbing his sides and showing Jax how to scratch behind his ears. The dog flopped to the floor and turned onto his back, his tongue lolling out of the side of his mouth.

"Pet his belly real gently," Kayla explained. "Like this."

Jax followed suit, carefully petting the dog's pink belly. His smile was huge.

"He seems great with Jax," Kayla said. "Were the kids in his original family this young?"

"One was," the worker said. She hesitated, then added, "The kids were the only ones who were upset about dropping him off. Mom and Dad were cold, but the kids couldn't stop crying."

Kayla's forehead wrinkled and her mouth turned down. "How sad."

"It was. They said they were going to get another dog, one that didn't have anything wrong with him. The kids just kept bawling." She swallowed. "They wanted to keep Paddington."

"That's terrible!" Kayla glanced down at Jax and bit her lip, obviously stopping herself from saying more so as not to upset Jax. But he was rolling and playing with Paddington, apparently oblivious to their conversation.

Tony and Kayla looked at each other over the squirming mass of dog and little boy. That gaze communicated everything: neither one of them would ever put children through that if there were any way around it.

There was a sound outside the little room, people walking by, and Paddington let out a deep, loud bark that made them all start, then laugh.

"He doesn't bark a lot, but when he does, it's loud," the worker said. "Do you think you might take him? I gotta be up front. He'll be a lot of work. He hasn't had much training, and he's likely to lose what vision he has. He's also likely to grow some more, according to the vet. These big breeds take a while to mature."

Jax held the dog's head and looked into his eyes. "We'll take you home, Paddington. You can 'tect me real good."

That was likely. Most thieves or intruders would be intimidated by Paddington's size and loud bark, even though from the looks of things, he'd probably drown bad guys with drooly licks rather than attacking them.

But far more important than the guard dog element was the happy expression on Jax's face as he hugged the Saint Bernard—gently, as instructed—around its burly neck.

"We'll take him," Tony said.

Jax's eyes glowed. "He can be my dog? Really?"

"Really, kiddo." It felt so good to be able to do this for Jax.

"Yes!" Jax couldn't contain himself then, jumping and whooping, which made Paddington start to jump and run, too.

"You know, I think this will be a good match," the kennel worker said.

Kayla was all smiles. "I'm so glad. I think he'll be a great dog for you. Good choice."

Her approval, the warmth in her eyes, felt good. Way too good.

Doing all of this together felt too good, as well. Tony needed to be very careful, or Kayla would become part of their growing family.

CHAPTER THIRTEEN

ON MONDAY EVENING, Sylvie dished up Big Bobby's favorite pasta and handed him a plateful. She was back in Filmore, and it was as if she'd never left. Cooking for Bobby had always been one of her main sources of joy. The man was the perfect audience. He definitely loved to eat.

She wasn't sure how he'd been managing without her. Possibly, eating less healthily. He'd gained so much weight in the past year—he was well over three hundred pounds now, which was way too much even at his height—and she'd been alarmed at how out of breath he'd gotten when he'd carried her bag upstairs.

He'd changed. Just three weeks away was enough time to make that obvious.

Thing was, she'd changed, too. Not physically but mentally, maybe even spiritually. She wasn't the sweet, content, compliant woman who'd gone on a fool's errand a few weeks ago.

"It's good to have you home," Big Bobby said between bites. "Been eating too much takeout. Restaurant food doesn't live up to this."

"Glad you like it. Salad?" She held up the bowl, even though she knew in advance what he'd say.

"Nah. You know me. I'll fill up on the good stuff instead."

She served herself—more salad, less pasta—and then spoke up. "You know, you should start eating healthier. You're not getting any younger."

"I'm as young at heart as my young girlfriend," he said, winking at her.

She smiled back. It was a running joke with his friends that he'd robbed the cradle. He was thirty years older than she was, a difference that had seemed fine when she'd gotten together with him. She'd been desperate, and he'd been kind. A father figure, something she'd never had before. As for him, he liked having a younger woman on his arm.

Things felt different now. She could see that they had less in common; he wanted to stay home or sit in a bar drinking with friends. She liked to get outside and walk, and to her own surprise, she'd been enjoying church and community activities in the short time she'd been in Pleasant Shores. No way would Bobby join her in any of that.

They ate quietly for a few minutes, and Sylvie looked around the dining room. It was small; the whole place was small, a little ranch, but cozy on this December night. The good smells of bread and marinara filled the air, and the house was warm from the heat of the gas fireplace.

"Sure is nice to be in a house instead of a motel room," she said, just making conversation. That part was true; she'd started going a little stir crazy at the Chesapeake Motor Lodge. If she stayed in Pleasant Shores, she needed to start looking for an apartment.

If she stayed. That was the thought that had been dancing around the edge of her consciousness throughout the day, and throughout the drive.

Going to Pleasant Shores had catalyzed her. All those hours in the motel room alone, the walks along the bay, the reading for the book discussion group, the friends she'd started to make, even the church services—and the pastor—had made her take a second look at her life in Filmore. She wasn't sure it was even possible to change, but she did want to try.

At the same time, she owed Big Bobby so much. Not only had he saved her from the streets, but he'd taught her what love was, really. She'd grown up not knowing a man could treat a woman well.

They'd been together for eight years, since she was twenty-four. That was a lot of history. It wouldn't be easy for either of them to let go.

He wiped his mouth and looked at her with eyes that were still piercing. "Had another visit from Little Bobby," he said. "He's worried and I am, too. What have you learned about that little boy?"

"I think he's fine," she said as nerves attacked her stomach. "He's just living his life. Settling in, from the looks of things. Getting to know other kids."

"And he remembers nothing about that day his mom was shot. Right?"

She pushed her own plate away, half-empty. "I just don't know." On the spot, she decided she wasn't going to tell Bobby what Kayla had said, that Jax had seen his mother on the ground. "And since he seems to kind of recognize me, I can't ask him what he remembers. Just the fact that it's me asking could spark memories better left alone."

"Wait a minute. He definitely recognized you?" Bobby's bushy eyebrows drew together.

"I'm not sure." She leaned back in her chair, sipped wine. "When he first saw me, he stared in a funny way. I've caught him doing it again a couple of times."

"He hasn't said anything?"

"No. Well…" She hesitated. "He did say I was in his bad dream."

"Not good." Bobby's eyebrows lifted and little beads of sweat broke out on his forehead. He sighed, shook his head. "I want out of this life, Syl. I'm too old for it."

She was glad for the change of subject. "There's nothing wrong with leaving your work to the next generation. Take it easy." She'd been encouraging that for the past year, as the strains of his wrong-side-of-the-law lifestyle had started to show on him.

"The younger guys, they have no morality. No sense of honor."

Sylvia pressed her lips together to keep from saying *you're not exactly a choirboy.* At least, that was the word around Filmore, though Sylvie had never heard anything specific about him being violent toward anyone.

She did know for sure that he'd hurt people terribly due to his prominence in the local drug trade.

His eyes were vague now, unfocused. "I don't need more on my conscience." He seemed to be somewhere else, thinking of something painful.

Maybe a lot of things.

She carried their plates into the kitchen and brought back a glass of his favorite after-dinner wine. When he saw it, he smiled and scooted back from the table. "Give me a hand standing up," he said, and she braced herself and helped him pull himself out of his chair. He picked up the glass of port and made his way over to his big double recliner. "Come here, girl," he said. "Sit with me. I've missed you."

So she climbed in beside him and he put his arms around her. He'd been like that since they'd first gotten together, giving her the sort of warm affection she'd never known. Back then, of course, he'd wanted more than cuddling, and she'd given it to him, out of gratitude and, eventually, out of love.

Lately, it was more about companionship than passion.

Which wasn't nothing.

"I want you to talk to the child," he said finally. "It's important we know what he knows. Find out for sure he doesn't remember any details of that day, and you can come home."

You can come home. The thought of that sent confusion through her. She didn't want to come home. Did she? Did she want this to be her home, and Big Bobby to be her man?

Just like Big Bobby, she was starting to want out of the life she'd made for herself.

He brushed back her hair and kissed her a little, and she felt...if not romantic love, then some other kind. She really did care for the man. He was the closest thing to family that she had.

"Family is family," he said.

His words were an eerie echo to her thoughts. "What do you mean?"

He looked up at the ceiling and slowly shook his head. "I have to take care of my son."

"Why are you thinking about Little Bobby now?" A terrible suspicion gripped her. "Is he the one who shot Jax's mom?"

He was quiet for a long moment. Then: "It's way too complicated. You don't want to know."

Her heart pounded so hard he could probably hear it. "Why did he—whoever did it—why did they shoot her?"

"Stupidity," he said. "Leave it at that. Like I said, you don't want to know."

"You're right. I don't." Because if she knew, she'd have to report it to the police. Would have to tell Tony what she suspected his nephew had seen, how she'd happened to hear the gunshot while walking in Big Bobby's neighborhood and rushed there to find a little boy crying beside a car, had gotten him to recite his address, had taken him home. Revealing all that would cause chaos to break loose, both in Pleasant Shores and in Filmore.

Best to stay on the surface, to not try to figure it all out. She lay her head against Big Bobby's shoulder and closed her eyes. With the gas fire sending its warmth into the room, the television on low, and Big Bobby's arms enfolding her, she felt embraced by the familiar.

Her life here was so much better than what she'd grown up with, what she'd experienced as a young woman on the streets. As Big Bobby's woman, she'd been safe. She'd thought it was the most a girl like her would ever get, and maybe it was.

Except she'd experienced something new in Pleasant Shores. A community. A different kind of man. The opportunity for some kind of adventure.

There, where people hadn't known her past, she'd started to make real friends.

She wanted to go that in direction, she was pretty sure. But how could she leave Big Bobby, in his age and infirmity?

On the other hand, how could she stay with a man who still worked to get drugs into the hands of addicts, who might even know his son had killed someone and was trying to protect him?

Her heart felt tugged in two directions. Part of growing older and getting perspective, she guessed. With every door that opened to you as an adult, another one closed.

She burrowed deeper into Bobby's embrace and stroked his arm, her eyes filling with tears.

It felt like goodbye.

"I DON'T MIND at all," Kayla said Tuesday morning as she walked in the door at Victory Cottage. And she didn't. Just seeing Tony's smile made her nerve endings tingle.

Then she looked around at the scattered toys, shoes, and jackets in the living room, and her eyes widened. Tony hadn't seemed like the messy type. "Rough morning?"

"Very." Tony's mouth quirked to the side in a wry expression. "Paddington didn't sleep real well, and that means that Jax and I didn't, either."

"I'm sure he'll get better," Kayla soothed. "Just like kids, a big change probably makes dogs feel discombobulated." She hung her purse and jacket on a hook by the door.

"Let's hope." Tony looked around the room and sighed. "When he started chewing on shoes, I realized I need more dog stuff. Toys and chew treats and a tie-out. I really appreciate your coming over to stay with them while I run to the pet store."

Paddington came running into the room, followed by Jax. The big dog banged into an end table, and the lamp on top of it tilted.

Tony caught the lamp before it could crash to the floor and then put a restraining hand in front of Jax, who was making another round through the room. "Whoa, buddy, slow down. Paddington still needs time to get the lay of the land."

"Seems like he's already started on that," Kayla said. Indeed, the big dog seemed to mostly have a sense of where the furniture was. He sniffed around the couch and coffee table. "Seems like he's comfortable with Jax, too. He must be used to kid shenanigans."

"I think so, but he needs to rest, as well. Give him a break, Jax, okay?"

"Okay," Jax agreed. He climbed into a chair, his eyes following Paddington's every move.

"You listen to Miss Kayla while I'm gone, too." Tony ran a hand through hair that it looked like he hadn't had time to comb. "I'll just grab my stuff and take off. Back in an hour, I hope."

"Take your time." Kayla walked over to the dog, who'd sat down beside the couch, panting. "Hey, Paddington, how's it going?" She rubbed his back and sides, and his fluffy, white-tipped tail wagged.

Tony snapped his fingers. "That's what else I need. I'm

going to get another brush. The one we were using didn't make much of a dent."

"I helped brush him," Jax said proudly. He scooted over to sit on the other side of the dog. "I love him so much."

His obvious joy put a lump in Kayla's throat.

As he walked out the door, Tony paused and smiled back at her. "You can't know how much I appreciate this, Kayla. You're a good sport."

"Glad to do it." *I'd be glad to do anything for you and Jax.*

Oh, brother. She was getting *way* too emotional for her own good.

Jax, of course, quickly distracted her from her thoughts. He tugged Kayla into the kitchen, Paddington trotting behind, and showed her the big bowls they were using as food and water dishes. "He likes to eat and drink a lot!" Jax explained.

As if to illustrate the truth of that, Paddington drank heartily, then turned and trotted away, his whole muzzle dripping water.

Kayla grabbed a paper towel and wiped the floor, even though she had a feeling it was a losing battle. "How'd he learn where his food and water dishes are already?"

"Cuz he's so *smart*!" Jax bounced up and down. "He's big and smart and he's *my dog*!"

Again, Kayla's throat tightened. It was good to see Jax so happy.

There was a knock on the front door. Paddington woofed.

"See, he's a guard dog!" Jax said as he ran to open it.

Kayla followed, the hairs on the back of her neck standing up for some reason she didn't understand. When she saw Norleen and Rhianna standing on the front porch looking in, she got it. Her middle school experiences had given her a sixth sense about mean girls. She probably needed to get rid of that, now that she was an adult.

As she reached the door, she wondered why Norleen was dropping in at Tony's place.

"Guess what, I got a dog!" Jax shouted. "Come see, come see!"

Kayla's heart plummeted. "Hi, Rhianna," she said to the little girl, who was already rushing across the room to Jax and Paddington. And then, with considerably less enthusiasm, "Hi, Norleen."

The woman came in, her gaze sweeping the room. "Where's Tony?"

"He's out buying dog supplies. He and Jax brought Paddington home yesterday."

The big dog was sniffing Rhianna.

"Come see him, Mom!" the girl said.

Norleen crossed the room and gingerly petted Paddington's head. "What's wrong with his eyes?"

"He's mostly blind. His family gave him away and that's how we got him." Jax wrapped his arms around the dog's neck and hugged him fiercely.

"Gentle," Kayla reminded him.

As soon as Jax released Paddington, the big dog moved closer to Norleen, panting up at her, twin strands of drool hanging down from either side of his mouth. Norleen, who was wearing tight black pants made of something that looked like leather, wrinkled her nose and stepped back, but not before he'd gotten a little drool on them.

Score, Paddington.

"Come on and see his stuff," Jax said to Rhianna. "He has a hu-u-u-uge dish, and he's gonna have lots of new toys."

After Kayla had ascertained that the dog was fine with Rhianna—who in any case was less rough than Jax—she sat down on the sofa. She had the feeling this visit was unexpected, because otherwise, why had Tony called her to come babysit Jax and Paddington? Why hadn't he just had Norleen do it, if he knew she was coming over?

On the other hand, maybe Norleen and Tony were on a drop-in basis with each other. "Is Tony expecting you?" she asked. "He'll be back in an hour, he said."

Norleen perched on the edge of a chair, tapping the toe of her high-heeled boot. "I'll wait. We had lunch plans, but you know how absentminded men can be. He probably forgot all about it."

"Uh-huh." Was Norleen telling the truth? Kayla had never experienced Tony as absentminded. At any rate, she wasn't going to offer Norleen a beverage or anything, since this wasn't her house. If she and Tony were so close, let her get it herself.

"You're looking really cute," Norleen said. "More grown up all the time."

Kayla felt somehow insulted. "Is that a compliment?"

The kids came back into the room, the dog following. Just looking at them lowered Kayla's blood pressure.

"Of course it's a compliment! You look great. It's like you got some style."

Kayla looked down at her Christmas sweater and faded jeans. "I guess?"

"I mean, back in middle school, you never wore anything that wasn't three sizes too big."

"I was trying to cover my brace, you know that," she said. "Jax! No pulling Paddington's tail."

"Sorry." He let go and went back to rubbing Paddington's side.

Norleen was biting her lip. "Look, I know I teased you some about the brace. I'm sorry."

"You teased me some?" Her voice rose to a squeak, and heat flashed through Kayla's body as she stared at the woman. "Actually, you made my life completely miserable. That's why I changed schools."

Norleen's hand flew to her mouth. "Oh, no, I don't think I did anything that bad. A couple of jokes."

"That's not how I remember it," Kayla said. "You had names for me, and you got your friends to trip me so you could laugh about how hard it was for me to get up."

Norleen's face flushed. "You were always so sensitive."

Kayla's eyes narrowed as she studied Norleen, trying to remember. Was that true? Had she been oversensitive?

Or was Norleen trying to justify her own bad behavior? After all, who tripped a kid with a back brace? It would practically be a federal offense these days.

"Anyway," Norleen said, picking at a perfectly manicured fingernail, "it wasn't me so much as the boys who teased you."

An image of a whole crowd of kids laughing at a lunch table flashed onto Kayla's mental screen. Norleen had definitely been in the group. "Not true. You were in on it."

"You make it sound like a conspiracy. I might've said a few things, but I never meant to make you feel bad."

Could that be true? Doubtful, but Kayla waved a hand. "It's all in the past. And the teasing made me focus more on my schoolwork, so there's that."

"You did well. You have a great career." Norleen frowned at the floor. "I wish I could've gone to college."

That bit sounded honest, and fit what Mom had said about Norleen. And, following Mom's example, Kayla ought to be kind. "What would you have studied in college? It's never too late, you know."

"I always liked math and accounting." She lifted her hands, palms up. "But I've forgotten everything I knew. I'm a mom and I can't afford college now, anyway."

"There are programs for women like you. Special scholarships for returning students, stuff like that."

"With my grades?" Norleen sighed. "I don't think so. My program is to find myself a rich husband."

"Oh." Did women still do that? "Uh…any prospects?"

Norleen laughed. "Yeah. We're sitting in his living room."

That remark twisted Kayla's stomach. *Be nice*, she reminded herself. "Is Tony rich?"

"No, but he'll get there. He's educated, and he works hard. He could support me and Rhianna. Believe me, I found that out right away."

Kayla was pretty sure Tony's counseling degree wasn't going to make him a millionaire, but it wasn't her place to disillusion Norleen.

Paddington flopped down on his side, panting, and Jax and Rhianna lay between his front paws and back paws, side by side, heads on his belly.

"Oh, I have to take a picture of that. It's adorable!" Norleen pulled out her phone and snapped several photos. "I love how well they get along. And if Tony and I got together…well, they'd be wonderful siblings, and I could stay home and take care of them."

Getting ahead of yourself much? But maybe she wasn't. She'd made herself at home in Tony's place and appeared quite confident.

But Tony had kissed Kayla, not Norleen.

Or maybe he'd kissed both of them. Maybe he'd acted sweet and tender to Norleen, just as he had to Kayla.

Maybe that was why he'd been so awkward after their kiss. And why, this morning, he'd called her a good sport.

She was the good sport, and Norleen was the prospective girlfriend. At least, that was how it usually went for Kayla.

Funny, Kayla had felt so confident when she'd tried on

clothes with Amber and Erica. Their admiration and praise seemed to have sunk in.

Now, in Norleen's company, her confidence had slipped away. Maybe it hadn't really been there to begin with.

"So...how come you're here?" Norleen asked now. "Did Tony need a babysitter or something?"

"Exactly," Kayla said. No use pretending there was more to their relationship. "He needed someone to watch Jax and the dog while he ran out for supplies."

"Well, that was real sweet of you to do it," she said. "I'm here now, though, so if you want to go ahead and leave, I'm sure you have a lot to do."

Seriously? "I agreed to stay until he came home."

Norleen shrugged. "Whatever you say." She walked over to the door and picked up a soft-sided cooler. "I brought lunch for us and the kids. I'll just go get it ready."

No question who was the "us" she was referring to. Kayla's heart plummeted. If Norleen was on a "make yourself at home in the kitchen" basis with Tony, then Kayla had no business interfering.

Jax would love to have a sister to play with. And a mother figure. And Tony would have a super attractive woman on his arm.

Kayla was still pretty sure Norleen wasn't a very nice person. She'd admitted she wanted to use Tony for his money. But Kayla couldn't tell him that. It would sound like sour grapes.

Tony banged through the front door, arms full of bags. Kayla hurried to help him.

"Don't say it," he said, grinning. "I went a little overboard."

"Do you think?" There were dog toys overflowing from one of the bags, treats of various sorts from another.

"Uncle Tony brought toys!" Jax ran over to his uncle and started rummaging through the bags. "Here, Paddington, catch!" He rolled a big stuffed ball, made to look like a bowling ball, toward the dog.

Kayla was about to correct him—Paddington couldn't see a ball—but then she heard the bell inside it. Paddington lifted his head, listened, and started sniffing.

"The saleslady said we should show him the ball, maybe even put a little food inside, so he could hear and smell it," Tony explained, showing Jax the little hole where you could put a treat.

Rhianna came from the kitchen. "Mommy made us lunch," she announced.

Tony blinked. "Norleen and Rhianna are here?"

Norleen came out. "We sure are. And I made sandwiches for all of us. Peanut butter and marshmallow fluff."

"I *am* hungry," Tony said doubtfully. "And I didn't fix Jax much breakfast. He probably is, too."

"I love peanut butter. Can Paddington have some?" That was Jax.

"Come on," Rhianna said, beckoning. "Mommy set the table!"

Norleen came out. "Lunch is served," she cried merrily.

Kayla had never felt more like a fifth wheel. "So long, I have to go," she said. She wasn't even sure anyone noticed when she left.

LATE TUESDAY NIGHT, Tony followed his new acquaintances, Isaac Roberts, William Gross, and Evan Stone, into the Waterman's Bar.

The place was crowded and loud. Strings of old-fashioned, multicolored Christmas lights crisscrossed the ceiling, alongside silver foil icicles. Inflated Santas stood in two corners, and signs painted with dubious Christmas statements—"Be Naughty, Save Santa the Trip" and "Don't Call Me a Ho Ho Ho"—decorated the walls. The crowd, mostly men in flannel shirts and jeans, seemed to favor draft beer.

They snagged seats at the corner of the bar and ordered a pitcher. Evan asked for a glass of soda.

It was Evan who'd invited Tony to come out deer spotting with them. Since Jax was having a sleepover with Davey, Tony was at loose ends and that was why he'd agreed to go. Surprisingly, it had been kind of fun.

"Did you see that last buck?" Isaac asked. He and William had been in one truck while Evan and Tony had been in another.

"We saw him." Evan raised an eyebrow. "Even I was tempted to take a shot." Hunting deer at night was against the law, and after this experience of deer spotting, Tony could see why. The large spotlights mounted on the tops of the trucks made the deer freeze, constituting an unsportsmanlike advantage.

"I never thought much about the 'deer in headlights' saying until now." Tony lifted a foamy glass and drank deep.

"First time deer spotting, huh?" Isaac, who owned the town's hardware store, asked the question.

"Yeah." Tony had known of the practice back in Filmore, but there, illegal shots would definitely have been taken. Probably because someone needed venison to feed their family.

"Gonna make some mighty fine hunting." Isaac tipped back his chair. "Not that I have time to do it. The hardware business is booming."

"This close to Christmas?"

"Sure. We've got all the last-minute gifts you need. Get your lady a snowblower and she'll be yours forever."

William snorted. "Even Bisky wouldn't look kindly on a snowblower. Now, a new outboard for the boat, maybe."

"Gonna be a while before she's back out on the water full time," Evan said. "When's the baby due? January?"

William nodded, smiling into his beer.

"You ready to be a dad?" Isaac asked William, and then broke off. "Sorry, man."

"No problem." That puzzled Tony, and it must have shown on his face. Both Evan and Isaac looked uncomfortable.

"I've already been a dad," William explained. "I lost my teenage daughter three years ago. She was shot by an intruder." He looked into his beer like he could see sad memories there.

"Wow. I'm sorry for your loss." Tony shook his head. "That just sucks."

"Yep." William let out a sigh and straightened his shoulders. "I'll never forget Jenna or, really, get over it. But I'm pretty excited about the new baby coming along."

The guys at the other end of the bar shouted at the TV, something apparently happening in the game, which provided a good shift of focus. Tony wouldn't mind talking to William sometime about how he'd gotten through such a devastating loss, but now wasn't the time.

Drinking and listening to the men around him, Tony tried to forget the things on his mind. Jax, he reminded himself, was safely settled at Paul and Amber's, as was Paddington. Jax had agreed to the overnight if he could take his dog, and Paul and Amber had been okay with it. Paddington and Sarge had gotten along fine, and the boys had been ecstatic. Amber had moved a few fragile items onto higher shelves in anticipation of running boys and dogs.

So Tony could rest easy and relax in regards to Jax and the dog.

Kayla, though, was another matter. He couldn't get her out of his mind.

She ran hot and cold. Hot, for sure, during their kiss. But then she'd told him he needn't take it seriously, implying that she didn't. She'd been friendly and companionable helping with Jax and the dog earlier, but then she'd disappeared with barely a goodbye.

Tony didn't understand, but it was for the best that she wasn't serious about him. That way, he wouldn't be tempted to get involved in her life only to skulk out of it when he inevitably let her down. He knew he wasn't the right man for her. She deserved someone better, much better.

Especially since getting involved, and then having to break it off when things went south, would hurt Jax, too.

In fact, he should probably start seeing less of her now, even as friends, since Jax was getting so attached.

Who are you kidding? You're attached, too.

Determinedly, he focused on the conversations around him. He played a couple games of pool and had a second beer. Soon, the married guys, Isaac and William, headed home.

"One last drink?" Evan asked. "Nobody's waiting at home for me."

"Me, either." He'd already told the guys about Jax's sleepover.

They left the pool table and found seats at the bar. "So what's on your mind?" Evan asked.

Tony held up his mug to the bartender, raised two fingers.

"Coke for me," Evan called. "I don't drink," he added to Tony. "And I'll ask again: what's on your mind?"

"What do you mean?" he asked Evan as the bartender brought over their drinks.

Evan shrugged. "Maybe I'm mistaken," he said. "Seemed like you weren't all there tonight. You worried about your boy?"

"A little." Tony shoved a ten at the bartender and waved away the change. "Plus the fact that I don't understand women."

"Who does?" Evan chuckled. "I assume you're talking about Kayla the preschool teacher."

So it was obvious. Great. "She was real friendly yesterday, did me a favor helping with Jax and the dog. And then she disappeared, and she's not answering my texts. Well, text," he amended. He hadn't wanted to harass her by sending more than one.

"What happened in between the friendly and the cold?"

Tony thought. "I came home, and Norleen had dropped by with lunch. Plenty for all of us, but Kayla ducked out. Barely said goodbye."

Evan sipped beer. "That Norleen is a piece of work. She made me want to run for the hills, and you, too. Why should Kayla be any different?"

"I don't know. I just thought women were more, you know, understanding." Wasn't Kayla a friend of Norleen's? They'd gone to school together, at any rate.

"Understanding of a rival? I don't think so." Evan sipped beer.

"A rival for what?"

"For you, dude." Evan smiled, his forehead wrinkling. "Are you dense?"

"I guess I am," Tony said slowly. "I used to do okay with women, but that was…before. Why would either of them be interested in a guy like me? I even told Kayla how I screwed up back home. She doesn't want anything more than friendship."

"That so?"

"I *think* so." And it was an uncomfortable subject with a guy he didn't know well. "Speaking of Norleen, I was hoping you'd kind of take her off my hands. You seemed to be getting along fine at Crabby Christmas."

Evan shrugged. "She's pretty. But she wants to replace her wedding ring ASAP, and I'm not the marrying kind."

"I hear ya." They sat awhile longer, watched some rerun football game that was on, and nursed their drinks while some of the men around them got plastered.

Finally, they left and walked up the docks to where they'd left their cars. The wind off the water was cold, and the moon flashed in and out from behind clouds. Tony drew a breath of the bay air he was starting to appreciate. "I never used to think I was the marrying kind, either," Tony said. "I've made it this far and stayed single. But lately...I'm having a different attitude."

"It's the kid," Evan said right away.

Was it? "I mean, it's not like I need a woman to help me raise him or something. I just..." He shrugged. "The bar scene and girl-of-the-week game was getting old, even before I had the responsibility of Jax."

"I don't deny that." Evan reached his car. "Plus it's Christmas. Hallmark movies and all." He unlocked his car. "If I don't see you, enjoy your Christmas."

Tony waved and drove home, thinking about the uncomfortable reality that he'd enjoy his Christmas more if Kayla were involved.

CHAPTER FOURTEEN

KAYLA HAD TO FORCE herself to go to the Book Club Christmas party on Wednesday night.

She'd woken up this morning feeling blue, and it wasn't hard to figure out why: Tony. Tony, who seemed to be getting together with Norleen.

She might be wrong, but from the cozy way Norleen had fixed lunch at his house, she assumed the two were on a familiar, drop-in basis.

At Crabby Christmas, Kayla had been willing to take action, spruce herself up and try to get Tony's attention. But that energy had deserted her now.

She'd had her first kiss, and it hadn't changed anything. Or rather, it had changed *her*; how she felt about Tony and herself and their relationship. It had put everything onto a higher plane, intensified everything. That might have been good if they'd ended up getting together, but since they weren't...ouch. It just hurt.

No self-pity, she told herself firmly. She cleaned her house, sorted through and posted a few cute pictures from the school's Christmas party, and wrapped some gifts. There was nothing more to do in the way of Christmas preparations, and she was off from teaching this week. The best thing was to go to the party, hang out with women friends. After all, she'd read the book.

She walked into Lighthouse Lit right behind Sylvie,

smiling to see the bookish winter wonderland. White garland with red berries circled high on the walls. A tall tree, real from the smell of it, stood in the corner, decorated with book ornaments. There was a pretty box for book donations. Handmade snowflakes decorated the window, and the kids' area had a realistic-looking Santa reading a book.

Mary's goldendoodle, Coco, lay in the midst of the circle of chairs, her head up and alert as she watched everyone come in. Even she was dressed for Christmas, sporting a red-and-green bandanna.

"She knows we'll bring treats." Kayla reached into her purse and pulled out a large biscuit, decorated with a red ribbon. She waved it at the dog and then handed it to Mary.

"You're sweet. Come in, sit down." Mary beckoned them toward the circle of chairs. "We're a small group tonight."

The door jingled again. "Oh, there's Amber. And Bisky may come, but she said she'd be late." Mary gave hugs all around, even to Sylvie, who looked surprised at the friendliness.

"It's a busy time of year," Amber said, "but when I saw what book we were discussing, I couldn't stay home."

"*Resolutions for Superwomen*. It's definitely a catchy title," Mary said. "And it's a short book, which is what we need during the holiday season. But before we discuss, let's eat and drink."

She beckoned them toward a dessert spread that made Kayla groan. Bourbon balls, a nut roll, a plate of fudge and another of colorful spritz cookies. A big heated container of hot chocolate stood at the end of the table, alongside a bowl of whipped cream, a jar of peppermint sticks, and a small bottle of peppermint schnapps.

"Heavenly," Amber said. And so they talked recipes and Christmas preparations. Bisky stuck her head in the door to apologize for not staying; she'd agreed to help her daughter with some last-minute shopping. As soon as Bisky left—laden with a container of cookies Mary pushed on her—Ria called to say things at the motel were crazy, so she couldn't come, either.

"More to eat for you ladies," Mary said, "and plenty to take home if you like."

Amber served up mugs of hot chocolate and then went around offering everyone hits of the schnapps. Kayla debated for only a minute before loading a small plate with fudge and cookies. Sylvie hesitated, too, then filled a plate. "Christmas is only once a year," she said. "I'll worry about the calories in January."

"They don't count on the holidays." Mary sliced the nut roll and handed around the bourbon balls. "Especially when you're fueling a book discussion. Eat up, everyone."

Finally, they made their way over to the chairs and sat down, pulling out their books or e-readers.

Mary led the discussion. "Let's talk about the concept of resolutions first. Who makes them? If you do, how did last year's resolutions go?"

Kayla's face heated, and she looked over at Amber and made a zipping motion over her mouth. No way was she going to let the group know about her silly kissing resolution.

Amber gave her a thumbs-up; she understood. "I resolved to write every morning from nine to twelve," she said. She wrote wonderful nonfiction books, including one about cancer, and was planning a travel book. "It was too ambitious, what with getting married and adjusting to having a young child again."

"And a husband who wants to spend time with you," Mary replied. "Totally understandable. But think how you could troubleshoot for next year's resolution."

"I need to get a writer shed outside of the house," Amber joked. "Only I know I'd be going back inside all the time to see what Paul and Davey were up to."

"How about you, Sylvie?" Mary asked.

Sylvie laughed, looking self-conscious. "I don't make resolutions."

"Any reason why?"

"Honestly?" Sylvie blew out a sigh. "It hasn't seemed like I had enough control over my life to dictate how it should go."

Kayla was curious about the woman. Despite working with her these past few weeks, she didn't feel like she knew her well. "Is that still the case going forward?"

Sylvie lifted her hands, palms up. "I just don't know. Lots of decisions in my near future. Leave it at that."

Mary nodded. "I understand. Kayla? What about you?"

"I've made resolutions," she said, blushing, "and even, kind of, kept them. But I don't think I'm making the right kind."

"What do you mean?"

Kayla sighed. "I made a resolution that I thought would get me on track toward what I wanted. It didn't work out that way."

"Cryptic," Sylvie said.

"Seriously cryptic," Amber agreed, her lips twitching with a smile she was trying to hide.

"But resolutions can be private. You don't have to share them if you don't want to," Mary said.

"Suffice it to say, it's about men. Men, and family, and the future."

Sylvie smiled at her. "That's me, too. I have stuff to figure out about men, one man in particular. But how do I make that be my resolution?"

"And that's where our book comes in," Mary said. "What did you think of her approach?"

"No, uh-uh," Amber said, waving a peppermint stick at Mary. "You can't get away with making us tell about our resolutions, and you don't tell yours."

"Last year, I didn't make one. I was just so worn out from all the issues in my life. Now, I'm ready to go forward again."

"Bravo!" Amber clapped. "Here's to new beginnings." She lifted her mug, and the rest of them followed suit.

"Cheers, to all of us," Mary said. "And by the way, just like our author says, resolutions don't have to be about accomplishments we can check off a list. They can be about self-care. Mine, for example, is to get outside every day, rain or shine, and be mindful in nature."

"I love that!" Amber said. "You have to be specific, though. How long?"

"Oh, I'll start with an hour. That's about the minimum Coco needs as a walk."

To Kayla's surprise, Sylvie spoke up. "You know what, I *do* have a resolution. I'm resolving to make a decision about my current relationship. And whether I stay or go, I'm going to journal, like she talks about in the book. Figure out what helps me feel good and what doesn't."

"That's a fine resolution," Mary said.

"I'm going to figure out how to be close to a man without getting all insecure," Kayla said. Her cheeks heated to reveal that about herself, but to her surprise, both Mary and Sylvie nodded.

"I'm totally insecure around men," Sylvie admitted.

"I was, for many years," Mary said.

"You?" Kayla couldn't believe it. "But you're, like, a model."

Mary snorted. "I *was*. Now, I'm a seventy-something woman. Either invisible, or…" She trailed off, a tiny smile curving her lips.

"Or a sex object, to your next-door neighbor." Amber waggled her eyebrows, making Mary laugh.

Kayla smiled, too. She'd heard that Mary and Kirk James were an item, or that he wanted them to be. "Men. Can't live with or without 'em."

"I do think," Mary said, "from my advanced age, that it's important to be strong in yourself before you can be with a good man. Treat yourself well, be secure, respect yourself."

Kayla looked at Sylvie, who was looking at her, the same skeptical expression on her face that Kayla wore. "How, exactly?" she asked.

"For me," Amber said, "it was about being honest about my past and accepting it."

Mary nodded. "I'm a work in progress, but making peace with the past was a big part of it for me, as well."

Sylvie turned her copy of the book over and over in her hands. "The trouble is, my man saved me from the streets. I owe him, and being with him seemed like a step in the right direction at the time, but now… I'm less sure it was."

Interesting. Kayla would never have guessed that Sylvie had such a rough background.

"Give yourself a break," Amber said. "You knew what you knew, then. You know more now. Forgive yourself if need be, and then move on."

Easier said than done. "I always feel so dumb about my past." Kayla looked around at the other women. "I don't know why I let my scoliosis, and wearing a back brace, govern my school years, but I did."

Amber went over to the food table and brought back

the plates of cookies and fudge, which she passed around. Kayla snagged another piece of fudge.

Mary patted Kayla's arm. "Just because someone else has bigger problems, that doesn't mean yours aren't important."

"Wearing a brace would be really hard on a middle school or high school girl," Amber said. "Teasing and bullying are awful things."

"Definitely," Mary said. "Bullying drove Ria's daughter Kaitlyn to take too many pills. She nearly died."

Sylvie gasped. "How awful. I thought Ria had such a perfect family."

There was a knock on the store's front door, and Mary went to let in a last-minute customer.

"No such thing as a perfect family," Amber said. "The point is, it's serious and it's worth working on, and we're here for you. Both of you," she added, looking at Sylvie.

Sylvie blinked. "You're choking me up," she said. "But it gives me the courage to take action. At least I hope so."

"I'm going to take action, too," Kayla said. "Not sure what the resolution will be, but I have an intent to get over the past and move forward."

Now, if only she could do that. If only she could get over Tony and figure out what she really wanted, which would *not* be a meaningless first kiss. Or at least, if it was a kiss, it would have to be meaningful to both parties, not just to her.

"Maybe," Amber said, "you shouldn't give up on your whole past resolution. The focus could have been wrong, but is everything that happened a complete loss? Could you salvage something, if you felt stronger in yourself?"

Kayla thought about kissing Tony. *Was* it a complete

loss? Should she give up on him because another woman was showing interest in him?

Or should she take action to explore whether there was any chance between them?

ON THURSDAY MORNING, Tony dropped Jax off at Goody's Ice Cream for a preschool friend's birthday party. Then he turned toward Kayla's place, Paddington at his side.

He was determined to talk to her rather than letting things fester. He wasn't the right man for her, but he also didn't want to leave things uncomfortable and negative between them.

As he and Paddington turned the corner, though, he spotted Kayla parking and climbing out of her car. Just the sight of her made him happy: blond hair blowing around messily, a warm red headband, ski jacket, and jeans that even from here he could see fit like a dream.

"I was just coming to see you," he said as they got within hearing distance.

"Funny," she said, kneeling to scratch Paddington's ears. "I was hoping to see you, too. Want to walk by the bay, or is it too cold for you?" She lifted an eyebrow and gave him a half smile, challenging him.

She wanted to see him! He tried unsuccessfully to tamp down the happiness that welled up inside him. "I can take it if you can," he said, and as they turned toward the bay, he took her hand and squeezed it for a minute before forcing himself to let it go.

It was sunny and cold, and Paddington trotted along beside them, tail high and wagging, pausing often to sniff along the side of the path.

"You'd never guess he was blind," Kayla commented. "How's it going with him? Is he sleeping better?"

Tony nodded. "I guess all the playtime has tired him out. He's been sleeping straight through." He paused. "The reason I wanted to see you—"

"I was wondering—" she said at the same time. Then they both broke off.

"Ladies first." He was really curious what she would say.

She sucked in a breath and straightened her shoulders. "I was wondering whether you and Norleen are together," she said, lifting her chin as she looked over at him. "After we kissed, I thought...well, I thought we had something that might go somewhere." Her cheeks flushed red, and she laughed a little. "And you have no idea how hard it was for me to admit that."

He couldn't resist putting an arm around her shoulders, just because she looked so sweet and vulnerable. "We could. We might, if..." How to say it? He squeezed her shoulder once and then removed his arm. "Look, I'm not into Norleen at all. I'm just, well, I'm not a good bet for any woman."

She studied him from under long, long lashes. "Really? Why's that?"

He blew out a sigh, his breath making steam in the air. Paddington tugged at his leash, and Tony pulled him back when he tried to follow a cawing gull right into the bay.

Tony didn't know how much he should talk about all the reasons he wasn't right for her.

How to explain that his temper made him say things he shouldn't say? He'd told her about Stella, but obviously, he hadn't made it clear enough: he'd pushed her to destruction, causing her death, causing a little boy to lose his mother.

He didn't deserve even a little bit of happiness, not after that.

This time, it was Kayla who slid an arm around his waist, nudging her way under his shoulder, nestling against his side as they walked ever more slowly. It felt perfect. She *fit* perfectly against him. His heart seemed to twist in the wind, back and forth, ready to expand out of his chest, then turning away, trying to shield her from danger.

He appreciated that she wasn't pressing him to tell more. They walked along together, and he struggled to stay focused on why this was a bad idea. Why walking down the bayside path with a beautiful woman on his arm was not for him.

He wasn't here long, not much longer. He was so attracted. Why not give into it, just a little?

"I'm not asking you to marry me," she said after a few minutes, practically echoing his thoughts. "I just thought it might be worth exploring a little, that's all."

He pulled her fractionally closer. "If things were different, I'd go for it in a heartbeat," he said.

She looked up at him. "It was my first kiss," she reminded him, her voice a little teasing. "And now I'm wondering, was it really as good as it seemed?"

He raised his eyebrows, staring at her. She was so sweet, so innocent, but some playful, all-woman part of her knew how to flirt.

"Well?" she asked, still in that teasing voice. "What do *you* think?"

Their steps slowed to a halt, and he couldn't take his eyes off her.

She was looking at his face. His lips.

His heart pounded hard, a mixed drum solo of thrill and worry. He let the dog's leash slide to his wrist, forked a hand through her soft, messy hair. "We'd better find out," he said, his voice a little hoarse. And then he lowered his lips to hers.

Things escalated fast this time. She just tasted so good,

and she wasn't afraid now, she was into it, pressing closer, responding eagerly when he deepened the kiss. The bay, the shops across the street, the few people out and about, all of it faded and there was only Kayla, kissing him back.

Finally he lifted his head and studied her flushed face. "Was it as good as you remembered?"

One corner of her mouth turned up. "Better," she said. She looked a little dazed. "Wow, even better."

He looked around, felt Paddington tug at the leash, heard his deep bark as another walker with a dog came toward them. Reluctantly, he stepped away. "If we weren't out in public…"

She stepped back, adjusted her headband. "I'm scared to ask you to finish that sentence."

He wanted to ask her out in the worst way, wanted to ask her over. Wanted to spend time with her, private time.

Don't do it. Think.

Paddington saved him by lunging at the dog passing by, requiring all of Tony's focus to hold him back, and then the moment was over. But as they continued strolling along the bay, Tony was reeling.

What was he going to do about the feelings developing between them?

As SHE STROLLED beside Tony, their hands linked, Kayla tried to breathe deeply, to stay calm.

Being here with him felt so good. That kiss had felt so totally, amazingly good.

Would they kiss again?

The sun sparkled like glitter on the rippling bay, but the cold breeze made her snuggle closer to Tony. When he squeezed her hand, her heart soared as high as the swooping seabirds.

Was Tony the one? Could he be the answer to her dreams of love and a family?

He said he wasn't a good bet for anyone, but he was wrong. He was kind and funny and sexy. He was a great father figure to Jax. He'd even turned into a good preschool volunteer.

Paddington's ears perked up at the increasingly loud gulls, and he barked and tugged at the leash. "Whoa, boy," Tony said, easily restraining the big, rambunctious dog. Of course he did. With those muscles?

Kayla's face heated at her own thoughts.

A car slowed, then stopped beside them.

"Uncle Tony! Hey, Miss Kayla!" Jax called from the open back-seat window.

"Jax!" Tony let go of Kayla's hand and hurried over, and she followed, wondering if something was wrong.

"Is the party over already?" Tony asked Jax.

"It got all dark!" Jax said.

"The power went out at Goody's," the driver explained, and when Kayla looked closer, she realized it was Sarah, one of the preschool moms. "Oh, hey, Kayla. We were having a birthday party, but it came to a sudden end." She looked at Tony. "I've been trying to call you, but when I didn't get an answer, I figured I'd bring Jax home. I have an extra booster seat. But then he saw you and wanted to stop."

Tony clapped a hand on his pocket. "My phone's been turned down," he said, as guilt flashed across his face. "I'm sorry to put you to the trouble."

Kayla felt her own cheeks heat. Had the woman seen her and Tony walking, hand in hand? "Come on out, Jax," she said, opening the car door. She helped Jax climb out.

"Paddington!" Jax threw his arms around the big dog's neck, and Paddington gave him a sloppy kiss.

Tony apologized again, but Sarah waved it off and drove away.

Jax looked up at Tony. "You and Miss Kayla were holding hands," he observed.

Tony flushed. "You're right, we were." He opened his mouth as if to explain further but then closed it again. He didn't seem to know what else to say, but that was fine because Jax was already focusing on Paddington and the swooping gulls.

"Can I hold his leash?" he begged, his eyes widening into a puppylike pleading expression. "I can do it like you showed me. Please?"

Tony smiled, and that made Kayla smile, too. Jax was so cute, it was hard to deny him anything. And Tony clearly loved his nephew more and more all the time. It was great to see how their relationship was growing.

"Okay, buddy. Just while we're on the path. When we get to the streets, I'll need to take it back." He extended the leash to Jax and helped him loop the handle around his wrist and grasp the length of the leash. "It seems like he knows to be more gentle when Jax is holding him," he explained to Kayla.

Jax walked ahead with Paddington, and indeed, the dog was much calmer with Jax walking him.

Tony took Kayla's hand again.

His palm was calloused, harder than hers. He held her hand firmly, and the pressure was warm, the touch seeming to sizzle its way to her heart.

Unlike other girls, Kayla hadn't had a boyfriend growing up. She'd never gotten to hold hands, didn't have the awkward, sweaty experiences her friends used to talk about while she could only listen enviously.

No, her first hand-holding experience was with a real man, who knew just how to touch her. His thumb moved over her hand, stroking it gently, and Kayla's skin felt supersensitive. She could barely catch her breath.

Was this what love felt like?

"He's pulling me, look, he's pulling me!" Jax's voice was delighted. Paddington, indeed, was tugging the leash a little, making Jax screech and laugh.

"Whoa, Buddy, don't get too excited." Tony smiled and looked down at Kayla. "He's rowdier now than when I dropped him off at Goody's."

"Pretty sure he's on a sugar high." Kayla hoped her own voice didn't sound as breathless as she felt. "Maybe we should keep walking, wear them both out some more." It was fine with her to walk all day, as long as she could be with Tony and Jax.

"Good idea." Tony looked down at her and squeezed her hand, and she smiled up at him.

Paddington's loud bark broke through Kayla's focus on Tony. At the same time, Jax screeched, now sounding upset.

"I dropped it! I dropped the leash! Wait, Paddington!"

Sure enough, the Saint Bernard was galloping toward the bay, trailing his leash.

"Paddington! Stop!" Tony's command was loud and sharp.

But Paddington must have smelled a couple of gulls on the edge of pier that extended out into the bay, and he raced after them. There was a splash, and the big dog disappeared into the water.

"He couldn't see and he fell in!" Jax ran toward the end of the pier, Tony following at a run.

Kayla rushed after them, her heart pounding hard. There was another splash as Jax hit the water.

Oh, no, the water's way too cold. She ran faster.

Tony reached the end of the pier in seconds, far outpacing Kayla, and by the time she got there, he had a soaked, coughing Jax firmly in his arms. The bay wasn't deep here, and Tony could stand.

All that was visible of Paddington was his head as he paddled through the water. Since Tony had Jax and was wading toward the little beach, Kayla focused on Paddington. "Come on, Paddington, come here!" she called, kneeling on the pier.

Paddington's hearing was acute, and he paddled toward her, but a seagull cried out and Paddington turned toward the open water again.

"No, Paddington!"

Her scolding had no effect.

She couldn't let the big dog swim farther out into the bay. Who knew how long his stamina would last or how the currents would affect him?

From long-ago memory, she thought of a dog program that had said you shouldn't yell at a dog to make him come to you; rather, you should entice him with big, exaggerated gestures.

But how did you do that with a dog who was blind?

"This way! Come on, boy!" She clapped her hands and made her voice loud and happy. "Let's go! Let's get a treat! Come on, Paddington!"

It worked: the big dog turned and began swimming toward her. She backed down the pier toward land, calling and clapping and promising walks and treats and dinner, keeping her voice upbeat.

He paddled alongside the pier at her urging. As soon as

he gained his footing, Kayla eased herself into the freezing bay far enough to grab his leash. Her heart pounding with relief, she guided him out of the water. He shook himself, spraying her with more cold water.

"Oh, Paddington!" She laughed and then hurried toward Jax and Tony.

Jax was wrapped around his uncle monkey-style, the way he'd done continually when they'd first arrived in Pleasant Shores, and Kayla had the fleeting thought of how far he'd come.

"Is Jax okay?" Kayla slipped out of her jacket, keeping a tight hold on Paddington's leash. "Here, wrap this around him and we'll run to my car. I'm parked right over on Front Street."

Tony hesitated. He tried to take off his own coat, but the movement made Jax cling on tighter.

"Do it! I'm fine." She handed him her dry coat, and he quickly wrapped Jax in it. He held the boy close as they jogged toward her car.

"That was my fault." Tony sounded out of breath. "I should never have let him hold Paddington's leash."

Of course, he was blaming himself. "All's well that ends well," she said. "Jax is fine. Aren't you, buddy?" She reached over to pat the child's arm. Paddington tugged at the leash and looked back at her, his mouth open, panting. "And look at Paddington. He loved his swim! He wouldn't mind jumping right back in."

Jax's teeth chattered.

"I should have been more careful." Tony shook his head.

More beating himself up. "This kind of thing happens all the time," she reassured him. "Kids are kids. You didn't know Paddington would go off like that." She reached back and rubbed the big dog's head—he was trotting along with what seemed like a smile. "Look at you, boy, you're laughing at all of us!"

"Paddington's laughing?" Jax peeked out around Tony. "He *is* laughing! Look, Uncle Tony!"

Tony glanced over and nodded, but his lips were pressed close together.

"He'll be fine," she said, patting Tony's arm and pulling out her keys to unlock the car. "They'll both be fine. I'll put the heater on high and we'll be home in a flash."

He put a hand on her shoulder and squeezed, and she went still, turning back to look at him.

"Kayla. You're the best, really. Thank you for the reassurance, as well as the help." He leaned forward and kissed her, lightly.

She reached up and touched his face. "I care about you."

"And I care about you, a lot." His eyes held hers, and there was promise in them. "Now's not the time, but I want to spend some time talking to you. About…stuff."

"Stuff, huh?" She smiled, her heart singing.

"Yeah, stuff. But first, I need to get this kiddo dry and warm." Tony helped Jax into the car, then turned to her. "Do you have towels we could sit on? And one to rub Paddington dry?"

Good, he was getting back to normal, thinking about the little things. "One for you and Jax." She got it out of her trunk and tossed it to him. "And one for Paddington." She gave the dog a quick rubdown and urged him into the back seat, where Tony was buckling Jax in. Once in the car, she noticed the time. "Oh, man, I'm going to have to rush to get ready for the kids' event at the bookstore tonight."

Tony and Jax were both quiet on the way home, and even Paddington seemed a little subdued. But Tony kept a hand on her shoulder, and it felt wonderful.

They'd all had a scare. Kayla was so fond of all of them, and so happy to drive them home and help them.

"Thank you, Kayla," Tony said as they approached Victory Cottage. "You saved Paddington and we appreciate it."

"What's life without a little excitement?" She pulled into the driveway, and Tony opened the door and got his cold, wet child and dog out of the back seat.

"Later," he said, giving her a meaningful look that was over too soon.

"See you tonight at the store event," she said, and then drove the rest of the way home, humming.

She could hear it in her own tone: she sounded like a woman in love. She *was* a woman in love. And she really, really liked the feeling.

SYLVIE HADN'T KNOWN when she might have the chance to put her book-club plan into action. The very next day, though, Bobby came to see her.

He hadn't given her much warning; he said he'd had a spur of the moment desire to visit, and here he was. Surprisingly, he'd agreed to go out to take a walk after dinner, so they were strolling through the lit-up downtown area of Pleasant Shores.

Last-minute shoppers hurried through the cold air and snow flurries, some calling out greetings. It was surprising how many people Sylvie had gotten to know in just a few weeks here in town.

"Seems like you've made yourself at home here," Bobby commented.

"I like it." Maybe that was a way to initiate the breakup conversation: make it more about locales than people.

"Don't get too comfortable," he said. "I've missed you, and things have cooled off back in Filmore."

"Things have cooled off?" She frowned. "What does that mean? Since when were things hot there?"

"Since you happened to find Jax crying and took him to his uncle's place," he said. "That was real good of you, but it worried a few people. I know you didn't see the shooting, but not everyone believes that."

"Wait a minute. You had me come here for my own safety, too? I thought I was just watching out for Jax."

"Two birds with one stone." He put an arm around her, pulled her closer, and she didn't resist. Bobby was so many memories for her, so much what her past eight years had been about.

"I'd like to see the boy," he said now.

It took a minute for her to understand what he was talking about. "You mean Jax?"

He nodded. "I don't want to talk with him, I'd just like to see him."

It was a strange request. "I'm not sure how... Oh, wait." She looked back down the pedestrian mall. "I think he might be going to the kids' event at Lighthouse Lit. We could walk by there."

They turned around and sure enough, when they looked through the windows of Lighthouse Lit, a crowd of kids and parents were inside. She pointed. "There's Tony, so... let's see. Yes. Jax is the one in the red sweater. Did you ever meet him?"

He nodded. "He's a cute kid."

There was something odd in his voice. Wistful. She turned to study his face.

His brow was furrowed and he watched Jax with a strange intensity. His eyes were shiny, as if...

She looked at Jax just as the boy got up and chased

after another child, running close to the window where they stood.

Bobby stepped back quickly, like he didn't want to be seen. But he didn't take his eyes off the child.

Something about Bobby's behavior didn't match the story he'd told her. He'd made it sound like having her keep an eye on Jax and find out what he knew was just part of his usual effort to track everything going on in Filmore's criminal underworld. When she'd visited, she'd learned that he thought Little Bobby had been involved in Stella's shooting.

But he was looking at the child almost as if Jax were… She stared at Bobby. "He's not your son, is he?"

Bobby didn't answer. Instead, as Jax passed close to the window again, he took her arm and tugged her down the walkway. "I've seen enough. Let's go."

"He's your child." Sylvie heard her voice going shrill and didn't care. "That's why you wanted me to watch out for him. That's why you had an interest." Her heart pounded so hard she felt like her chest was going to explode. "You had me looking out for a kid you had with some other woman. For Stella's child." Her mind raced as she tried to count back. "When were you with her?"

It couldn't be true. He'd deny it.

But he didn't. He just limped along, faster than normal, looking at the ground, the storefronts, anywhere but at her.

She stopped, tugged his arm to make him stop, too, and stared at him. "That's why you wanted me to come here."

"That's part of the reason," he said, his voice soothing. "It was to protect him, and to protect you, too. Little Bobby is volatile. This is a safe place. He doesn't know where you are."

"Stop patronizing me!" Sylvie's own anger shocked her.

She'd mostly fallen out of love with Bobby, wanted to break up with him, but even so, the evidence of his betrayal made her hot with rage.

On some level, clearly, she did care about Bobby. He wasn't a good fit for her anymore, but this still felt like a huge blow.

They walked back through town in silence. Sylvie's mind raced. Why hadn't Bobby been willing to have a child with her, when he'd had one with Stella? How long had he been seeing Stella? Did Jax know Bobby? Did Bobby visit him, pay child support? Jax was so cute…how had she not seen that he had the same dark eyes as Bobby did?

And if Little Bobby had shot Jax's mother…if Jax was Little Bobby's half brother… Her head spun. "What did you see in her that you didn't see in me?" was the question that came out of her mouth.

He looked at her then, his expression startled. "What?"

"You had a kid with her when you'd never let me go off birth control."

Bobby shook his head, his palms lifting. "Getting her pregnant was an accident, a mistake," Bobby said. "Look, I was just seeing her for a couple of weeks, back when we had that rough stretch."

"A kid's never a mistake," she said automatically. "Does he know you?"

"Not as his father," Bobby said. "I've visited Stella a few times, seen the child, but not for months now."

"Because she died! Because your *other* son shot her down!"

He reached for her hand, but she jerked it away.

On the main street of town, a black SUV sped past, nearly hitting a couple who'd ventured into the crosswalk, swerving, then squealing off. Sylvie was surprised into forgetting her anger for a minute. She hadn't seen that kind of reckless driving in Pleasant Shores. It must be someone from out of town.

Big Bobby was staring after the SUV. His face had paled.

"What's wrong?" she asked.

"That car. That was Little Bobby's car."

Sylvie looked at him, then at the disappearing taillights. "How could that be? You said he didn't know where Jax and I were."

"He must have followed me here," Bobby said slowly. "Although why…" He turned to look at her, growing even paler.

"He's after Jax," Sylvie said. She broke into a run back toward the bookstore. "We have to warn them."

CHAPTER FIFTEEN

TONY FINALLY GOT Jax into his jacket and headed out of the bookstore. The Christmas event had been really fun, for kids and adults alike.

Kayla had been adorable, dressed in a Mrs. Claus outfit with steel-rimmed glasses on her nose. She'd read a story in varied, expressive voices and passed out packets of what she called reindeer food. The kids obviously loved her, Jax as much if not more than the others. She was so open and natural with children, it was no wonder.

She'd not paid special attention to Tony, giving him the same impersonal smile she gave the other parents, and then she'd turned and started gathering her things, along with the other storytellers. He knew he shouldn't wait for her. He should head home with Jax.

He should *especially* go home because of how much he wanted to stay. He couldn't get Kayla's kiss out of his mind. Couldn't forget what a help she'd been when Jax and Paddington had gone into the water. His feelings were heating up faster than he could control them.

Bottom line: he wanted to be with her.

But look at how he'd let Jax fall into the bay. Just like with Stella, Tony hadn't protected Jax.

He'd done so well at fulfilling his role in the military, but when it came to the interpersonal stuff, especially when it came to family, he was a failure. No way could he get involved in Kayla's life. The risk of letting her down was too great.

As they walked out, Evan Stone joined them. He was wearing his uniform. He'd read the kids a Christmas story with a police officer at its center. "I'm glad I saw you. Do you have a minute?"

"Sure," Tony said. He glanced down at Jax. "Run up as far as the snow pile where Davey's playing," he said, pointing.

Jax did, happily, and was soon tossing snow with Davey and a couple other kids while the parents watched, laughing and talking. For the hundredth time, Tony felt grateful for how far Jax had come.

"What's up?" he asked Evan.

"This probably isn't a big deal, but you might want to have Kayla take down that social media post with Jax in it," he said. "She posts pictures from the Coastal Kids school events sometimes, and even though the audience is limited, it's not real secure."

Tony frowned. "I tend to stay away from social media. I didn't realize she was posting pictures of the kids."

"I mean, he's just in a couple of the group shots, but if someone searched pages related to the town, they might be able to see him."

Tony took that in. "Thanks. I'll talk to her." In fact, that would give him an excuse to have a conversation with her. Maybe he'd run back to the shop and talk to her now.

He looked toward Jax and saw that some of the kids and parents were leaving. Only Paul remained, supervising Davey and Jax. So Tony's conversation with Kayla would have to wait.

A large black SUV pulled up beside where the kids were playing. The window opened. There was a familiar bark.

Then everything happened at once.

"Paddington!" Jax cried, and ran toward the vehicle.

"Jax! Stop!" Tony took off, his heart a pounding fireball in his chest.

A man dressed in dark clothes got out of the SUV and came around toward Jax.

"Hey!" Paul had been squatting, helping Davey with his shoe, but now he gave Davey an abrupt order and then ran toward Jax and the man.

As for Tony, he was running as fast as his legs would carry him, faster than he'd ever run in his life. "Jax! Get back here!"

Jax looked over his shoulder, eyes wide, and Tony realized he never yelled at Jax. But he was yelling now. "Come here! Right now!"

He could hear Evan Stone running behind him. How could this have happened so quickly? When had Kayla posted those pictures?

He was closer now, trying to take in what he was seeing. Why was Paddington in some stranger's passenger seat, paws out the window, big head lifted to sniff the air?

The dark-clad man, unlike Tony, was smiling as he beckoned to Jax, encouragement on his face. He said something and then picked Jax up, put him in the back seat, closed the door, and ran around to the driver's side.

Paul reached the vehicle and tried to open the rear passenger door. Tony was close enough to hear the locks click.

The car roared off.

Paul had his phone out, snapping pictures of the license plate. Tony could hear Evan shouting into his phone.

"Text those to the police," Tony barked at Paul.

"On it," Paul said. Davey ran to him, and he put an arm around the boy as he spoke into the phone.

Tony took off after the rapidly receding taillights, his pumping arms and legs fueled by utter panic.

Then there was a squeal of brakes. Less than a block away, the SUV swerved, apparently to avoid another vehicle, and then there was the sickening sound of metal hitting metal.

"Jax!" Tony ran faster as horrible images flashed through his head. *No, no, no, no.*

He reached the vehicle just as the man in black half climbed, half tumbled out, looking dazed.

He was holding a gun.

KAYLA WAS HALFWAY to her car, carrying her supplies, when she heard a commotion down the street. Screeching tires, a crash, shouts, and loud, deep barking.

She heard children's high, scared voices, dropped her things, and took off toward the chaos.

There were some shouts and a struggle on the ground—it looked like Tony was wrestling some guy—and then Paul came up from behind and stepped on the man's gun-holding hand, hard. The man groaned and let go, and Tony decked him into unconsciousness.

From the wrecked SUV, which had apparently hit a lamp post, she heard more barking. She rushed over, peered in a back window, and saw Paddington's big blocky head with two little arms around it. She tried to open the rear door—stuck—then hurried around to the driver's side. She climbed in and knelt between the two front seats, reaching back for Jax.

"Come on, buddy, let's get you out of here," she said, grasping him by the armpits and tugging.

"Paddington was helping me not be scared," he said,

clinging to the dog. "But he bumped against the door when we crashed."

"We'll get him out as soon as we get you out," she said. "I promise. Let go."

Reluctantly, Jax let go of the dog and Kayla eased him gently into the front seat and then out of the car just as Tony approached.

Jax saw him and burst into tears, and Tony took him from her and held him tight.

A police car pulled behind the SUV, sirens blaring for a moment then going quiet, lights flashing. From a block away she heard another siren, probably an ambulance. The noise made Paddington lift his head and howl.

Kayla found a way to unlock the SUV's rear doors, did so, and then turned off the vehicle. She hurried around to the outside and opened the door, holding Paddington firmly by his collar. She ran her hands over the dog and winced when one of them came away red.

There were people talking all around them now. Kayla saw that Tony had Jax, and Paul had Davey. So the kids were accounted for. Still holding Paddington's collar, she looked around, trying to figure out what was going on.

Sylvie was pushing herself to a sitting position. Sylvie? Why was she here?

An EMT was working on an enormous man who lay silent next to her.

Kayla pulled off her belt, hooked it through Paddington's collar, and walked the dog over. "Sylvie, what happened?"

The woman was breathing hard, her eyes flickering from Jax and Tony, to the black-clad man now being read his Miranda rights, to the unconscious man beside her. "Long story. Complicated."

It definitely seemed that way. Kayla asked the first question that occurred to her. "Why is Paddington here?"

"Bait for Jax, I think." Sylvie blew out a breath, her eyes big and scared.

Kayla sat down on the cold sidewalk beside the woman. "Are you okay? Can I do something for you?" She could see that Sylvie's arm was scraped.

"I'm fine." Sylvie waved away her concern, opened her mouth, closed it, and then started talking. "You know Jax witnessed his mother being killed?"

Kayla nodded, her heart lurching.

"Well, the killer realized that Jax could identify him, so he came looking for him. At least, that's what I've been able to piece together." She turned toward the EMT who was working on the big man still unconscious on the ground. "Is he going to be all right?"

"We'll get him to the hospital as soon as he's stabilized. Looks like he took a pretty solid hit from that SUV. He's lucky it didn't run over him."

"He basically dove in front of it," Sylvie said. Her chin quivered.

One of the police officers then came over and knelt beside Sylvie. "I need to ask you a few questions," he said.

Kayla backed off, head swirling with the confusing events, and led Paddington over to Tony and Jax.

"Paddington!" Jax said, and rushed to hug the dog, who licked his face.

Kayla handed the makeshift leash to Tony. "I think he'll need a vet visit," she said. "He's bleeding from the shoulder."

"Thanks." Tony took the leash, looked away from her, and then looked back. "Why did you post that social media picture of Jax?"

Of all the things he could have said, that wasn't what she'd expected. "What?"

"Evan told me to tell you to take down the pictures, since Jax could be identified. But it's too late. He already was."

Kayla clapped a hand to her mouth. "That's how this guy found him?"

"Looks that way." His face was closed, his voice grim.

"I'm so sorry, Tony," she said, her stomach churning. "But...you signed the release form, right? Surely you wouldn't have done that if there was a chance—"

"I didn't," he said flatly.

"I'm pretty sure you did. It was in the paperwork you did early on."

He threw up his hands. "You may be right, but I was scrambling at that point. You should have known better than to give me that form then. You should never have posted the pictures."

He turned away and picked up Jax.

"I'm so sorry!" Her whole chest hurt at the thought that she could have been the cause of this nightmare.

He waved a hand, not looking at her. "Look, I'm sure this was more my fault than yours. It was me who didn't stick close enough to him tonight. But just... I need a break. It's not going to work out between us."

"You...what?" With police barking orders and spectators talking and lights flashing around them, he was dumping her?

She opened her mouth to say...what? What could she say when she felt so numb?

He turned away, Jax in his arms, urging Paddington to walk beside them.

Even if he wasn't blaming her entirely for what had happened, the message was clear: he didn't want to be with her.

MUCH LATER THAT NIGHT, Tony finally got back to Victory Cottage. He helped Paddington out of the car and tried to guide him inside, but the big dog whined and strained toward the car's back door.

Loyal creature. He didn't want to leave Jax.

The emergency vet had examined Paddington, tended to his wound, and assured Tony that he would heal up just fine. On the way home, once Jax had fallen asleep, Tony had called the therapist's emergency number and told her what had happened. She'd listened, asked Tony to describe Jax's behavior after the incident, and said that he'd be fine, no need for an extra appointment. She'd talk to them after Christmas.

He hadn't had the heart to tell her that they wouldn't be here.

The thought arose that Dr. Liz was much better than the therapist they'd had back in Filmore. Jax had really connected with her and her dog. Was Tony doing the wrong thing, taking Jax away from the counselor who'd helped him?

Probably. He was screwing up so much that his head spun with it.

He had no idea what was right, but he had to get out of here. Too many bad things were happening. Too much danger, too much confusion. So he'd stick to his decision and leave.

Once he'd put Jax to bed, with Paddington sleeping heavily on a blanket beside the boy's bed, and taped up cardboard where the intruder had broken a window to abduct the dog, Tony started packing.

He was still shaking from the risk to Jax. Still berating himself for not protecting his nephew better, and then for his genius move of blaming everything on Kayla.

A phone call from Evan Stone had let him know that the incident tonight had probably stemmed from a complicated series of links to Stella's death. Nothing to do with anything Kayla had posted on some social media site.

Tony had screwed up, big time. The only thing he'd done right was to blurt out something to end things with Kayla, for her sake.

His father's dying words echoed around and around his head. *You're in charge of the family now. They're your responsibility.*

And he'd promised he'd take care of them.

He'd failed miserably with Stella, of course. He was almost used to the guilt and shame of that. He'd had a scare of a similar, but much milder sort when Jax and Paddington had gone into the bay.

Tonight, he'd almost lost Jax.

What if Jax had been taken, had been killed? The images evoked by his thoughts squeezed a vise around his chest and sent horror jolting through his body. He half ran into Jax's room, sat down on the edge of his bed, and brushed a hand over his solid, safe limbs.

He made himself take deep breaths. Jax was okay, physically, at least. Who knew what psychological ramifications would emerge from what he'd been through?

At least Tony had pulled away from Kayla. He'd hurt her, he knew, but it was nothing compared to the disaster that would strike if they got involved.

A car pulled up outside and Tony tensed, hurried downstairs. He didn't own a weapon—didn't think it wise with Jax in the house—but he armed himself with a baseball bat and went to the door.

Evan Stone. He put the bat down and opened the door.

"Just wanted to let you know everything's under control," he said. "The man who tried to abduct Jax is in the hospital, but we have a twenty-four-hour guard on him. We spoke with Sylvie and the other man on the scene, and we'll interview them again tomorrow. They're tied in with this somehow." He frowned at the cardboard-covered window, then looked at the open boxes in the room. "You're leaving?"

"Yeah." Tony didn't have it in him to do a long explanation. Didn't even know what he'd say. "I'll leave a forwarding address."

"What's Kayla think of your moving out?"

Tony shrugged.

Evan tilted his head to one side, his forehead wrinkling. "You're letting that go?"

For her, Tony thought. He'd screwed up too badly. She deserved better. He shrugged again. "Complications," he said. "Look, I gotta get going."

Evan studied him for a long moment. "Stay in touch," he said.

Tony nodded and watched as Evan went to his car and drove away. He wouldn't stay in touch. He needed to make a clean break.

He'd go back to Filmore where he belonged, resume his life there, take up the VA job. Jax was better now and could be settled in a day care. They'd be near Tony's brother and sister.

It would be okay. Safer. Less confusing.

He finished packing, carried loads out to the car, and finally picked up Jax and led Paddington to the car. He really should leave the dog here, find another home for him, but he couldn't do that to Jax. Couldn't do it to Paddington, not after he'd been a better protector of Jax than Tony was.

He eased Jax into his booster seat, helped the injured dog climb in beside the boy, and started driving.

SYLVIE WAS STRESSED and angry, even devastated...but she still didn't want to disappoint the children just three days before Christmas. She'd agreed to help at the party to distribute the gifts they'd wrapped, and she was going to show up and do her best. Especially since Kayla had backed out. Primrose was helping, and the elderly twins, but they needed someone agile enough to get up and down, over and over again, distributing the presents to the individual kids.

She tried to stay focused on the positive project as she walked to the restaurant where the party was to take place. But the events of last night kept coming back to her.

She'd never forget the terror of seeing Jax—and Big Bobby—at such terrible risk. Big Bobby, who was Jax's father.

She couldn't believe that Bobby's request for her to watch over Jax had been based on a lie. Not just a lie, but a long-lasting deceit. He'd concealed the fact that he'd fathered a child with another woman, and no doubt many times when he hadn't come home to Sylvie, he'd been visiting Jax. And Stella, too. Sylvie didn't want to think ill of the dead, but she had to figure that Stella had allowed Bobby to remain involved, both romantically and financially, in her life and Jax's.

Bobby had never wanted to have a child with Sylvie, and so she'd given up her chance of that. It turned out he hadn't stuck to the same rules with the other woman in his life. She felt like a fool.

And yet, maddeningly, she was also worried about him. He'd been taken to the local hospital last night as a precaution, after diving in front of his son's car and sustaining a hard blow to the head that had knocked him out for a time. Due to his size, there was concern about his health and his heart. She'd called the hospital to check on his status but hadn't visited. She didn't know whether he'd been released or not, and she wasn't going to call him. She was still too angry.

The web of lies he'd woven, and involved her in, could have led to a child's abduction and worse.

She pushed open the door to the back room at DiGiorno's, and the sound of excited kids' voices and Christmas music swept away some of her dark thoughts. It looked like about fifteen kids, ranging in age from two to ten, clustered around the tall Christmas tree or ran wildly around the room. Parents chatted and scolded and sampled cookies and punch from a table along the side of the room.

Primrose drove toward her on her scooter. "Thank you for coming, dear. I wasn't sure you would after what happened last night. Are you all right?"

"Mostly." She could tell the woman wanted to know more. "Jax is fine, and the man who tried to abduct him is in police custody. So we can hope that all's well that ends well."

Primrose put a hand on Sylvie's arm. "How are *you*, dear? I can tell you're upset."

Sylvie forced a smile. "Thank you for caring. I'll be fine, eventually."

A loud "ho ho ho" came from the back of the room, and there was Santa, with a bag of gifts—the gifts they'd wrapped. And Santa was... Yes. It was the pastor, padded and fake-bearded, enthusiastically opening his bag to spill out enough brightly wrapped gifts for all the kids.

Sylvie went to help distribute the gifts, and the pastor winked at her. His simple, open smile touched her heart.

After years of being involved with a complex, difficult man, she appreciated Steve's goodness and simplicity.

The party went on, and it was a balm to Sylvie's wounded soul. No matter her personal problems, children would always love gifts and Santa. Moreover, seeing these kids interacting happily with their parents reminded her that not everyone had the same sort of miserable issues she'd had with her own mother. These parents were comfortable receiving help, and the committee who'd wrapped the gifts were happy to give it. No judgment involved.

Her phone buzzed, but she ignored it. She couldn't think of anyone who had her number that she'd want to be in touch with. She helped some of the little ones to open boxes and figure out how to operate their toys, then walked around picking up napkins and cups and half-eaten platefuls of cake.

"Sylvie." The deep voice, as familiar as her own, made her heart skip a beat. She turned, and sure enough, there was Bobby at the door of the room. Wearing the same clothes as yesterday and with a full day's growth of beard, a bandage on his head, he definitely looked the worse for wear.

What was he doing here?

He beckoned to her and she hurried to him, not wanting him to come in and disturb the party's mood.

"How did you find me?" she demanded.

"There's an app on your phone," he said.

Sylvie's jaw almost dropped. "There *is*? Who put it there?"

He didn't answer, probably because the answer was obvious. "Sylvie, we need to talk."

She shook her head. "I'm busy doing something I agreed to do. I don't want to talk to you. You lied to me and betrayed me."

"Little Bobby's in custody," he said, "here in town, for abducting Jax. We need to get him out and then go to Filmore. I think Jax's uncle took him back there."

That statement was wrong on so many levels. "Little Bobby needs to be in custody. That's what happens to criminals. And Jax needs to be with his uncle."

Bobby shook his head. "Bobby's my son."

"So is Jax!" Sylvie lifted her hands, palms up. "That doesn't give Little Bobby immunity. And besides, he abducted a child who turns out to be his brother, or half brother at least. What do you think he was going to do with Jax, buy him a Christmas present?"

"He wouldn't have hurt the boy."

Sylvie wasn't so sure. "Well, if he thought Jax had witnessed him shooting Stella—"

"Don't." Bobby closed his eyes like he couldn't stand the picture she'd painted. "And don't be mad. We have to work this out."

She opened her mouth to protest.

"For Jax's sake," he said.

He was going for her soft spot, but Sylvie shook her head. "Jax is yours. Not that I think you should raise him, but he's definitely not my responsibility." Even as she said it, she felt awful. She didn't want to care about Jax, but she did. He was an innocent victim.

"I should have done things differently," Bobby said. "Taken charge of the boy, rather than leaving him to Stella and her family."

"No. Leave him alone." Sylvie crossed her arms. "You haven't been involved or helped so far. Just leave him to his uncle and these good people. If you don't, I'll...well, I'll do something." If she tried, she could pull together enough evidence to convince the authorities that Big Bobby wasn't a suitable guardian for a child, even if he was the biological father. She'd do it, too.

Big Bobby must have seen that resolve in her eyes, and he waved a hand. "You're right, it's not as if I'm going to sue for custody. I just, well, I want to see him sometimes, make sure he's safe." He reached out, took her hand. "And I want you back home."

He looked shaky, pale. Sweat beaded on his forehead.

She took his hand, pulled him to a bench in the hall lobby, and sat down. There was no easy way to say it other than to just blurt it out. "Bobby, it's over. I'll send someone to get my things, or you let me know when I can come pack up."

He stared at her as if he couldn't believe what he was hearing. "Because of something that happened five years ago? A two week affair?"

"Because you made a dupe of me, lied to me, and...well, because I want something different. I don't like all the secrecy and crime in Filmore."

He looked away, his breathing hard and audible.

She forced herself to say the rest of it. "I'm moving on. It's time for me to move on."

He turned back toward her. "I took you off the streets."

She softened. "You did." She squeezed his huge, weathered hand. "I'll always be grateful that you did. But... I feel like I've paid that debt." As she said it, she knew it was true. She'd kept house for him and given him the physical affection he needed, listened to his complaints, rubbed his aching back. And it had been willingly done, but now... now, things were different. *She* was different. She wanted to start new. "I'm sorry, Bobby, but it's time. I want a new life, and I'm starting one here." She felt something roll down her cheek and realized she was crying.

Bobby looked at her, really looked at her, as if he was trying to read her. Then he shook his head and sighed. After a moment of silence, he spoke again. "I always knew this day would come."

He *had*? Sylvie had always assumed she'd stay forever with Bobby.

He stared at the floor for a long moment, then spoke. "You're too good for me, Sylvie, but I thank you for all you've given me, and I'm sorry for the wrong I did." He kissed her forehead and pushed himself to his feet.

There was so much to say, and yet there was nothing to say. She looked at his weathered face, his huge burly body, the dark eyes she'd fallen in love with. She bit her lip. Should she change her mind?

But what she'd said was true: it was time for her to move on, out of her past and into a new future.

He nodded once, turned, and limped out, his big body lurching, his shoulders square.

She watched him until he was out of sight, headed into the dark and cold. Wondered how long he could make it in the world he lived in, which wasn't kind to age and weakness. But what she felt for him now was what someone would feel for a wayward father, and it wouldn't be right to share his home and his bed.

She sat for a long time, as the noises of the happy Christmas party blared around behind her. She was too spent to think.

A while later, someone came and sat beside her. The pastor, still in his Santa outfit, handed her a bunch of napkins to dry her tears. "You okay?"

She wiped her eyes and blew her nose and smiled at him, a watery smile. "I will be," she said.

The noise of the party was fading now. People were starting to leave.

He gestured in the direction Bobby had gone. "Friend of yours?"

She let her eyes close for a minute as images of all the years she'd spent with Bobby flashed across her mind like a movie. "He has been, yes." She opened her eyes and looked at Steve. "Not anymore." Saying that brought on more tears.

He nodded and just sat beside her while she pulled herself together. She supposed he was used to being around emotional, upset people.

"Thank you," she choked out. "I'll be fine."

"Did you get a chance to read the book I gave you at all?"

She tried to smile. "I have. It's helped."

"And will we see you at church Christmas Eve?" He gave a self-conscious laugh. "It's a beautiful service. Not too much preaching, lots of singing."

With an effort, Sylvie pulled her thoughts out of the past. She didn't know what the future would hold, but she could think as far ahead as Christmas Eve, at least. "I'll be there," she said.

KAYLA PRACTICALLY slunk into the Gusty Gull on Saturday night. She hadn't wanted to come, not at all. But Amber had texted her and Erica had called, and short of turning off her phone, she realized she wouldn't be able to get them off her back.

Plus she didn't especially want to stay at home hating herself.

As soon as she was fully inside, she deeply regretted coming. The Gull was in the middle of its annual Christmas party, and things were getting *very* festive. She waved to a couple of people she knew and ducked to avoid being spotted by Norleen, who was sitting at a table with her middle-school posse, drinking and laughing.

"Over here!" Erica yelled, and Amber waved her arms wildly.

Kayla dodged a line of aging dancers and made her way to their tiny table, squeezed in tight with many others.

"Tell us everything," Amber demanded. "No, wait, get a drink first." She flagged down a waiter and ordered three big fruity drinks.

Erica leaned close and put a hand on Kayla's arm. "I hear Tony left the Victory Cottage program and went back to his hometown."

Kayla swallowed hard and nodded. She couldn't speak. He'd texted her to say they were leaving to spend Christmas back in their hometown, that the incident probably wasn't her fault, and that she shouldn't try to get in touch.

"Was that something you knew about? Did you expect it?" Erica practically had to shout over the noisy crowd.

Her throat too tight to answer, Kayla shook her head.

Erica studied her for a minute, then grabbed Amber's arm. "We can't talk here. You and Kayla stay and get the drinks. I'll get someone in the back room to trade places with us."

Amber nodded, then turned and laughingly fended off Henry Higbottom, who wanted her to dance with him. Normally, Kayla would have loved this event, the casual informality of it, the way almost everyone in town was here.

Now, she felt vulnerable and exposed.

Amber looked at her, still laughing, and tilted her head to one side. Then, her expression darkening, she scooted over and put an arm around Kayla. "That scum," she said. "You're going to tell us about it, and we're going to get back at him."

Kayla shook her head, half smiling at Amber's vehe-
mence, but afraid if she let even a few of her feelings out,
she'd cry.

Finally, drinks in hand, they made their way to the small,
somewhat quieter back room where just eight tables held
people mostly eating meals. Erica waved them to a corner
table. "Come on, this is as quiet as it gets."

Amber urged Kayla into a seat against the wall and sat
down beside her. With Erica across the table, Kayla was effectively trapped. "Look, guys, I can't stay long," she said.
"I appreciate your trying to cheer me up, but it's fine. I just
need to kinda…lick my wounds."

Only saying that made her think of Paddington, licking
Jax's face. She'd never see either of them again. Her eyes
filled with tears and she grabbed napkins from the dis-
penser and wiped them, angry with herself. She shouldn't
have gotten her hopes up. Shouldn't have let herself come
to care so much.

"Oh, honey." Amber put an arm around her again. "I'm
so sorry. I know how it can hurt."

"I just don't understand why he left so suddenly," Erica
said. "Do you?"

Kayla nodded and blew her nose. "He got mad at me,"
she explained, "because I posted a picture of Jax on social
media. He thought that was how that awful man found
him."

Erica frowned. "Is he right?"

"I don't think so. He texted to say he was wrong and…"
She sucked in a deep breath. "Anyway, Sylvie was trying
to explain to me how she and the really big guy already
knew Jax, from before. That had something to do with the
guy who tried to kidnap him. It doesn't make a whole lot
of sense."

"Didn't Tony sign a waiver about pictures?" Amber asked. Having a son in school, she was familiar with the yearly paperwork.

"He did," she said. "I brought that up, but he said he was signing everything in a hurry, and didn't realize what it meant, and I should have known. Or checked."

Amber blew out a snort. "That's ridiculous. Sounds like he was looking for someone other than himself to blame."

Kayla thought of the misery on Tony's face. "He was blaming himself plenty, too," she said. "It's just that…well, I guess I was a contributing factor. I thought…" Her throat tightened again, and she shook her head. "Never mind."

"You thought he cared for you, right?" Amber sucked down some of her drink. "So did everyone else in town. It was pretty obvious."

"It never was obvious to me," Kayla said. "He never made any promises." Unless you considered a few amazing kisses a promise. Which he obviously didn't. "Anyway—" she choked out the worst of it "—he said he needed a break, that it wasn't going to work out between us. When he texted, he said not to get in touch."

"Out of nowhere?" Erica shook her head. "Man, I thought he was a nice guy."

Amber narrowed her eyes. "Did you and Tony ever… you know, get romantic?"

Kayla stared at the table, ran a finger around a liquid condensation ring, and nodded.

"You had your first kiss!" Amber practically yelled.

Erica smacked her sister's arm. "Would you stop broadcasting things to the world?" She turned to Kayla. "And… wow, really? It finally happened?"

Kayla nodded miserably. "And then he dumped me. Just my luck."

Erica pressed her lips together. "No, it's not just your luck. It's not something you deserve, either. I can't believe Tony treated you that way."

"He shouldn't get away with it," Amber said. "Someone should give him a good talking-to."

"But don't you see?" Kayla looked from one sister to the other. "Even if he feels bad about being mean, he didn't care enough to give me a second chance. As soon as something happened, his reaction wasn't to try to work it out. His reaction was to leave." She gulped and forced it out: "To cut me off entirely."

"Which was completely wrong," Erica said. "And what it tells you is, he's not right for you. But you *can* find a good guy."

Kayla grabbed another napkin and blew her nose. She didn't want another guy, she wanted Tony.

"And you *deserve* a good guy," Amber said. "Now that you've kind of practiced with Tony, you're ready to find the right person. The big leagues!" She made a dramatic gesture with her drink, sloshing some of it over the side.

"Cheers to that!" Erica, normally quieter, raised her voice along with her glass.

Kayla had to laugh a little, even though her heart hurt. "You guys are the best," she said. "Thanks for dragging me out and cheering me up."

"Here's to real love in the new year," Amber said. "A new resolution, to find a love that lasts."

"Second the motion," Erica said, giggling. "Or the resolution, or whatever."

"Raise your right hand," Amber joked, grabbing Kayla's hand. "I, Kayla Harris, do solemnly swear to find true love—"

Kayla tugged back her hand, laughing. "Stop. Love isn't like that. You can't just resolve and then find it."

"Worked for kissing," Amber argued.

"Sort of. But I want it to happen naturally. And—" She held up a hand to halt Amber's protest, sitting up straighter. "And I know I did nothing wrong with Tony."

"That's right," Amber said. "And you're a beautiful, kind woman."

"You had scoliosis, but we all have physical problems," Erica said, one hand going to her abdomen.

Amber reached out and squeezed Erica's other hand. "That's right. We both have our scars and our issues, and we found love. And you can, too."

Kayla blew out a sigh. "I hope so. I really hope so." Through her tears, she saw the Christmas lights and her friends' blurry faces.

Love was a splendid thing. And now she could admit it: she'd fallen in love with Tony and his sweet nephew. She'd started to hope she could form a family with them. The hurt she felt, finding out that wasn't going to happen, wouldn't go away anytime soon.

But she'd survive it, because she was strong, and because she had friends like Erica and Amber, and a community full of people who helped each other find a second chance.

So she lifted her glass and tried to laugh with her friends, but her heart told a different story.

Oh, Tony, we could have been good together. Really, really good.

CHAPTER SIXTEEN

THE MORNING OF December 24, Kayla slept in and woke up feeling marginally better than she had since Tony had left.

She'd spent a day wallowing in misery. Almost two days, really, but then she'd been dragged to the Gusty Gull last night and she'd figured some things out.

It was true that she was a decent person who deserved love. That her scoliosis didn't define her, and neither did her lack of experience with men. She might have made a mistake posting pictures of the kids, and she'd taken them down, but Mom had checked and Tony had definitely signed the release form.

All the logic in the world didn't erase her sadness, though.

She'd thought she and Tony had something. She'd put herself out there with him and he'd totally bailed.

Which meant, as Amber and Erica had said last night, that he wasn't worth it. It might even be the case that she'd find someone better, someday.

For now, she had to acknowledge that she was in for a rough holiday. She didn't get over things quickly; they didn't roll off her back. She was sensitive.

She also knew that she had to get her mind off Tony. She'd already checked her email, but there was nothing except last minute sale information; everyone was busy with their own holiday preparations. That was clear from all the mock-irritated social media posts: so much food to cook! So many relatives to host! So many gifts to wrap for the kids!

Kayla had already wrapped all her Christmas gifts. They sat in a cheery stack beside her little tabletop tree.

Including...

She picked up the big plastic dump truck she'd gotten for Jax, lovingly wrapped in truck paper. It was from a recent kids' movie featuring trucks that talked and had feelings, and all the kids were obsessed with it.

He would have really, really liked that gift. But because she and his uncle hadn't been able to make things work between them, Jax wouldn't get it.

Oh, he'd be fine. Plenty of people would love him, buy him gifts.

Plenty of women, she thought, and then shook her head. Not her business, not her problem.

She'd return the gift to the store where she'd bought it. It wasn't like a preschool teacher had vast amounts of extra money. Buying it had been a stretch for her. Plus she'd heard that the gift was scarce now, hard to find. Let it make some other kid happy.

She ripped the pretty paper off, crumpled it into a ball, and stuffed it in the trash. Wiped her eyes and blew her nose, put the truck in a shopping bag, and walked toward downtown and the little toy store.

It was chilly and brisk, but people were out. Christmas Eve day was big for shopping, even when it fell on a Sunday. Some shoppers looked cheery, stuffing bills into the Salvation Army kettle on their way into the hardware store. Others, bundled against the wind, looked tired and frazzled, especially the parents tugging little kids by the hand.

Kayla stuck a bill in the kettle herself—after all, she was about to get a nice refund—and then marched into the toy store. She made her way through the crowd of frenzied shoppers, unzipping her coat as she started to sweat. The store seemed too small and too warm.

Maybe coming here today hadn't been her brightest idea.

Kids begged and whined and shouted, and Kayla could see in their parents' eyes that they were having similar thoughts: coming to the toy store with kids in tow, at this time of year, was a bad idea.

One of the whining voices rose over the others. Rhianna.

And that meant Norleen was here. Even more, coming to the store seemed like a bad idea. She did *not* want to see Norleen today.

She heard Rhianna again, closer this time.

"I told you, if you fuss we have to leave," Norleen said. From the sound of it, she was just on the other side of a shelf from Kayla.

"But I want a Daniel Dump Truck!"

"They're all out of those. C'mon, let's look at the dolls."

"Can we get one?" Rhianna's voice was hopeful.

"No, I told you, your father didn't send money like he was supposed to. You'll get a couple of things, but not the big stuff like they have in here. We're just looking, remember?"

"I want more toys!" Rhianna's voice rose in a wail. "Other kids have more toys!"

A surprise wave of sympathy washed over Kayla. People were looking at each other and then in the direction of Norleen and Rhianna, who had a really loud voice. It was hard when your kid melted down in front of others, no question. Even for Norleen.

"Come on. We're leaving." Norleen's voice sounded strained.

Kayla stepped to the end of the aisle in time to see Norleen and Rhianna head for the door. Norleen took a swipe at her own eyes with a tissue before reaching down to hug Rhianna and wipe her face.

That was surprising to Kayla, but it shouldn't be. Of course Norleen loved her daughter, and it would be hard not to have enough money to treat your child at Christmas. Norleen hadn't been in town long enough to connect with the organizations that bought toys for disadvantaged kids, apparently. Not that Norleen had ever seemed disadvantaged; she and Rhianna both had pretty, new-looking clothes.

But Kayla knew that appearances weren't everything. If there was a deadbeat dad in question, Norleen and her daughter could be wearing clothes they'd bought when she and her husband were still together. A lot of times, families plunged into poverty after a divorce.

She thought about what Mom had told her. How she and Norleen had been friends and played together when they were small, but had been put in different classes. How Norleen had struggled with school, had fallen behind.

When she'd become such a beauty in middle school, it had been a way for her to get the attention and positive strokes she'd lacked before, and she'd ridden that wave all the way to an early pregnancy and marriage, one that hadn't worked out.

Like any mother, she loved her daughter and wanted the best for her. How hard it would be to walk through a toy store with your child and not be able to buy them what they wanted.

Norleen had been cruel to Kayla years ago, but she'd had her reasons. Now, Kayla had a good life, a job she loved, great friends. She was attractive enough, and was healed from her scoliosis.

Norleen's healing might well take longer, coming from a deeper ill.

Kayla's heart went out to the other woman and she almost called out a greeting, but she wasn't sure she was up to an interaction with Norleen. And then she lost the choice, because Rhianna spotted her and tugged her mother's arm. "Miss Kayla is here!"

Norleen turned back, blinking rapidly. "Hi, Kayla," she called, obviously trying to conceal her teary feelings. "Good heavens, what are you wearing?"

Kayla glanced down at her old sweater and jeans. "Um... clothes? I didn't actually give my outfit a thought when I came out today."

"I can tell, girlfriend." Norleen's voice sounded a little croaky, but she cleared her throat and lifted her chin. "How are you gonna find yourself a man?"

Kayla studied the woman. It was like she was speaking Klingon. "Why would I look for a man in a toy store?" *And why would you talk that way in front of your impressionable daughter?*

Norleen smiled. "Single dads, you know?" She flashed a smile and stuck out her chest as a man walked by. He smiled back, and the woman with him gave him and Norleen a dirty look.

"Mommy, I want my truck!"

"We don't have the money for it!" Norleen snapped.

Kayla wavered. Should she hand the truck she was returning to Rhianna? Wouldn't that undermine Norleen as a mother?

Norleen winked at another man passing by, and he raised an eyebrow and looked her up and down. "See?" Norleen said to Kayla as the man continued on, looking back over his shoulder a couple of times. "That's how it's done. You should try harder next time."

Kayla sighed. Norleen was Norleen. She knelt to hug Rhianna. "Merry Christmas, honey," she said. "Be nice to your mom," she added in a whisper.

She turned back into the store and made her way to the counter. She put the item down. "Return?" the tired-sounding clerk asked.

Kayla nodded, then shook her head. "Actually," she said, "I changed my mind."

It took less than an hour to go home, rewrap the gift, and find Norleen's address. She put a "from Santa" label on it and dropped it off secretly in the woman's front door.

She still felt miserable about all that had happened. But picturing Rhianna's happiness made her feel a little better, boosted her faith in herself and her ability to heal. She'd get there. She'd be okay.

IT WAS CHRISTMAS EVE. Tony was back in Filmore. And it wasn't awful.

His brother and sister were surprised but glad to see him and Jax. They'd discerned that something was wrong and had rallied to make Christmas good for all of them. His sister had brought over a decorated Christmas tree and a pile of the gifts she'd planned to give Jax when she came to Pleasant Shores after Christmas. His brother had ordered a takeout feast from a local restaurant, and they'd gone to early Mass. His siblings had raved over Paddington, and they'd found a big red bow to tie around his neck and walked him around the old neighborhood, earning smiles everywhere.

Tony had kept a close eye on Jax, worried about the effect the brief abduction had had on him. But the boy was more obsessed with the fact that Paddington had helped him when he was scared. He wouldn't leave the dog's side, and for now, that was okay. Tony could afford to take a little more time before returning to work, stay home with Jax and help him readjust to his hometown.

He would contact Mary about the fact that he wouldn't be returning to Pleasant Shores to live in Victory Cottage or work at the preschool. Not now, no need to disturb her holiday, but he'd express all his gratitude for what the program had done for him and try to make amends for his own shortcomings.

The Victory Cottage program, the counseling and the refuge and the preschool, all of it had helped. He was a better man than when he'd started out there, and Jax was definitely healing.

"Jax seems like he's doing great," Vince said now, echoing his own thoughts. They were sitting in the old front room, a football game on the TV, while Jax played with the new handheld video game he'd been allowed to open early. He lay on his back, his head on Paddington's midsection, while the big dog lay on his side.

"He is," Tony agreed. "Even with what happened right before we left Pleasant Shores, he didn't backslide. He's stronger."

"That man shot Mommy," Jax said conversationally as he played.

Both Tony and his brother snapped to attention, looked at each other, and then focused on Jax. "What man, buddy?" Tony asked.

"The man in the car," he said. "That's why I was scared, but Paddington helped me be brave."

"Could you tell the policemen about that sometime soon?" Tony asked. He didn't know how much credence would be placed in a four-year-old's returning memory, but it might be a brick in the wall.

Jax nodded. "If Paddington's there," he said.

"I'm sure that would be fine." Tony quickly texted Evan Stone about Jax's comment.

There was a return text almost immediately. The man in question was still being held in custody. Evan would report Jax's words and they'd go from there, after the holiday.

He showed Vince the texts, not wanting to upset Jax. But everything was becoming clear. The reason the man had tried to kidnap Jax was that he suspected Jax would remember and was worried about the boy identifying him.

"So you don't think you'll go back?" his brother asked.

"Nah." Tony tried to sound blasé. "It's done us some good, but it's time to get started with real life." He looked around the room where he'd spent most of his childhood, watching TV with his brother and playing board games with his parents and siblings.

"You running from something?" Vince threw over his shoulder as he walked into the kitchen.

Tony didn't answer, but he thought about it. *Was* he running? He'd thought he was running away from Filmore to the idyllic town of Pleasant Shores, but maybe he'd gotten it backward.

"Well, are you?" His brother returned with two beers, handed Tony one, and popped the tab on the other.

"I… Look. There was a woman, but I screwed up."

"Why am I not surprised?" Vince grinned.

Tony glared at him. "Thanks a lot."

"We all screw up with women. It's in the male DNA."

Well, that was probably true. It was just that Tony had never cared about a woman as much as he cared about Kayla. "Basically," he said, "I blamed her for what happened to Jax, even though it wasn't her fault. And then I dumped her."

"Yeah, that just might make her mad. Can you talk to her? Because I haven't seen you be this way about a woman for a long time. Maybe ever."

"I could talk to her, but…why open that door? I don't want to get involved. I told her that."

"Because of Stella." It wasn't a question.

"Yeah."

"Because you're to blame for what happened to her."

The stark words surprised Tony. "Yeah." But even as he said it, he thought about what Kayla and Evan Stone and the others had said. He still blamed himself, but maybe not 100 percent.

His brother ran a hand through his hair. "Did you know Stella came to my place after she left yours?"

"What?"

Vince nodded. "She wanted to know if she could stay there. I told her, sure, but she couldn't use drugs or go out. She got mad and left."

"Wow." He hadn't known that.

"And then," his brother said, "she went to Pam's place. Tried to drop Jax off, and Pam said fine, but she had to stay and take care of him. Stella didn't want to do that, so she left and went downtown. You know the rest of the story."

Tony was blown away by the fact that his siblings had done basically the same thing he had: criticized Stella and set boundaries for her. Probably not as harshly as Tony had, but in any case, it hadn't worked. "Why didn't you tell me before?"

"We all kept it to ourselves. I felt like a jerk about it. But a week or so ago, Pam and I were talking, and it came out she'd done the same thing. We were going to talk to you when we came to visit. I mean, it's not like we all did the best job ever, but we were on the same page."

"Wow." Tony didn't know what to say. "So none of us helped her."

"That's one way to look at it," Vince said. "Turns out all of us had given up on the soft and kind approach, and we'd all independently turned toward tough love. Which might have worked, except…"

"Except it didn't." They both swigged beer. Jax had fallen asleep on Paddington.

"I want to show you something," his brother said. He walked over to the built-in bookshelf by the fireplace and pulled a photo album off the shelf. It was one Tony hadn't seen.

Stella had made it for Jax. It was a collection of photos of all four of them, Tony, Pam, Vince, and Stella, when they were kids. Having fun, riding bikes, going to the lake. Back when Filmore had been a better place to be. Declining even back then, sure, but still with some good neighborhoods and good people.

The captions she'd written in were all about love and family.

Tony's throat tightened as he paged through. So many photos had him carrying Stella on his back or holding her hand. He'd really been close to her, tried to take care of her. And the way she'd looked up to him… When he'd finished, he couldn't speak.

"The drugs got her," his brother said, "but she was a good person. We had a good family. Not perfect, but good. It's just, everything doesn't always turn out the way you want it to."

Tony swallowed hard, nodded.

"If you're really coming back," his brother said, "you

should get involved with the movement to bring Filmore back to what it was. That's what you should do for Stella. Not beat yourself up for the rest of your life."

"I'll think about that."

"That woman you screwed up with," Vince said. "She's a teacher, right?"

"She is."

"There are Head Start programs in need of good teachers here," he said. "Maybe she'd like to take a look. I'm sure she could get a job."

"I wouldn't want to bring her from Pleasant Shores to here," Tony said. Kayla was too good, too pure, for a place like Filmore.

"You could at least have her to visit, ask her."

The thought of talking to Kayla, bringing her here, telling her about his childhood...it lit a fire in him. An unreasonable fire. "That's assuming we have a relationship," he said. "Which we don't."

"But you could," his brother said. "If you could eat crow and apologize and tell her how you feel."

"You think you know it all," Tony grumbled.

"You're older, but not necessarily smarter." His brother stood and headed for the kitchen, whacking Tony's shoulder on the way. "I'm going to bed. See you tomorrow."

Tony should sleep, too, but he felt wide-awake. He carried Jax up to bed and tucked him in, then tapped on his brother's door and let him know he was running out to the convenience store.

Once in the car, though, he knew he wasn't headed for the store.

Fifteen minutes later, he was in downtown Filmore. He got out of the car and walked toward the little park where Stella had lost her life.

He wasn't alone. On the street that bordered the other side of the park, a car door slammed. He could hear quiet voices from that area. In a doorway, a man and a woman argued, their voices rising to shouts, then sinking down again.

Stella, Stella, this was no place to bring a child.

No place for her to be, either. Out of all Filmore's rundown neighborhoods, this was the most dangerous.

What could she have been doing here, except looking for her next high? Because he knew she'd cared about Jax, had loved him deeply. She hadn't been a bad person, or stupid.

The drugs, the disease of addiction, was the only magnet that would have been strong enough to override her urge to take care of her son.

He actually remembered bringing Stella and his other siblings to this park as a kid. They'd ridden their bikes, Stella on his handlebars, a few dollars in Tony's pocket to buy them all ice cream. His parents had both worked, and as soon as Tony was old enough, they'd gladly stopped hiring babysitters in the summer, putting him in charge.

He'd sometimes railed against the responsibility, but he'd known he was essential to his family, and he'd liked that feeling. He liked to be useful and needed. It was why he'd gone into the service, become a petty officer, taken leadership whenever he could. It was why he'd become a counselor and decided to work at the VA.

He liked helping people, and he thought of himself as making a difference in people's lives. That was what he'd wanted to do.

That was why what had happened to Stella had nearly destroyed him: it had made him feel like he wasn't himself. Like he wasn't who he'd thought he was.

He strolled through the park, avoiding a couple of pairs

of people. No need for him to get caught up in any danger or violence, not now. Jax needed him.

He reached the spot where Stella had been found—he'd visited here with one of the cops, trying to understand—and knelt on the ground. There was a beer bottle and a sandwich wrapper and other, less savory trash.

He should come clean this park up.

Had Stella remembered their happy times here, before she'd died? Had she even, maybe, been trying to recreate that, bringing Jax here? If so, it had been incredibly misguided, but maybe it had been a last little bit of light in her troubled and drugged mind.

He lay back on the grass and looked up at the stars, keeping his ears open for anyone's approach. In some ways, this was a foolish risk, but he wanted to know what she'd experienced, at the end.

All of a sudden, he remembered lying with her on the ground at their house when she was small, looking up at the stars, telling her about them, how far away they were, making up the details he didn't know. Why had they been out so late? He didn't remember, but he did know he'd told her that her name meant "star."

She'd cuddled close to him and listened, or he'd thought so, until he'd looked over and seen that she was asleep.

He'd stayed a little while, just enjoying the feel of her head on his shoulder, her warm little body next to him. The trusting way she'd been with him.

Oh, Stella. Why did you go the wrong way?

He looked up at the stars. Maybe, from their faraway perspective, a plan was visible, one he didn't understand. Or maybe not. Maybe it was all random.

Whichever was the case, since he was a stronger person,

he needed to help others. That was a message his parents had drilled into him, and he believed it.

He'd failed with Stella. No matter how much Kayla told him only toddlers blamed themselves for everything that happened around them, and no matter that his siblings had also pushed Stella too hard, that didn't negate his own culpability.

He was starting to realize, though, that everyone made mistakes. Sometimes, big, ugly, major ones.

Did it serve the world, did it serve Jax, for Tony to obsess about his mistake and his guilt?

Was there maybe another way he could help the world?

Caring for his nephew, sure, but maybe there was more he could do for Filmore, like his brother had said.

And maybe it wasn't all about making things better for other people who were strangers. Maybe, he could make things better with someone closer to home and closer to his heart.

He'd been wrong to accuse Kayla, wrong to back off from her after the closeness they'd shared. He hated to leave things in such a bad place with her.

Was there anything he could do to fix that?

Because if he wasn't just going to curl up and die from guilt, then he was going to have to live in the world. Of course he was; he had to take care of his nephew.

And he had to set right what he could. Kayla had been nothing but kind and good to him. And he'd thrown that goodness back in her face.

He had to apologize, and not just say he was sorry, show it. He had to make sure she understood that she wasn't to blame. Knowing Kayla, she'd be beating herself up for it.

Or maybe not, because just in the time he'd known her, Kayla seemed to have gotten stronger and more confident.

Maybe she was just rolling her eyes at how ridiculous Tony was, on the way to moving on with her life.

Either way, he needed to man up and apologize. But was Christmas the right day to do it?

And could he pull off a proper apology by tomorrow?

As THE LIGHTS of the church dimmed, Sylvie lit her candle from Ria's, next to her, and then passed the light to the next person down the row. Watching the flame move from person to person was magical.

She was glad she'd come. Though she felt blue from the breakup with Big Bobby, she'd accepted Ria's invitation to sit with them at church, had gotten a smile from Steve's encouraging text, and here she was.

The organ swelled with music, and the familiar words of "Silent Night" came right back to her, probably from childhood. All *was* calm and bright, or at least, getting that way. And the promised heavenly peace just might be coming to her.

There was a moment of silence when the hymn ended, and then Steve gave the benediction and they all extinguished their candles. The lights came back up, and people grabbed coats and helped kids into jackets and greeted each other.

There was hot chocolate and cider in the church lobby, and trays of Christmas cookies, and people lingered around, even though it was late. Ria and Drew were talking to friends, and Sylvie was glad to stay a little in the warmth and brightness. The thought of going back to her motel room to spend the rest of Christmas Eve threatened to bring her blues right back.

All the Christmas Eves of her past seemed to come marching by her, something like what had happened to Ebenezer Scrooge in *A Christmas Carol*. The childhood ones, disappointing or scary. Back then, an uneventful Christmas was the best thing to be expected.

It had actually been during the Christmas season that she'd met Big Bobby. He'd picked her up when she'd been shivering in a short dress and heels, her first night on the street. He'd taken her to a motel room and she'd lost it and cried. Instead of getting angry, he'd listened to her story and calmed her worries about the hustler she'd just started working for. Bobby had been big and strong and confident, much older than she was, and he'd simply taken her home. Later, she was pretty sure there had been some sort of negotiation, because he'd reassured her that there was nothing to fear.

He'd done so much for her. Saved her, really. But he'd also had other women, had a child with one of them. Life wasn't black and white; it was all kinds of shades of silvery gray. She'd done the right thing, ending their relationship, but the thought of her first holiday without him was lonely.

"We'll be ready to go in a few minutes," Ria said apologetically, as she snagged another cookie. "It's just, we like to talk to everyone, Drew especially. It's hard to make him leave."

"I'm fine," Sylvie said truthfully. "Take your time. I have a few people I still want to speak with, too." Mainly, she meant Primrose, she told herself. Not the pastor, who'd taken off his minister's garb and was making the rounds in a red sweater and Santa hat.

"Most of the young people are at Bisky's, I think," Ria said. "In fact, we can head over there if you'd like. That party goes on way into the night."

Sylvie shook her head. "Not unless you two want to go.

In fact, if you do, I'll probably walk back to the motel by myself. Just not in a party mood."

"Us, either. We'll go soon." And Ria waved and returned to her husband's side.

Primrose rolled up on her scooter. She wore a red sweater that looked like cashmere, soft black velvet slacks, and pearls. Her hair was newly done, her makeup perfect.

"You look so nice!" Sylvie said. "You put the rest of us to shame!"

Primrose waved a hand, but the color that rose to her cheeks told Sylvie the compliment had pleased her. "Church is the highlight of my Christmas holiday," she said. "May as well dress for the occasion. You look pretty, too."

"Thank you." Sylvie sat down on the edge of a chair to be at Primrose's level. "Do you have plans for tomorrow?"

"I'll go to dinner at Mary Rhoades's place," Primrose said. "She always invites a number of us single folks. In fact, you're welcome to join us, I'm sure."

"Thank you, but Ria and Drew invited me to dinner." It was nice that so many people opened their homes in Pleasant Shores. No one had to spend a holiday alone.

"I wonder where Pastor Steve will spend the day," Primrose said, eyes speculative. "Maybe Ria and Drew have an extra space at the table."

The thought was a nice one. "I like him," Sylvie admitted. "But..." She lifted her hands, palms up. "It's been a wild few days. Emotionally, I mean. I don't know if I'm coming or going, and I definitely don't have leftover energy for men."

"I understand." Primrose smiled at her. "Let's compare notes after tomorrow. We single women have to stick together."

"I'd like that," Sylvie said, and hugged the older woman.

She watched Primrose move toward the exit and then noticed Steve making his way toward her. Her heart gave a little extra skip. She stood to meet him.

People kept stopping him to talk and greet and hug. That was what life would be like for whatever woman got together with him: open and expansive, social, lots of people involved. It was who he was. His congregation clearly adored him, and he fully met that adoration and returned it, kneeling to laugh with a preschool-aged child, gently hugging an elderly woman, bouncing a crying baby to make him laugh.

He was clearly into it, high on it. But he kept glancing in her direction.

Finally he reached her. "I'm glad you stayed," he said, eyes frankly appreciative, and she was glad she'd worn her prettiest green dress, knowing it brought out the color of her eyes. "You look great."

"Thank you." She smiled at him, feeling suddenly shy. "It was a wonderful service."

"It's always good when there's more singing and less preaching," he said, easily self-deprecating. "Do you have a place to be tomorrow?"

She nodded. "Ria and Drew invited me over."

"Good." His eyes were steady on her.

The place was emptying out now, people calling greetings to one another, a couple of ladies putting cookies away, a teenager carrying the big carafe of hot chocolate toward the church kitchen.

Drew and Ria walked toward the door, slowly, talking and laughing. When Ria glanced back, Sylvie waved a hand, putting up a finger to indicate she was coming. "I have to go. Merry Christmas, Pastor Steve."

She put out a hand as if to shake his and ended up opening her arms for a hug. He smiled and pulled her close—not too close, nothing disrespectful, but she could smell his faint cologne and feel his muscular chest against her. She had to admit she liked it.

He squeezed her a little closer before letting her go, and when he did, his eyes lingered on her face. "I'd like to see you in the new year," he said.

She lifted an eyebrow. "For Bible study?" She was pretty sure that wasn't what he meant, but he was easy to tease.

His smile broadened. "Yes, of course. Tuesday mornings or Wednesday nights. But I meant socially. There are a couple of nice restaurants up the coast we could try."

He was asking her out, and it was tempting. She liked what she knew of him, wanted to know him better. And the thought of a nice date, of someone treating her like she was special, appealed to her in all kinds of ways.

But she'd centered her life around a man for too long. "I appreciate the offer," she said, "but I need to see how I am by myself for now. Maybe a walk along the bay." But that sounded romantic, too. "Or maybe Bible study really is the best place to start."

His face fell a little, but he quickly got back his smile. "The Bible is always the best place to start," he said. "Friends, then?"

"Friends," she said, giving him another quick, awkward little hug. "Merry Christmas."

CHAPTER SEVENTEEN

CHRISTMAS DAY STARTED cold and overcast, with wind whipping the bare tree branches. Kayla's mood matched the weather, but she was determined to fight through her feelings, if not for herself, then for those she was spending the day with.

Here in Paul and Amber's place, it was warm and bright. The big Christmas tree still sported a few wrapped packages. Paul, Amber, and Davey had of course opened theirs in the early morning, as evidenced by the big stack of toys.

"Sarge got a ball that moves by itself!" Davey told Kayla, holding up a big green-and-yellow ball and rolling it toward the big bloodhound. The dog watched the ball's movements from his spot by the fire.

Davey lowered his voice. "It's for exercise, because he's lazy and kind of fat."

"Aw, that'll be fun," she said. "Is your mom in the kitchen?"

"Yeah, and Miss Meg, and Aunt Erica."

"I'll go help, and you can show me your gifts later, okay?"

"Sure!" He knelt and started examining the stack.

Kayla headed into the kitchen, crowded with three bustling women. Erica, carrying a tray of vegetables and dip to the table, gave her a one-armed hug.

"Smells great in here," Kayla said. "I brought a pie and

some cookies, as ordered. And I did cheese straws, too, for appetizers."

"Yum. Put it down here." Amber cleared a space on the crowded counter, then gave Kayla a hug. "Glad you're here. You're the last one."

Kayla's heart fell, just a little, and she realized a tiny part of it had hoped Tony and Jax would be coming, which was totally ridiculous. They'd left town, gone back home.

Not that she was feeling fond of Tony right now, anyway; in fact, she was furious and hurt. So it was especially annoying that she wanted to see him so badly.

"I was a little lazy this morning," she said to Amber, by way of explaining her lateness. She put an arm around her mother, who was stirring something on the stove.

"Oh, my goodness, I was anything but lazy. Price of having a little one." Amber put out a hand to stop Davey, who was running through the kitchen, followed by three dogs: Trey's former K-9 German shepherd, and Erica's goofy goldendoodle, and Sarge. "Slow down, honey. Why don't you go in the TV room and hang out with the men?"

Davey looked thoughtful, clearly debating inside whether he would rather run through the house or be an honorary man.

"Take them these," Amber said, and put Kayla's plate of appetizers into the child's hands. "Careful. Take them right to Daddy. He'll know how to keep them away from the dogs."

The chore—and the fragrance of the cheese straws—made Davey cooperate. The dogs followed him out of the kitchen, nudging to try to get first place.

"He's so cute," Erica said. "And such a good kiddo."

"I hit the jackpot," Amber said.

"If you ladies have this," Kayla's mother said, "I think

I'll go catch the rest of the game with the guys. Keep them from thinking a strict gender divide is right."

"Go for it. We'll eat in about forty-five minutes," Amber said.

Paul stuck his head in the kitchen. "Anything I can do?"

Amber kissed him. "Just keep the drinks refilled. And I'll need you to carry the turkey to the table in a bit."

"Will do."

"He's making my slug of a husband look bad," Erica said, her smile belying her words. "Actually, Trey worked all night and he's watching Hunter, so I can't complain."

A little later, Davey wandered back into the room. "I wish Jax was here to play with."

His words pierced Kayla's heart. What was Jax doing today, for Christmas? Had he gotten the truck he'd wanted?

Amber took a quick look at Kayla, then brushed a hand over Davey's head. "I know, honey, but you have to teach Hunter to play."

"He's too little," Davey complained. He leaned on Amber's leg, his eyes droopy. Of course. He probably hadn't gotten much sleep.

"Tell you what, let's set you up with a video until dinner's ready," Amber said. "You need to rest up for the parade this afternoon, anyway. Lots of your friends will be there, and you can show off your new bike." She made a face at Kayla. "His grandparents got him the fanciest kid's bike I've ever seen."

"Okay." Davey allowed himself to be led out of the room.

"Help me check this turkey," Erica said, beckoning Kayla over to the oven.

Kayla studied it doubtfully. "Did you get the kind with the pop-up thermometer?"

"No, and I should have. I hear you're supposed to wiggle the leg—" Which she did, using an oven mitt. "Um… I don't know, maybe another twenty minutes and we'll take it out."

"Sounds good. Now, what else can I do?"

"Split these brussels sprouts and toss them in some olive oil. We'll put them in as soon as the turkey comes out. I forgot about them."

"Sure thing." Kayla set to work. She didn't need to mope about being single on Christmas. The fact that she and Mom were spending the holiday here meant she didn't have to endure a litany of distant relatives' questions about why she was still single.

Of course, Mom had brought Finn, the man she'd started dating this fall. She'd kept it low key until now; Kayla had barely seen the man. But today, he was invited to a holiday gathering.

Just maybe, Mom had found love. And Kayla was happy for her, she truly was.

Lots of people were entirely alone on the holiday. She needed to be thankful for Mom, and for Erica and Amber and her other friends.

I wish Jax were here, too. And his uncle.

She finished chopping the brussels sprouts, then found some fresh garlic to add in. She drizzled on olive oil and ground in fresh pepper and sea salt.

"Those look perfect." Amber had come back into the kitchen, and she put an arm around Kayla for a quick squeeze. "Now, can you do the same with some broccoli?"

"Of course." She narrowed her eyes at Amber. "You're not trying to keep me busy, are you?"

"It's the best thing," Amber said quietly. "I really am sorry you can't be with Tony and Jax today."

"It's okay," Kayla said, her watery eyes belying her

words. She swallowed hard. "I'm grateful for what I have, and that includes the invitation for Mom and me to spend Christmas here."

"We're so glad you came." Amber patted her shoulder. "Now, I have to get that turkey out."

Things got busy then, with Paul coming into the kitchen, and then Trey and Davey and Hunter. Amber put Paul and Davey to work setting the table, and Trey got the job of filling water glasses. "Just about my skill level," he joked.

Kayla slid the trays of vegetables into the hot oven to roast, and helped with the table setting and the rolls, and finally everything was on the table. They said grace, and dug in, and everything was delicious. Kayla could almost forget about Tony and Jax.

Almost.

She forced herself to chat and help serve food and, afterward, to take control of the cleanup. They were preparing to leave for the parade when the sound of a dog barking just out front caught everyone's attention. Especially the dogs, who started barking and rushed to the front door.

"That's Paddington!" Davey yelled, and rushed toward the door.

Paul followed him, stopping to glance out the front window. "He's right."

Kayla put down the dish she'd been carrying, her stomach freezing into ice. Tony and Jax were here. Why?

TONY LISTENED TO his nephew's happy laughter and reflected that it was a good thing he'd gotten Jax a new bike for Christmas. It couldn't compare to Davey's pricey model, sleek with enough chrome to satisfy a car fanatic. But Jax's bike was sturdy, had training wheels, and gave Jax a way to participate in the parade. Jax had insisted he wanted to walk to the parade with Davey, so they'd dropped their bags at Victory Cottage and hurried right over to Paul and Amber's place.

The whole group ended up walking together to the parade. Davey and Jax were at the front of the crowd, pushing their bikes, Davey explaining about the bike decorating station.

The eager expression on Jax's face made Tony glad they'd decided to come back.

They'd had a nice visit with his brother and sister, had opened gifts and eaten breakfast together early this morning. But Tony hadn't been able to stop thinking.

He'd spent the past months feeling guilty about Stella and overwhelmed with becoming Jax's full-time caregiver. But after the conversation with his brother, and the trip to the park where Stella had died, it was as if a fog had cleared. He could see into the future now, a little at least, and he wanted Kayla to be a part of it.

The trouble was, he'd hurt her badly. Would she accept his apology?

Things weren't looking great so far; Kayla seemed to make a point of being far away from Tony. Once they'd reached the park, she stayed beside Erica and Hunter until they got swept away to ride in a big sleigh with other parents and small children. Then she huddled near Paul and Amber.

Fortunately for Tony, that hiding spot was doomed to disappear, too. Amber patted Jax's shoulder and then looked at Tony. "We'll take the boys over to the decorating station."

"I'll go, too," Kayla said.

Amber gave her a meaningful frown. "No need," she said, and hustled the kids off in the direction of a big, tented structure, Paul walking beside them.

Was Kayla afraid he was going to jump down her throat again? Why wouldn't she be, when that was what he'd done the last time they'd seen each other?

Kayla turned toward her mother, standing beside a tall, well-dressed man who'd been introduced as Finn. Clearly, Kayla wanted to cling to the last remaining barrier between herself and Tony.

Find something else to do, he willed Meg and Finn.

"Will you mind terribly if I head home?" Kayla's mom said. "I think I feel a migraine coming on."

"Oh no, that's not good!" Kayla said. "I'll come with you."

"No, dear. Finn will take care of me. You stay and enjoy the parade." She winked at Tony, turned, and hurried off toward the parking area, Finn beside her.

Wow. His intentions toward Kayla must be obvious. And Meg seemed to be on his side. That was a little surprising, but good news.

And there was no time to waste, since Jax could return, needing him, at any moment. "Can we talk?" he asked Kayla.

A blast of music drowned out her answer, coming from a float with members of the high school band. They all seemed to be tuning their instruments at once.

He reached out to take her hand, but she kept her own close to her sides. Okay. So she wasn't going to make this easy. That was her right. He beckoned her over to a bench that was set back from the parade route and slightly sheltered by some bushes. "Do you mind sitting with me for a minute? I need to talk to you."

"O-kaaay," she said. She followed him and sat down on the very edge of the bench.

Nope, not easy. "Listen, Kayla, I want to apologize. I

should never have accused you of causing Jax to be abducted by that man. I was wrong to even think such a thing, when all you were doing was trying to help."

She studied him, nodded, and looked away. "Okay."

What was that supposed to mean?

But he could read it well enough. She'd accepted his apology, but was still hurt. "You're such a good person," he went on, feeling his way. "I should have known you'd never do anything but help a child. You've meant the world to Jax."

"He's a great kid," she said.

It was the same generic thing she'd say about any child. And she still wasn't looking at Tony.

This wasn't going the way Tony had hoped. He'd pictured the whole scenario with Kayla being her usual sunny self, but she wasn't. She was distant and seemed uncomfortable.

He was the one in the wrong, so it was up to him to keep the conversation going and to steer it in the direction he'd planned. He squared his shoulders and went for it. "I hope I didn't ruin my chances," he said.

"Of what?"

Game time. "Of a relationship with you."

The Christmas carols cut off, and a man's jolly voice came over the loudspeaker. "Ho ho ho, everyone, we'll start in about fifteen minutes. Kids, let's get lined up."

Fifteen minutes was all he had. Amber had texted him that she and Paul would take the kids over to where the parade started, but he couldn't expect more than that.

"You said you needed to back off, and that it wasn't going to work." She met his eyes, lifting one eyebrow. "You texted me that I shouldn't try to get in touch."

"Yeah." He looked across the crowd and then back at

her. "Believe it or not, I did that for you. I thought I wasn't a worthy person, thought I'd screw up and let you down. And I might, but... I'm starting to make peace with what happened. To hope for more."

Kayla looked at him, and for the first time, there was a faint smile on her face. "I'll always be your friend," she said. "And a friend to Jax, as well."

So that was the way it was going to be, then: the dreaded friend zone. Well, it was what he deserved. But he looked at her beautiful face and knew he couldn't give up; he had to try harder. "Is that all you'll be?" he asked.

"I don't know." She looked troubled. "I don't understand what you're offering."

The speaker was giving more instructions. Children shouted. A red-suited Santa Claus walked around the crowd, throwing candy.

This wasn't the perfect location for what he had in mind, but suddenly, he realized what *would* be the right spot. "Hang on," he said. He took out his phone and texted Amber, making sure she was okay with getting Jax started in the parade.

She was.

"Will you take a little walk with me?" he asked Kayla.

"But..."

"I want to ask you something," he said, "but it's too noisy here." If that wasn't a hint of what he planned, nothing was.

But Kayla's face didn't brighten. "I do want to see the parade," she said.

"This will be quick." It shouldn't be, but if she was going to say no, then the parade would provide a way to escape the awkwardness.

Think positive.

They walked a block to the Coastal Kids school. The playground was deserted. A light snow was starting to fall.

"Do you remember when we met for the first time?" he asked her.

"Of course. I thought you were kidnapping Jax." The corner of her mouth turned up, just a little.

"And I thought you were nosy and interfering," he said. "And cute."

Her cheeks went pink. She looked over at the school as if she might want to escape there.

"I was a mess then," he went on. "I'm still a mess, but not as much. And you're a big part of why."

"Why you're a mess, or why you're better?" There was a teasing look in her eyes now.

"Why I'm better. Even though we started off on the wrong foot, you didn't hold it against me. You helped with Jax, and accepted me as a volunteer in your classroom when I was pretty bad at the job."

She let out a little laugh. "You improved quickly," she said.

"All I had to do was to watch you. You're great with the kids. Great with Jax."

"Well." She sounded uncomfortable and looked off in the direction of the parade route. "Is that what you wanted to talk about?"

"No." He was sweating despite the cold. "I want to tell you how much I care for you. I know we've only known each other for a short time, but I feel like I know your heart. I know my own heart, too, now."

She studied him without speaking.

"You're a good person, Kayla, and you make me want to be a better man."

He guided her to sit on the bottom of the sliding board

and then knelt in front of her. "You make me want to spend the rest of my life with you. Is that something you'd even consider?"

KAYLA CLAPPED HER hand over her mouth and stared at the man kneeling in front of her. Was she dreaming?

Around them, the snow was heavier now, big wet flakes. From the park came the distant sound of music and an announcer, but the little playground felt like a snow-globe world of their own.

"I know it's a bad time to ask, right after I was so mean to you. Right after you saw for yourself the trouble that's following me and Jax around."

Kayla's head was spinning. She tried to bring herself back to earth. "The man who tried to abduct Jax is in police custody, right? You're safe now?"

He nodded, still kneeling in front of her. "We're so lucky Jax wasn't more traumatized." Then he frowned. "But that brings up another challenge to this marriage proposal. Jax is always going to be with me. If you marry me, you get him, too."

He'd said *marriage proposal*. He'd said *if you marry me*, as if the outcome was in doubt. She wasn't dreaming. He was proposing marriage.

"It's a huge plus that he's crazy about you, but it's also a lot to ask."

He thought *Jax* would be a dealbreaker? She shook her head. "I love Jax. He's a wonderful part of the package."

Her insecurities surged up, suddenly and hard. Was he proposing so that Jax would have a mother?

After all, she wasn't the girl who got the sexy, handsome guy. She was the helpful friend type, always single. The one who got invited to the party so she could babysit the kids. The one with the crooked spine. No way could a guy like Tony have feelings for her.

And then she realized how ludicrous this situation was. She was considering herself the girl who'd always be single, in the midst of a marriage proposal.

Her spine wasn't curved anymore, and even if it had been, that didn't make her less deserving of happiness. She squared her shoulders. "Are you asking me so that Jax can have a mother?" she demanded. "And stand up. You're getting soaked kneeling on the ground. Come sit on the bench with me."

She was being bossy, but hey, she was a preschool teacher. It was in the job description, which fit her to a T, and she wasn't going to apologize for who she was anymore.

His eyes narrowed, and then he got to his feet and took her hand and led her to the bench. "Kayla, I'm proposing because I love you. You're beautiful and—"

She raised a hand, waved the compliment off. "Don't kid a kidder."

"I'm not!" He looked shocked. "Have you looked at yourself? Your hair, your face, your figure…you're the whole package, and you don't have to doll yourself up like some women to look good. But it's more than that, way more."

She tucked that description aside to think about later and studied his face, trying to gauge his sincerity.

"You're absolutely kind and reliable. I don't have to guess whether you're in a good mood or going to be willing to help, because you always are."

"You make me sound like a Sunday school teacher," she said, but her heart was lifting a little.

He smiled and slowly shook his head. "You could be one, and that's not a bad thing. But I have feelings about you that are way different from Sunday school feelings. Sometimes when I look at you, I'm so attracted that I can barely breathe. That knockout figure, that innocence…" He put his arm around her, making her shiver. "When I found out I was the first to kiss you, I was blown away."

She laughed nervously. "I felt like such a loser."

"The guys who didn't date you before were losers, but it's my win," he said. "Or at least, it was my win to be your first kiss. I hope I can be your first…everything."

She knew what he meant, and the thought of a wedding night, of a romantic honeymoon with Tony…her heart started to pound faster. "You would be," she said, and stole a glance at him.

He brought her hand to his lips. "I would love that," he said. "But even more than that, I'd want to be there for you. Every day, through everything. More kids, if you want them. Kayla, I want to grow old with you, but you're killing me here. Is there even a chance you'll marry me?"

She felt his strong arm around her, the warmth of his body beside her, and she knew she wanted that, too, for the rest of her life. And she believed him, she realized. She believed she *could* be loved, and she believed Tony did love her. Her anxious, ugly-duckling, middle-school self should see her now.

Only she felt somehow…kindly toward that younger self. Looked at her with compassion. And watched her fade away.

Then she turned to the man she loved. "Yes, Tony," she said. "I love you and Jax, so much. I would be honored to marry you."

EPILOGUE

The Next Year, December 26

TONY STOOD AT THE FRONT of the church, sweating.

It wasn't that hot. The old church was actually poorly insulated, leaving plenty of ways for the Chesapeake wind to come in. The flames of the many red and white candles flickered, and out in the pews, he could see that lots of people had their coats draped around their shoulders.

No, he was sweating because it was finally, finally the day he got to marry Kayla.

They'd waited because they wanted to make sure Jax was used to the idea, and because Christmas was romantic to them, since they'd met during the Christmas season. Most of all, they'd waited because Kayla deserved a real courtship. But it had been a challenge, and Tony was past ready to be married to her and to start spending their lives together.

The bonus of putting off the wedding was that Stella's killer was in prison. That chapter of their lives was behind them, and he and Jax could start clean, building a family with Kayla.

"You'll be fine," Pastor Steve, who was officiating the ceremony, said in low voice.

"This is the worst of it," Paul added.

"Is it that obvious that I'm nervous?"

Tony's brother snorted, under cover of the organ music that was starting to get louder. "You're sweating. Just think how lucky you are that you found someone to put up with you."

Tony knew it; he was lucky in many ways. Lucky to have these men in his life. What a thing, that he had too many friends to ask them all to be groomsmen, right here in Pleasant Shores. But William had turned him down, saying he wanted to be available to Bisky and their daughter, who was just learning to walk and was a real handful. Drew, too, had said he'd just as soon attend the wedding with his wife and daughters.

Tony was luckier still, or blessed maybe, that his nephew was healing from the traumatic death of his mother. His counseling sessions were once a month now, and were mostly just a chance for him to play with Mixter. Every now and then, he'd get sad or something would prompt another memory, but for the most part, he was a normal, mischievous, happy five-year-old boy.

Most of all, Tony was blessed to have found the love of his life. Kayla was everything he hadn't known he'd needed. A truly good person who thought of others first. Fun and lighthearted, wonderful with Jax. Beautiful and sexy and pure.

He ran a finger inside the too-tight collar of his tux shirt. He hadn't wanted to wear a tux, but Kayla and her mom and friends had assured him that he, and all the men, would look "amazing" in black tuxes with red bow ties and cummerbunds. He glanced over at his groomsmen and had to admit, they did look pretty sharp.

He heard a muffled bark and shout in the back of the church and tensed, but the noise was quickly silenced. The people in the pews had heard it, though, and they were chuckling and murmuring.

Looking out at all the guests, he felt a wave of fondness. They'd become his community, and he was going to miss them. But he and Kayla had committed to spend at least a year in Filmore, she teaching in a Head Start program, and he working with the VA's drug program. It was a trial, to see whether they'd like to live there on a permanent basis.

Tony couldn't fathom anyone preferring Filmore to Pleasant Shores, even though he'd grown up in Filmore. But Kayla had gotten to know his brother and sister, had spent time in the town and seen the need, and she wanted to help, at least for a year. After that, they'd see.

In any case, they'd spend summers here in Pleasant Shore.

There was a change in the music, and the congregation's murmurs got louder as Jax came down the aisle in his suit and red bow tie. Beside him was Paddington, walking nicely on a red leash and wearing a red bow around his neck. Strapped onto the big Saint Bernard's back was a pillow holding Tony's ring. Jax held an identical pillow, to which was affixed Kayla's ring.

Now sweat dripped down Tony's back. Sure, he knew that the rings Jax and Paddington carried were fakes, and that his brother held the real rings safely in his pocket…but still, he didn't want Paddington to go nuts and run around the church, drooling on everyone in their finery. The dog had been seriously trained by Bisky's daughter Sunny, but he was big and this was an unusual event for him, a crowd of people inside, in a church.

Seeing the smiles of the guests, though, made Tony start to relax. Kayla and her mom and friends had been right to include Paddington in the ceremony. And seeing Jax's proud expression as he guided the big dog up the aisle showed him that it had been wise to give Jax such an important role. After all, Jax's family was changing with this marriage, and he deserved to play a major role in the ceremony.

Dog and boy arrived safely. Jax hugged Tony, as coached. He was getting to where he didn't like public hugs as much as he'd used to.

The moment Tony let Jax go, Paddington jumped up, paws on Tony's chest, imitating Jax. Tony would have gone off balance if it weren't for his brother steadying him from behind. Sunny hurried up from the audience and Erica, who'd been walking down the aisle in her fancy red dress, quickened her step to almost a run. Together, they helped Jax guide Paddington to his proper location in the front row, where he flopped down with a loud sigh that made everyone laugh.

Erica took her place, and Amber walked down the aisle and joined her.

And then everyone was standing and murmuring and turning toward the back of the church. Kayla started down the aisle toward Tony on her mother's arm, and every rational thought went out of his head.

This was his first sight of her in her wedding gown, for tradition's sake. Her white dress was fitted on top—wow, fitted in a really good way—with some red Christmassy trim that made her stellar figure even more...well, nice. She'd tried to describe the gown to him, had talked about balancing out the white of a gown with the red and green of the season, but it had all gone over his head. Now, he got it. She looked stunning.

She reached the front of the church, hugged her mom and then turned to him, her eyes full of tears. It was all he could do not to take her in his arms and kiss her, right then and there.

He didn't, of course. He made it through the ceremony, said his vows, put the ring on her finger. And *then* he kissed her with all the passion and promise he felt inside.

AFTER THE PHOTOGRAPHS and their grand entrance at the reception, hosted in the warm back fireplace room of DiGiorno's, Kayla sat down at one of the tables and traded out her heels for glitter-decorated sneakers. She sighed with relief. "Oh, that's so much better."

Amber took her fancy shoes and put them somewhere, taking charge as the excellent matron of honor that she was. "I still can't get over your dress," she said, picking up the bottom of it to admire the red velvet, shot through with gold stitching, that made up the train.

"I can't get over yours. You look beautiful." All the bridesmaids wore red velvet dresses with cap sleeves and long white gloves.

Amber bent down to give her a hug. "I'm glad it went well. You deserve a beautiful wedding. You deserve all the happiness in the world."

"Thank you for everything." Kayla felt teary, but in the good way—with a joy that kept bubbling up inside her.

Wreaths of greenery and poinsettias, woven through with twinkle lights, graced every table, and the cake, white with a cascade of red roses, looked spectacular. Waiters made the rounds with hot drinks, cider and hot chocolate—with and without peppermint schnapps—as well as more traditional soft drinks and cocktails.

"I feel funny not helping," Kayla said. "Do you think I should pass out drinks?"

"No," Amber answered. "Your mom can run the show."

She pointed out Kayla's mom, who stood talking with Mary, Sylvie, and Primrose. Sure enough, Mom's eyes scanned the room; clearly, she was watching to make sure that everything was under control.

Jax rushed over and leaned on Kayla, a candy cane in his mouth. His sticky hands gripped her dress, leaving red peppermint marks, but it was fine. The dress could be cleaned. She put an arm around him and kissed the top of his head, still in awe that she was going to officially be this wonderful little boy's mother.

Bisky and William's toddler chose that moment to pull on a tablecloth, nearly bringing the centerpiece down on herself. Before Kayla could get up to help, multiple people rushed over to steady the wreath and comfort the startled child. Jax rushed over to see what was going on. Amber started to follow and then turned back. "Stay and sit," she ordered Kayla. "We'll handle it."

"And *that's* why we decided to have twinkle lights instead of candles on the table," Kayla's mom said, sinking into the chair Amber had just vacated. She was holding a big, flat package. "I know it's unorthodox, honey, but what do you think about opening one present now?"

"Whatever you think. Should I get Tony?" He was standing with a group of the men, talking and laughing, so handsome it made her heart hurt.

As if he felt her eyes on him, he turned to her and smiled. She loved that about him, how attentive and affectionate he was.

"This gift's really just for you," Mom said. "From the kids, and I know some of them won't stay late."

Kayla ripped open the package and then put her hand to her chest and studied the large canvas. Covered with children's handprints, with a small school picture in each, it had a large, painted caption: *We Wish You a Happy Marriage*. Kayla's eyes filled with tears as she made out the names of kids from earlier years, including Davey and yes, there was Jax. "When did you do this? I know you had to be involved."

"It's been an ongoing project," she said. "They all wanted to wish you the best."

Kayla's tears overflowed then. "I'm going to miss Coastal Kids so much, Mom."

"I know you are." Mom got a little choked up, too. "I'll miss you, too. But it's only for a year, right?"

"Right. For now." Kayla was actually thrilled about the opportunity in Filmore. She'd loved working at the private school, but there were kids in Filmore who needed her help much more.

Primrose and Mary were at a table talking, and after her mother left to check on the food tables, Kayla walked over and sat down to join them. Ria and Drew came over and sat with them.

"She's making all kinds of excuses to get out of dancing with me," Drew complained.

"I don't know why," Ria said, "but I'm just so tired and nauseated."

Mary studied her. "Have you considered you might be…"
Ria gasped.
Drew's jaw dropped.
Ria put a hand to her mouth. "Oh, my goodness, I'd stopped hoping. We've been so blessed with our two beautiful daughters…"

"And a grandson," Mary reminded them wryly. "Are you ready to start over with diapers again?"

"Congratulations," Primrose said, glee in her voice.

Kayla bit her lip to keep from laughing. If Primrose

knew Drew and Ria suspected they were pregnant, everyone else would know soon, as well.

"Now we have to dance," Drew said, "so we can talk this over."

"I...have to go chat with some people," Primrose said.

"I'll come with you." Mary stood. She'd try to contain Primrose, most likely. And most likely, she'd fail.

Kayla looked out at the dance floor and was delighted to see that Sylvie and Pastor Steve were dancing.

She felt a hand on her shoulder. "Time to go soon," Tony whispered into her ear. "And I, for one, am ready."

Kayla looked up into his warm brown eyes. "Me, too," she said, holding his gaze. She'd loved every minute of the wedding and reception, but now, she was ready to be alone with her new husband.

"One last dance?" he asked. It had been a delight for both of them when they'd realized they both liked to dance and were good at it, together.

She nodded and soon was in his arms. The candlelight flickered, and the fragrance of pine and bayberry filled the air. She snuggled closer. "I'm so glad we got married at Christmas," she said.

"I'm so glad you're finally my wife." He stroked her hair, then eased her over to the side of the dance floor. "Oh look, mistletoe," he said, pointing upward and feigning surprise. Then he kissed her, long and slow. It swept Kayla away so much that it was only when he stopped and lifted his head that she realized everyone was clapping.

"Get a room," Tony's brother yelled.

"We're about to," Tony called back, earning more laughter and applause.

Tony leaned close to Kayla. "Seems like a great time

for us to take off," he said. "And I have a surprise for you and Jax."

They collected Jax and slipped through the back of the restaurant. Outside, Kayla gasped. There was a sleigh and horses waiting for them.

"Horses!" Jax cried. He was sleepy, but the sight of the sleigh still excited him.

Kayla climbed in with Tony's help and then held out her hands to help Jax climb into the sleigh. Tony followed and tucked a fur robe around all of them. They were going back to Kayla's place tonight, with Jax. In two days, once everything had settled down and Jax was used to the changes a bit more, they'd leave on their honeymoon.

It wasn't a conventional wedding night, but Jax came first. Kids always came first. It was one of many things they agreed on. They wrapped their arms around each other, and Jax sprawled in their laps, sleepy again.

In the starlight, as the horses trotted toward home, Kayla looked from her new son to her new husband. Satisfaction as bright as Christmas filled her.

Her first kiss had been important and meaningful after all. It had turned into deep, true love and a family.

* * * * *

Read on for a bonus prequel novella featuring Kayla's mother, Meg, and her summer romance! And if you're curious about Dr. Liz's background, sign up for Lee's newsletter at www.leetobinmcclain.com *to receive a free short story about how she and Mixter came to settle in Pleasant Shores.*

SECRETS OF SUMMER

CHAPTER ONE

Meg Harris jerked awake, checked the clock and groaned. It was 2:45 a.m.

Tap-tap-tap. Click-click. Silence, then just as she was dropping back off, there it came again. Click-tap-click-click-click.

She was used to noise—she did run a preschool, after all—but the annoying tapping from the other half of her duplex was different. It pounded on her brain like a gremlin with a tiny hammer.

At forty-eight, she already wasn't a great sleeper. *Thank you, perimenopause.* And every time she woke up, she thought about her thesis, due in two weeks.

Getting her master's degree was a lifelong goal, and she hoped to use it to kickstart this new phase of her life, but she was blocked, blocked, blocked. She'd already negotiated two extensions. These two weeks were her last chance.

She threw back her too-hot covers and climbed out of bed, glad to notice that the noise had stopped. She'd get a cup of chamomile tea and do some brainstorming. Hopefully, she'd come up with a way forward. She had the academic section done, and the bibliography was perfect, but the final, creative part was doing her in.

It was insecurity. She lacked confidence in her creative ability, just like she lacked confidence in herself as an attractive woman. Two areas of weakness in what was otherwise a really great life.

Her dachshund, Oscar, lifted his head and looked at her as if to ask, "Do I have to get up?" He was eight years old and getting lazy.

"Go back to sleep," she said, giving the dog a quick ear rub.

There came the tapping again, this time accompanied by a scream. And then a sharp crack, like a gunshot.

A gunshot? *Was* it one?

Oscar woofed half-heartedly, as if he didn't know, either.

Heart racing, she reached for jeans instead of her robe. Should she go next door or call the police herself?

Breathe. It's probably nothing.

In her small Chesapeake Bay town, crime was rare, and it would be embarrassing if the noise next door were just a too-loud TV show. After all, the walls here were thin. But tourists dominated Pleasant Shores in the summer, and although her landlord tried to vet the short-term renters, occasionally, someone not so great slipped through.

Downstairs, she popped a teabag into a mug and stuck it in the microwave, then looked out the window at the parking spaces in front of the duplex. Her quiet street was deserted, peaceful, bathed in starlight.

A loud bang from next door made her jump. Another scream and more clacking. Oscar trotted downstairs. His awkward gait usually made her smile, but not tonight. She was annoyed. Annoyed her temporary neighbors had awakened not only her, but also her dog.

She did want to get back to sleep at some point. At the risk of sounding like a cranky old lady, she was going to have to go next door.

She opened her front door, ordered Oscar to stay and

headed out. The August heat enveloped her as she marched over to the other half of the duplex. She banged the knocker, rang the doorbell and then backed down the porch steps in case she needed to flee.

The noises stopped. After a minute, she heard footsteps trotting down the stairs. The door flew open to reveal an enormous pair of sock-clad feet. She looked up to a slim midsection, broad shoulders, hair graying at the temples and...

When she focused on the man's face, she gasped. "Finn? Finn O'Conner?"

What on earth was her late husband's business lawyer doing in Pleasant Shores?

He looked stunned, too. He leaned forward and squinted out into the night. "Meg? Is that you?"

She nodded. "It is. What are you doing here?"

"What are *you* doing here? Since it's..." He pulled a phone from his back pocket and looked at the face of it. "It's 3:00 a.m."

"I came over about the noise." She gestured upward. "We share a wall. I heard screams and gunshots, and then this irregular tapping sound. Woke me up."

He clapped a hand to his forehead. "I'm sorry. I was right in the middle of... Well, look, the yelling and gunshot sounds came from some videos I was watching. Would you like to come in? I can offer you coffee, with or without a shot of bourbon." He held open the door.

Which suggested he was here alone. When he was photographed as a major donor at the charity events he attended, he usually had some extremely young, extremely attractive woman on his arm. A different one every time, if Meg was remembering correctly.

Still, he was a good guy. He'd gone to school with her

and Randy, and he'd been a big help with Randy's estate, but then they'd lost track of each other. They hadn't spoken in years.

She had to look a sight, her hair a tangled mess down her back, her jeans and sweatshirt faded, her face bare of makeup. Not exactly the way you wanted your former sweetheart—because they'd been that too, briefly, as teenagers—to see you. But oh, well… she was past the age of being obsessed with her looks. "Sure, I'll come in for a minute, if I'm not interrupting anything," she said. "And I'll take that shot."

"I HAVEN'T SEEN you since Randy died," Finn said as he led Meg inside. This flash from the past at 3:00 a.m. felt fairly surreal.

As he gestured her into the kitchen ahead of him, he noticed that her long, wavy red hair was threaded through with silver. It looked good on her.

She looked good, just as good as the day she'd married Finn's former best friend. Slim and fit, with that athletic way of moving that reminded him she'd been a gymnast and cheerleader in high school. Way fewer lines on her face than he had, which probably meant she'd led a more peaceful life.

He pulled out a chair for her at the small kitchen table and then set about making coffee, wondering how to play this scene. He hadn't realized the walls were so thin, that he'd have to come up with some explanation for the noise. There were two secrets he needed to keep from her, one about himself and one about her, or rather, her past. That meant he needed to get into lawyer mode, where schooling his features was second nature.

He'd lead with questions so she didn't start asking too

many. "What brought you to Pleasant Shores?" he asked. They'd grown up in a town a few miles inland, and most everyone had come here to Pleasant Shores for recreation and fun, but the last he'd heard, she'd been a teacher farther up the coast.

"A job opened up running a preschool here," she explained. "I needed a change, and Kayla was having some problems in middle school, so…" She lifted her hands, palms up. "All of a sudden, I've lived here twelve years. It's home now."

"And Kayla's doing well?" He found two mugs and poured coffee. Although he'd mostly focused on Randy's business, and then later on his estate, he'd met Kayla twice. Once, as a scared and worried ten-year-old whom he'd met visiting Randy at the hospital. Then once more, at her father's funeral.

"Really well. She's a teacher at my school." She leaned back in her chair. "I don't know if you knew her scoliosis got worse. Wearing a brace made her adolescent years a little tough, but that and some surgery fixed things. She's well and happy now."

He hadn't known that, and he felt for Kayla and for Meg, too. From the way she was talking, it sounded like she hadn't remarried. And though he'd deliberately *not* kept track of the woman he'd always regretted letting go, he couldn't help but be glad she was single.

It sounded like she'd raised her daughter alone, helped her through some serious struggles, which was an achievement to be proud of. "If you work together, you must be close. That's terrific."

Meg nodded. "She's a real blessing. So, how long are you renting this place? I know Primrose usually doesn't let it for less than a week."

"I'm here for two. As long as you don't file a noise complaint against me." He broke the seal on a bottle of bourbon and splashed some into her coffee. "Cream?"

She shook her head, raised her hand like a stop sign when he offered to add more bourbon. "Yeah, why were you watching scary videos in the middle of the night?"

"I, uh, was looking up some stuff on my laptop and the volume was turned up high." That much was true. He'd wanted to make sure he was describing the sound just right.

She tilted her head to one side, probably curious because he hadn't answered her question. "I'm saving up for a single-family home with some real walls, but for now, I get to listen to some weird stuff." She took a sip from her cup, studying him. "So the laptop explains the screaming and gunfire, but what was that clicking and clacking?"

He hadn't intended to, but he poured some whiskey into his own cup of coffee. "I was working on something, writing on an old typewriter."

"Oh, a typewriter!" She smiled. "I was trying to figure out what it was. That's it."

"I'm sorry it woke you up," he said. "I can work downstairs, on the other side of the house. And keep my computer volume down."

"Sure, but…if you have a laptop, how come you're using a typewriter? A manual one, from the sounds of it."

He sat down at the table, looked into her honest green eyes and found that he wanted to tell her the truth. "I write legal thrillers. Under a pseudonym. Using my dad's old typewriter seems to bring out the creativity in me."

"Would I know your work?" she asked politely.

The skepticism was most people's reaction, and he preferred it, but for some reason he decided he didn't need to keep his writer identity a secret. "I'm Alex Marsh," he said.

Her eyes widened. "*You're* Alex Marsh?"

"Yeah, but don't tell anyone. I like my privacy."

"You always did," she said. "Wow. That's really cool. Congratulations on your success."

"Thanks." So he'd blurted out one of his two secrets. Hopefully, that was all he'd do.

Clearly Meg had become a competent and successful woman. A happy one. She could handle knowing the rest of the truth, but why burst her bubble?

She seemed so different from most of the women he dated, but then again, she was the type you married.

If you were the marrying kind, which he wasn't.

CHAPTER TWO

THE NEXT AFTERNOON, Meg returned home from errands to see Finn sitting on the front porch, laptop awkwardly perched on a coffee table. Just looking at the tall, lanky man bending over to type made her back hurt. Made her heart pound a little harder, too, but that wasn't important.

It was eighty degrees and humid. What was he doing outside?

She set her grocery bags inside her front door and called over. "Is that comfortable?"

He stood and laughed ruefully. "Not really, but I don't like being cooped up all day. I'm trying to capture the sights and sounds, you know."

"Your book is set here?"

"In the general area." He waved a hand like he didn't want to talk about it. "Speaking of writing, I thought you said you were working on your thesis today."

She made a face, annoyed with herself. "I'm supposed to be, but I decided I couldn't live another minute without oregano and paper towels."

"Procrastination." He nodded as he stacked the papers he'd had strewn out on the table. "I'm very familiar with it."

"If you only knew." She was embarrassed to confess to him how uncreative she really was. Part of the problem was her subject: kids with disabilities in literature. It hit a little too close to home.

"Happens to all writers, from time to time," he said.

"But what do you do about it when it happens to you?"

He tilted his head to one side, shrugged. "Take a break or a walk."

"Done both."

"Sometimes I talk things through with my editor," he said. "Do you have a thesis advisor?"

"I've burned her out with all my questions." She lifted her hands, palms up, trying to make a joke of it. "I'm a hopeless case."

He leaned against the porch rail and studied her, all long, loose limbs, genuine interest in his eyes. "What's your thesis about?"

"Children's literature. I focus on kids with disabilities, how they're portrayed."

"Interesting. You have part of it done?"

"Most of it, but I'm stuck on the creative part. I have to write either a short story or the start of a longer work, kind of putting the principles I've learned into action. I don't know where to begin." She shrugged, self-deprecating. "I just don't have the imagination."

His eyebrows came together and he shook his finger at her, mock scolding. "Sounds like an excuse. Have you tried brainstorming with someone else?"

She shook her head. "Pleasant Shores isn't chock-full of writers." Goodness, she sounded whiny. She'd have chewed out her daughter if she came up with that many excuses.

Hands on his hips, Finn pinned her with an intense gaze. "I'm a writer. I'll brainstorm with you."

Her heart gave a flutter. What was this vibe she was getting from him?

Most likely, she was just imagining it, and that was pathetic. "You're a famous thriller writer. I'm a nobody."

"It's the least I can do for keeping you awake all night."

She blushed at the image his words evoked, other reasons a man like Finn might keep a woman awake all night. She waved a hand and turned back toward the house. "Don't worry about it."

"Wait, Meg." He walked over to the divider between their two porches. "I'm serious about that offer. I would be happy to help you brainstorm, especially if you'd let me do it over dinner."

His words made her feel breathless. "I don't... Well." She'd been about to say she didn't want to do it, but she'd be lying. "That would be a wonderful help, but I at least ought to cook. If you take me out, and brainstorm with me, the transaction's unequal."

A car drove by, windows open, country music blaring. From the bay, a breeze chilled her sweaty skin. She looked into his amber eyes, eyes she'd always found interesting.

He studied her. "Is that how you look at it, a transaction?"

She shook her head rapidly. "I don't know." Restless, she took the broom propped against the wall and brushed a few sticks and leaves off the porch. She felt like a frumpy old lady, wearing her faded jeans, sweeping her porch, complaining about her woes. "I'll be fine, but thanks for the offer."

"You don't have to cook. I'll pick up pizza." He hesitated, then added, "You don't know me all that well, despite the past. Maybe working at your place isn't the best idea. Do you know of any place where we could use a whiteboard or chalkboard? That always helps me capture good ideas."

His thoughtfulness touched her. "There's my school, but—"

"I'll knock on your door with a pizza, and we'll take it

to your school." He held up a hand, stopping her protest. "Six o'clock. See you then." He turned and disappeared into his side of the duplex, leaving Meg to wonder what had just happened. Had she agreed to a date or a work session?

And which did she want it to be?

WHAT HAD HE been thinking, asking Meg to dinner? Actually insisting on it.

Shortly after six, Finn followed her toward what looked like an old house converted to a school. He knew what he'd been thinking, or rather feeling: lonely. His usual active dating life had paled lately, and most of his friends had families to keep them busy.

Plus, Meg was pretty. He looked at her now, punching a code into the keypad lock at the door of the big old house, which according to the sign was the Coastal Kids Early Learning Center, and admiration filled him.

She was competent and successful, here in her element. That alone drew him to her. Of course, she was attractive in other ways, too. Right now, she wore a skirt made of some kind of athletic material that flared out around her pretty legs. Just a plain red T-shirt, but it showed off her figure. And those flat sandals that all the young women wore now.

Toenails painted red. Nice.

She'd always been a pretty girl, but she'd blossomed into a beautiful woman.

And he didn't need to focus on that. "So this is your school," he said as they walked in.

She flipped on the lights and gestured toward the glassed-in office. "Yep. My joy and my frustration. I'm not even going into my office, because I know there's a ton of paperwork waiting for me there." She sounded a little breathless, and he wasn't sure what that was about. "We're getting ready for a new school year. Come on, we can use my daughter's classroom."

They climbed the central staircase. Kid-friendly pictures and posters decorated the walls, and when they went into the classroom, he was taken with the bright primary colors and tiny chairs. He put the pizza down on the big teacher's desk and walked around the room, looking at everything— the different play areas, the easels, the bright carpet with a rocking chair in front of it for story time.

Meg rummaged in the cupboards until she found paper plates, forks and napkins. She brought them to one end of a long table and served up pieces of pizza. "Dinner's ready," she joked.

He started over and then a bulletin board of photos caught his eye. One was labeled Miss Kayla, and he studied it for a moment. "She's really grown up, isn't she?"

"It happened too fast." Meg looked wistful as she handed him pizza and one of the sodas they'd picked up. "She was the center of my world for so long. I miss having that closeness, that sense of purpose."

He wanted to know whether she dated, whether there'd been anyone serious since she'd been widowed. She was the kind of woman who should have a boyfriend at least, maybe a husband.

She touched his back as she moved past him to grab a soda for herself, and the heat of her hand traveled right through his shirt to his skin, and then to his heart. What was wrong with him?

"You never had kids, did you?"

He shook his head. "I'm not the fatherly type."

"Any regrets?" She was looking at him, really looking. Like she cared about the answer, and it was refreshing. He hadn't realized how bored he was with his usual young, self-centered dates until this moment.

"Sometimes I have regrets." And he didn't want to talk about it. Didn't want to feel this warmth in his chest, this out-of-breath sensation. He took a bite of pizza, still standing, and scanned the room. "Let's use this big whiteboard. You have markers?"

"Um, sure." She handed him one.

He'd go into the teacher mode he used when he taught creative writing. That was the way to do it: keep things impersonal, professional. "Now, tell me anything you know about your story."

"I know nothing," she said, setting her plate aside and slumping, crossing those pretty legs. "I'm never going to be able to finish this thesis, especially in the short time I have."

He wanted to put his arms around her, comfort her. To clasp her against him and see how well they fit together. "Don't think about the time. Not to be all Zen about it, but just be here now with me." He stood at the board, marker poised. "Just one thing you thought you might not mind putting into the story."

"Don't you want to eat your pizza?"

"You're stalling." He took another bite and wiped his hands. "I'm used to eating and working. Tell me one idea."

She sipped her soda and traced lines in the condensation with the tip of a finger. "Well... I *thought* of writing about a girl with scoliosis, like Kayla had." She looked at him quickly and then went back to the finger painting, as if she was scared to know what he thought.

"Great idea." He wanted to encourage her, and would have tried to be positive about anything she said, but that *was* a great idea. Straight from her warm heart. He focused on writing it down, because he didn't need to be thinking about Meg's warmth and all her other assets. "What interests you about that?"

She was watching him, studying his face, and her own cheeks went pink. Like she'd forgotten what she was about to say. Like he had an effect on her, similar to the one she was having on him.

He restrained the *yes!* and the arm pump he felt inside, stood still, looked at the whiteboard. Like a teacher, waiting; not like an average ordinary guy who wanted to take her out on a real date.

She cleared her throat. "I'm not sure exactly what happened to Kayla, but middle school was a misery. Peer pressure and bullying. She's never opened up about it."

He wrote all that down. "Would she tell you if you asked?"

"I don't think so. She doesn't like to talk about it."

"Would she do a sensitivity read?" He saw her puzzled look and explained. "That's when you're writing about someone different from yourself, usually someone of a different race or age or ability level. You get someone who's in that group you're writing about to read it and tell you what you got wrong."

"You know… I bet she *would* do that." Meg sat up straighter. "Maybe that's why I've been so blocked. I didn't want to make her feel bad or infringe on her territory or be a helicopter mom. And I want to get it just right."

She cared so much, and he admired that about her.

He couldn't resist walking over to rub her shoulder a little. Just to relax her, he told himself, but the feel of her arm underneath his hand made him want more. A lot more. He covered his totally inappropriate feelings with a chuckle. "Yeah, an idea that close to home would be enough to block anyone. But if you don't have those things in the way, what could be elements of the story?"

The ideas poured out of her then. A dog, a mean girl, a support group. Coming of age, dealing with puberty at the same time you discovered you'd have to wear a brace for several years.

They carried on brainstorming until the whole whiteboard was covered with notes. At some point she grabbed another marker and stood at the board with him, adding lines and arrows to link ideas.

It was good working with her, fun. More fun than he'd had in a long time.

When they finally wound down, she studied the whiteboard and then reached over and patted his arm. "You have no idea what this means to me. You've fixed it!"

She was standing right in front of him. If he stepped forward a couple of inches, he could pull her into his arms, embrace her from behind.

With iron control, he took a step backward. Another. "Don't be premature. You still have work to do. You brought your laptop, right?"

She looked over her shoulder at him, nodded. Her eyes were half-closed. Had she been thinking about him the way he was thinking about her?

"Get it out." He kept his voice steady. *Be professional.* "We'll put things in order now. Then we can give you a task for each day."

The dreamy look fell from her face and was replaced by anxiety. "I have two weeks."

"You can do it." They kept working, and by the time he handed back her computer, there was a rough outline of the story. Which made him happy, because he'd helped her. For other reasons, too, reasons he didn't want to name, so he stood and started cleaning up the remains of the pizza. The feelings he was having about Meg were disturbing. He wanted, no, *needed*, for them to stop.

She studied the screen, her earlier anxious expression replaced with relief. "I *can* do it. You're a miracle worker." She stood and threw her arms around him.

He hesitated, then returned the hug, then wished he hadn't because of how great she felt in his arms. He loosened his grasp quickly, leaned back with his hands still on her arms and studied her happy face. "Glad to be of help."

Her color was high and her eyes went dark. He expected her to push him away, but she didn't. Instead, her gaze dropped to his lips for the shortest instant.

His chest felt tight. Up this close, he could see her thick lashes and the gold flecks in her green eyes. His pulse hammered.

He leaned forward. It would be a mistake, but he really, really wanted to kiss her. He couldn't fight it anymore.

Footsteps pounded up the stairs. "Who's there? The school is closed. I have the police on speed dial..." A silhouette appeared in the door, then the overhead lights switched on. "Mom! What are you doing?"

CHAPTER THREE

"You were kind of rude to him," Meg said to her daughter. After they'd left the school, all three of them, Finn had headed back to the duplex. Meg and Kayla were strolling by the bay.

The sun was setting, casting a golden light. Clouds dotted the horizon, gray lined with silver, and all of the beauty was mirrored in the bay. Fishing boats, dark shapes now, poked their masts into the sky, and a squat Chesapeake Bay lighthouse stood like a friendly sentinel over the town.

Meg inhaled the salty bay air. The lonely, haunting cry of a loon echoed, and she huddled into her sweater, more for the comfort than the warmth.

She was concerned about her daughter, who'd never seen Meg in even a slightly romantic situation before. That was because she hadn't been in one, but clearly it was long overdue. She'd *really* wanted Finn to kiss her. Her skin still felt hot, her heart rate elevated, her stomach full of butterflies. Who knew she had it in her to feel this way, after so long, and at her age?

But her daughter was her priority. She glanced over at Kayla. Good. The bay was working its magic on her, calming her down, mitigating what Meg thought she'd seen.

Then Kayla's eyes met hers and Meg realized they were as stormy as the bay was calm. "Maybe I *was* rude, and I'm sorry for that," she said, "but you were kissing him!"

"Not quite." Meg didn't want to get into the intricacies of what she had and hadn't done. The truth was, she and Finn had been about to kiss. Meg had wanted to, and surprisingly enough, Finn had seemed to share the feeling. The desire in his eyes had been a balm for the part of her that still hurt, so many years after Randy's death.

"He was helping me with my thesis," she explained. "You know how blocked I've been, and he's such an experienced writer."

Kayla narrowed her eyes. "C'mon, Mom. You expect me to believe that?"

Meg blew out a sigh as they continued to walk along the bike path. No bikes were out this late, but a few couples strolled ahead of them. They were nearing the tiny downtown of Pleasant Shores. Up ahead, the door of the Gusty Gull opened, light and noise and laughter spilling out as a happy, tipsy group emerged.

This was the trouble with grown children: they thought they knew how their parents should act and live. Plus, for all these years, it had been just her and Kayla. No wonder Kayla was upset at the thought that her mother might get involved with someone she didn't like.

Meg studied her daughter. Her long blond hair blew in the bay breeze. She wore casual shorts and her usual loose T-shirt, almost as if she were trying to hide her pretty figure. She was uncomfortable around men and shied away from relationships. Part of it had to do with her scoliosis, which had put a crimp into her experience of high school, when most girls started to date. But was part of it from something negative she'd sensed from Meg and Randy's marriage?

"There were a few sparks between us—you're right," she

said. "Nothing that'll amount to anything, but I'll admit, it felt nice."

"I don't trust him. He's a lawyer."

"And a novelist," Meg said, "and very successful at both." In an effort to soothe the awkwardness, she'd gotten permission from Finn to tell Kayla about his pen name.

Kayla hadn't been impressed. "He was hiding something about Dad," Kayla said now.

That startled Meg. "What do you mean?" There was a lot Kayla didn't know about her father, or at least, Meg hoped she didn't know it.

Kayla waved a hand and looked away. "Just a sense I had. Anyway, doesn't he date all kinds of women, younger women? You've shown me a couple of pictures over the years of him at charity functions, and he was always with a different woman." Her voice was troubled.

Her daughter's words hammered at the pleasure Meg had felt being close to Finn, sensing his interest and desire. Had it all been for show, a practiced routine? "He had a coldhearted family, honey," she said. "Maybe that's why he never committed to one woman. Which is sad, but it's really not for us to judge. He's here for two weeks, to finish a book, and that's all."

They turned and headed through downtown, past Goody's ice cream shop, doing a brisk business. The toy store and the bookstore, Lighthouse Lit, were both still open at this hour, the proprietors catching the last few weeks of summer business.

"Oh, Mom," Kayla said, taking her arm and drawing close as they walked. "I want you to be happy. I really do. If you want to date, date! I'd never stand in your way unless I thought you'd get hurt. I just don't think he's the right man."

Meg hugged her daughter. "I appreciate your taking care

of me. I really do," she said gently. "And this little flirtation with Finn isn't important. But you know I have to make my own decisions and live my own life."

Kayla pulled away. "I still feel like he's hiding something," she said.

Meg lifted both hands, palms up. "You're welcome to ask him any questions you like while he's here. In fact, maybe you should, for your own peace of mind. But as for me, I'm just grateful he got me unblocked on my thesis, and I'm going to spend the next two weeks writing it."

And trying *not* to think about the handsome man on the other side of the wall, clacking away at his noisy typewriter. The man who'd *almost* kissed her.

THE DAY AFTER he'd nearly kissed Meg, Finn found himself in the passenger seat of her car.

It wasn't what he intended. He shouldn't be here.

But he'd had to check on her this morning, hadn't he, to make sure she and her daughter weren't at odds after Kayla had burst in on them—fortunately or unfortunately, Finn kept alternating.

She'd waved off his worries and introduced him to her round sausage of a dog, Oscar. Of course he'd had to sit down and get to know the chubby fellow—he liked dogs—and they'd ended up talking about her book a little more. He was pleased that she was finding inspiration in the work they'd done last night.

He'd started to leave, explaining that he wanted to get out into the country and gather some impressions for his novel. He planned to set up shop and write for a couple of hours at a nearby nature reserve. "Good inspiration," he'd said.

"That's interesting." She'd looked thoughtful. "I should

do that sometime, too, since I'm setting my story around here."

What could he do except invite her to go along? She'd hemmed and hawed, saying she needed to walk the dog, but she'd finally agreed. And then insisted on driving, saying that she saw the sights and sounds here every day while he was less familiar.

So here they were, cruising along the narrow highway that ran up the coast. Overhead, the sky was a variable gray, light peeking through in spots, clouds moving rapidly from east to west. The bay, when he glimpsed it through the trees, was gray and choppy.

A rusty pickup passed them, its engine loud, a refrigerator unit on the back suggesting a haul of fish.

"Lots of traffic today," she remarked.

He looked back, then forward. The truck that had passed was disappearing in the distance, and there were a couple more cars behind them. Nothing coming the other way. "This is traffic?"

She smiled. "Okay, city boy. It's a lot of traffic for us, for a weekday."

They rode in comfortable silence for a couple of miles, but something was bothering him.

"You're sure Kayla wasn't too upset?" he asked.

Meg smiled wryly. "I talked her down. Felt like she was the mom and I was the guilty teenager."

"That's how I felt, too." They both laughed, but his own laughter was nervous, and hers sounded that way, as well.

Talking over Kayla's reaction was one thing. Talking about how close they'd come to kissing each other…that was what they were skirting.

He knew that bringing it up could evoke more of the same feelings, and he couldn't do that. He'd never been

especially wise about women, but even he knew it would
be a mistake to actually kiss her.

He couldn't get close to her when he knew something so
awful about her late husband, something he had to conceal.
And anyway, Meg was different. She wasn't a flavor-of-
the-week date. She was the kind of woman you stuck with,
only Finn couldn't stick.

"Here we are," she said, turning off the highway to a dirt
road and driving back through a stand of pines. She parked
by a rustic pavilion that held several tables. "This okay?"

"Perfect. Thank you for driving."

When he got out, the soft, humid salt air seemed to wrap
around him. Birds chirped steadily, interspersed with the
occasional loud *caw-caw-caw*. Interesting, he thought, taking a quick video with his phone to capture the sights and
sounds. He'd have to find out what types of birds nested
here, their habits. A breeze rustled through the leaves and
long-needled pines, cooling the sweat that had instantly
formed on his skin.

It didn't feel like home, no. He'd only visited this part
of the shore now and then. But it did feel welcoming, hear-
kening back to a simpler time before his world had filled
with clients and cases and deadlines. He'd been raised for
responsibility—"to whom much is given, much will be
required" was his father's favorite explanation of his own
hard work despite the family wealth—but the weight of
Finn's work had grown heavier on his shoulders. Especially his legal work.

And especially since the fiasco of Randy's unusual orders just prior to his death.

They settled down quickly, Finn at a picnic table, Meg
in a folding chair she'd pulled out of her trunk.

Finn swatted at a fly, then winced as another one bit him.

"Uh-oh. I have bug spray somewhere." She opened her trunk again, rummaged around and pulled out a spray bottle. "You do me and I'll do you." Her cheeks went pink as she handed him the bottle.

He laughed. "You'd better be glad I'm an old friend. Some guys might take that the wrong way." He sprayed her shorts-clad legs, back and front, her arms. "You'd better do your own face," he said. "Hold out your hands."

She did, and he sprayed some repellent into them. As she ran her hands lightly over her face, he lifted her long hair and squirted a little on the back of her neck.

She could have done that herself, too, of course. But he wanted to see the pretty, vulnerable back of her neck. Wanted to touch her soft, wavy hair that always smelled like flowers.

Her face was still flushed as she took the bottle and did a much more businesslike job on him.

They settled again, with laptops, and Meg got right to work. She typed steadily, smiling sometimes, occasionally consulting a small notebook or looking off into the woods.

Finn tried to focus on his own book in progress, but his concentration was spotty. Something about Meg reawakened his desire for love and a family, something he couldn't even consider with her because of the dark secret he knew and had to keep. He took a couple of deep breaths and then refocused on his screen.

Much later, she stood and stretched, and the sight of her brought him out of his reverie and back, with a bang, into the present moment. Wow. Meg was simply lovely, glowing with joy.

"I'm going to take a stroll through the woods," she said. "Want to come?"

Of course he did. They locked their things in the car and then headed down one of the paths.

It was actually a great way to get more of a feel for the area's natural beauty and wildlife. He looked up at the sky, hoping to spot one of the bald eagles that nested in the area. Instead, he saw a heron, headed toward the marsh, its *awk-awk-awk* distinctive over the chorus of crickets and frogs and smaller birds. A squirrel scrabbled up and around a tree trunk, chased by its friend or mate. Small pools of standing, brackish water alternated with marsh grass growing in clumps. A couple of turtles plopped lazily into the water at their approach.

Meg chatted happily about her project, and he smiled at her enthusiasm.

She laughed up at him. "I'm going on and on, aren't I? I'm just excited to finally have the ideas flowing. Thank you so much for helping me." She reached out and touched his arm.

He reached for her hand, clasped it and didn't let go. They walked a few more steps and paused, and then she turned to him, her face confused. And concerned. And interested.

He shouldn't have done it, but he couldn't resist those full, beautiful lips. He pulled her close and kissed her.

CHAPTER FOUR

MEG HAD NEVER felt anything like Finn's kiss. It wasn't the careless, passing thing she remembered from her marriage; he kissed her like she was the most precious and wonderful creature in the universe.

His hair. It was thick and wiry and she wanted to touch it. She *did* touch it, and ran her hands through it, and her fingers felt alive, supersensitive.

His lips were warm on hers and just firm enough, and electricity seemed to sizzle through her lips and into her heart. Waves of it danced there, shimmering through her stomach and veins.

And they kept on kissing.

Rather than rushing toward some other motive, Finn kissed her in a leisurely way, as if they had all the time in the world. Or maybe it was just that time stood still as they remained in place, kissing, kissing, kissing.

Finally, he lifted his head and looked down at her, one corner of his mouth turning up.

She sucked in air. "Wow. I haven't done that in a long time." *Ever*, she amended silently. *I haven't kissed like that, ever.*

He touched her lips with a gentle finger and then leaned closer. "It's like riding a bike," he said against her mouth. "You don't forget."

"I...don't think...it's like riding a bike."

He dropped a kiss on her again.

"At all. It's not like that at all." She reached for him then, clinging on, head spinning, legs weak.

From the direction of the parking lot, a car door slammed and children's voices rose.

"We might be getting company," she said. Reluctantly, she pulled away from the warmth of him.

He gave a low growl and pulled her against him. The children's voices came closer.

She stepped back, regretful. "We should go. I have a reputation to uphold in this town," she said. "Really. I can't have any of my kids' parents finding me kissing the mysterious stranger."

"Of course." He brushed a hand over his hair, held out a hand to her and then pulled it back. "No hand-holding, either, I guess."

"Right. Sorry."

So they walked back side by side in what felt like a comfortable silence.

Until they got to the parking lot and she looked at his face. What was that expression? Why was his forehead wrinkled like that? Why was he looking at the ground and not at her?

The ride home was quiet, but not quite as comfortable. Halfway there, he cleared his throat. "Meg, I'm sorry."

"No need—"

"Really, I am," he interrupted. His voice sounded flat. "I don't want... I'm in no position to have a relationship."

She tried to tense against the hurt of that, but it hit her anyway, square in the gut. Why wasn't he in a position to have a relationship when he seemed to be as rich as Warren Buffet? Was one of his usual arm-candy women serious, or was it just that he didn't care for her?

Hurtful phrases from the past came back to her in Randy's voice. "You're looking a little heavy" and "Can't you loosen up some?" and "Boy, it's obvious you don't have any experience." Over the years, she'd managed to wipe away that ugliness, or so she'd thought. But there it was again, right under the surface, released by another handsome man.

"I'm sorry," he said again. "I really don't want to hurt your feelings. You're a great person—"

"Stop." She said it sharply as she swerved to avoid a Sika deer. "You don't need to pretend. I'll be fine."

HE OPENED HIS mouth a dozen times to speak and then closed it. What could he say?

He could tell her he'd lied, that he *did* want a relationship. He hadn't, before coming to Pleasant Shores, but these few days with Meg had opened a window and he was looking through it, looking at something beautiful: love and family and connection.

He wanted a relationship, if he could have one with her.

But he couldn't, not with what he knew. He couldn't destroy her image of her past. She deserved her memories.

He'd loved kissing her. She was so sweet, yet so ardent and honest and real. They'd fit together perfectly.

Not only that, but she'd melted into him as if she wanted to be there, as if she belonged there. Not trying to jump him for sex, like some of the women he dated; not pretending to be more passionate than she was in the hopes of impressing him, getting him to take her somewhere exotic.

Meg was real, and that had made kissing her rare and sweet and hot.

The thought of never having that opportunity again made his chest hurt and filled his head and heart with despair.

Could he tell her the truth? She was strong, right? She could handle it.

But he'd been raised to take the burden on his own shoulders, not hand it off to someone else. Right now, there was only one living person who knew what Randy had really been like: Finn. And he couldn't tear down the man's false image. Not for Meg, and not for her daughter.

They pulled into the driveway, still silent, and he got out of the car and came around to open her door, years of drilled-in good manners coming to his aid. He took the cooler she'd brought and carried it toward the duplex, walking behind her, silent and miserable.

There was someone on the porch. Kayla. She stood waiting for them, arms crossed, unsmiling, Oscar beside her. "I need to talk to both of you," she said.

CHAPTER FIVE

MEG CLIMBED THE STEPS, beckoning for Finn to follow her, and frowned at Kayla. "What's this about?"

Oscar must have heard the worry in her tone. He jumped and propped his front legs on her shin, and she reached down to pet him, his soft ears a comfort.

"I'm sorry, Mom." Kayla put a hand on Meg's shoulder, her face distressed. "I just don't think... Well, you need to know about... You said I was welcome to talk to him. Well, I found this, and it made me feel like I had to."

She held up a notebook, brightly flowered, with a little gold lock and strap that had been opened.

"Your diary?" It had been years since Meg had seen it, but she remembered Kayla writing in it secretly, right around the time Randy had died.

"Yes, I dug it up," Kayla said, "because I wanted to see if I was remembering something right. I was." She paused. "I wrote down what he said to Dad."

"What he said to..." She looked over at Finn. "Do you know what she's talking about?"

He didn't answer. He was rubbing a hand over the back of his neck, his brow wrinkled, eyes on Kayla.

"When did you hear him say something to your father?" Meg asked Kayla. "Wasn't I always there?"

"There was a time, in the hospital," Kayla said. "You'd

stopped in the cafeteria for coffee, and I went on up. He was there." She nodded toward Finn.

Meg's heart sank for no reason she could name. "Go on."

"I heard them arguing," Kayla said. "He was yelling at Dad. Dad was sick and weak, and he was yelling at him."

Again she looked at Finn. He pressed his lips together and gazed off toward the bay.

"He said, 'I'll take care of it and I won't tell Meg.' Dad said something else, so quiet—he was weak—and Finn said, 'I'll give her the money.'"

Meg tried to process the words. That Randy had wanted to keep something from her was no surprise. But the rest... "What money?" she asked, looking directly at Finn. "Do you know what she's talking about?"

Finn frowned into the distance for another few seconds. She saw his shoulders rise and fall as he took a deep breath and let it out. Then he turned and looked directly at Meg and then at Kayla. "We should get comfortable," he said. "It's a long story."

Meg just stood there while he pulled over a chair from his side of the duplex. He opened the cooler and handed around sodas. Once she and Kayla had sat down, he did, too.

There was a breeze, a warm one. A family of tourists carried beach chairs and hauled a wagon filled with buckets and toys, headed in the direction of the beach.

Finn cleared his throat and looked at Meg. "Are you sure you want to hear this? It might hurt you." He shifted his gaze to Kayla. "You, too."

"I want to know," Meg said instantly. And then she bit her lip and looked at her daughter. She'd always tried to honor Randy as Kayla's father, tried not to say a bad thing about him. "But honey, maybe you don't—"

"I want to know, too." Kayla glanced at Meg and then frowned at Finn. "I want to know what you did with Dad's money. Not for me—I'm fine—but Mom struggled so much…"

"Hey. We were okay." Meg patted her daughter's hand. "Let's hear Finn out."

He drew in a deep breath and let it out in a sigh. "Okay." Then he looked at the floor for so long that Meg thought he'd decided not to tell them. Her heart pounded. What was he remembering?

"Go ahead," she said. "We can take it." She reached over and squeezed Kayla's hand. "We're strong."

"I know you are." He looked into Meg's eyes, his own full of emotion.

She thought of their kiss. She had a feeling it was going to be their only one.

"I knew Randy had some flaws," Finn said. "He always did."

Meg nodded. "I knew that, too."

"Everyone has flaws." Kayla sounded impatient. "Get to the point."

"He… Well, there was an indiscretion."

Here it came. Meg glanced over at Kayla, concerned. Kayla had always held her father in such high esteem.

"What do you mean, an indiscretion?" Kayla asked.

He looked at Meg. "There was another woman," he said slowly. Then he paused. "I'm sorry to be the one to tell you."

"There was another…what?" Kayla's eyes were wide and shocked, and the color drained from her face.

Finn was quiet, as if letting them process it. Meg squeezed Kayla's hand.

Kayla looked at Meg, pulled her hand away and pressed a fist to her lips. "You're not even surprised," she choked out.

Meg's throat tightened, too, for Kayla. Seeing her daughter's pain made her own chest ache. "No," she said slowly, "I'm not surprised. I knew. Or was pretty sure, at least."

"You knew?" Finn stared at her. "I thought you idolized him."

"You never said a word!" Kayla burst out. "You always told me he was a good man. He *was* a good man. He was." But doubt had crept into her voice.

Unwelcome memories pushed themselves out of some closed chest in the back of her mind. Randy coming home late, saying he'd had a work meeting, smelling of alcohol and sometimes of a woman's perfume. Randy suddenly claiming their sex life was boring. Randy getting critical of her looks.

The signs had all been there, and she'd confronted him, but he'd denied it, over and over.

She tugged her mind back to the present, looked at her daughter's distressed face and then turned back to Finn. They needed to get through this. Kayla was going to be hurt, from the destruction of the image of her father, and while Kayla had asked for it, brought it on, Meg could have strangled Finn for what he was telling them.

But now that he'd started, he should finish. "Go on," she said. "What's this about money?"

"Yeah." Kayla's eyes narrowed. "Are you saying you gave Dad's money to…to some other woman?" Her voice rose to a squeak.

Oscar let out a woof and nudged at Kayla's leg, and she reached down to pet him.

Finn blew out a breath. "It's a complicated story."

"We have time to hear it," Meg said. She took a drink

of soda. Was she upset? Sort of—she didn't like the idea of Finn having some big secret about Randy—but she was beyond being surprised at anything her husband might have done. Truth to tell, she'd have left the man long before his death, except for Kayla.

The big disappointment was that Finn was involved in Randy's shenanigans. She'd thought he was better than that. "Maybe we all need a beer instead of soda," she suggested.

"Mom!"

Finn gave her a half smile. "If you're serious, I'd love one."

She went inside, half listening to see if he and Kayla talked, but the silence was deafening, so she hurried back out with three light beers. "All I've got," she apologized, handing them around.

Kayla cracked hers open. "We're waiting to hear," she said to Finn.

Meg pressed her lips together. Kayla wasn't near tears anymore, but her sharp tone betrayed her anger and pain.

If she thought Finn had taken money away from her family—which Meg still found hard to believe, even though he wasn't denying it—and she'd just learned her dad wasn't the paragon she'd always held him up to be...it couldn't be easy. Again, she reached over and squeezed Kayla's hand.

Finn set down his beer and leaned forward, elbows on knees. "As Randy's lawyer and friend, I visited him several times in the hospital. On my last visit, he clearly had something on his mind. When he explained that he'd gotten involved with a woman who was into drugs and down on her luck, I guess I did yell at him. We had heated words, at any rate."

Kayla's lips compressed into a thin line, but she didn't speak. Meg's muscles tightened. She didn't really want to hear the rest, nor did she want Kayla to hear it, but Pandora's box was open and there was no closing it.

"He told me he had bearer bonds in his desk drawer at work, and that he wanted them to go to her, to help her get her life together."

"Wow." Meg blew out a breath. So Randy had cared for his lover—one of them at least—enough to want to fund her recovery.

"Bearer bonds," Kayla said. "They're, what, not in anyone's name?"

"Right, so ownership can't be traced. They're not issued in the US any longer, but you can buy them in certain countries, and some banks will still cash them." He opened his mouth as if to say more and paused. "Anyway. There are a lot of legal issues I can explain if you're interested."

"He went to some trouble to do this." Meg was still struggling with the implications. Had Randy known he was dying earlier than he'd told her? How long had Finn known? As Randy's business lawyer, had he been involved in some shady overseas transaction?

"Apparently," Finn went on, "he'd promised to send her to rehab before he'd gotten sick."

"That's so wrong." Kayla's breathing was ragged, and her voice was thick. "Why should he pay for his mistress's problems when Mom had to struggle all these years?"

"I didn't struggle so much." Meg thought back to the years immediately following Randy's death. "We always had shelter and enough to eat, and eventually, everything got pretty comfortable."

The soothing words were for Kayla, and they were true. Inside, though, she was reeling about something else.

Finn had known all this, after they'd reconnected, and hadn't told her. He'd kissed her, knowing what a dupe she'd been. Knowing that he'd taken money that should legally be hers and Kayla's, and given it to some drugged-out other woman. She couldn't look at him.

"Let me finish," he said, and something in his voice made her look back at him. "I did go and find the bonds. They added up to about fifty thousand dollars, and that's what I gave to your dad's…whatever you want to call her."

"That's a lot!" Meg blurted out, indignant. "I didn't know he was holding back that kind of money." It was an amount that would certainly would have eased the way for them.

"It is," Finn agreed, even though it had to be pocket change to him at this point in his life. What did he know about the struggles an ordinary family faced? "I gave her that money," Finn said, "out of my own accounts. So you got all the money Randy had, including the bearer bonds. I cashed them out for you and included the money in the estate. It was only right. Especially with all the hospital bills and the debt Randy had gotten you into."

Meg stared at him. "You paid Randy's mistress out of your own pocket?"

"Yeah. It was the only thing I could figure out to do. I didn't want to disillusion you two when you were already grieving. Working on estates with our firm, believe me, I've seen plenty of that. It's an ongoing issue in the legal community. Sometimes it's better not to reveal everything you find out when going through the decedent's papers."

Kayla's anger seemed to have deflated. "That was… generous," she admitted. "I don't know how to feel. I thought…" Her voice broke, and she swallowed hard. "I thought Dad was better than that."

"Oh, honey," Meg said. "He was a good man in so many ways. He just didn't have the faithful gene." She met Finn's eyes. He knew. She was still glossing over Randy's flaws for Kayla's sake.

"I'm going to have to think about all this," Kayla said, standing. She turned to Finn. "Look, I'm sorry to have accused you of stealing. I guess I should be thankful for what you did."

"I'm not looking for thanks," he said quickly. "I'm just sorry you lived with this worry all these years."

"I didn't, not really. It was seeing you that piqued my memory." She looked at Meg. "Still, Mom...be careful, okay? I don't want you to get hurt."

"Of course. Thank you for caring so much." She stood and hugged her daughter, felt her shoulders shaking, and that made Meg's own eyes tear up.

When they finally let go, she leaned back, still holding Kayla's forearms. "We'll talk."

Kayla nodded and then hurried to her car.

She and Finn watched her go.

"Do you hate me for what I did?" he asked her.

"No! It was a generous thing. More than Randy deserved." She checked her own feelings to make sure she was telling the truth. She was. "Whatever happened to the woman?"

"She did go to rehab," he said. "And the money should have given her a little stake to get on her feet afterward, as well. But I didn't stay in touch."

She nodded, her head spinning.

"Meg, now you know why I said I wasn't in a position to have a relationship. I didn't feel like I could, with that secret standing between us. And I didn't want to tell you the truth and break your bubble." He shook his head. "I should have known that you would be aware of Randy's issues and mistakes."

"I learned about them pretty quickly in the marriage." She sipped beer and stared out at the bay. "Stayed with him because of Kayla. It's an old familiar story."

They sat quietly for a few minutes, watching the gulls swoop, listening to their harsh cries.

"You're a good woman, Meg," he said. "A wonderful woman. You didn't deserve what Randy did."

"I don't know about that," she said.

She'd started to feel alive and attractive, with the wonderful positive attention from Finn. But today, she'd been plunged back into the reality that she hadn't been enough for Randy. She reached down for Oscar and pulled him into her lap.

After a little dog therapy, she stood. "I have a lot to think about," she said, "so I'm going to say good-night." Before she could change her mind, she turned and carried the dog and her bag into the house.

THE KNOCK ON her door a week and a half later made Meg jump up. She started to hurry toward it and then deliberately slowed her steps. It probably wasn't Finn, and even if it was, he was probably just coming to say a polite goodbye.

She'd seen him packing his car earlier. She'd thought he planned an early departure tomorrow, but maybe he'd decided to leave a day sooner.

And that would be fine. She drew in a deep breath, composed her features and went to the door.

Seeing him threw her emotions into turmoil again, especially when he smiled that crooked smile.

And then he said the last thing she'd ever expected: "Want to go on a boat ride to the art festival over on Teaberry Island?"

She tilted her head to one side. "What? I thought you were leaving?"

"I am. It's my last day, and I take off early tomorrow. But I wanted to clear the deck so we…" He paused. "Well, I, but hopefully we, can go check this summer festival out. Get a little inspiration, you know?"

He was springing this on her last minute and she didn't know why, didn't know what to say.

Time had sped by since Kayla had confronted Finn after the nature reserve day. The day they'd kissed. Meg had worked like crazy her thesis, finally gotten it done and turned in. And though she and Finn had greeted each other going in and out, and one night had shared burgers and a beer at the Gusty Gull, there hadn't been any more romance between them.

"Please?" he said. "I don't want to leave without spending at least a little more time with you." He checked the time on his phone. "Plus, the ferry leaves for the island in forty-five minutes, and we have two seats reserved."

She felt her eyebrows shoot up to her hairline. "We *do*? You were that sure I'd go?"

"I've always been a hopeful guy, but no pressure. You can say no."

Could she really, though?

If she went, it would mean one thing; if she refused, it would mean another. But she wasn't ready to make that choice. "I'll go," she said slowly, "but listen, this doesn't mean… Well, it doesn't mean more romance. I'll go as your friend. If you want me to."

Then she felt like she'd been forward. Maybe he'd just come over as a friend after all.

An emotion flickered across his face and was gone. "That's fine," he said. "We'll go as friends."

But you could hardly take a boat ride to Teaberry Island on a summer day that didn't feel at least a little romantic. The waves of the bay sprayed mist against Meg's face, and she laughed. Finn reached over to wipe it off and his hand lingered. The gulls swooped overhead and the sun warmed their backs.

The island was an artist's paradise. So naturally beautiful, with mostly small houses and a cute tiny downtown, and rows of paintings and crafts on the lawn of the town park. He bought her a stained glass suncatcher shaped like a crab.

She imagined a story about a kid living on a tiny island, loving her home but wanting to see the big world, too. She told Finn about it and he lifted a brow, nodded, asked her questions to get her to think it through.

Wouldn't it be wonderful to have that type of connection with someone, that meeting of the minds, on a regular basis? Maybe even full-time?

Finn held her hand a couple of times, and poignant regret stabbed her heart. She enjoyed this man's company, cared what happened to him. Liked the way the sun shone on his hair and made his eyes sparkle.

They sparkled more when he was looking at her. Twice, she caught him doing that, studying her like he was memorizing her, but he made no move to kiss her.

And after all, that was what she'd requested: just friends. Right?

It had to be that way. Jumping into a superficial relationship with Finn now, when he was leaving, when his life was so different from hers...well, it just didn't make sense.

The boat ride home took them into the sunset. She didn't want the day to end, didn't want him to go, but she knew it wasn't meant to be between them.

After they'd left the boat and were strolling through the quiet streets toward home, Finn spoke. "Meg, since I came here I've developed feelings for you. You've always been a terrific person, but now…" He raised his hands, palms up, and a smile lifted one side of his mouth. "I've fallen for you. I don't know how else to say it."

His words seemed to suck the air from her lungs. They weren't what she'd expected to hear. She studied his face.

He seemed sincere, but it was such a rearrangement of all she'd thought about herself that she couldn't quite wrap her mind around it.

"I'd like to pursue that," he went on, "although I understand if you're not interested after all the water that's passed under the bridge."

She looked away from his handsomeness, his appeal, and let her gaze sweep out over the bay, its blue reflecting the sky. She saw a few sailboats, not as many as last week. Tourist season was ending.

So much had gone on in these past two weeks, from Finn to her creative work. She was on the verge of achieving her dream.

A man had derailed her dreams once before, dreams of a good, happy family. And then she'd lost him, and she'd had to shelve her dreams in the interest of just plain surviving. How could she know Finn wouldn't do the same?

For better or worse, she was wiser now, more cautious.

When she'd figured out what she wanted to say, she turned to him. "I understand why you did what you did all those years ago, about Randy. And today's been wonderful. But right now… I just need time to absorb everything. And I have my work to do." She lifted her hands in apology. "I appreciate you, and everything you've done, but I'm not ready for more just now."

CHAPTER SIX

A MONTH LATER, at midmorning, Finn approached the biggest redbrick building at Bayshore University. The air was a little cooler now. Instead of tourists, students dominated the town just a few miles up the coast from Pleasant Shores.

Amid the small crowd walking out of the building, he spotted her.

Meg had the biggest smile on her face. She was dressed in a skirt and jacket, wearing heels, and she looked…amazing.

The man at her side was a good-looking guy, too, and they laughed together.

Primal possessive anger rose up in him, but he forced it away. It wasn't surprising she'd be with someone. She could have flocks of men around her if she wanted to. Maybe he should put the flowers back in his car.

But he'd brought them, and he cared, and he wasn't going to give up without a fight. He'd respect her choice, of course, but he knew what it was to complete a big project. At any rate, he'd congratulate her. He strode toward them, and when he got close, called her name.

She looked over and her eyes widened. She paused, then turned back to the man. Finn kept coming closer, so he heard what she said to him: "See you. Thanks for everything, Dr. Hypes."

"I'll call you," he said. "See how the degree's sitting with you."

She looked surprised. "Um, I guess."

It was a little endearing that she didn't know the guy was hitting on her. He pulled his flowers from behind his back just to make sure the guy understood he wasn't the only one interested in how the degree was sitting with Meg.

"The thesis really was terrific. One of the best I've read." The man touched her arm, glanced at Finn and walked away.

Meg's eyes sparkled with newfound confidence. It looked good on her.

"I wanted to congratulate you for finishing your defense," he said. "I assume you passed?"

"I did," she said slowly. "How did you know where and when?"

"A little bird told me." He handed the flowers to her. "Congratulations. That's quite an accomplishment."

She took a deep whiff and smiled. "A bird named Kayla?"

He nodded. "She seemed to feel she'd been hard on me. So when I called her, she was kind enough to give me the information. Plus, she was sorry she couldn't be here herself." Apparently, Kayla was needed to supervise the preschool in Meg's absence.

"Thank you for the roses," she said. "They're beautiful." She inhaled them again, and the pleasure on her face tightened every muscle in his body. He wanted to see that look on her face every day.

"I remembered that you liked them." On their one fancy date together, back in high school, he'd brought her a few roses, and she'd loved it.

Of course, he'd told Randy, who'd taken advantage of the insider knowledge to win her heart.

He brought his other hand from behind his back: a small bottle of champagne in a shiny gift bag. "Do you think we can find a spot to share a glass of this? I have cups." He held the bag open to reveal a couple of plastic wineglasses. "I scoped out a secluded spot over by the little bridge."

"It's worth a try." She smiled up at him. "I do feel like celebrating."

Heat flickered inside him as he led her to where a stone bridge arched over a creek. Beside it were a couple of benches, with bushes blocking the main quad from view. Thankfully, aside from a few students visible in the distance, it was deserted.

"What if I get in trouble and they rescind my degree?" She was joking, looking around, and he loved it, loved how relaxed and fun she was.

"You're not really nervous." He popped the cork and the champagne flowed.

Laughing, she caught it in her wineglass and then held his up to fill.

He raised a glass to her. "To a successful woman on her way to bigger successes."

They both sipped, and she raised an eyebrow. "You spared no expense," she said. "But I can't believe you came back for this."

"I care about you, Meg. A lot. In fact…" He hesitated. "I'm house hunting in Pleasant Shores."

She gazed at him over the rim of her glass, then took another sip. "You're looking for a second home?"

"Maybe a first home," he said. "Since the place is starting to become a writer's paradise."

She smiled. "I guess it is. I, for one, am planning to finish my book in my free time from running Coastal Kids."

"I'm glad." She had talent, and he wanted her to succeed. Wanted to help her, but he didn't know if he'd get the chance. "Hey, listen. Would you consider coming with me to look at houses?"

She tilted her head to one side, like she wasn't sure what he was asking.

He wasn't sure himself.

Her expression cleared and she brushed her hands together briskly. "I guess it *would* be good for you to have a local perspective. I'm happy to provide it for you."

That was Meg, never assuming it was her own appeal that would make him want to be with her. "It would," he said. "But also… I was hoping if you helped look, you'd have a little stake in the place. Hoping you'd spend a little time there."

Her eyes widened. He could see a pulse quicken in her very lovely neck. "What do you mean?"

Here it was. Time to share the vision that had been haunting him ever since he'd left Pleasant Shores a month ago. "I mean, I'd like to host you for dinner. Find a place with a deck where we could watch the sunset and have a glass of wine. One with some good office space so we could write together. Wood floors, so we could dance in the moonlight, all by ourselves."

Her breath caught. "I… Wow. I don't know what to say."

"You don't have to say anything. Just come help a guy find a house."

She considered, and a tiny smile rose on her face. "You do make it sound appealing to spend some time there."

He pulled her into his arms. As she smiled up at him, as he stroked her hair, he felt the secrets and the pain of the past slip away.

He hoped they'd spend more than a little time there. Hoped they'd spend a lot of time.

Maybe even the rest of their lives.

* * * * *

*Read on for a sneak peek at the final book in
Lee Tobin McClain's The Off Season series,*
Forever on the Bay, *coming this spring!*

CHAPTER ONE

EVAN STONE TIPPED back his chair in the middle of the Gusty Gull, laughing at someone's dumb joke. Here among friends and off duty, he could relax. There'd been a time when even being in the vicinity of a bar had been a risk, but not anymore.

He tapped his thumb on his thigh in rhythm with the music—eighties pop, "Girls Just Want to Have Fun"—and breathed in the smell of fried fish and crab cakes. Life was good in his adopted Chesapeake hometown, and he was content.

He felt his phone vibrate and glanced at the face of it.

Got a minute? Need some help.

He did a double take, stood, and strode out into the chill of an early-March night. Cassandra Thomas, his late best friend's younger sister, never, but never, asked for help.

What's wrong, can you talk? he texted back and then, too impatient to wait for an answer, tapped the audio call button.

She answered immediately. "I'm okay, I'm sorry to bother you." Her voice sounded fine, just a little… funny.

His tight shoulders relaxed some, and he leaned against the bar's outside wall. "What's going on?"

"I'm worried about Mom."

"She's gotten worse?" Cassie's mother struggled with anxiety and depression, and it had gotten more acute since the death of her only son, Cassie's brother.

Cassie sighed into the phone. "Not exactly. It's just, since I didn't get this artist-in-residence job I applied for, she's canceling her trip. Do you think you could talk to her, reassure her that I'll be safe staying here in Harrisburg? She really needs to get away, and she might listen to you."

"*Are* you safe there?" Cassie had lived with her brother after college—Josh and Cassie had been unusually close—but after he'd been killed four months ago, she'd moved back to her mother's home so they could help each other cope.

"Yes. Yes, I think I'm safe."

"You don't sound sure." Cassie was nine years younger than Evan was, but he'd grown up next door. Since Josh was his best friend, Evan had spent a lot of time at their house, and he could recognize the doubt in Cassie's voice.

"No, I know I'll be fine here. And I get it, why Mom's so anxious. She's afraid for me. She only has one child left. But she's not getting better sitting around thinking about what happened."

"Any signs of the guy who…" He trailed off, not wanting to say it.

"Noooo…" Her voice was uncertain. There was a pause. "No," she said more firmly. "I mean, only in my nightmares."

His gut clenched. "I'm sorry, Cassie."

"I know you are." Her voice was husky now. "We all are. And Mom really needs this trip, but I made the mistake of telling her I thought I spotted the, um, the intruder, once, and—"

"You spotted him?" Evan's hand went sweaty on the phone. "Where?"

"I *thought* I spotted him. I'm sure, now, I was wrong. It

was at a park where I was walking Ace. I'm fine, but Mom's turned into the queen of all worriers."

Evan blew out a breath. The last time he'd seen Cassie and her mother had been at Josh's funeral. Her mom, barely able to contain her grief. Her mom's straight-backed live-in fiancé on one side, and Cassie on the other, a pale shadow of the lively woman she'd started to become with Josh's help.

"Did you tell the police you thought you spotted him?"

She made a disgusted noise. "No."

"Why not?"

"They've basically stopped working on the case. Whenever we call, they just pass us off to victim services."

The idea that no one was trying to find the thug who'd created this misery made a slow, angry fire simmer in his gut, but he'd think about that later. Right now, Cassie needed him.

She was twenty-eight but looked ten years younger and in terms of life experience, she *was* young. In some ways.

"Give Mom a call tomorrow, would you? Not tonight, she's upset."

"I'll talk to her. And...look, what if we could find you a low-cost rental here in Pleasant Shores? It's safe, and I'm here." As soon as he said it, he thought of all the reasons it wasn't a good idea.

"Hmm. Maybe. Josh and I loved it there when we were kids." She cleared her throat. "It would have to be *really* cheap, though, and take dogs."

"I'll ask around." Really cheap places in a waterfront community were rare, but it *was* the off-season.

"Thanks. Love you. Bye." Her voice was a husky whisper that sent an electrical surge down his spine. Which made him feel like a jerk.

Take care of her if anything happens to me, but don't

you dare try to get with her. Josh's prescient words echoed in Evan's mind as he pocketed his phone and turned back toward the door of the Gull.

He would call Cassie and Josh's mom tomorrow, but he doubted he could be convincing. The truth was, *he* worried about Cassie. He'd figured she was safe, living with her mom and burly stepfather-to-be, but if they left her alone in the family home in Harrisburg...

Cassie's mom had helped Evan out a lot over the years, and he cared about her. She needed to get away from the site of all her heartache. Cassie probably did too, for that matter. Evan blew out a sigh, thinking. He'd check online tomorrow, see if there was anything vacant near him, cheap, and safe. A tall order.

Evan's friend William ducked his head as he came out the door. "You left in a hurry. Everything okay?"

"Yeah. An old friend's sister, having some trouble." Evan led the way back to their table. He didn't feel like participating in the jovial conversation, not anymore, but he'd left his coat. "I should take off."

"Want a beer first?" It was a guy Evan didn't know well who'd stopped by the table. He held up a pitcher and a glass.

Evan's friends turned as one and glared at the newcomer.

"What?" the guy asked.

"It's fine. Chill," Evan said to his friends. He did feel a slight tug, more of a dryness in his throat that only alcohol would fix, but it was nothing unmanageable. He gestured at the table. "I'll finish my soda, but then I have to go. Early shift tomorrow." And a cop in a small town couldn't be late to work.

He sat down and the conversation got general, someone continuing a story he'd started, the rest listening and laughing.

"So your friend's sister is having trouble?" William asked, scooting his chair back away from the others.

"Yeah. Trying to find her a new place to stay." Evan debated whether to say more, but only for a minute. In the short time he'd known William, he'd come to trust him as much as he'd trust any man. "She needs to get away somewhere safe, make a fresh start, to get over the fact that her brother, my friend, was killed." He paused, took a drink of soda, and forced the memories and the regrets out of his mind. They'd been childhood best friends, and back then, Josh had basically saved him. Had tried to save him again when they were older, but Evan had pushed him away and they'd ended up running in different directions. Now that Josh was gone, Evan thought a lot about all the lost opportunities.

"Killed like in an accident, or murdered?" William could ask the question because he was familiar with violence, had lost a daughter to it. He understood that it was okay to bring up a bad experience, talk about it, that something like that never really left your mind for long.

"Murdered. Shot."

"Sorry, man." They were both silent for a couple of minutes. "Are there safety issues for her? The sister, I mean."

"I don't know. Her mom thinks there are." Add the unsolved murder of her brother onto Cassie's health issues, and Evan totally understood the worries.

Take care of her if anything happens to me.

The noise at the table had risen. One of the guys was leaning in, telling a joke that had the others roaring.

"You know," William said to Evan, "the guy at Victory Cottage is about to move out, and the person Mary had planned to have there next can't come."

"Yeah?" The Victory Cottage program was for victims

of violent crime and their families. They came to stay for three months, got counseling, volunteered in the community, and generally found healing. William had been a participant and was solid now.

Evan was happy for William, but why had he brought up Victory Cottage when they were talking about Cassie? And then he got it. "You think Cassie could be a candidate for Victory Cottage?"

"Might be. She's a victim, right?"

"Yeah, she is."

"And now that you're living next door, it's more secure. If she *is* at any risk, or feels herself to be, she'd have some protection." Having a local cop rent the place next to Victory Cottage was a recent addition to the program, and a smart one, after the cottage had been broken into by a lowlife from a resident's past. Evan had been glad to oblige, since he was the only single guy on the force. He kept an eye on the place, his cruiser parked in the driveway serving as a deterrent to criminals and a reassurance to residents.

Evan thought about what it would be like to bring Cassie to Pleasant Shores. She already loved it here, based on a couple of childhood visits. It was safe and the location was beautiful, right on the shores of the Chesapeake. The town wasn't pretentious, but a real fishing village full of ordinary people for most of the year. And sure, the tourists would descend in the summer, liven things up, but it never got tacky-crazy like some of the beach towns over on the Atlantic shore.

Evan could protect Cassie better here. He'd felt neglectful of his promise to do that—no surprise, neglect was his calling card—but he hated that he was letting Josh and Cassie down after all their family had done for him.

Bringing her to Victory Cottage would solve Cassie's problems and her mother's, too.

The trouble was, the last few times he'd seen Cassie, before Josh was killed, he'd gotten a *feeling*. She'd grown up, come out of her shell, turned into an interesting woman. And a very pretty one.

Josh had seen what was going on before Evan realized it, consciously, and had called him on it. "No way. I love ya but I also know ya. You're not dating Cassie. Ever."

Josh had been right, of course, and Evan had promised.

Now Josh was gone, and Cassie needed Evan. There was a solution at hand.

But staying away from Cassie while protecting her up close and personal—while living next door to her—was it even possible?

CASSIE THOMAS SET the last carton on the desk of her childhood bedroom and looked out the window for the tenth time. Where was Evan?

And how many times, back when she was a kid, had she looked out this very window, hoping for something to happen, someone to spring her from her soft, comfortable prison?

Bear, her big apricot-colored labradoodle, jumped his front paws to the windowsill beside her, standing like a person to look out.

"We're going on an adventure," she whispered into Bear's shaggy ear, and he nudged her with his nose as if to say he was excited, too.

She straightened the cover on her single bed and put the packing tape and scissors into a neat stack on her desk. She'd replaced her childhood posters with good nature paintings, had brought the neutral comforter and pillow shams from Josh's house, but the room still felt like it belonged to a kid. She'd packed up her dolls and supplies, but she wondered if her passion for dollmaking—a child's pursuit, according to most—was what kept her feeling stuck in the past.

"We can all back out." Her mother's voice quavered a little, and Cassie turned to see Mom leaning against the doorjamb, eyes red.

"No way. You're doing that trip, Mom." She worried about her mother traveling far away from her therapist, but a trip back to Ireland where she'd been born had been a lifelong dream. Cassie and Donald had strategized about ways to help Mom stop spiraling into darkness, and that was what they'd come up with. Mom's counselor had agreed, and though Mom had protested, just looking at brochures and websites had gotten her more energized than she'd been since Josh's death.

"I just feel better when I can see you," Mom said now.

"I know you do." She went over and pulled Mom into a long hug, and Bear came over to lean against the pair of them. "But I'm excited about this Victory Cottage program, and with Evan living next door, you know I'll be safe. He's just as protective as…" She trailed off, her throat tightening.

Mom recovered first, stepping back and patting Cassie's shoulder. "I know you'll be safe. And it'll be good for you to get away, too." She straightened her shoulders. "We can do this."

A car door slammed outside. Bear barked, and Cassie moved back to the window. There was Evan, climbing out of the driver's side of a pickup truck and going around to the passenger side. He opened the door and helped a slender, white-haired woman climb out. Who was that?

Evan looked good, of course. Her friends had always

thought he was hot. Short hair befitting a veteran and cop, broad shoulders, his weathered face reminding her that he was thirty-seven—Josh's age—and had already lived a life full of action and ups and downs.

Mom came over and stood at her side. "He's a good man in a lot of ways," she said out of nowhere. "But he's not for you. Dating-wise, I mean. You know that."

"Of course." She glanced over at her mother, puzzled. Why would Mom feel the need to tell her that? Evan was Josh's friend, not hers. He thought of her as Josh's annoying little sister. Right now he was being kind, because she'd asked for help. But once she got on her feet again, once the three-month Victory Cottage program was over, their relationship would go back to the occasional text or phone call.

The doorbell rang, and Cassie turned to go downstairs, but Mom put a hand on her arm. "I mean it," she said. "Evan's a recovering alcoholic, and kids of alcoholics can get drawn into the same patterns. You need to be cautious."

"I'm not going to fall for Evan Stone just because..." She trailed off, not wanting to say "you fell for Dad." Mom had suffered enough, they all had, and she didn't need to be reminded that marrying a heavy drinker had been her own choice. "I'm not in the market for romance," she amended. Her childhood illness had pushed her toward being quiet and quirky, and men weren't interested. Which was a good thing, because relationships meant dependence. Cassie had had enough dependence to last a lifetime. Anyway, she had things to do, a business to run.

She and Mom went downstairs, Bear running ahead of them, and there was a flurry of introductions. The white-haired woman turned out to be Mary Rhoades, who'd started the Victory Cottage program, and she somehow herded Mom and Donald, into the kitchen so Evan and Cassie could carry her things out to the truck.

"Mom, take Bear," Cassie said, and Mom called the big dog. He trotted into the kitchen. He'd comfort Mom by his loving presence, help her keep it together.

"That was brilliant, bringing the Victory Cottage woman along," Cassie said to Evan once they were upstairs.

"I know your mom will like her," he said. "And she'll offer a little more reassurance than I could provide. Mary's great."

"Thank you so, so much for this. It's the only way Mom would agree to the trip, and she really needs to go." She wrapped her arms around Evan in a big hug, just like always.

Just like she'd always hugged Josh.

A heavy feeling settled behind her eyes and made her throat hurt. She'd never feel her brother's embrace, never hear his ready laugh again.

Evan tightened his arms briefly around her as if he could read her thoughts and then let her go quickly, half pushing her away. "None of that, we've got work to do."

He tested the weight of a carton before letting her carry it, waved away her protest that she could carry more as he picked up three of her actually heavy boxes and started downstairs.

She needed to make sure he didn't expect to keep her in Bubble Wrap. "You know I'm healthy now, right? No more cancer. I lift weights at the gym." She flexed her arm to show her decent biceps.

He raised an eyebrow, one side of his mouth quirking up. "So now you're Wonder Woman?"

"I could take you," she said, the words coming out automatically before she could even remember why: she'd used to make that threat to him and Josh, back when she was a little kid trailing after them.

Then, though, it had been "I could take you both." Now, there was only one of the duo to joke around with. That heavy feeling settled behind her eyes again.

Evan must have had the same thought, because his smile slipped away. They walked through the living room and outside, loaded the boxes into the truck, and then returned to the house. Inside, he stopped before a family picture, Mom, Josh, and Cassie. "Hard to believe he's gone." She saw him swallow hard.

As they headed through the house and up the stairs, he kept looking around, and it hit her: he hadn't been here for years. He had to be remembering all the days he'd hung out with Josh in their living room. They'd been as close as brothers at one time. She wrapped an arm around him as they reached the top of the stairs. "It's hard, I know."

"Yeah. Let's go." He extricated himself, and they carried the rest of her things downstairs.

They loaded the last boxes into the truck, and then he looked over at his old house. "Who lives there now?"

"A nice family. They have a couple of young kids."

"Good." He laughed, but it sounded forced. "About time your mom had some decent neighbors."

"Oh, Evan." His parents had continued to live there until a couple of years ago, when they'd moved south. "Your parents settled down in the last few years." They'd slowed down their drinking, Mom had told her, because both of them had developed some health problems. There were fewer loud, late-night parties. Mom had even started taking them cookies at Christmas, and once, she'd driven Mrs. Stone to a doctor's appointment.

She turned to tell Evan all of that, but he was looking

over at his old house, his eyes far away, and she knew he was seeing into the past. She swallowed what she'd been going to say. He had a lot about his family and childhood that he needed to process; she got that.

Mom, Donald, and Mary came out the front door, Bear pushing his way past them to run to Cassie.

Mary followed the dog and put a hand on Cassie's arm. "Your people are delightful, and I've promised to keep them updated on your well-being, within the bounds of your privacy, of course," she said. Something in her wise blue eyes told Cassie that she'd gleaned some knowledge of the issues in their family, just in that short time she'd spent with Mom and Donald. Or maybe Evan had filled her in. "I'll let you say your goodbyes. We'll have a good opportunity to get to know each other during the drive to Pleasant Shores." She opened the back door of the truck and climbed easily into the back seat. From her face, Cassie would have guessed her to be in her sixties, but she moved like someone significantly younger.

"I'll sit in back with Bear," Cassie protested.

But Mary scooted over and patted the seat beside her. "You sit in front and your dog can join me back here. Bear reminds me of my doodle, and I'll enjoy his company on the way to Pleasant Shores."

"If you're sure." Cassie gestured, and Bear jumped readily into the back seat of the truck.

Mom was crying a little, and Cassie went to hug her, her own eyes brimming. She turned toward Donald, wanting to tell him to take care of her mother, but he had Evan off to the side of the driveway, talking seriously to him. Evan was nodding, rubbing the back of his neck.

They turned and started toward the truck, and Cassie caught the end of their conversation: "Don't take offense,"

Donald was saying. "But you know what I mean. She's young. Inexperienced. Not right for someone like you."

"Donald!" Cassie's face went hot. "I don't need you to—" She broke off, not even knowing what to say. Donald had managed to insult both her and Evan, and she didn't know how to fix it.

"I get it." Evan shook hands with Donald. And then he said something about traffic and climbed into the truck, not offering to help her in.

As they headed out of Harrisburg, Cassie looked over at Evan, who was staring straight ahead. There was an awkwardness between them that had never been there before. "Look, I'm sorry about Donald," she said. "Every now and then he decides he needs to be my overprotective father figure and throws out something ridiculous like that. Don't give it another thought."

"Don't worry about it," Evan said.

"Parents have trouble letting their nestlings fly," Mary said, and the conversation got general as they cruised onto the highway. The awkwardness passed, although Evan didn't do much of the talking.

Underneath hers and Mary's getting-to-know-you chatter and the quiet music Evan had turned on, though, Cassie kept wondering.

Why would both Mom and Donald emphasize that she and Evan weren't right for each other? Wasn't that obvious?

*Don't miss the final book in The Off Season series
by Lee Tobin McClain!*

"We need a housekeeper because I can't chase you down every other—" Tucker suddenly remembered they had an audience. "We can talk about this at home."

Nan, spritely at seventy with short silvery hair, grinned big and inclined her head toward the other woman.

"Clara needs a job," she said.

"I don't think so," Clara shot back.

"You need something to do," Nan insisted.

"She doesn't want the job." Tucker winked at the woman and watched her cheeks turn rosy.

Flirting was an art he'd learned late in life, and he still wasn't too accomplished at it. He'd never been a ladies' man.

"No, I really don't," she answered. "I'm only here temporarily."

Should he feel relieved or let down?

"You should introduce us," he told Nan.

"Tucker Church, I'd like you to meet Clara Fisher," Nan said. "She's one of my kids."

One of Nan's foster daughters. She'd had a dozen or more over the years. He held a hand out. "Clara, nice to meet you."

It was a long moment before Clara slid her hand into his. Then she stepped back, putting space between them.

"Nice to meet you, too. But I'm afraid I'm not interested in a job."

She gave his niece a genuine smile, then her gaze lifted to meet his. "I think that we probably met in school, but you were a senior and I was just a freshman."

He couldn't imagine forgetting Clara Fisher, with her dark brown eyes that held secrets and a smile that was captivating. He found himself wishing he could make her smile again.

Shay elbowed him. "She doesn't want the job," she whispered. "Can we go home now?"

"Of course she doesn't want to work for us. She's probably heard the stories about you running off two housekeepers." He gave Clara a pleading look.

"Would you take my number? In case you change your mind?"

"I won't change my mind," she insisted.

He had no right to feel disappointed. She was a stranger. And yet, he was.

"Well, we should go," he said as he walked Shay toward the door.

"I bet she can't even clean," Shay said under her breath.

He didn't disagree. But Clara looked like a woman who was trying to put herself back together. He needed someone strong who could stand up to Shay.

The woman who replaced Mrs. Jenkins couldn't have soulful brown eyes and a smile that made him want to take chances.

Don't miss
Her Christmas Dilemma *by Brenda Minton,*
available December 2021 wherever
Love Inspired books and ebooks are sold.

LoveInspired.com

IF YOU ENJOYED THIS BOOK
WE THINK YOU WILL ALSO LOVE

 LOVE INSPIRED

INSPIRATIONAL ROMANCE

Uplifting stories of faith, forgiveness and hope.

Fall in love with stories where faith helps guide you through life's challenges, and discover the promise of a new beginning.

6 NEW BOOKS AVAILABLE EVERY MONTH!

Get 4 FREE REWARDS!

We'll send you 2 FREE Books <u>plus</u> 2 FREE Mystery Gifts.

FREE
Value Over
$20

Both the **Romance** and **Suspense** collections feature compelling novels written by many of today's bestselling authors.

YES! Please send me 2 FREE novels from the Essential Romance or Essential Suspense Collection and my 2 FREE gifts (gifts are worth about $10 retail). After receiving them, if I don't wish to receive any more books, I can return the shipping statement marked "cancel." If I don't cancel, I will receive 4 brand-new novels every month and be billed just $7.24 each in the U.S. or $7.49 each in Canada. That's a savings of up to 28% off the cover price. It's quite a bargain! Shipping and handling is just 50¢ per book in the U.S. and $1.25 per book in Canada.* I understand that accepting the 2 free books and gifts places me under no obligation to buy anything. I can always return a shipment and cancel at any time. The free books and gifts are mine to keep no matter what I decide.

Choose one: ☐ **Essential Romance**   ☐ **Essential Suspense**
(194/394 MDN GQ6M)   (191/391 MDN GQ6M)

Name (please print)

Address   Apt. #

City   State/Province   Zip/Postal Code

Email: Please check this box ☐ if you would like to receive newsletters and promotional emails from Harlequin Enterprises ULC and its affiliates. You can unsubscribe anytime.

Mail to the **Harlequin Reader Service:**
IN U.S.A.: P.O. Box 1341, Buffalo, NY 14240-8531
IN CANADA: P.O. Box 603, Fort Erie, Ontario L2A 5X3

Want to try 2 free books from another series? Call 1-800-873-8635 or visit www.ReaderService.com.